TREE MAGIC

HARRIET SPRINGBETT

TREE MAGIC

This edition published 2020 by Impress Books.

First edition published, 2017.

13-14 Crook Business Centre, New Road, Crook, County Durham, DL15 8QX

ISBN 13: 978-1-911293-63-7

To Lumineuse, who lit the way

And Cycy, who paved it

TABLE OF CONTENTS

PROLOGUE

MERISTEM

"What's meristem?" asked Rainbow.
"It's one of the plant tissues that trees are made from," he said.
"Meristem cells divide and form new cells. Primary meristem is
what makes trees get taller and their roots go deeper."

THE SEED

Rainbow thought she'd died in the accident. She had to be dead because she could see Amrita Devi, and Amrita came from a Bishnoi legend.

Amrita was hugging a silver maple tree on the edge of a wood. A heaven full of trees seemed fitting to Rainbow, though lightning had split this particular maple and one of its two branches was almost dead. It needed some good hugging.

The Bishnoi girl was exactly as Rainbow had imagined: small and sprite-like with long black hair, and wearing a colourful sari in pinks and reds. Rainbow's mum had told her the legend nine years ago, when Rainbow was four. According to the fable, Amrita had tried to save an ancient tree from woodcutters.

Amrita lifted her head from the trunk and beckoned to her. Rainbow crept through the silence to the silver maple and mirrored Amrita, lacing her arms around its trunk and hugging it. Then she closed her eyes and let herself be drawn into the tree's reassuring comfort. It was as if she, Amrita and the maple were one, holding and healing each other. This was definitely heaven.

She opened her eyes to tell Amrita how great it all felt. But Amrita raised a finger to her lips and pointed towards a figure that had just arrived. It was another Rainbow.

This Rainbow looked angry. She kicked through decaying leaves, her hands shoved deep into her jean pockets. When she heard Amrita's low call, she stopped and stared at them both. Her face was shock-white and her lips frozen blue.

Amrita stretched a hand towards her, inviting her to join them at the silver maple. But this strange Rainbow refused to come closer. Amrita pleaded, her voice an ethereal shimmer. "Xylem and phloem, xylem and phloem," she said. "You're not cambium. You shouldn't have divided. Come! Be healed!"

The strange Rainbow ignored Amrita's peculiar entreaty. She turned her back and stamped away.

Rainbow realised she'd been holding her breath. She let it out in a sigh of relief. She didn't want to share Amrita and heaven with this imposter. She tried to catch Amrita's eye and smile at her, but Amrita was no longer as solid as before. The whole of heaven rippled, like a bubble in a breeze. The colours weakened. Each separate entity blurred into a red-gold fuzz of whirling leaves. Then the bubble burst.

Other pictures began to form in Rainbow's mind, pictures from real life: her rough hands, a breaking branch, a red car. She wasn't in heaven, after all. There was a smell of disinfectant and she felt emptied, as if she had vomited all her insides and only the shell of her body was left. Had Amrita taken her gift away? Under her cheek, the coarse cotton of the pillowcase was cold. Her eyelids flickered open.

She was in a hospital bed.

She couldn't remember what had happened or why she was here. She closed her eyes and felt herself fall, spinning through a fringe of cascading autumn leaves. Cracks of splitting wood echoed around her head. She fell for a long time.

When, at last, she struggled through the leaves and reached the surface again, the memory of a red car roof rushed towards her. She blinked it away and clung to consciousness. Reality filtered through the leafy eddies. She remembered the heavy branch under her hands, her hands on the branch, the branch in the air, the branch on the car ... and the man in the car.

It was too much to bear. She closed her eyes and tried to slip back among the leaves to her woody heaven. The leaves had gone. She squeezed her eyes tighter shut. There was no longer any heaven. All that remained was an unsteady memory of a girl in an Indian sari, quivering like a watery reflection. Rainbow blocked out the disturbing images of squashed red metal and concentrated on the girl. She was sure it was Amrita Devi. She remembered the day she'd learnt about her.

She remembered how, aged four, she'd watched Mum climb out of the workroom window and had decided that this time she'd follow her. She remembered wriggling out from behind the piano, scrambling up onto a footstool and looking out of the window to see where Mum had gone.

Mum was striding across the garden towards the woods. Her long, orange-spangled skirt caught on wet tufts of grass and spread into a triangle behind her. Rainbow struggled through the window and jumped down onto the lawn.

Mum was about to be swallowed by the dark greens and browns of the Dorset trees. Rainbow raced after her: round the pumpkin patch and the rhododendrons, under the snarled chicken wire, across the hayfield and into the bracken at the edge of the wood.

Mum stopped at the foot of the big oak tree and stared up into its canopy. She threw out her arms in their wide, purple sleeves. Rainbow followed her gaze. There must be something special up there. Mum seemed more distracted than usual and Rainbow expected to see a dragon or a Buddha. But there was nothing of any particular interest – simply branches, twigs and leaves.

She ran forward to tug on Mum's skirt. Before she could reach her, Mum stepped up to the trunk of the tree, wrapped her arms around it and laid her face against the bark.

Mum's closed, kohl-dark eyes shut Rainbow out, so she sidled up beside her and leant her tummy against the tree. Her arms were too short to go far around. It didn't matter. She felt grown-up. Now she knew where Mum disappeared to when she'd been crying. Rainbow had Big Ted for the times Bob made her cry. Mum didn't have a teddy, so she obviously had to make do with trees.

She was wondering why Mum had chosen trees rather than something that would fit in bed with her and Bob, when Mum sighed. Her arms slipped down. One bumped onto Rainbow's head.

"Ow!"

"Rainbow! What are you doing here? I thought Bob was looking after you."

"I hid from him. Why are you hugging the tree?"

Mum smiled down at her, took her hand and led her to a tree stump. She sat cross-legged with her back to it and pulled Rainbow onto her lap. Rainbow snuggled up to make the most of Mum's attention.

"Tree-hugging makes me feel better, love."

"How come? You could hug me instead."

"I am hugging you. Look." Mum gave her a squeeze. Rainbow closed her eyes and burrowed into the earthy smell of Mum's skin.

"Trees affect our chakras. They absorb our negative energies in the same way they absorb the carbon dioxide we breathe out," said Mum.

"What's carbon dioxide?"

Mum laughed the tidy laugh she used with people who didn't interest her. "It's too difficult to explain to a four year old. Shall I tell you a story instead?"

Rainbow rubbed her head against Mum's shoulder in a vigorous nod.

"It's a legend told by the Bishnoi people about a girl called Amrita Devi. She lived in India a long, long time ago. She understood how important trees are. One day, the Maharajah's tree cutters came to cut down a tree in her village to build a new fortress for the Maharajah. Amrita threw herself in front of the men's axes, hugged the tree and declared that if they wanted to cut down the tree they'd have to kill her first. Wasn't that brave?"

"What happened next?"

"There are two versions. One says she saved the tree and the other says she died."

"Maybe she did both," said Rainbow. She twisted her finger around a coil of her brown hair and entwined it with a long strand of Mum's silky, black hair.

Mum's arms slackened. Rainbow glanced up at her face. She was gazing up into her tree.

"Yes," Mum murmured. "Maybe her soul split into two and created an Amrita who died and an Amrita who lived. Perhaps they coexisted in parallel worlds."

Mum was getting her faraway look. Rainbow frowned. "I meant that the *Marjah's* men could have killed her but then decided not to chop down the tree after all."

Mum wasn't listening. She'd begun to float away. Rainbow tugged on a black line of her hair.

"Can I come with you next time you hug a tree?"

Mum kissed the top of her head. She eased Rainbow out of her lap and disentangled their braid.

"If you like, but don't tell Bob."

Rainbow grinned and hopped from one foot to another as her mum swept dead grass from her skirt.

"It's another secret? Like the *weejee* board?"

Mum nodded and held out the other hand for Rainbow to take.

Rainbow remembered grasping it and following Mum back to the house. She remembered thinking that next time she caught her mum with the Ouija board, she'd ask her to talk to Amrita as well as Dad.

And, as she lay in the hospital bed, Rainbow realised that Amrita was the seed from which everything had grown.

PART ONE

THE TRUNK

1990

CHAPTER ONE

Rainbow wriggled the last few metres home through the August-long grass on her belly, aiming for the hole in the chicken-wire fence. It made her feel like a kid again, playing Red Indians with an invisible friend, though at thirteen she was too old for games. Her knees and elbows were an angry red and she was itching all over, but she daren't stand up. She had to know whether Fraser was there.

She parted the grasses in front of the fence and peered into the garden. There was no sign of Fraser's red Porsche but this wasn't reliable evidence, as he sometimes walked up from the village to work with Mum and Bob. She sidled round the back of the rhododendron bushes to the weeping willow and then climbed up the rope ladder to her tree house.

Everything was quiet. She sat down on the floor, let her legs swing over the edge of the platform and surveyed her hilltop kingdom. A crown of woods around the house separated it from the village at the bottom of the hill. It could almost be a castle, except that castles were grand and her house was just big and untidy, and overgrown. She had a good view of its crumbling walls from her tree beside the front gate.

The kitchen door slammed. She stilled her legs. Bob appeared, followed by Fraser. They strolled to Bob's white van, which was parked in front of the house. Rainbow's tree was a good twenty metres away; there was no reason for them to look up and see her.

"Jasmine's so clumsy, man. I *mean* … the mixing desk! I'm always telling her not to take her coffee in there," said Bob.

Most of his thin, grey hair was scraped back into the ponytail he'd made of it last week. The rest straggled around his frown-lined face, and he was slouching from a bad mood.

"She didn't do it on purpose," said Fraser. "Anyway, the insurance should cover it."

They leant on the open doors of the van, waiting for the heat to escape. Fraser smoothed down his hair and looked around the front garden.

"What's Rainbow up to? My Becky said she couldn't go to the fair with her today because she's too busy."

Bob looked up to where she was sitting. Rainbow drew her legs back inside the tree house and closed her eyes.

"In there, as usual," he said to Fraser. Rainbow heard him suck a last drag out of his cigarette and stamp it into the stony drive. "Up to no good; as bad as her mother."

Footsteps came down the drive towards her tree. "Hi, Rainy," Fraser called.

She opened her eyes and saw him standing below, his fatherly smile beckoning her to share confidences.

"Why aren't you at the fair with Becky? You told me you loved all those dizzy sensations. School starts on Monday and it'll be too late then," said Fraser.

"I hate the fair," she replied.

It was easy to resist his warmth, now that she knew she couldn't trust him.

"Worried you're not tall enough for the best rides?" He chuckled.

She pulled her knees up to her chest and glared down at him.

"Actually, Rebecca and I don't hang out any more."

She slithered backwards into the far corner of her tree house, where she was invisible to him, and wound her arms around the trunk of her tree.

Fraser's voice invaded her den: "Make up with her quickly, then. I've missed not seeing you around."

His feet crunched back up the drive to the van. She hugged her weeping willow hard. She had to grow. Mum wasn't short, but for all she knew about her dad, he could have been a midget. Maybe that was why she was small for her age. If she could catch up with her classmates, she'd no longer be the odd one out. Mum said it didn't matter if she was different from everyone else. But Mum didn't understand. She didn't notice the way normal people looked at her.

An ant scuttled up the trunk to her arm. A trickle of others followed the same path. She moved her arm to a nearby branch and watched the ants continue along their highway. Could the tree feel their scurrying feet? They must make it itch … all those ants, flies and birds: even her. She tickled the branch in front of the ant, imagining the tree swaying a branch-rippling response and giggling. Nothing happened. She let her hands rest on the branch and listened to Bob continue to moan about Mum.

At last, the men got into the van. The doors slammed and the engine grunted into life. It whined as Bob backed along the drive and into the lane. Rainbow looked at her hands against the rough crevices of the bark. A strange warmth emanated from the branch. She pressed harder. The heat increased. She plucked off her hands in surprise and turned them over. Her palms carried a slight imprint of the bark. She ran a finger over the subtle ridges and watched them fade away. The sensation made her shiver. Her neck was goose-pimply, reminding her of Mum's expression about someone walking over her grave.

She shook off both the sensation and Mum's saying, picked up her sketch pad and leafed through the pages. The drawings of Patti's kittens, which had seemed so perfect when she'd sketched them that morning, now looked flat and amateur. The real kittens were rounded, lively and perfect. How could she persuade Mum and Bob to let her have one of them?

"Rainbow, lunch!"

Rainbow slid down the ladder and jogged to the house. She pushed the door to the point where it stuck on the curling lino and then squeezed through sideways into the dim kitchen. Mum was leaning against the cooker. She was smoking, as usual, and stirring something in a saucepan.

Rainbow wrinkled her nose. She could smell tomatoes through the smoke.

"You haven't made soup, have you?" she asked.

Mum glanced into her saucepan as if she'd forgotten what she was cooking.

"Don't you like soup?"

Rainbow raised her eyes to the cobwebs on the ceiling

and sighed. Most mums knew what their children liked and disliked. Sometimes she wished Mum was normal, like Rebecca's mum.

"Not home-made. You know I don't. It's not fair. How come Bob gets to eat out while we have to use up his tomatoes? Aren't there any tins?"

"Home-made soup is better for you. It'll make you grow, love."

Mum served them both a generous helping of orange, grainy water and then draped herself over the chair opposite Rainbow. She fixed her eyes on the music manuscript beside her bowl as she ate.

"Mum, was Dad a midget?"

The spoon paused on the way to Mum's mouth, wobbled and then slowly delivered its contents.

"A midget?"

"Short. Like me."

Her mum snorted. "He was lacking in everything, including height. Eat your soup."

Rainbow knew there was no point in persisting. Her searches for photos of Dad in the cardboard box on top of Mum's wardrobe had been fruitless. She'd given him imaginary features according to the snippets she wormed out of Mum. Now, she readjusted her image of Dad, giving him short arms and short legs, and shortening his brown ponytail into a crew cut. He still smiled and had twinkling green eyes, though he was only five foot two.

Mum finished her soup. "I've got to work on Jeff's song this afternoon, love. Are you all right on your own?"

Rainbow nodded.

"Good girl." Mum scooped up her Indian box and a pouch of tobacco, then swept across the corridor into her creative corner. Rainbow knew what was in the box: pellets of hard, brown hash. The one she'd licked had made her think of dirt. It had an aftertaste of Dettol and chocolate.

She washed up the dishes, put a bar of chocolate into her pocket and then peeked into her mum's workroom. Mum was sitting at the piano, one hand jiggling a keep-fit routine while the other spidered words over a scrap of paper. She was a blues songwriter when she was in this room. When she crossed the corridor to the recording room, she became a blues singer. Bob accompanied her on his guitar and, more recently, Fraser had started to join them on the keyboard.

Rainbow wandered back outside. The tomato experiments in Bob's vegetable plot stood to attention against their wooden posts. She stopped, the taste of soup still sour in her mouth. An idea fizzed in her mind. There were dozens of tomatoes, enough for a month of soup.

She carried a bucket to the plants and gathered most of the ripe ones, leaving a scattering in the way Mum had shown her when picking wild flowers. Then she lugged the bucket down the drive.

It was awkward to carry, so she paused by the front gate to change hands. She rubbed her left hand down her jeans to ease her stiff fingers and looked up at her tree. The thick willow branches tapered into yellow fronds, like a shaggy haircut, and her tree house lay behind like a half-hidden face: a tatty, ugly face. It needed a facelift.

The tree house had been there for years. Bob had built it for her one summer when he'd been given a lorry-load of second-hand wood. It had a leaky, sloped roof, planked walls, a solid floor and one window for spying. At first she'd been proud: it was the smartest tree house in the world, and she would skip out to it after lunch every day while Mum and Bob had their siesta. Later, when the novelty wore off and she wanted to stay indoors, Bob got angry.

"I haven't spent all that time making you a den for nothing," he'd say, pushing her outside.

She left the bucket of tomatoes by the gate and climbed the ladder. She'd spent her summer holidays here rather than in the house with Mum and Bob's storms, and it was starting to feel cramped inside. The ceiling was too low for her to be able to stand upright. She ran her hands over the crocheted rug she'd taken from Mum's wardrobe. What could she do to make her den feel bigger? Maybe she should take down her summer holiday sketches and paint the walls white instead. She didn't want to have to ask for Bob's help.

She turned to the trunk side of the tree house and watched the line of ants. There was a mutiny in the ranks. When they reached a certain point on the branch, they hesitated, turning right, then left, before scurrying back down and upsetting those following them.

She moved closer. The point causing the problem was where she'd pressed her hands that morning. She thought about the heat flow she'd felt; the goose pimples. Then she put her hands back in the same place.

The tree felt warm, then warmer still. She closed her eyes and rested her cheek against the trunk, concentrating on the bumpiness of the bark under her palms. She could sense the sap flowing beneath them.

The tree really was alive. Yes, alive: not just living. It was breathing, had a heart that was beating, was growing. She knew because she could feel it. The bark was stretching under her hands, warming them with its effort.

She opened her eyes and drew back her hands. The bark was lighter in colour. She circled the branch with her hands and then slid them backwards and forwards. The branch was narrower where her hands had rested.

This was weird. She must have imagined it.

She moved her hands up the branch and tried again. Heat. Pulse. Melting hands.

She hadn't imagined it; the branch had stretched.

Her heart thumped and her hands trembled. She turned them over and stared at the slight bark imprint on the palms. Other than that, they looked the same as ever: stubby, fat-fingered and rough.

She had magic hands!

Exhilaration swept through her body. She jumped up and whooped. Her head hit the ceiling. She rubbed it hard, and kept rubbing. It had to be a dream. People couldn't grow trees like this in real life.

She slithered down the ladder, raced indoors and burst into Mum's workroom.

"Mum! Pinch me."

Mum was stretched out in the armchair. She opened her eyes and blew out a funnel of smoke.

"Rainbow, I'm working. What's the matter?"

Rainbow leant over the sagging armchair and thrust her arm into Mum's lap.

"Sorry, but you've got to pinch me. I think I'm dreaming.

I've just made my tree grow."

"That's nice, love."

Mum pinched her gently with the hand that wasn't holding the joint and then took another drag. Her eyes closed.

"Mum!" She shook her mum's shoulder. "I've got magic hands!"

"Then magic yourself away, love. I really must finish this song."

Rainbow looked down at her unimpressive, magic hands and shrank to her normal size. She backed out of Mum's workroom, eased the door closed behind her and went into the kitchen. She was stupid to have expected Mum to be excited. Magic was part of Mum's everyday world, though she called it spiritualism. It was what started the arguments with Bob.

She thought about Mum's seances, her Ouija board, her crystals and tarot cards. What she'd just done with the tree didn't feel spiritual in the same way. It was real. It was fun. It could even be useful. It was nothing like Mum's boring magic.

She sped out of the house and climbed back into her den. She hugged the trunk and searched for the part of the branch she'd grown. When she found it, she stroked the lighter bark, feeling for cracks. Had she hurt her tree? She laid her ear over the branch and concentrated on the tree's breathing. It didn't seem to be in pain. It felt normal. Apart from excitement constricting her chest, she felt normal too.

She tried again on a different branch, and laughed out loud when she saw the branch had stretched. Then she stood up, her head and shoulders hunched under the ceiling, placed one hand on her stomach and the other on her back, closed her eyes and willed herself to grow.

Nothing happened.

Perhaps she could use her magic hands to raise the ceiling. She'd only need to stretch the trunk, because the two branches that held up the roof came off the same part of it. She wound her arms around the trunk and rested the side of her face against it, listening for its sap-beat. There it was. She closed her eyes and breathed in the dust of its dry odour. Then she asked it to grow. Silently, squeezing with her arms, she willed it to stretch.

It creaked a slow sigh, stiffer than the branches. Tree dust swirled before her nose. She sneezed and then opened her eyes. Her arms were heavy, as if she'd lifted the tree. There was no change to the ancient bark of the trunk, no lighter colouring, no warmth. But there was a gap between the walls and the roof of her tree house.

"Thank you, Tree," she whispered.

She stood up. Her tree seemed to have known why she wanted it to grow, because her head was now slightly lower than the ceiling. She raised her chin and looked through the all-round gap. She had a great view of the fields and woods around the house now. Tree-growing was dead useful.

She rubbed the trunk and pulled the chocolate out of her pocket. She wanted to do something for the tree in return but couldn't imagine what would give it pleasure. Not chocolate, she was sure of that. She cracked off two squares and let them melt on her tongue.

Outside, Mum was leaning from the kitchen window, staring over the side garden towards the woods. She must have finished the song and was probably contemplating going on one of her treks.

Rainbow dropped the rest of the chocolate into the wooden box she'd sneaked out of Fraser's car last week and climbed down the ladder. She must deal with the tomatoes before Bob got back.

CHAPTER TWO

Rainbow hooked the bucket of tomatoes over one arm and lugged it out of the front gate. Then she changed arms and began the march down the lane that led to the village a mile away.

Three of the first four houses were empty and she had only sold enough tomatoes to earn two pounds by the time she arrived at the Drunken House, on the outskirts of the village. The Drunken House was the local horror spot, the place you had to go into alone if you lost at Forfeits. She'd only lost once, but the memory of invisible eyes watching her as she'd stood in the hall and counted to ten had been burnt into her mind forever. She'd stopped playing Forfeits with the village kids after that.

The house lurked on the inside of a bend in the dank lane and had been empty for years. Ivy-clad trees grew on the steep bank opposite, and its cold brick walls huddled in their shade. There weren't any neighbouring houses. It crouched alone, full of ghosts who were just waiting for her to run home alone on a dark night so they could reach out and grab her.

Rainbow hurried past, clutching her bucket. She could feel the house's dampness creeping out to her. It willed her to push open the rotting door and sacrifice her warm body to its hunger.

She broke into a run. An urge to look into the front window nagged at her. She steeled herself against it and fixed her eyes on the road. Then she was safely past. She dared a glance back at the window.

A man stood inside. White light sizzled from a wand in his hand and he was holding a mask to his face. He was too solid to be a ghost. She stopped. He lowered the mask, examined something in front of him, and then made bright light again. She blinked and looked down at her feet. There was a white stain in her eyes as if she'd stared at a naked light bulb for too long. She dropped her bucket and rubbed them. Then she blinked again and looked around. The image started to fade.

Behind her, the front door of the Drunken House creaked open. She grabbed the bucket.

"Can I help you?"

She turned around. The man was standing in the doorway, the mask in his hands. A heavy, brown apron hid all but his shiny head and scuffed boots. He was old – about the same age as Mum and Bob – and limped. He had warm, brown eyes and crinkled skin, a bit like Bella, her friend Patti's dog. He took a step towards her.

She took a step back.

"What are you doing with that mask?" she asked.

He looked down at his mask, back at Rainbow and then in through the window.

"Did you look at the arc?"

"I was watching you make light," she replied.

"You should never look directly at the arc. That's why I wear a mask. Can you see all right?"

He bent down and stared at her eyes.

"I'm fine. Why are you in the Drunken House?" She'd never seen anyone inside before. "Are you exorcising it?"

He started to smile. His lips curled at the corners like Hercule Poirot's moustache.

"I'm renting the cottage. I arrived yesterday. The removal men broke one of my sculptures, so I'm welding it back together. Why do you call it the Drunken House?"

"Because it's haunted."

"Is it?" He didn't look particularly worried. "Have you seen the ghost yourself?"

"Yes. It was over there in the corner," said Rainbow.

"How do you know it was a ghost?"

She'd expected him to tell her not to be silly, like Fraser had done.

"It was kind of vague," she said.

"I haven't seen anything vague yet but I'll keep an eye out for it. My name's Michael, by the way. Michael Jallet. And you're …?"

"Rainbow Linnet."

He dropped his mask. "Rainbow?"

She nodded. People often reacted like that when they heard her name. It usually marked the beginning of the sideways looks.

"That's unusual," he continued. "Do you live in the village?"

"Up on the hill." She picked up the mask and handed it

to him. "Would you like to buy some tomatoes?"

"In Wymer Hill House?"

She nodded. "I'm selling tomatoes. Do you want some?"

Michael glanced into the bucket.

"How much?"

He wouldn't have any tomatoes in his garden if he'd just moved in.

"Twenty pence each."

"That's expensive. Did you grow them yourself?"

"Of course," she lied.

"So you're a gardener. Will you give me a reduction if I buy them all?"

"Okay." That would save her dragging the bucket any further. "But I need at least three pounds."

"Come in and we'll count them, then we can agree on a price."

He turned and limped the few steps into the house without waiting for her answer.

Rainbow hesitated: he was a stranger. But he was disabled. She could easily run away. And he seemed harmless.

Things had begun like this with Fraser. He'd been interested in her because she was Rebecca's friend. He'd invited her on family outings. She'd been to the zoo and the cinema with them, and soon she'd started to wish he were her father. He'd teased her, listened to her, given her advice and made her laugh. He'd been everything that Bob wasn't – and that Dad might have been, if only he hadn't died.

Rainbow wasn't sure she wanted to take the risk of getting to know Michael. She decided she'd sell him the tomatoes and then leave.

She followed him into the Drunken House. The invisible eyes were watching her. She concentrated on Michael. From behind, she could see that he wore a faded black T-shirt and a patched pair of shorts under the apron. His bad leg was criss-crossed with purple scars.

"What's the matter with your leg?"

"I had a motorbike accident."

She left the front door open behind her. "Does it hurt?"

"Only if I stand for too long."

He led her through the dim hall. The fug of damp bricks she remembered hung indoors. In the front room, this mingled with a new, blacksmithy smell of hot metal. Cardboard boxes were piled up around the room, which still had a desolate feel to it. She shivered. Michael eased himself into a chair at a wood-wormy table.

"Put the tomatoes there," he said, tapping the table.

She caught sight of his hands and spent longer looking at them than she usually would. They were the opposite of her own: as delicately shaped as a princess's, yet veiled with old man's skin.

The tomatoes on the top were still whole. She counted them out and tried to stop the bottom ones squidging through her fingers.

"Thirty-eight," she said. That would be … sixty … eight … well, more than three pounds.

Michael screwed up his blob of a nose.

"The last ones are a bit squashed. I wouldn't pay twenty for those. How much for the lot?"

"Five pounds."

"Four."

"Okay." She frowned at his outstretched hand.

"Always shake on a deal," he prompted.

She shook his hand. The warm shock of its scaly dryness mesmerised her. Their hands fitted together in the same way her hands fitted the bark of her weeping willow. He was a tree, a human tree, and for a perfect second she was cocooned in safety.

"Nice to do business with you, Rainbow," he said. "Would you like a drink?"

"No, thanks."

She looked around the room. The physical contact with Michael had changed the atmosphere. She couldn't feel the invisible eyes anymore and she no longer wanted to leave, despite her resolution not to get to know him.

There was a crate on the bare, stone floor in front of the fireplace. On top sat a metallic fish shape. A thick lead linked a black box to a clamp, which held the stick she'd seen in his hand.

"Is that your welding kit?"

"Yes. And that's one of my sculptures."

The way he said it, proud in a careless kind of voice, made Rainbow look at him instead of the fish.

"You made it?"

"Yes. Do you like it?"

She studied the flat sculpture.

"It's odd. Is it supposed to be a fish?"

"It's a flying fish. Look, the metal around the edge holds the resin and chips of coloured glass in place."

He picked it up and passed it to Rainbow, who turned it over. It was dead cool, apart from the metal rod sticking out of its belly.

"What's the rod for?"

"It goes into the ground to make the fish look as if it's flying. You have to see it outside with the sun on it. Do you want to see the others? They're in the garden."

Her previous visit had been too fraught with terror to allow her to explore. She was intrigued by the idea of a garden hidden from the road.

"Okay."

He led her through a tiny kitchen to the back door. He was right: with the sun rippling through the blue, green and yellow glass of their bodies, the fish looked exotic in the weedy jungle of his garden. There were other sculptures on the flattened-grass side of the yard: a huge spider made from metal; a sun-eye; and several figures she couldn't identify. She picked her way around the nettles to look more closely while he explained how he'd made them. Then he showed her a tumbledown shed.

"This is going to be my workshop and art studio," he said.

"Really? Do you draw and paint as well?"

"I sketch."

"Can you do caricatures of people?"

"Of course."

Perhaps it would be worth getting to know Michael after all.

"Would you teach me?"

"If you like." He smiled his curly smile.

"When?"

He rubbed his bald head. "It'll have to be after work."

"Oh. Isn't sculpturing your job?"

"Yes, but I need another job to pay the bills. A day job."

Rainbow twisted her finger into a loose curl of hair.

Michael perched on the huge spider. "You look puzzled."

"It's just that Mum and Bob haven't got jobs. They're musicians. I thought artists were like musicians."

"Well, if they're commercially successful, I suppose they don't need day jobs too."

"So you're not successful?"

"Not anymore," he said.

"What do you mean, not anymore?"

"I used to make sculptures to sell, ones people asked for. That made me plenty of money but it stopped being art. And I lost a lot of things that were important to me. Sometimes, if you use your gift to earn money, you end up making sacrifices."

She nodded, pretending to understand. He talked as if she were a grown-up.

Michael continued: "So is your mum successful?"

"I don't think so."

He was waiting for her to say more, but it felt wrong to talk about Mum to a stranger. She picked up her empty bucket.

"I must go," she said. "I've got to get to the village shop before it closes."

He stood up and accompanied her to the front door. "Come back and see me soon. If you'd like drawing lessons, you could pop in on your way home from school."

"I'll think about it," said Rainbow.

CHAPTER THREE

When Rainbow reached her front gate, after her visit to the village shop, she saw that Bob's dented van was parked askew behind Mum's yellow Mini. That meant he was either in a good mood or a stinker. When he was his normal grumpy self, the van would be slotted neatly between the Mini and the compost heap.

She climbed into her tree and emptied the Yorkie bars and her change into the box. Then she glanced out of her new spying gap. Fraser wasn't loitering in the garden, so she left her den and ventured into the house.

Once she'd made her usual crab-like entry through the sticking door into the kitchen, she saw that he wasn't there either. Muffled laughter came from the recording room: Bob's. He was in a good mood then. His coat and a leather jacket she didn't recognise were thrown over the back of a chair. The jacket could have belonged to any of the multitude of musicians and groupies who came and went like Bob's moods.

She lined up the tins of tomato soup she'd bought from

the shop inside the food cupboard, then pulled out the leather jacket and slipped her fingers into its pockets. Keys jangled. She drew them out. They were on the plastic key ring Rebecca had made at school. The jacket belonged to Fraser. Rainbow's key ring was somewhere under the pile of papers and mouldering food on the kitchen table.

She dropped the keys back into Fraser's jacket pocket, pushed it under Bob's and wiped her hands on her jeans. She didn't want any contact with Fraser ever again. She'd been wrong to think he was the perfect father.

When Rebecca had arrived in the village earlier that summer, Rainbow had started to spend all her free time at Rebecca's house. Her home was like an Enid Blyton story; her mum fussed over her and her dad played games with her and listened to what she said. That was why Rainbow had confided in him.

She stalked the voices to the recording room and peeped around the open door. Through the sweet, smokey haze she could see Bob sitting on the rolled-up mattress. Mum and Fraser were sprawled on cushions. Bob was fingering a guitar that Rainbow hadn't seen before.

"I've got to have it," he said.

"You've already got seven too many." Mum's voice was sharp.

"But it's a bargain. You're selling it for next to nothing, aren't you, Fraser?"

Fraser looked from Bob to Mum. Before he could speak, Mum cut in: "We've got more important things to spend the cash on."

"What, like mending the mixing desk you spilt coffee on?

Or have you signed up for another inspirational retreat?"

Mum and Bob glared at each other. Fraser eased his guitar out of Bob's clenched hands.

"Look, I'll do you a special deal," said Fraser.

Rainbow sighed. She returned to the kitchen and pulled down a packet of multicoloured pasta twirls. She'd do her favourite meal of pasta mixed with fried courgettes and garlic, held together by tons of grated cheese. That would stop Mum making some horrible tomato concoction.

As she was emptying the pasta into the saucepan of boiling water, Mum, Bob and Fraser appeared, laughing together as if there had been no argument over the guitar.

"How's my favourite sparrow?" asked Fraser, tweaking her hair.

Rainbow jerked her head back, out of his reach.

"Doing dinner again, love?" asked her mum.

"I haven't done enough pasta for Fraser," said Rainbow, "though I expect there's some tomato soup left from lunch."

"It's okay. He's eating with his family," said Mum. She hummed as she opened the fridge.

"Rainbow's a wonder," said Fraser. "I can't imagine my Becky doing any cooking. She's far too busy painting her face with make-up, or buying new clothes."

"At thirteen? I was still playing with dolls," said Mum. "And I was trying to smoke without coughing," said Bob. They laughed. Bob handed around cans of beer.

"Let's celebrate our new mission," he said. "To blues, and to hell with short-sighted recording companies."

Rainbow helped herself to a Coke, ignoring Mum's frown. With Bob in a good mood, Mum wouldn't nag her about sugar and healthy food.

"Come and tell us what you've been up to today, Rainy," Bob continued, leading the way outside.

I discovered I've got magic hands, thought Rainbow. The unspoken words sent a delightful shiver down her back. No, she wouldn't say anything about her tree, not while Bob was in a good mood, and certainly not with Fraser there. Instead, she set the timer for the pasta, dashed to her tree house for her sketchbook and then joined them at the bald bonfire spot.

"So, what mischief have you been making?" Bob ruffled her hair – something he hadn't done for months – and made a space for her beside him on the log.

"I went to see some kittens. Look, aren't they sweet?"

She opened her sketch pad and showed Bob.

"Nice pictures, honey."

Bob closed the book and shoved it onto Mum's lap.

"This is your way of telling us that you want one," said Mum.

She smiled at Rainbow, opened the pad and studied the drawings.

"Yes. Please, Mum. They're going to drown them if nobody gives them a home."

Mum stopped turning the pages. "Who's *they*?"

"The farmer."

Rainbow felt herself colouring under Mum's scrutiny. "All right, the Bellamys."

Mum stiffened. Her smile shrank into a thin, straight line. "What were you doing *there*?"

"I didn't go on purpose. I met Patti on my walk and she

invited me in."

Rainbow fixed her eyes on the hole in the knee of Bob's jeans so that Mum wouldn't spot her lie.

"I hope you're telling the truth, Rainbow. Next time you must refuse."

Rainbow dared a glance at Mum. Her eyes were narrowed in suspicion.

Rainbow bit her lip. "Why don't you want me to go there?"

Mum frowned at Fraser, who quickly averted his eyes to the charred logs in the ash. "I've already told you," she said.

"All you said was that you had an argument with Mrs Bellamy. I don't see why your argument should stop me seeing Patti. Mrs Bellamy won't tell me, either. It's not as if I'm a kid anymore." Rainbow could hear her voice starting to whine. She stopped.

"We're not having a kitten, Rainbow, and certainly not from the Bellamys."

"I'll look after it. You needn't do anything."

"No."

Bob laid a hand on Mum's arm.

"Come on, Jaz. If any kid can look after a pet, it's Rainbow," he said.

"You've changed your tune," Mum muttered.

"Don't be such a misery," said Bob. "Who cares where the cat comes from?"

Mum's expression hardened further, then crumpled. Rainbow thought Mum was going to cry and she wished she hadn't mentioned the kitten.

Fraser cleared his throat.

"If you made up with Becky, you wouldn't need a kitten

for company. You could come round to our house."

Rainbow ignored him. Mum wasn't crying. She just looked resigned, like the times when Bob decided to play at a gig she disapproved of and she couldn't find a reason to stop him going.

"Please, Mum. I promise I won't go round to Patti's again."

Her mum sighed and took a long gulp from her beer can. "All right."

"Thanks, Mum. Thanks, Bob, you're fab!" Rainbow jumped up and clapped her hands, dropped a kiss onto Bob's greasy hair and hugged her mum. "Can I get it now?"

"I thought you were doing dinner," Bob said.

"And you've just promised not to go there again," said Mum.

"Oh, yes. I'll ring Patti and ask her to bring it over."

Rainbow checked the timer and rushed back indoors. A kitten! She'd have to go and get it, though. She wanted to see them all before she decided which one would love her most. She'd sneak off tomorrow, before Bob changed his mind and before Mum got up.

She'd only been on the phone to Patti for a minute when Bob threw open the kitchen door and signalled that he wanted to use the telephone. Of course, it was Saturday: first the garden, then the house would be overrun by musicians and groupies until the early hours of Sunday morning.

She relinquished the sellotaped handset of the red dialphone and took her pasta up to her bedroom to eat. On her bedside table was the copy of *Just Seventeen* Patti had lent her. She flicked through it as she ate. It was the first time she'd had the magazine to herself. Before long, she was absorbed in the articles she and Patti had pretended to scorn that morning, fascinated by the strange details of other people's lives.

❧ ❧ ❧

That evening she was attracted downstairs by laughter. Usually, the early-soirée murmurings of adult conversations crescendoed into *forte* voice-battles and then subsided into *pianissimo* humming and strumming. Mum was the Grand Finale, her husky voice rising through the contentment around the fire, tingeing the atmosphere with melancholy.

Tonight, however, the party sounded fun. She was curious to see what was amusing them so she slung her jeans on over her pyjama shorts, pulled on a jumper and jogged downstairs. An abandoned glass of beer sat on the kitchen table. She swallowed a mouthful and grimaced at its bitterness. Coke was far nicer. She tried a second sip, but it was no better. She eased open the kitchen door and crept outside.

Mum and Bob's friends came from the pubs and festivals where they gigged. Rainbow nodded hello to the few who noticed her. The laughter had died down. People milled around the bonfire, the hammocks and the kitchen window, where the tin bath Mum and Bob had picked up from a tip had been turned upside down and now served as a table for bottles. The biggest group was gathered around Mum; the groupies were sitting on logs and listening to her recounting an anecdote. Rainbow sidled up and sat down outside the circle, wondering what could be so enthralling.

Mum was different in a group. Rainbow watched her shake

her hair and raise her arms in imitation of some politician. She was in constant movement, leaning forwards with her hands outstretched; shrugging her shoulders; looking round at her audience. None of these people would recognise her faraway mum during the daytime hours.

Nothing was any different tonight, after all. The longer she studied her mum, the smaller Rainbow felt in comparison. A man in a black silk shirt and tie jumped up to fill Mum's glass as soon as it was empty, but Bob wrenched it out of his hand and filled it himself. He glared at Silk Shirt. Mum, apparently oblivious to Bob's gesture, stood and stretched. Then she bent down to listen to an earnest girl who couldn't have been much older than Rainbow. She laid a hand on the girl's shoulder and said, "It's the creative process. Don't worry. I'll help you out if you like."

The girl's back straightened and she appeared to expand with importance. Rainbow stood up, her chest burning with a sudden hate for the stranger, and shoved two men aside to reach her mum's elbow. Mum saw her and stiffened.

"Rainbow! Aren't you in bed yet?" Her voice was bright and clipped.

"I had a nightmare."

Rainbow slipped her hand around Mum's arm and pulled her close. Mum patted her head and then unhitched her elbow from Rainbow's grasp.

"Never mind, love. Off you go, back to bed," she said, and turned back towards Earnest Girl.

There was no point trying to compete. Rainbow took a step away and bumped into a man standing behind her. His beer spilt over her jumper and his sleeve. He stared down at her in surprise. A wave of hair hid most of his face but the little she could see showed he wasn't as old as the rest of the men. He looked like the model called Brad she'd seen in *Just Seventeen*.

"Aren't you a bit young for this kind of party?" he said.

"No, I'm eighteen," she lied. She swept back her hair like she'd seen Mum do.

"Gosh, I'm sorry. Where did you come from? I didn't see you earlier."

Rainbow waved an arm airily towards the house. "I was on the phone to the gallery. I'm exhibiting at the moment. Someone made an offer and I had to negotiate."

Brad raised his eyebrows. "An exhibiting artist at eighteen? Wow! Can I get you a drink?"

"I'll have a beer."

"Cool. Don't go anywhere."

Brad strode off towards the tin bath. Rainbow folded her arms and watched him rinse out a glass and fill it with beer. It was lucky she'd read 'Ten Sure Ways to Grab His Attention'.

When he handed her the glass, she tilted it to her lips for several seconds so it looked as if she were drinking it.

"So what kind of stuff do you do?" asked Brad.

Rainbow shrugged. "Everything really. Contemporary, of course; abstracts."

Brad nodded and she quickly described the modern-art exhibition Fraser had taken her to at the beginning of the summer, pretending it was hers. Brad's attention slid from her face. He was staring at something behind her. A hand touched her shoulder. She turned around.

"Rainbow! How come you're still here? Who's your

friend, love? Are you going to introduce us?" Mum held out her hand and shook Brad's. "I'm Jasmine Linnet."

"Alastair Knight," he replied, "from *Barely Blues* magazine. I loved your gig last week at the Seaman's Arms. You've really got something special. I hear you write for other singers too?"

"Oh, has Rainbow been giving my secrets away?" laughed Mum.

She put her arm around Rainbow's shoulders. Rainbow shrugged it off. She must look about ten years old to Alastair.

"You should be in bed, love," added Mum. "Go on, now."

Rainbow struggled to find an honourable way of leaving. Alastair took a step closer to Mum and asked when she was performing again. He seemed to have forgotten he'd been talking to Rainbow. It was just like when Mum had met Fraser for the first time, last month.

Rainbow sloshed her beer over Alastair's foot and stamped back to the house.

CHAPTER FOUR

Rainbow's first thought when she woke up was that she could get her kitten that afternoon. She rushed downstairs, ready to forgive Mum for stealing Alastair away from her last night, and whirled into the kitchen.

Her cheerful "Morning!" fell into the vacuum between Mum and Bob, who were sitting at the table, eating breakfast. Rainbow plumped into a chair and studied them while she ate her cereal: Bob's mouth was a short, straight line and Mum had slipped into sadness. Last night's laughter had disappeared into the sky with the smoke from the fire.

Mum spilt milk over the letters that had been pushed to one side to make room for the bowls. Bob growled at her. Mum sighed, mopped up part of the mess and stirred her tea. Stirring was a bad sign – she'd given up sugar several months ago with the arrival of the health-food fad, and only stirred her tea when she was particularly distraught. Bob rolled a cigarette and lit it instead of eating his usual toast and home-made jam. It was difficult to breathe in the same room as them. Rainbow bolted down the rest of her cereal and stood up.

Mum held out her arms. "Give your mum a hug, love."

Rainbow gave her a quick squeeze and started to extricate herself.

"Leave the girl out of it," Bob snarled.

Rainbow's arms went slack. "Out of what?"

Neither replied.

"Leave me out of what?"

"Nothing, love. Bob's not feeling well. He had too much to drink last night."

"Shut it, Jasmine!"

Rainbow glared at Bob and wound her arms back around Mum.

"Shall we go and hug some trees?" she whispered.

Mum stroked Rainbow's thick hair. "No, love. I've got to finish Jeff's song. He's coming to pick it up today."

"You can work in my tree house if you like."

"I'll never make it up the ladder. I'll be fine in my workroom."

Rainbow took her bowl to the sink, scowling at Bob as she passed. He'd cleared up the rest of the spilt milk and was organising the disarray of papers, unnoticed by Mum, who carried her mug of tea into her workroom. Tidying up was Bob's way of preparing for a fight.

Rainbow had to get out of the house. She couldn't go to Patti's home yet because Patti was away this morning. She knew what she would do. Upstairs, she picked up her rucksack and then went to her tree house.

Sitting cross-legged in her den, she studied the tree limbs that framed the walls around her. Nothing else needed growing. She stood up, leant out of the doorway and searched for a branch to stretch. Dozens arched above her. If she could climb onto the roof, they would be accessible. She dragged her wooden box to the entrance and pulled herself up, kicking against the trunk and twisting herself into the fork of the roof branch. Once there, she looked across the garden and the woods, towards the village in the valley below. The Drunken House was hidden in shadow.

To one side of her, a thin branch split away from a larger one. She laid her hands on it, shifting them slightly higher until they felt comfortable. Then she closed her eyes and concentrated.

At first it was an effort not to open her eyes and look; not to think about something else. It was like when she tried to see behind her eyelids: to begin with, her eyelids would flicker and she'd only see darkness. Then, gradually, shapes in hues of orange would start to appear.

After a few seconds her hands seemed to pass through the superficial layer of bark and touch an element more intimate to the tree. It was the closeness of a heart-to-heart conversation, without the heart and without speaking. The word 'soul' came into her mind. There was something comforting and natural about the feel of the tree in her hands, and she remembered the reassurance she'd felt as a young child when she'd hugged trees with Mum.

When she'd stopped travelling through the bark and could feel the calmness of the tree's soul, she started to imagine it stretching. Her fingers moulded around the branch, squeezing slightly. She felt it glide lengthwise and opened her eyes. The branch was young and impressionable: growing it took little effort.

The next branch she tried was even smaller. This time, as she felt it move, she exerted more pressure with one hand and created a slight bend in the branch. She giggled at the result: this was fun! She could make a spaghetti tree. Were there other tree-stretchers she could share this magic with? She would have to find out more about trees and treeshapers.

Before she could experiment further, she heard the kitchen door slam. It was too hard for Mum. It had to be Bob. She slithered out of the fork, swung herself back down into her den and watched him stride along the drive. He looked like a bull, snorting in rage, bursting for a fight. She hoped he hadn't attacked Mum. What would it take to calm him down this time?

"Rainbow!" he roared.

She decided to try her 'innocent' face. She poked her head out of the doorway.

"What?"

"Get down here."

"Why?"

He swore at her. "Get down here this instant and I'll tell you why," he snarled.

It was one of his worse moods – he didn't usually swear until she retaliated – so she stayed in the safety of her shelter. The innocent approach was pointless.

"Come up here if it's so important."

"Cut the cheek! You and your mother, you're dirty swine, the pair of you, leaving your trash all over the place. I'm fed up with being the only one who tidies the house. D'you hear me?"

"Sorry, Bob. What trash?"

"Apple cores, clothes, papers...."

"That was me, not Mum," she lied.

"Well, you're a disgusting pig."

Rainbow nodded and cast her eyes down. Did she need to do a bit of crying? Probably not – he seemed to have run out of puff already. She would have to remember that the 'sorry' technique finished him off more quickly than the 'speaking back' one.

He was still staring when she raised her face with the 'shamed' expression.

"What have you done to your tree house?" he asked.

He must be referring to the gap between the walls and the roof. He'd be angry if she mentioned the word 'magic' and she didn't want him forbidding her to grow branches.

"Oh, you mean the roof?" She coughed to gain time. "I took the top planks off to make a window."

"I'm coming up."

He struggled up the rope ladder, grunting with each step. She checked that nothing stolen was visible and then sat down on the box.

"It's bigger than I remember," he said.

"You haven't been up here for years."

He examined the gap. Rainbow tapped her foot on the floor and rehearsed her lie in her head.

He scratched his chin. "How did you manage to do such a clean job?"

"I guess I've got workman's hands."

He glared at her. "Well, you'd better not have left my tools lying around."

He took a last suspicious look at the gap and then groped his way back down the ladder. Rainbow breathed a sigh of relief. She would have to be more careful in future.

CHAPTER FIVE

The thought of her magic hands filled Rainbow with a sense of power. At the same time, she was reluctant to tell anyone. She could already feel the weight of people's stares and hear echoes of them referring to her as a weirdo. It was time to find other people who could shape trees and to learn more about her skill. She didn't even know what it was officially called.

She spent the rest of the morning searching for information. There was nothing about it in Bob's gardening or biology books, and nothing in Mum's secret stash of books about spiritual magic either. What she really needed was a specialist tree book. No doubt Patti's family had one – they had as many bookshelves as there was wall space. She would look when she went to pick up her kitten that afternoon.

Lunch was a strange affair. Mum was caught up in her song-writing. She didn't notice when Rainbow tipped the remains of the home-made soup down the petal-holes of the drain and heated up a tin of the tomato soup she'd bought at the shop. Bob looked even more distracted. Several times,

Rainbow turned to see him stroking his chin and staring at her.

"What did you do with the wood you took off?" he asked at last, having fidgeted all the way through the meal.

"Off what?"

"Your tree house."

"I chucked it onto the woodpile," she said, and escaped outside to fetch her kitten before he could ask any more questions.

🌿🌿🌿

She had thought she'd choose the black one, but when Patti opened the shed door, Rainbow saw a new cat. It was mostly ginger, tainted from perfection by one white leg, and lay on its side in a cardboard box.

"Where's that cat come from? It wasn't here yesterday."

It was smaller than the other cats but bigger than the kittens.

"It was Mr Landing's. You know, our neighbour. He moved house yesterday. Mam couldn't bear the idea of the cat being abandoned, so she said we'd have it. It's divvy; completely brain-damaged."

They approached. It was concentrating on something in a corner of the ceiling. Rainbow looked up to see what had caught its attention, and saw a cobweb trampolining under the weight of a trapped wasp. Patti wriggled her fingers and tried to divert the cat, but it ignored her. She pulled aside the stack of discarded wellies and captured her favourite black kitten instead.

Rainbow dangled her fingers over the ginger cat's head. It rolled over and tried to catch them with its front paws, kicking against her arm with the hind ones. Rainbow slipped her other hand under its back and picked it up. It stretched over backwards as she cradled it, arching the knobbles of its spine, and reached lazily for the ground with its front legs.

"Look, he's an acrobat!" she said, holding him out to show Patti.

"A failed one," Patti replied, hissing her contempt as the cat overstretched, lost its balance and tumbled onto the floor.

"He didn't even land on his feet," said Rainbow. "He's the one I want."

"Won't you take the black one? Otherwise they'll drown him."

"Rubbish. Your mum would never drown a kitten and your dad wouldn't know how to. Anyway, he's too busy working. Your older brothers might, but they're away. That leaves little Jimmy, and he's too nice to drown anything. Come on, let's tell your mum I've chosen Acrobat."

They burst into the kitchen. Patti's mum was washing runner beans from the garden. Rainbow showed her Acrobat and then asked if she could borrow a book about trees for Bob. Mrs Bellamy dried her hands and helped Rainbow choose the thickest one.

"What do you want the book for?" Patti asked, once they were outside again.

"I told you. It's for Bob. I've got to go now. See you at school tomorrow."

She stuffed the book into her rucksack, gathered Acrobat into her arms and pushed the gate shut with her knee.

When she reached the deserted playground, she released Acrobat into the grass. She plumped down beside him and took out the book. In the section entitled 'Topiary: Shaping Your Trees', there were no pictures of people bending branches with their bare hands. The section didn't mention specialists who could change the shape of trees either. Tree-hugging was shown in the part called 'Trees through the Ages', but she couldn't find anything about alternative growing techniques.

Acrobat pounced around her. Either he was playing with insects that were too small for her to see, or he had some cat form of invisible friend. She shut the book, shoved it back into her rucksack and tickled Acrobat's tummy. Then she scooped him up onto her shoulder and continued her journey home. She would have to resort to asking somebody.

Acrobat seemed to like his form of transport, although he dug in his claws when she tried to run. They came to the Drunken House and Acrobat made a wild jump for the hedgerow. He must have sensed the horror emanating from it, even though Rainbow could no longer feel the invisible eyes. She scrambled up the bank to retrieve him and then turned to slither down.

Michael stood on the opposite side of the road, leaning on his door frame.

"Hi, Rainbow. What's that you've got?"

"Hi. It's Acrobat, my new cat." She jumped down onto the road. "Isn't he cute?"

She held him out to show Michael, who limped across the lane and took him into his hands.

"A ginger tom. You know gingers are always male?"

"How can you tell?"

"It's just a fact. I know lots of useless trivia."

Rainbow thought about the lack of information in the tree book.

"Do you know anything about growing things?"

"A bit. Why? Do you want to grow some more vegetables to sell?"

Acrobat fidgeted in Michael's hands. Rainbow took him back. He clawed up to her shoulder and settled himself like a scarf around her neck.

"No. It's about trees."

"I might be able to help you, then. My father ran a tree nursery. What do you want to know?"

"How they grow."

Michael shifted his weight from his good to his bad leg and then back again.

"Trees are plants, Rainbow. You plant a seed – an acorn, for example – then you water it and let it grow." He paused. "Is that what you mean?"

Rainbow nodded.

"Why don't you come inside? I need to sit down."

They crossed the road, Rainbow's hands on Acrobat's head and rump, and entered the gloomy house.

"Would you like a drink?"

"No, thanks. I can't stay long. So trees grow like plants. How else?"

Acrobat scrambled down from her shoulders and skittered across the table, then dived to the floor and padded towards the kitchen. Rainbow took off her rucksack. Could he smell ghosts?

Michael scraped up a chair, lowered himself into it and stretched out his scarred leg. He started to massage it.

"What else do you want to know? How to graft them? How to treat them against diseases? How long they live?"

Rainbow hesitated.

Fraser had ruined everything the day Rainbow had invited Rebecca home for the first time. When he'd come to their house to pick Rebecca up, Rainbow had hugged him as usual and started to tell him about Rebecca falling off the rope ladder.

Then Mum had appeared. Fraser had stopped listening. Rainbow had pulled on his sleeve, but he'd ignored her. She'd left him to Mum and gone up to her bedroom to continue the mosaic she was making with Rebecca.

When she came back down ten minutes later, to ask if Rebecca could stay a bit longer, she overheard him say her name. She crept closer. He was recounting the secret she'd told him about Mrs Jones – and laughing at her. Mum was laughing, too. The more Mum laughed, the more detail Fraser went into. He made Rainbow sound ridiculous.

She'd never felt such a glut of tearing hate before: Fraser had promised he wouldn't tell anyone how she knew Mrs Jones was an alien. She'd run back upstairs, told Rebecca that Fraser was in a hurry to leave and dashed to the toilet so she wouldn't have to face him. She'd avoided him ever since.

Standing in Michael's front room, she wondered if Michael would betray her too.

"I just need to know whether you can force them to grow," she said.

"You mean by putting them in a greenhouse or using fertiliser?"

"No, by stretching them with your hands."

Michael stopped rubbing his leg. She waited for him to make a joke. He stared out of the front window.

"I've never seen it done," he said, slowly, turning back to face her. "But that doesn't mean it's impossible. Why do you want to know?"

"It's for my school project."

"We could look in a book."

"I've looked. There's nothing in Patti's tree book. Have you got any books?"

Michael nodded at the piles of boxes. "Buried somewhere in there. Who's Patti?"

"My friend. Can we look at them?"

"If there's nothing in a specialist tree book, I'd say you couldn't stretch them. Wouldn't you?"

"I s'pose so."

"So if someone found a tree that stretched, I should think it would be quite exciting. Extraordinary. I'd like to see a tree like that."

Rainbow frowned. Her hands were magic, not the tree, weren't they? She jumped up from the table.

"Let's do an experiment."

"An experiment? You mean, try to force a tree to stretch?"

Rainbow nodded. She led the way out to his garden and pointed across the weeds. A young tree shaded the corner between the workshop and the boundary wall. Its branches were low enough for Rainbow to reach.

"That one."

"The ash?"

"Whatever it is; the one by the wall."

She stood against the lowest branch and felt it grate her forehead. She would try to grow the trunk below this branch, which would allow her to walk underneath it afterwards.

Michael was watching her, his arms folded.

"So how shall we start?" he asked.

"If you look the other way, I'll try to stretch the trunk."

He turned his back. Rainbow laid her hands and cheek against the crevasses of the trunk. Closing her eyes, she let her fingers crawl over the ash's skin. She felt as though she were a great distance away, looking down onto a neverending mountain range of ridges and valleys. One part of the bark felt right. She let her hands rest there. The bark nestled into her palms until it and her hands were one. She pressed slowly. Her fingers stretched out and her hands flattened into the bark. She willed the ash to stretch. She coaxed it to taste the pleasure of stretching after a long sleep.

The sap pulsed upwards from the heart of its trunk to the extremities of its twigs. Then the ash settled back down into its meditative peace. Rainbow opened her eyes and released her hands. Her arms were heavy and her palms were marked with the imprints of the tree's ridges. It was as if there had been an exchange. She understood that the tree would keep the mark of her growth and she would keep a shadow of its imprint.

She didn't need to try to walk underneath the branch to know that she could. Her instinct told her the ash had responded. She dropped her arms, stood back from it and admired its shape and solidity. How strange that she hadn't noticed the beauty of its symmetry, the music of its leaves caressing each other in the slight breeze. It had so much character. She wanted to grow with it, to live the season changes with it, to breathe its greenness as it changed to brownness and withdrew into slumber.

"Rainbow, are you all right?" Michael shook her shoulders. "Rainbow?"

The force of Michael's concern hit her. She struggled to wrench her eyes from the ash and blinked several times.

"Oh! Yes, I'm fine. It's so powerful."

"Sit down for a minute. You've gone white."

She dropped onto the grass. Michael hurried away to fetch a glass of water. So it *was* her that was special – her hands – not simply her weeping willow.

He came back and passed her the glass. "Does this happen often?"

"No. Yesterday was the first time," she said.

Michael glanced at the tree and then lowered himself to the grass beside her. "I meant the trances."

"Oh! So did I," she lied. She tipped up the glass to hide her face.

"It grew, didn't it?" he said.

"No, nothing happened."

"Let's have a look." He limped to the trunk and studied it. "I can't see anything. Come and stand against this branch again."

Reluctantly, she stood up and walked towards the ash. Michael had his hand on the branch and his eyes fixed on her. There was no escape, unless … she took the last two steps awkwardly and touched the branch with her forehead.

"You see. Same as before," she said.

Michael ran his hand over his bald head.

"Even on tiptoes, you barely touch the branch. It's incredible."

Rainbow scowled. "I was on tiptoes before."

"Listen, Rainbow. Is this really for a school project?"

"Yes."

"Then I think you should leave it out. It's too unusual to write about in a project. What do you think?"

Rainbow turned around. "Where's Acrobat gone?"

Michael laughed and laid a hand on her arm. "Come inside. I've got something to show you."

CHAPTER SIX

Rainbow followed Michael indoors. Acrobat was curled up on her rucksack in the front room. She sat down at the table and stroked him while Michael hunted through one of the cardboard boxes. He soon found what he was looking for and slumped a thick photo album onto the table. Then he drew up a chair beside her.

The brown-and-white photos he showed her looked more like drawings than the proper colour photographs she was used to seeing. There were babies in flowing white dresses, children posed like grown-ups and a severe granny sitting in a high-backed chair with an ornate walking stick in her hands. Michael flicked through the pages, slowing down once or twice when Rainbow wanted to study a particularly interesting photo: three girls in stripy swimsuits standing on an empty beach, flower-encrusted hats skinned to their heads; a family picnic complete with rug, hamper and crockery. She wished she had a photo like this of her dad.

He reached a frilly-edged photo of a grizzled man leaning on a rough-cut staff, and stopped. He squinted and passed his index finger over the old man.

"Here he is."

"Who is it?" she asked, intrigued by the shepherd. "He looks like Patti's pictures of Jesus."

"This is my great-grandfather, the one who started our tree nursery," said Michael. "When you asked me about stretching trees, I said I'd never seen it done. But I *have* heard of it. There were rumours about my great-grandfather being a wizard. When I was five, and fascinated by witches and wizards, my great-grandfather died. He must have been at least a hundred years old. After the funeral, everyone came back to the house and I heard two old ladies talking about his magic. I already knew he had healing hands and could make people well, but these ladies were gossiping about his magic with trees. They were telling each other about the times he'd changed the shapes of trees. They talked about how he'd cured trees of diseases, repaired their damaged bark and rebalanced them when they'd been uprooted. So I asked my grandfather what they meant about his father's magic. But he growled at me and threatened me with a hiding if I ever spoke about it. He was wicked with a belt."

"So other people *can* make trees grow?"

"Well, I haven't heard the like of it since, and the rumour was never confirmed by anyone, so it can't be very common. And when something isn't very common, we have to be careful what we say."

Silence pressed in on her. It felt as if Michael were sharing a huge secret with her, not the other way around.

"You mean keep it secret?"

"Yes. It would be best for the moment. How many people

know about your gift?"

"No one really. Bob saw what I'd done to grow my tree house but I think he believed my lie."

Michael didn't look reassured. "What about Jasmine?"

Rainbow jerked up her chin. "How do you know my mum's name?"

"They told me in the pub. Does she know about your gift?"

"No."

"Good. I shouldn't mention it to her – mothers tend to over-worry."

"Not mine. I did tell her I had magic hands, but she wasn't listening and just told me to magic myself away."

Michael shook his head, smiling slightly.

"What do you think would happen if people knew about your gift?"

Rainbow crossed her arms and considered.

"If it's really spooky, I expect the newspapers would do a piece on me and I'd get lots of money. And everyone at school would call me a weirdo and not want to hang around with me."

"Right. You'd be exploited. Do you know what that means?"

"Of course."

"Your life wouldn't be your own. You'd be like a celebrity, but worse. People would treat you as an oddity. That wouldn't be much fun, would it?"

"I'm used to that. At school they give me sideways looks every time I ask a question."

"Do they?"

"They did. Now I don't ask questions."

Michael grinned and then shook his head. "Actually, being

exploited would be far worse than the sideways looks. You'd better not mention your gift for the time being. When you're older, you can think about whether you want to use it as a basis for your life's work."

"You mean as a career? Shaping trees?"

Her mind flitted back to an old story, a legend her mum had told her years ago, before she'd started school: something about a foreign girl risking her life for a tree. *Rita something? Rita Devi? No, Amrita Devi. That was it.*

"Maybe," said Michael.

"I like the sound of that," she said.

"Good. It'll be our secret. Can you keep secrets?"

The memory of Fraser and Mum laughing together over her secret about Mrs Jones flitted into her mind. She frowned. But Michael didn't know Mum. Rainbow vowed she would never let him get near her. As long as they didn't meet, it would be fine.

"*I* can keep it secret," she said, "but what about you? Do you promise not to tell anyone?"

Michael held up a finger and drew it across his throat. "Cross my heart, hope to die." He paused for a moment, then continued: "If you like, I can teach you what I know about trees. Then when the time comes for you to decide whether you want to develop your gift, you'll already be a tree expert."

"You bet! I don't know anything about them." Rainbow scooped up Acrobat from where he was pawing a panicking beetle on the floor. "But I've got to go now. School starts tomorrow."

She began the new school year reluctantly. Each day was a trial to be passed until she was free to do the things that really mattered: shaping trees and sketching. Michael was the key to both, and she sketched or learnt about trees with him most evenings on her way home from school. Sometimes she'd watch him sculpting and other times she'd ask for help with her homework. His job sorting mail in the local town meant that he worked early in the mornings and was always at home by late afternoon.

He told magical tales about his travels in Europe on his motorbike before his accident. He'd never lived in one place for more than a year, and admitted that he found it impossible to settle down. Sometimes he'd regretted running away, but when she asked him why, he changed the subject. Rainbow imagined a lonely girl standing on top of a hill with tears running down her face, watching him leave. She didn't press him for more details.

More than anything, they talked about trees. Rainbow told him which ones she'd shaped and brought him leaves so they could identify them in the book he'd given her. The only disappointment was that he couldn't walk very far because of his leg. He never accompanied her on her tree-research trips to the surrounding woods.

One Saturday afternoon in late October Rainbow couldn't stand being shut indoors any longer. She'd spent all day hoping for the sun to appear so she could grow some trees but it was still gloomy outside and would soon be dark.

As soon as Mum and Bob had wandered their separate afternoon ways, she shoved open the sitting-room window and breathed in the essence of decomposing leaves. An autumn mist shrouded Wymer Hill. Rainbow wished she could live in a parallel world where there were no rules and no school; just her and nature and Acrobat … and Michael. She loved this season. Early autumn meant swirling leaves, gales and drizzle before the crunchy frosts of November arrived. On windy days she was powerful: a witch running through the fields, the wind buffeting her, hair whipping around her face as she twirled to the whistling fury in the treetops. The wind gave her power. It could make her fly, she was sure. She could almost hear voices in it, calling to her, beckoning her to climb to dizzy heights and launch herself into its invisible embrace.

Today, however, was calm and dank. She left the window open to fill the stuffy room with damp October air and pulled on her favourite red anorak. Calling Acrobat, she picked her way through the wet grass to the tree house. Acrobat shook each paw as he lifted it, making their progress tortoise-like.

"Come on, Fatty Batty!"

Autumn had stripped her weeping willow of leaves. She hoisted Acrobat onto the pole she'd placed at an angle between her den and the ground as a bridge for him, and climbed her rope ladder. She'd made another change too: the roof was now lined with some plastic sheeting Michael had given her, which meant she could spend time here when it was raining.

In her box she kept the guide to common trees that had belonged to Michael's great-grandfather. Her favourite pages were the black-and-white photos of different barks. She could imagine them under her fingertips as she studied them. This helped soothe the ache when she hadn't touched a tree for a few days. On each page there was a space for notes. Here, she drew the trees she'd shaped and wrote how each one felt to her hands. Some trees were easier to shape than others; some made more of a whistle than a creak while they stretched, and some left deeper marks on her hands.

She'd already worked on half the trees in her book. Today, the page fell open at the beech tree. She studied the picture of the canopy shape, the sketches of the leaf and beechnuts and the photo of its bark. She wouldn't have time to do any growing before night fell but she could search for a beech. She turned down the corner of the page, slipped it into her rucksack, and left her tree house. Acrobat poked his nose around the plastic sheet that acted as the door, twitched his whiskers and returned inside.

"See you, Bats. Don't let anyone in," called Rainbow.

She dragged open the five-barred gate that separated the garden from the muddy lane and walked down the hill, stepping around pothole pools, her hands buried in the fur of her pockets. She thought she'd seen a beech tree on the way to the village. The trees passed, looking down at her sleepily, as if she was stationary and they were moving. She stopped at the oak she'd stretched on her way home from school the week before and examined its bark. The place where she'd laid her hands showed no signs of damage.

It didn't take long to find the beech tree. She was a redheaded beauty, almost symmetrical, the exception being the side hanging over the lane. Tractors had mauled the branches on this side as they towed trailer-loads of hay up the lane, giving the tree the look of a home-haircut. Rainbow fingered her own hair, remembering the disastrous fringe and her classmates' sniggers. Mum hadn't understood why she'd grown out the fringe.

On the side of the lane, in the passing space that was already thick with a batter of fallen leaves and mud, lay a topping of beechnuts. They were prickly under her booted feet. She bent down and studied the hollow-cheeked pyramids, then slipped a few clean ones into her pocket.

The bark of the beech tree surprised her. It was as smooth as it looked in the photo and reminded her of wallpaper. Its irregular, horizontal knife-scores gave it relief. They lipped up as she ran her fingers up and down the trunk. She would enjoy growing this one. Its trunk divided into tributaries at the height of her shoulders, so she would be able to climb into it easily. Not today though: it was too wet. And it was starting to get dark.

She wondered whether she had time to visit Michael. It wouldn't be the first time he'd lent her a torch so that she could turn it on if any cars came along the lane on her way home. It was a five-minute walk to his house. The previous evening he'd mentioned an idea for a shared drawing project. She'd been working on caricatures, and her favourite was a girl she liked to draw sitting in trees or hugging their trunks. She called the character Amrita and had told Michael what she remembered of the Bishnoi legend.

Her decision was quickly made. She jogged down the lane to join her best friend in the Drunken House.

CHAPTER SEVEN

"You're late again!" Bob bellowed. He was downstairs.

"It's your fault for setting a rehearsal at such a stupid time. On a Sunday, too," shrieked Mum.

Rainbow, sitting upstairs in her bedroom, wondered why they had to shout when they were in the same room as each other.

"Four o'clock is reasonable for any normal person. Look at the state of you!"

"Just because *you're* dressed up for that slut, it doesn't mean I have to be."

Rainbow covered her ears with her hands. For a moment, all she could hear was the reassuring pound of blood coursing through veins and a slight creaking as her fingers stiffened and relaxed. Then Mum and Bob's voices forced their way into her cocoon.

"Shut up!" Rainbow yelled. "I'm trying to do my homework."

Acrobat, curled up on her lap, dug in his claws and stretched. There was silence.

Ten minutes later Mum put her head around Rainbow's

bedroom door. She was heavily made-up and dressed in purple and black with orange trimmings.

"We're off to our rehearsal, love," she said. "Will you be all right on your own?"

"I always am, aren't I?"

"Yes, you act more maturely than a certain person I could mention."

Rainbow refused to be drawn in. "You'd better go. You're already late."

She turned back to her maths homework and pretended to be absorbed in the figures. Mum dropped a kiss onto her head and left the room.

"Rainbow! Don't let the fire go out," shouted Bob.

Rainbow tickled Acrobat's ears with her right hand and twiddled her pen in her left. Mum was starting to talk about Bob in the same tone of voice she used for Dad, on the rare occasions she mentioned him. She'd married Bob when Rainbow was only a year old and Rainbow couldn't remember being on her own with Mum. Would Bob leave them too? She wouldn't care if he did, except that she'd have to cope with Mum alone. She imagined Mum turning wild, wandering aimlessly around the countryside and singing her depressing songs until ivy grew over her and transformed her into a gnarled statue. At least Bob kept Mum in touch with reality. Dad had given up on her.

She dropped her pen in surprise. There was no Dad-ache! She usually felt a longing when she thought about her dad. But since she'd met Michael and started to learn about trees, the hollow inside her seemed to have closed up. Michael meant much more to her than Fraser had ever done. He was her secret, her accomplice. She mustn't let Mum bewitch him.

Acrobat miaowed. He shook himself out of Rainbow's grip and fell to the floor, his tail wagging.

"Oh, Bats! I'm sorry. I didn't mean to hurt you."

She picked him up and squashed her face into his ginger fur.

"Let's go out. Maybe Michael will help me with this maths."

She took one last despairing look at her maths homework. It was taking forever to finish. The numbers stared stubbornly back at her. They refused to team up and rearrange themselves into brackets. She folded her answer sheet into four and slipped it into the back pocket of her jeans. Mr Cunningham talked about solving problems with numbers, but Rainbow couldn't get to grips with this concept. How could you solve a problem with numbers? She wondered whether she could solve the Mum and Bob problem with numbers. Which ones would it take?

She threw on her red anorak, left the house and jogged down the road to Michael's. A yellow stain of light in the mist outside his window showed he was in. She knocked at the door. While she waited, she pulled the beechnuts out of her pocket and examined the starred husks. They were bristly, but the bristles didn't hurt the toughened skin of her palms as they once would have done.

"Hello, Rainbow." Michael opened the door wide.

"Hi. Are you busy?"

"No. I had a friend here, but he left a minute ago."

She stepped inside and shut the door against the

October chill.

"Shall we finish our picture?" he continued. "I've hidden it away so I'm not tempted to look at your half, and so you don't look at mine."

"Where have you put it?"

He tapped the side of his nose. "It's safe under its tiled roof."

It would be easy to follow him and discover his hiding place but her concern, for the moment, was her maths. She asked if he'd help her and he agreed. She took off her coat and hung it on her hook. After two months of occupation, the Drunken House was warm in the middle but still a little damp around the edges.

"So who's your friend?" she asked.

"A bloke called Fraser. You may know his daughter. She's called Becky."

"*Fraser?*"

"Oh dear. It sounds as if you don't like them."

"I hate him."

Michael rubbed his head.

"Does he know I come here?" asked Rainbow.

"I don't think so. Why?"

"Good. Don't ever say my name to him. Please."

She couldn't bear to think of Fraser talking to Michael about her; to imagine them laughing together over things she'd said and done.

"You haven't mentioned my gift to him, have you?"

"Of course not." Michael paused. "Do you want to tell me why you feel so strongly?"

Rainbow shook her head. She pulled her homework out of

her pocket and put it on the table. Michael stared at it.

"Talking of secrets," he continued, "does your mum know that you visit me?"

"No. Why?"

"Doesn't she wonder where you are?"

"Mum doesn't notice I've gone, let alone wonder where I am. Bob knows I'm out, but he thinks I'm defying Mum and hanging out at Patti's."

"Maybe you should tell them."

"No."

"Why not?"

"Things are better like this," she said.

"I don't want you to get into trouble."

He looked disappointed. Had Fraser told him that Mum was beautiful? Or was he sad because she wouldn't explain herself? She pushed the maths paper away.

"Look, if I tell Mum about us, she'll feel guilty about not noticing I've been out. She'll make a fuss and want to meet you. Then she'll bewitch you, and you won't be my secret anymore. You'll be like all the others who come up to the house. You'll end up being Mum and Bob's friend instead of mine."

"Rainbow!"

"Well, it's true. You don't know what she's like."

"I think it would be normal for her to want to know who I am. I'd want to meet me, if I was your mum ... or rather, your dad."

"Bob's not my dad. He's my stepdad."

"I know, you told me."

"Anyway, my dad's dead, so *he* doesn't care about meeting you.

Nor does Bob."

"Dead? You didn't tell me that."

She shrugged. "He died after he left us."

Michael picked up the maths sheet. He folded it in half, then in half again, and again.

"What's the matter?" asked Rainbow. "You really want me to tell Mum, don't you?"

Michael put the paper back down.

"I think I'd better come to your house and tell her myself."

Fraser had ruined everything. But Michael looked determined. Maybe he was right: if Fraser learnt she was friends with Michael and then told Bob, Bob would forbid her to come back.

"In that case you must promise you'll still be my friend and not theirs," she said. "And that you won't talk to them about my gift."

"Of course. Nothing will change that."

Michael smiled, but the twinkle didn't reach his eyes.

They bent over the homework together. An hour later, Rainbow ran home with the unlit torch in her hand. She didn't want to see the threatening shadows at the edge of the light beam.

🌱🌿🌱

The next day was dry and sunny, perfect for tree-growing. Rainbow was always amazed how the weather could pass from one extreme to another overnight. This Monday evening had been stolen from September, stuffed into the last week of October and uncovered from between the layers of misty days.

The sleepy sun was irresistible.

Thoughts of the beech tree had riddled her all day and she'd spent her physics lesson sketching it from memory. On the way home from school she stopped in front of it. At last, the moment she'd been looking forward to had arrived. Her hands skimmed the beech tree's bark. She wasn't sure whether its warmth came from the late afternoon sun or the contact with her hands.

These days her hands had a pachyderm's skin and were always warm. They'd become less sensitive to everything other than trees, and she constantly dropped dishes and plates. It seemed that by developing this new sense she was slowly losing an old one.

She found a handhold, pulled herself halfway up into the branches and wriggled her legs and torso until she was balanced between the triple trunks. Then she searched with hands and eyes until she discovered her next stopping place: a fork where a branch cut her view of the field below her into two. With each movement, a few more russet leaves danced to the ground and she rose higher above the lane, climbing up the beech's face beneath its heavy fringe.

When she reached its eye level, she stopped to rest. She was breathing heavily. In the hedge by the passing space lay her school bag, dusted by leaves; a reminder that she couldn't stay too long. Had the beech been able to see, it would have had a good view of the tractors chuntering up the lane to decimate its trailing branches.

Her breath returned to normal and she lowered herself until her pelvis fitted in the crook between two of the trunks. She wrapped her legs around the one in front of her and put her hands on a thick branch. Her cheek, laid against its skin, felt the tree's chill. She began to massage the branch in her search for the right place. Only her hands could find these zones, and usually it took a few seconds, a dozen at the most, to find one.

She spent a minute caressing the beech in vain. It wasn't unwelcoming, like the horse chestnut had been on that wet day last week. She'd respected its unwillingness and left it until the weather was dry. No, the beech was as cold as a dead body: as cold as her cheeks when she'd fallen into the Blue Lake last spring. It needed warming up.

She closed her eyes. Her hands hovered. The heat from her body dissipated through the papery bark, and the coolness of the branch seeped up through the crevasses in her palms. She was surprised. There was normally an exchange of heat. She concentrated on sucking up the cold into the pores of her skin and searched for the willingness that was so slow to surface. It was as if the beech were asleep.

There was still no response. She opened her eyes and lifted her cheek. She was as tired as the beech: cold and heavy and tired. She fidgeted and started to shiver. Either she'd lost her gift or it didn't work on beech trees. Perhaps this particular branch didn't want to be stretched. She changed position and sat on another branch, her back to the trunk. This one was slimmer and grew straight across the lane. It would have been perfect for a swing.

She let her hands dangle, shook them and opened and closed her fists to bring back the warmth. Once they were warm again, she trickled her fingers over the bark and then placed her palms flat against it. Right here. This was the niche. She relaxed. Warmth crawled through the fibres. Contact. She recognised the phase of mutual recognition. This always preceded the easing out of fibres, which she would then guide into shape with her hands.

The beech was extraordinary! She could feel no movement, no creaking or sighing, no aroma of green dust. It was a silent, invisible mover.

Or was it refusing to move?

She opened her eyes. Her hands were in the same place. The branch was unchanged. She had asked and the tree had refused.

Part of her wanted to stop, to leave the tree alone. It was clear that it didn't want to grow. Or was it testing her? Her resolve strengthened into stubbornness. She wanted it to grow. She wanted to see whether she could force it despite its reluctance. She wanted to master it.

She laid her hands back in place and pressed harder. The beech quivered deep in its internal cells. She insisted. Waves of determination flowed through her hands and urged the branch to stretch. She dominated its resistance. She was powerful enough. She would overcome its laziness.

At last, the branch's fibres began to draw apart. She began to smile in triumph – but the smile quickly froze on her face. Where was the normal vibrancy? Instead, there was a twanging sensation, as if the fibres were ligaments she was overstretching to snapping point.

This wasn't right.

As the thought hit her, she felt the fibres twitch under her hands. This was wrong. All wrong. She stared at the branch, expecting to see it ripping apart. Nothing showed.

She put her hands back, to feel what was happening. Fibres were still twanging. And she could hear a strange, growling crescendo. The twanging accelerated. She pressed her hands down and tried to calm the vibrations under her palms. She stroked her hands towards the trunk, trying to ease the ligaments back to their original position.

A flash of red broke her concentration. She glanced down into the lane. A car was approaching. She realised that the strange growling noise was its engine, not the tree. It was Fraser's Porsche. Fraser. He was coming to her house to ridicule her in front of Mum.

The beech! She'd stopped concentrating for a split second. Under her palms the twanging heightened to a groan and then a silent screech. She had to stop the branch. She didn't want it to break. She forced all her energy through her palms. The branch teetered on the edge of catastrophe; hovering, waiting. All it needed was a little more effort to draw it back.

And then she had an idea.

It was a terrible, murderous thought. She pushed it away and willed the fibres back into place. But her hesitation had been fatal. The branch's fibres edged further apart. She redoubled her efforts. The red Porsche was still approaching. She held on. If she could pump enough energy into the branch, the car would be through, out of danger. She concentrated with all her strength.

The car slowed down. What was Fraser doing? *Go on, go on!*

It stopped beneath her. The passing place. *Get out of there, Fraser!* Yellow car coming the other way. It was too much for her. Fibres screamed. The branch cracked. She couldn't hold on any longer.

Golden leaves flew around her. She and the branch were falling. There was an explosion of red. Screams. Under her broken body she could feel the cold, cold branch. And under the branch, pressed against her nose, she saw squashed, blood-red metal.

More screams. Slamming doors. Mum's voice, howling. But under her, under the splinters of metal and wood, there were no sounds.

Then she heard Fraser swear. He was alive.

Mum's voice came closer. She could let go. Sounds mixed, danced together, entwined, danced away. She was part of the branch. She was drifting elsewhere, dead bark and drying sap imprinted on her cheek.

PART TWO

CAMBIUM

1990

"What's cambium?" asked Rainbow.
"Cambium is a secondary type of meristem. It divides to produce cells called secondary xylem and secondary phloem. They make the tree grow wider."

CHAPTER EIGHT

Phloem and Xylem

Phloem

Rainbow woke up in a hospital bed. Pain throbbed in her right leg. She opened her eyes and looked along her shrouded body to her feet. Her right leg was swollen with a plaster cast, making the left one seem shrunken. She wiggled the toes of her left foot and saw the sheet bow like a puppet in response. Her body was fine.

There was an empty space in her mind between landing on the roof of Fraser's car and opening her eyes in the hospital ward. Empty, except for the fleeting scent of Amrita. She had seen Amrita. She had seen another Rainbow. Amrita had tried to give her a message about healing, about splitting into two. But that wasn't the proper legend about Amrita. The proper legend was of a girl who had sacrificed herself to save a tree.

The end of the legend troubled her. Had Amrita died in her attempt to save the tree, or had she lived and saved it? She was sure that Amrita had lived and saved the tree, but she couldn't understand why this suddenly seemed so important. Nor why she felt as if part of herself had died.

"Rainbow?"

She looked up. Mum came into the room and rushed to the bed. There were tears in her eyes. The reality of the accident chased away Rainbow's thoughts about Amrita.

"Mum!"

Mum kissed her, straightened her pillow, stroked her hair, squeezed her hand. Rainbow felt a gleam of joy: Mum was fussing over her. But she looked sad. Rainbow swallowed.

"Fraser?" she asked.

"Fraser's fine. But I'm afraid there's some bad news, love."

Rainbow's delight slithered into the sheets. She wished Mum had saved the bad news for later.

"There was a man in the car with Fraser," continued Mum. "A man from the village. I'm afraid he died in the accident."

Rainbow's throat seized up. Only a whisper could escape: "Who?"

"No one you knew. And it wasn't your fault, love."

"But what was his name?"

Mum's eyes shifted slightly to the left. "Knowing his name won't help you get better. It was an accident. You must try to forget it."

"I need to know his name!"

Mum hesitated. "Well, if you're sure. He was called Michael Jallet."

Rainbow's eyes closed before her mum finished saying

his name. She willed herself back towards the spinning leaves of unconsciousness. But it was no good. She couldn't escape from reality, from the horror of what she'd done.

She reached out for Mum, who gathered her into a hug. Even the reassurance of Mum's arms didn't lessen the pain inside. She had killed her best friend.

Xylem

Rainbow wakes up in a hospital bed. Pain throbs in her right leg. She opens her eyes and looks along her shrouded body to her feet. Her right leg is swollen with a plaster cast, making the left one seem shrunken. She wiggles the toes of her left foot and sees the sheet bow like a puppet in response. Her body is fine.

Her mind flicks back to Amrita, the tree protector. She knows now that Amrita died in vain. This revelation came to her while she was unconscious. She remembers the moment of icy shock, like the time she'd fallen into the freezing water of the Blue Lake. First there was the warm hospital bed and the reassuring beep of machines as she struggled through spinning leaves. Then came Mum's voice.

There was an Arctic flash. Separation. Shock.

Then she'd seen her old self and Amrita hugging a dying tree. She was outraged at them both; furious at them for not knowing.

Now, though, she can't remember exactly what it is they don't know. The moment has frozen and won't thaw into sense. The idea of trees sickens her. She doesn't want anything to do with trees anymore, nor with Amrita. She knows with all her heart that Amrita died without saving the tree. She doesn't know why she's so sure, but she's certain that it doesn't matter now.

Pain spreads up from her right leg and she forgets about Amrita. Mum arrives and peers anxiously at her through smudged eyes. She says her name, kisses her, straightens her pillow, strokes her hair. But the sound of her low, throaty voice puzzles Rainbow. Something isn't right. Her subconscious nudges her towards a haze she can't quite remember.

"What happened?" she asks.

"There was an accident, love. You were climbing trees and a branch broke under you. Do you remember?"

"Yes. Fraser's all right though, isn't he? I heard you tell me while I slept."

Mum nods and opens her mouth to speak again, but Rainbow interrupts.

"What happened while I was asleep?"

Mum shifts in the plastic chair, uncoils her long legs and reaches into her bag. "Nothing. I sat beside you and the nurses looked after you."

"Oh." Rainbow frowns and searches for the source of the strangeness she can feel inside her. "You said something while I was asleep; something important."

Mum riffles through her bag. "It must have been a dream."

"No, I'm sure it was real."

Rainbow struggles to sit up, studying her mum. There's a desperate look in Mum's eyes, like in Patti's pony's eyes on windy days when he gallops from one end of the field to the other without respite.

"I said lots of things, love. I was worried."

Mum *does* look worried. Rainbow summons up her

courage: "Didn't you mention Dad?"

"No, of course not. Why would I do that?"

Mum must be really worried about something because her voie is devoid of the usual Dad anger. She clears her throat, perches on the edge of the bed and takes Rainbow's hands in her own.

"There is something I must tell you about the accident. There was a passenger in the car. He wasn't as lucky as Fraser. I'm afraid he passed away."

Rainbow squeezes her eyes shut. "Who was it?"

As Mum's mouth closes over Michael's name, Rainbow's stomach begins to cramp. She turns away from Mum, retches and then digs her fingers into her hair and starts to scream.

It isn't the cramps that make her scream. It's the recollection of that glacial flash. She's just remembered what Mum confessed while she was unconscious.

Phloem

Hours seemed to pass before Rainbow found the strength to release herself from the safety of Mum's arms. The knowledge of what she'd done lay heavy in her head, like a bandage she couldn't think through. Michael was dead. She'd killed him with her stupid antics in trees. If only she'd listened to the beech. If only she could go back in time and change what she'd done.

Mum smoothed back Rainbow's hair. She looked whiter than ever and her eyes wore their worried wrinkles. She would have been the last person to see Michael alive: her and Fraser. Maybe Mum had got everything wrong.

"Are you *sure* he ...?" She couldn't bring herself to say

the word.

"Yes, love. I'm sure. Try not to think about him. It was an accident. You must concentrate on getting better now. How's that leg?"

It was easy for Mum: she hadn't known Michael. She was probably glad that it hadn't been Fraser. If only …

"Rainbow? I knew I shouldn't have given you a name to focus on. It wasn't your fault. Now, how's your leg?"

Her leg hurt, but it was nothing compared to the pain of knowing she'd killed her best friend. She bit her lip, tasted salt and buried her face in her pillow. Of course it was her fault. She shouldn't have forced the beech, but she couldn't tell Mum. Her gift was a curse. She'd never use it again, never mention it to anyone else. Never, ever share the secret she'd shared with Michael.

Xylem

When Rainbow stops screaming and opens her eyes, the world has changed.

Nurses cluck around them, ethereal as ghosts. Mum is sitting on the hospital bed beside her, leaning over to stop Rainbow wrenching out her hair. Rainbow lets her hands drop, shakes off Mum's hands and stares at her. Although she looks exactly the same, she's not the Mum Rainbow thought she knew.

"Rainbow! What is it?"

Rainbow's mouth is full of acid. It's the taste of hate spiced with guilt and self-disgust. It's too much to take. She can't swallow this on her own.

She searches Mum's eyes for help in dissipating the

poisonous cocktail that's threatening to burn her from inside. She can forgive Mum for lying, if only Mum will admit the truth and help her deal with it.

"I killed him," she whispers.

"No, love. It was an accident."

"I killed him," she insists.

"You mustn't say that. It was an accident."

"Mum–" The word tastes foreign in her mouth.

"No. You must move on."

Rainbow swallows. Self-contempt floods her insides. If only she could say the words, challenge the confession she thinks her mother made while she was unconscious. But she can't; it's overwhelming. She's drowning. In a few seconds she'll no longer be able to breathe. One, two, three …

A determination she didn't know she possessed kicks in and she fights for survival. She's got to block out the past, separate herself from it, begin again … pretend it never happened.

The further she can distance herself from the person she was *before*, the easier it will be to forget about the accident. The easier it will be to turn her back on the terrible gift Michael encouraged. She mustn't torture herself. She mustn't think about how things could have been if her mother had told her the truth when it mattered. She's got to become someone who is as different from the person she was *before* as possible.

"Forget the accident and concentrate on getting better," soothes her mother.

Rainbow concentrates.

Phloem

Rainbow remained under observation for a week. At first she slept for much of the day. When she awoke she'd find Mum looking down anxiously at her. For the first millisecond she felt a wash of happiness at having Mum's full attention. Then her memory cut in and the weight of Michael pulled her back down.

On the third day she found a trick to stop herself thinking about Michael: Amrita. The two of them were linked in her mind. She would make her thoughts glide over Michael's name to land on Amrita's: Amrita, the tree-hugging survivor.

Each day she was able to linger a little longer on Michael before passing onto Amrita. When Mum and Bob came to take her home, she could visualise him sitting in his chair with his bad leg stretched out in front of him before she had to move onto Amrita.

On the last day she limped down the corridor and into the lift. She felt like a VIP, with Mum on one side and Bob on the other. She smiled her goodbyes to the nurses and experimented with her new crutches. But when she squeezed into the Mini, her throat constricted. Driving past the Drunken House was going to be the big test.

"We thought you might like to sleep downstairs until your leg's out of plaster," said Mum as she turned the Mini into their lane.

"Whatever."

"What would you prefer, love?" Mum's eyes sought Rainbow's in the rear-view mirror.

"Upstairs will be fine."

They approached the Drunken House bend. Rainbow closed her eyes.

"Watch the road!" cried Bob.

The Mini bumped into a pothole; the one just in front of the Drunken House. Rainbow's eyes opened of their own accord. She could see Michael in the front room. She could see the flash of his welding arc. Mum accelerated past. Rainbow blinked and craned her neck to see his face.

It was trick of her brain, a trick of the light. The house was empty. The hollow windows of its eyes stared hopelessly back at her.

"You'll see Acrobat in a minute," said Mum, her voice bright. "Everything will soon be back to normal."

Xylem

Rainbow concentrates on how to get better, how to get better than she was *before*. Mum – no, *Mother* – has refused to acknowledge what she said while she was unconscious. Mother has refused to help her. She's alone so she will speak to no one.

The first thing she has to change is her name. She's stopped thinking of herself as R–, and there's a hole where her name should be. This feels right. It matches the vacuum around and inside her. But she needs a name to plaster over the R– that she was *before*. She mulls over the Myras, Lorenzas and Chloes she has been during her childhood games. They won't do. She needs something ordinary. Something as plain and ugly as the lie she now knows she is.

The answer comes on the afternoon Mother drives her home from hospital in the yellow Mini. Bob is there too.

He makes an effort to walk slowly as she hobbles along the hospital corridor on her crutches. Her doctor is with them and she overhears Bob ask him if her silence is due to brain damage. She doesn't hear the doctor's answer. Perhaps her brain *has* been dislodged by the fall. Maybe the perpetual sickness in her throat and the memory of Mother's words are the result of an illness in her head. But she refuses this false, easy solution. There is no illness: only Mother and her lie. Everything is Mother's fault: even – especially – the accident.

The lift glides down to the ground floor. Mother tries to hug her, but her touch makes R– retch. In the car, R– slides her hand away from Mother's insistent grasp. She has become a stone. Are there such things as hollow stones? Bob and Mother talk to her but the words refuse to line up properly. She feigns sleep.

The car lurches into the Drunken House pothole. She resists the urge to open her eyes. *I can do it*, she thinks.

She succeeds.

Home appears disturbingly unchanged. She doesn't look at the weeping willow. The path to the front door is difficult to manoeuvre, but she refuses Bob's help.

"We thought you'd be better off sleeping downst–" he begins.

"I'm going up to my room."

She pushes away the Coke Mother offers her and struggles towards the stairs.

All afternoon Bob and Mother traipse up and down the stairs to check she's all right. They whisper to each other outside her door. The old R– would have loved the attention, but all she can feel through her numbness is a vague frustration that they won't leave her alone.

Her sketch pad is on her bedside table. She picks it up, wrenches out each page and throws both used and unused paper into the bin. This is good. Encouraged by the ease of changing things, she lurches into her mother's bedroom. The cardboard box of souvenirs is on top of the wardrobe. Inside, there are photos of herself as a baby, crumpled newspaper cuttings, paperwork and the Ouija board. Last time she opened the box she only looked at the photos. This time, she deals with everything.

Mother calls up to tell her that dinner is ready. She has prepared R–'s favourite dinner of pasta and courgettes and Bob has cleared the table. It's birthday treatment. So why doesn't she feel like the lucky birthday girl? Instead, she is struck by a sense of emptiness. How false everything seems. Mother smiles with her mouth, not her eyes. Bob doesn't grumble once. R– leaves most of her food and waits until they finish eating to make her announcement.

"You will call me Mary from now onwards."

Bob looks surprised. "Mary, Mary, quite contrary. Isn't Rainbow nicer?"

He obviously doesn't know the truth.

The effect on Mother, however, is satisfying. She grips the edge of the table with one hand and her glass with the other. The new voice in Mary's head whispers that it serves her mother right.

"What's the matter, Mother? Don't you like my choice?" She should be feeling frightened and sorry now. Somewhere inside, that's exactly how she feels. But she won't let this weakness surface. This is Mother's last chance to admit the truth and close the widening gap between them. It still hurts too much to challenge her directly.

The contours of Mother's face blur, as if she's about to collapse. Mary holds her breath and counts the seconds. She's ready to accept the truth.

"No, I'm … just surprised," says Mother.

Disappointment bubbles inside Mary. But the good thing about being a stone is that stones don't have feelings.

"I'm finished with Rainbow," she says. She pushes back her chair and reaches for her crutches.

Upstairs, Mary locks the bathroom door and opens the medicine cabinet. The scissors are inside. She slices them through her hair and throws sixteen handfuls of lifeless brown strands into the bin. Then she runs Bob's electric razor over the back of her head. What's left of Mary's hair must be dyed black.

Phloem

Bob helped Rainbow up the path to the front door. In the kitchen, he pulled up a chair and took her crutches away for her. Rainbow leaned on Mum and then sat down. Mum offered her a Coke. She accepted before Mum could change her mind.

Through the kitchen window she could see her tree house in the weeping willow. It was exposed now the whipping branches were leafless. She sighed. That was where it had all started. She dragged her eyes away and looked to the right: the woods. To the left: more trees. She turned her back to the window and focused on Acrobat. He was lapping up the dregs of the milk she'd poured into his saucer. Even Acrobat reminded her of Michael.

"What would you like to do this afternoon, love?"

She had no idea. Nothing inspired her.

"Shall we invite Becky around?" asked Bob.

"No!"

Mum and Bob exchanged glances.

"I think I'll go up to my bedroom."

She clambered up the stairs with Mum on one side and Bob just behind her. Then she hopped up to her bed, dropped the crutches and stretched out. Acrobat jumped up with a purr and nestled down by her left foot.

Mum smoothed back Rainbow's hair. "Can I get you anything else, love?"

"I expect she'd like some peace," said Bob. "Fraser gave me this pile of work for you. It's stuff you missed at school." He plumped a bag onto the floor by Rainbow's bed.

"I'll pop back in half an hour," said Mum.

Rainbow nodded. She picked up the bag and slipped out Rebecca's French book. She'd only been absent for ten days, but vocabulary and grammar lessons filled several pages. On the last one there was a gap and then a pencilled message in Lucy Carter's writing:

Rainbow = un arc-en-ciel
Evil Eye = le mauvais oeil

Rainbow bit her lip and tasted blood. She shut the exercise book, shoved the bag to the floor and picked up her sketch pad instead. She flicked through the pages. Trees. Amrita. Amrita. Trees. She found the clean pages and skipped one.

Acrobat was washing himself at the foot of her bed. She picked up her pencil and started to sketch him.

Xylem

Mary decides to take a week off before she goes back to school. During the week she hears Bob and Mother argue more frequently and knows she's at the core of their disputes. She hears the word 'teenager' and snorts at their stupidity. It hasn't even occurred to Mother that she could be at the root of the problem. R– would have felt sorry for Mother and relented, but Mary must be as hard as R– was soft. She lets them argue and takes Bob's side as often as possible.

This morning she pulls open the curtains and prepares herself for the sickness that wrings her guts into knots when she sees the trees around the house. She concentrates on the dull grey concrete of the patio until the nausea passes, then swings her crutches into position to attack the day.

On her first day home she told Mother she didn't want to see anyone, so no one has visited – apart from Fraser, who she refuses to see. Today, she feels ready to go out. It's time for the world to meet Mary.

"I want to see Patti," she says at breakfast.

"Good idea," says Bob.

Mother clears her throat. "You promised–"

"She needs to get out of the house," says Bob. "I'll drop you off after breakfast."

"I don't want her going there," says Mother.

Mary sits back and listens to them spit words at each other. She refuses to feel protective towards Mother and lets Bob flatten her with his scorn. Within seconds she sees tears in

Mother's eyes. She joins in the fight at Bob's side.

"If you won't explain your problem with the Bellamys to me, I don't see why I should avoid them. Anyway, I'm taking the cat back," she says.

"Acrobat? I don't understand. You adore him. What's come over you, Rainbow?"

"It's *Mary*!" she shouts.

Mother turns away, her head bowed.

Mary pinches her leg. She must defy the old R–'s instinct to break down. One, two, three, four … The pain passes and Mary cools back to stone.

"Let's go, Bob," she says.

"Are you sure about the cat?" he asks.

Mary pulls an empty cardboard box out from under the table and thrusts it into his hands.

"Yes. You'll have to get it out of the tree house. I can't go up there with crutches."

🌿🍃🌿

Mrs Bellamy glances over Mary's head at Bob and then lets the cat out of the box. It uncurls with a miaow and pads away from the front door to the shed. Mary averts her eyes from the cat to the stripes on Mrs Bellamy's apron. There are twenty-three of them.

"Come in for a coffee, Bob," says Mrs Bellamy.

"He can't. He's in a hurry to get to Fraser's," says Mary.

Mrs Bellamy folds her arms. Her tea towel drapes over her apron. She looks at Mary, then Bob.

"I see there have been some big changes in the

Linnet household."

"Yeah. Difficult times," says Bob.

He raises a hand in farewell and says he'll be back that afternoon. Mrs Bellamy watches him leave. When she turns to Mary, her expression is pensive.

"Come and have a chat before you disappear upstairs to see Patti," she says. She steers Mary into the kitchen, nods towards a chair and goes back to stuffing her chicken.

"So, tell me what's happening at home," she continues. "I see you've changed your hairstyle. That means something's going on inside that head of yours."

Mary ignores the chair and leans on her crutches instead. "I've changed my name too. Rainbow is too childish. I'm called Mary now."

Mrs Bellamy is bent over the chicken and Mary can't see her reaction.

"Mary Linnet. So the accident has made you feel older?" Her round face pops up again.

"Yes." It's true: she does feel older.

"And with those crutches you must be confined to the house instead of running around the countryside like you usually do. How're you bearing up?"

"Same as ever. Bob and Mother fight all the time."

"Mother? Is 'Mum' too childish as well?"

Mary shrugs. "By the way, there's something I want to ask you: why doesn't she like me coming here?"

Mrs Bellamy finishes the chicken and puts on the kettle. "I told you: we had an argument a long time ago."

"About what?"

Mrs Bellamy cocks her head to one side. Her eyes narrow,

as if she's thinking something over. "It seems to me that this Mary is looking for answers."

"So give me some. You know what Mother's like." *She's a liar*, the voice inside Mary's head adds.

"I can't tell you, you know that. It's up to your mum to explain. She'll tell you as soon as she's ready. So, when are you going back to school?"

Mary sighs and answers Mrs Bellamy's questions about her convalescence. At last, Mrs Bellamy releases her and she goes upstairs to see Patti.

🌿🌿🌿

Patti's *Just Seventeen* magazine slips from her hand onto the floor.

"You can't just change your name!"

Mary tosses the jagged edge of her black fringe out of her eyes.

"Why not? Rainbow is a kid's name. Your mum didn't blink an eye. She understands."

Patti pushes her glasses up her nose and tucks her ginger hair behind her ears.

"Well, maybe you can, then."

Mary nods towards Patti's pile of magazines. "Look at those models and singers. They've all changed their names."

She spots a packet of chewing gum under the heap of clothes on the floor, and helps herself to one.

Patti frowns at her *Just Seventeen*. "I guess it's kind of glamorous. Maybe I should change to Patricia. Patti is a bit babyish too."

Mary stops chewing. This is something new. She's seen Patti copy Lucy Carter, but never her. "It won't help you get into Lucy and Rebecca's gang," she says.

Patti isn't listening. "No, not Patricia. Trish. That'll be my new name."

She picks up a pen, rummages around for a piece of paper, and practises signing 'Trish' with a flourish. Mary sits down on the bed and leafs through the magazine on the pillow. After a few minutes Trish suggests they go outside and play with the kittens.

"I can't. I'm allergic to cats now. I've brought back that stupid ginger one."

"Acrobat? But I thought—"

"Let's listen to some music instead."

She fingers through Trish's cassettes, ignoring her stare. "Haven't you got anything less wishy-washy than the Beautiful South?"

Trish sits down. "But you love them."

"Not anymore. What about Public Enemy?" Mary outstares Trish, who lowers her eyes.

"You've gone all hard and defiant since your accident."

"So what?"

Mary feigns carelessness, though she feels a kernel of triumph inside. Killing off R– is more satisfying than she ever imagined it could be.

Trish tilts her head to one side, reminding Mary of Mrs Bellamy. She smiles slowly. "What are Lucy and Becky going to make of you?"

PART THREE

BRANCHES

Rainbow, 1991

CHAPTER NINE

By the time Rainbow was able to walk properly, the Drunken House had fallen back into neglect. Its dead windows were boarded against intruders as if no one had spent late summer and early autumn breathing life back into it.

One April day, six months after the accident, she freewheeled down the hill on her bicycle, her teeth gritted against the freshness of the spring air. She stopped in front of the Drunken House.

She was hoping something had been left behind, an object she could take to keep Michael's presence closer to her. His face was already fading from her memory. She could picture him running his hand over his egg of a head and hear his booming laugh, but she couldn't remember what colour his eyes were.

She left her racer propped against the window sill and edged through the brambles sprayed against the side wall. Michael had cut them back to make an access path to the rear of the property. The recent sunny spell had given the thorny tendrils the incentive to stretch out and reclaim what had been theirs for years. Her arms bled and she grumbled as she picked a path to the gate.

It was padlocked. She smashed the lock against the metal bars. She had to get inside. The wall was as high as her tree house. She had recovered most of her right leg muscles but she knew it was too high to scramble over.

She could see the ash tree on the other side of the gate. Her eyes followed the lines of its lower branches. The oak behind her was the only solution. Up into the oak, along the branch and down into the branches of the ash on the other side.

She shuddered. The thought of laying her hands on the bark of a tree, even to help her enter Michael's garden, was too sickening to contemplate. She yanked at the padlock and willed it to spring open. It didn't. She turned her back on the secret garden and pushed back through the bushes into the lane.

At the front of the house she ran her fingers around the window boarding and searched for a hole to lever a board away. There was nothing. The owner had done a serious job. Perhaps he thought Michael had exorcised the house's reputation and that druggies would come and squat in it.

She could hear a car coming from the village. It sounded like the nippy hum of the Mini engine, pushed to its limits by Mum. She always waited until the last second before changing gear. Rainbow pushed herself away from the facade and turned her bike around to face homewards. A few moments later the dim lane was filled with bright yellow. Mum slowed to a stop and turned her head sideways to speak through the gap where the window was stuck.

"Are you all right, love?"

"I'm having a rest. You were quick."

"Don't overdo it. See you at home in a minute."

Mum smiled at her – the worried smile that had replaced the old, vacant one. Then she pipped the horn and drew off without looking behind her. Rainbow waited until the car had disappeared around the corner. Then she dropped her bike and searched under the stones in case Michael had hidden a spare key.

The whine of an engine reversing filled her ears. Before she could spring back into place, the Mini hurtled backwards towards her. It pulled into the side of the road and Mum opened the door.

"Mum! You shouldn't do that. There could have been something coming the other way."

"I just wondered what you were doing at that old house."

"I'm not at the house. I stopped for a rest."

Rainbow wiped her earthy hands on her jeans. She still hadn't told Mum she'd known Michael. Mum had somehow found out that Rainbow knew where he'd lived, and Rainbow didn't want her to guess anything more.

She could now spend whole minutes at a time thinking about him, but the idea of speaking his name and explaining how much he'd meant to her was overwhelming. In any case, there was no point telling Mum about the art lessons now that he was dead.

"His family came and took his things away," said Mum. She reached out and touched Rainbow's shoulder.

"I know, you said."

"I expect some new people will come to live here now."

Rainbow nodded and pulled up her bicycle. Mum rested on the Mini door frame and watched her.

"It wasn't your fault, love. You know that, don't you?"

Rainbow straddled her bike. "Yes."

Of course it was her fault. She was the one who'd killed him with her stupid antics in trees. She wished she'd never discovered her gift.

"Don't listen to what anyone says," continued Mum.

Rainbow's head jerked up. "What do they say?"

"Fraser told me the kids at school have been giving you a hard time."

"Oh, *them*. I don't care what they say."

Mum's eyes were sad. "Don't hang around here. It won't do any good. Why don't you come back with me? Bob can pick up your bike later."

"No, I'm fine. I need to exercise my leg."

Mum slid back into the car and motioned Rainbow to pull out in front of her. Rainbow wobbled into action and puffed her way up the lane with Mum following like a sheepdog. She'd come back another time. There had to be something for her inside the house; an overlooked object she could keep as a souvenir. She must get it before the next lodger moved in.

🌱 🌿 🌱

She was sitting on the floor behind the settee, skimming through a copy of *Lady Chatterley's Lover*, when she heard Mum and Bob arguing outside the door. She slid the book back under the tasselled russet settee cover and waited in her hiding place between the wall and the back of the settee for the voices to pass.

They didn't pass. Mum walked into the sitting room. The tassels lifted a few centimetres as Mum sat down.

Bob followed.

"You don't practise anymore," he said, "that's why. We were continually covering for you last night. It's not good enough."

Rainbow frowned. Their arguments rarely touched on their music.

Mum let Bob pull her performance apart without defending herself at all. This was really bad. Rainbow sensed a shift into a darker future.

"You've lost the plot, Jaz," Bob said. "Where's your bite? Where's the movement? You looked more like a school kid reciting lines than a performing blues singer."

"I've got other things on my mind right now." Mum's voice was dismissive.

Rainbow grinned as she imagined how frustrated Bob must be looking.

"Like what? Rainbow's better. She's off her crutches. She never mentions the accident." Bob sat down too.

"Exactly! She doesn't talk about it."

"So she's over it. Full stop. Turn the page," said Bob.

"I'm worried about her. The kids say she's got the evil eye."

"They're teenagers, Jaz."

"And she hasn't got any friends."

"Goddammit! Get over it, Jaz. She's a tough thing; much tougher than you give her credit for."

"But she's being victimised."

"Stop mollycoddling her and concentrate on your own

problems. You haven't written a song since the accident and now you can't even sing decently."

"I'm going to take her out of school."

"What?" Bob exploded. "Because of some smart-arse kids? Besides, where else would she go?"

"I could get a teacher in. Or teach her myself."

"You really have lost the plot. We can't afford a teacher, and you wouldn't last two minutes. Since when have you had the slightest interest in her school work?"

The tassels bounced back and touched the ground. Mum swept out of the room. Rainbow heard Bob mutter a swear word as he followed her.

She stood up. She'd love to leave school, but the idea of Mum giving her lessons was ridiculous. Mum saw complications in the simplest explanations. Rainbow had felt more confused than ever on the rare occasions Mum had explained something to her. If Mum took her out of school, she'd have to make sure someone else gave her lessons. But Bob would never agree to her staying at home all day. The best solution would be to show Mum that everything was all right. Things would go back to normal. Mum would get that distant look back in her eyes and start muttering song lyrics to herself again.

The trouble was, everything wasn't all right. For starters, Acrobat was padding all over the house, mewing, unable to settle in one place. Rainbow watched him claw his overweight body up onto one of the easy chairs, knead the frayed cushion and then plop back down onto the floor. He sniffed and miaowed at her. When she walked into the kitchen, he curled around her ankles and then crept into the open cupboard under the sink. She pulled him out and lugged him outside. He was too heavy to carry. She put him down. He looked up hopefully at her and then waddled along the overgrown path towards her tree house. Was he trying to show her something?

She hadn't been inside since the accident. Simply standing in front of a tree made her want to retch. Today, her curiosity overcame her dread and she followed him. His belly swayed comically from side to side. He needed to go on a diet.

He stopped at the foot of his pole bridge and started mewing again. Then he wobbled up to the top. Relieved by his safe arrival, she stared at the doorway and waited for him to reappear. He was taking his time, not that it mattered. She had plenty of time. She folded her arms and drummed her fingers on her biceps. What did she use to do on Sunday afternoons? Weekends, which had always seemed to pass in an instant, were now interminable. It was as if her life was on hold and, like Acrobat, she was unable to settle to any activity. Of course, she knew perfectly well what she'd done with every spare minute since Magic Hands Day last August. But she was trying to forget that period. The question was what she used to do before she found trees.

Her eyes wandered from tree house to tree. She took in the weeping willow's shape and the lime-green brightness of its branches. The longing to touch it rose up from her coiled intestines like a snake. *I've tasted it and now I'm addicted*, she thought. That's what Lucy Carter said when she boasted about being a smoker. *You must stop, it's bad for your health*, she replied to herself. Everyone knew that smoking would kill you, but people did it anyway.

There was a thud inside the tree house. Rainbow called out Acrobat's name. He mewed, but didn't reappear.

"Are you all right, Batty?"

There was no miaow in reply.

"Batty?" She took a step towards the rope ladder. She didn't want to climb up there. She couldn't even place a foot on the first rung. She took another step closer and looked up.

Acrobat peeped down at her. She breathed out a sigh of relief.

"I'm going indoors," she said to him.

He miaowed and returned inside the cosy den. That night, he didn't come indoors for his dinner.

CHAPTER TEN

Rainbow shivered. The April night was cold. She shouted Acrobat's name into the darkness.

"Where did you last see him?" asked Bob.

"In the tree house this afternoon."

"Well, get your arse out there and bring him in."

Rainbow wrapped her arms around her shoulders. "I can't."

"Of course you can." Bob handed her the halogen torch and gave her a push. "Don't be such a wimp."

Rainbow retreated into the kitchen, away from the black night.

"He's probably asleep."

"Well, make up your mind. Either go and get him or stop making a fuss. And shut the door. You're letting out the heat."

He stomped across the kitchen and into the music room.

Rainbow hovered on the threshold. "Grumpy git!" she muttered. She gripped the torch, stepped out of the house and slammed the door shut behind her.

The wind had dropped. Dew soaked through her trainers and into her socks as she picked her way to the weeping willow. She pointed the torch downwards. The trick was to concentrate on what she could see in the light – and not on the noises outside the wavering circle. Not on the screeches from the wood, nor on the sudden whirring of air as something passed above her. Not on the tock-tocking from the vegetable patch, nor on the regular swishing that could have been footsteps crossing the grass. She ignored the heavy menace of the thick air behind her. Instead, she studied the bruised grass on the path to her tree.

The drive would have been drier and less scary than the path, but she wasn't in a hurry to reach the tree. Acrobat always chose this path. She called his name. The solid sound of her voice would ward off any loitering ghosts.

At the foot of the tree she heard Acrobat answer. He miaowed, purred and then miaowed again. She could hear him moving about. But there was more movement than one cat could possibly make. Something else was in there with him. Perhaps he was cowering from the homeless tabby tom. The tabby regularly fought with the neighbour's Yorkshire terrier, and Acrobat would slink away when he saw him. The tabby's ripped ears, mangy fur and scars were not caused by neglect.

She shone her torch directly into the tree house. Three metres higher, the light was a pathetic yellow glow rather than the bright white she'd hoped for.

"Tabby! Get out of there!"

The only response was a plaintive miaow. Acrobat was in trouble.

"I'm coming up, Batty. Hang on in there."

It was easy to say. She placed the torch on the ground and

wedged it on a stone so that it shone up the rope ladder.
Then she glanced at the trunk and wiped her sweating palms
on her jeans. She wouldn't have to touch the tree. She could
climb up the ladder and then pull herself into the tree house
using the floor of the den. Coming down again would be
tricky; she usually swung herself out of the shelter using a
branch. If she lay on her tummy, slid backwards over the
edge and groped with her feet, she'd be able to get hold of
the ladder. So it was no big deal. She could do it. She wiped
her hands once more and grasped the third rung of the rope
ladder.

It was difficult to climb the ladder without touching the
tree. She usually climbed up the side of it, like a trapeze
artist, but this meant leaning her back against the tree. It was
out of the question now. Her legs stretched out in front of
her, making an L with her body, and she struggled to pull up
her weight. No wonder Mum never came up.

She grasped bar after bar, until her eyes were level with
the floor of the tree house. The light was at the wrong angle
to see much inside. In any case, her most pressing need was
to relieve her arms. She slotted her stiff fingers into a gap
between two wooden boards and yanked herself onto the
platform. She was in.

She rolled onto her side and squinted into the dimness.
Acrobat miaowed. She located him with her ears rather than
her eyes. His head rose out of the wooden box. He must
have nosed off the lid, because it lay with one corner propped
against the side. She sat up to caress him and peered inside.

"Where's that bully gone?"

She tickled him behind his ears. He purred richly. Then he

dropped his head back into the box and miaowed again.

"What have you got in there? A mouse?"

She slid her arms into the box and felt for Acrobat's front legs. Circling his tummy with her hands, she pulled him out.

Two things happened in quick succession: Acrobat wriggled in her grasp and slashed her face with a claw; and something dropped back into the box with a thud.

She released Acrobat with a cry of surprise. He'd never attacked her before. And neither had a male cat ever given birth to kittens. Michael had been wrong about ginger cats always being male. She grinned, despite the blood trickling down her cheek, despite the pain that came from thinking about Michael.

Acrobat mewed, purred and licked the kittens. Rainbow's eyes had grown accustomed to the dimness and she could see four mole-like shapes in the bottom of the box. She knew she mustn't touch them, in case her human odour caused Acrobat to abandon them. She contented herself with stroking Acrobat while she wondered what she should do.

"I'm going to get you some milk."

She reached absent-mindedly for the branch to swing herself onto the rope ladder, wondering how she would carry the milk up the tree. Her hands touched the branch.

Everything went black. She screamed. A din of white noise deafened her and she was glued to the trunk by a ferocious wind. It was like opening the window of a train as it hurtled through the night. Tree dust clogged her lungs. The willow sucked her in. She was no longer in control. Her hands were burning, clutching, writhing. Her body flattened into an infinitely thin skin around the trunk and seeped into the ridges of the bark. She was being absorbed; dissolving into the tree. The brightness of it! The life of it! The sap-beat. She was the sap-beat. The sap, beating her into the pulp of itself: powerful, thirsty and vengeful.

And then someone else's hands were clawing at hers. Warm hands. The hands yanked her away from the tree. It hadn't absorbed her after all. She heard her name being cried out. It was like that other time. The accident. Mum.

She let go, expecting to fall into swirling-leaf oblivion like last time. But the darkness of reality greeted her. She was sprawled on the ground, her arms wrapped around the trunk.

"Rainbow, love, what is it? Why were you screaming?"

She twisted away from the willow and collapsed into Mum's arms.

"It's the tree," she whispered.

"Did you fall?"

"I don't know." She held tight onto Mum.

"What happened? You were in a trance."

"I touched the tree." Rainbow calmed her ragged breaths. "It's been so long."

"This is because of the accident, isn't it?" said Mum. She stroked Rainbow's hair and eased out a twig lodged in a tangle.

Rainbow drew back and studied Mum. Mum looked strong in the torchlight. She looked protective, like Acrobat with his kittens. Rainbow needed Mum's strength. She needed her, even if it meant that Mum might float away into her spiritual explanations. She grasped Mum's hand in an effort to anchor her.

"No, Mum. The accident was because of this."

"It wasn't your fault. Don't pay any attention to the children at school."

"It was my fault."

"It was an accident, love."

"No. Listen to me." She took a deep breath. "I overstretched the branch and broke it."

There was a short silence. "Overstretched the branch?"

"Yes. It's because of my gift. I abused it. I forced the beech to stretch against its will."

"What gift?"

"I've got magic hands, Mum. I can communicate with trees and get them to stretch." Saying the words out loud made her gift seem more solid. There was no going back now.

Mum took Rainbow's hands in her own. She ran them across her cheeks, turned them over and then held them close to the torch.

"You're right. They've become healer's hands."

Rainbow looked for signs of Mum getting spiritual. But she could see nothing dreamy about her. In fact, she looked almost business-like.

"How can you tell?"

"I know a lot of healers, love, though I've never heard of anyone healing trees. What exactly do you do to them?"

Rainbow relaxed. Mum wasn't slipping into her faraway mode. Perhaps things would be all right. If Mum didn't get spiritual then Bob wouldn't get angry and he wouldn't leave them.

"Well, I touch the bark and concentrate, and the fibres ease apart and the branch stretches," she gabbled. She longed for contact with the tree again. She clenched her hands together in an effort to squash the ache.

Mum didn't ask any more questions. She simply nodded and then hugged her. They sat together in the wet grass, haloed by the dim torchlight in the dark of the night. Rainbow started to shiver. Mum eased her up, retrieved the torch and led her back along the drive to the house.

❧ ❧ ❧

"You're a different shape today," Rainbow told Mum over breakfast the next morning. Mum was sitting upright in her chair and digging into her yoghurt with unusual vigour.

"It's because our souls have made contact."

Rainbow's chest constricted. Mum mustn't say things like that. Even so, she tingled with complicity. She couldn't wait to demonstrate her gift.

"Don't start on that mumbo-jumbo again," muttered Bob. His pint-sized mug of tea obscured his face.

The day took an eternity to pass. After school, Rainbow cycled home from the bus stop as fast as she could. Would her gift still work, or had her experience with the willow yesterday been a warning not to touch trees ever again?

She dropped her bike inside the front gate and was about to speed to the privacy of the woods behind the pumpkin patch when she heard a miaow. Acrobat! She clapped a hand to her mouth and looked up at her tree house. How could she have forgotten him and his kittens? She hadn't even told Mum and Bob about them. Gingerly, she laid a hand on the bark of the trunk. Her body tensed in expectation of a shock wave.

There was nothing. She let out her breath and shinned up the ladder.

Acrobat climbed out of the box and nuzzled her. She stroked him and peered into the nest he'd made. There were four kittens – a ginger and three tabbies – and they looked like little logs of warmth, blunt-faced with squinty lines where their eyes were squeezed shut. They writhed over each other in search of their mother's protective mass. She could guess who the father was. They would either be divvy or fighters, or perhaps divvy fighters. She resisted the urge to touch them. Instead, she sat crosslegged, pulled Acrobat onto her lap and stroked him. Which traits, apart from shortness, had she inherited from her own father?

Acrobat padded back to look into the box. His swollen teats brushed Rainbow's fingers as he passed. Perhaps she ought to refer to him as 'her' now. She swung out of the den and slid down the ladder. Acrobat edged down his pole, and they walked through the grass to the house.

The Mini and the van were both there, the van parked ominously askew. Rainbow braced herself. She pushed open the door and followed Acrobat into the kitchen.

Mum and Bob were sitting on opposite sides of the table, glowering at each other. Rainbow headed straight for the fridge to fetch Acrobat's tinned meat and some milk. She could feel Bob's eyes on her.

"It's not the cat's dinner time," he growled.

"She needs it to feed her kittens," replied Rainbow.

"Kittens? Don't be ridiculous. It's a tom."

"I thought so too. But he's a she."

Rainbow sneaked a look at Mum. Her eyes were fixed on

Rainbow but she remained silent.

"How many? Where are they?" he said.

"Two. In the woodshed." There was no point taking any risks.

Mum interrupted before Rainbow could establish Bob's intentions.

"Rainbow, love, I think you'd better tell Bob what you told me last night."

Rainbow dropped the tin. "Mum! It's a secret."

She'd been sure Mum wouldn't say anything to Bob. Mum kept lots of secrets from him. He had no idea of the spiritual seances she held when he was out gigging alone.

"Bob won't mention it to anyone. And perhaps, at last, he'll accept that science doesn't explain everything."

"Come on. Your mum's getting weird on me," said Bob. "What's the trick?"

Michael had advised her to keep her gift a secret so that she wouldn't be exploited. But surely Mum and Bob wouldn't exploit her? Michael may have been wrong. He'd been wrong about Acrobat being a tomcat.

"All right."

She fetched the book that had belonged to Michael's great-grandfather from her tree house. The cover was damaged by dried blood, where Acrobat had given birth on top of it. Inside, however, the line drawings, black-and-white photos and Rainbow's notes and sketches were intact. She pushed aside the papers on the kitchen table and laid the book in front of Bob.

"I found this at the village fete last summer," she said.

She leafed through the pages and showed Mum and Bob

the notes she'd written next to the trees she'd grown. Mum admired Rainbow's sketches and read a couple of entries aloud. Bob hardly looked at the book.

"Yeah, yeah, but I want to know how you make it work," he said.

"I put my hands on the tree and kind of push."

"I don't believe you. It's not possible."

"Believe what you like. It's all the same to me."

Bob narrowed his eyes at Rainbow. "Is that what you did to your tree house?"

"Yes."

"You're lying," he muttered.

Rainbow put the book onto her chair and sat down on it, grinning. Bob looked seriously freaked out.

"You'd better give us a demonstration to prove it," he said.

Her smile disappeared. She suddenly regretted telling Mum and Bob. It felt as if she'd been unzipped and emptied. With her gift exposed, she had nothing left to hug to herself except the fading memories of her time with Michael.

Michael. He'd said her gift was part of her. Conviction gripped her. She had to use her gift, even if it meant people staring at her, like Bob was at this very moment. She didn't care about the looks. She was used to being different from other people, anyway. Michael had died because of her gift. If she stopped the work he'd helped her to start, she'd be rejecting what he'd given her.

She had to use her gift. For Michael. To keep her memory of him warm. And to stop the creeping ice-fingers of guilt from freezing him out of her reach forever.

"I need to work alone first. I'll show you after school tomorrow," she said.

CHAPTER ELEVEN

Rainbow stood in front of a young alder tree and studied her hands. They had softened over her treeless winter, thanks to Mum's lily-of-the-valley hand cream. The backs of her hands were idle-soft now, but there was nothing to be done about the palms. Neither cream nor willpower could erase the rough, cracked skin. She stroked them and struggled to remember the pleasant tickling sensation that stroking them used to evoke. The touch of her fingers came from a distance, as if her skin had developed its own bark.

Behind her, Bob slid the tongue of his steel tape measure in and out of its casing. He was frowning, his feet planted wide apart in stubbornness. He liked to think he was a scientist, his garden being his major scientific experiment. Yesterday evening, when she'd shown him her book, he'd been bewildered. By nightfall, his mood had worsened to disbelief and he'd accused her of wilful deceit. This evening, he looked determined to prove her wrong.

Mum had chosen the alder for Rainbow to work on. It had two trunks growing from the same knobble. Rainbow brought her face close to the first trunk and smelt its vigour. There were alders everywhere in Wymer Hill Wood. Last autumn she'd noted their energy in her book. Now it was spring, and she wondered if the rising sap would make the stretching even easier.

She felt uncomfortable in front of an audience. She'd asked them to turn away. Mum didn't mind, but Bob said she'd pull one of her tricks if he didn't keep her in his sight, and had refused. If she was going to spend her life doing this, she'd have to get used to people watching. Even so, she used her body to block his view of her hands.

The right spot was easy to find. She closed her eyes, concentrated on the connection and then asked the alder to stretch its trunk a little. The alder jumped to attention and responded eagerly. Rainbow felt an immediate responsibility towards it. She had to be careful not to let it overstretch itself.

Bob's voice encroached on her thoughts. "Have you finished yet?"

She stepped aside and showed him the curve in the trunk's profile.

"Goddammit!" He stroked his chin and then bent and slapped the tree. "How did you do it?"

Rainbow pushed his hand away from the alder. He flinched, stroked his skin where she'd touched him and then grabbed her wrist, which he turned over so he could examine her palm.

"Jeez! Look at this, Jaz."

Rainbow tried to pull away. Mum glanced at Rainbow's hand and then told Bob to let go. She seemed unfazed and had hardly looked at the elongated trunk.

"This is freakish," Bob said. He wiped his hands on his jeans as if the contact with Rainbow had dirtied him. "Do it again … on the other trunk." He knelt down, measured the height to the lowest branch and pointed to a spot halfway up. "Right here."

"I can't do it just anywhere," scorned Rainbow.

She stroked the trunk and took her time to settle her hands in the right place. Then she let Bob measure from the ground up to her chosen point. She felt like a magician, under pressure from an audience. Mum and Bob were holding their breath in expectation of silk handkerchiefs turning into doves.

She suddenly realised she'd made no mental contact with the trunk. She frowned and concentrated. Still nothing.

"We haven't got all night," grumbled Bob.

Rainbow tried to commune with the second alder trunk. It was a twin and, like Chris and Mike Loach at school, this trunk seemed to be the opposite of the first. It was slow, reluctant and uncommunicative. Rainbow opened her eyes and stood back.

"What's the matter? Lost your nerve?"

She didn't bother to reply. She laid her hands back on the trunk and ran them up and down. It was definitely the right place. Nowhere else was possible. She tried again. Her eyes closed and she opened her mind to all that her hands could feel. The fibres were vibrant and the sap-beat was strong. She could feel no resistance. There was no power struggle; the alder simply didn't respond. It was like having normal hands again. She let her arms drop to her sides.

"Your thing isn't very reliable." Bob was smug. He tossed

the tape measure from one hand to the other.

Mum came forward. "Can I look at your hands, love?" Rainbow held them out and looked at them cupped in Mum's beautiful, long-fingered hands. Mum had artiste's hands. Her fingers were stretched by octave-jumps and tipped with purple nail varnish. Rainbow's hands looked even more scabrous beside Mum's creamy ones. Not magic-looking at all.

Mum closed Rainbow's palms together like butterfly wings and held them tightly. "Try later," she said.

"No, now," said Bob. "I've not come out here for nothing."

"She mustn't. She'll hurt her hands."

"Rubbish! You're too soft on her."

"The show's finished, Bob. Go home."

"Rainbow, get over there and do it again," he said.

Mum released Rainbow's hands and spun around to face him.

"She's shown you once. It's enough."

Rainbow remained beside Mum.

"But I want to measure it. I need proof," said Bob.

Mum marched right up to him. She was slightly taller, Rainbow noticed. He stepped back. Mum jabbed his shoulder with her finger.

"Why? You saw the other trunk stretch. Isn't that enough proof for you? Her hands will bleed if you force her to continue."

"Yeah, yeah. You'll have me crying in a minute." Bob shoved his tape measure into his pocket and stamped away.

Mum fingered an alder leaf. Her gaze wandered over the tree and she lifted the leaf to her cheek. Rainbow knelt down beside the alder, placed a hand on each trunk and laid her forehead between them. She apologised and then stood up.

"I don't understand why it didn't work. It's the first time I haven't felt anything."

"Don't try to understand," said Mum. "Accept it. There isn't always an explanation. Our scientific knowledge is limited, so sometimes we have to be humble and just believe what we know in our hearts. It's the nature of life."

She strolled back towards the house. Rainbow watched her meander through the vegetable patches and stop to caress a plant from time to time. Was Mum right? Couldn't science explain everything?

❦ ❧ ❦

On Saturday morning Fraser breezed into their home and shut himself in the recording room with Bob for a blues session. He and Bob excluded Mum. Rainbow spied on them through the hatch window on her way upstairs to get dressed. They were actually recording, not simply smoking and strumming.

It had rained all week. Acrobat didn't want to move his kittens into her bedroom and it was too cold and dreary to sit in her tree house. She'd spent the evenings after school in her room, staring out of the window at the greening woods and looking through the coloured photos of *Trees in Western Europe*, a book she'd borrowed from the school library.

She pressed her nose against the glass of the hatch window and watched Fraser sucking up to Bob. It was strange to think that the same kinds of trees grew on the other side of the English Channel. How had forests managed to cross the sea to France and Germany? None of the books answered her question. She wondered who she could ask without getting sideways looks. Certainly not Fraser. And not Michael anymore.

Mum appeared from the kitchen, tapped her on the shoulder and motioned her outside with a tilt of her head. Rainbow wondered if she was going to be told off for spying. They weren't supposed to make any noise when Bob was recording, and she knew she hadn't broken that rule.

Outside, it had stopped raining. The sun came out. Mum sipped from a cup of herbal tea and Rainbow watched her step into the uncut grass. She didn't seem cross. Her wrap-over skirt loitered in the grasping, wet tendrils. Rainbow traipsed after her, swishing her hands through the long stalks until they dripped rain.

Mum walked towards the orchard beyond the pumpkin patch. She'd woven a willow shelter in the entrance to the orchard a few years ago and called it her 'boudoir', which sounded like something out of *Lady Chatterley's Lover*. It had three woven willow sides and an arch with roses growing over to make a roof. Underneath were a bench and a small table. The boudoir was the summer equivalent of her creative corner, and she'd chosen a view over the woods for inspiration. Rainbow considered the boudoir to be a miracle: the concept of Mum creating anything solid on her own was too difficult to believe. She had spent two complete weeks building it, to the exclusion of everything else. She hadn't looked after the roses properly though, and they trailed wildly instead of bushing neatly like Bob's hybrids in the front garden.

Mum stopped at her boudoir and pulled the plastic sheet off the bench. Rainbow plumped herself down beside her and waited. Mum was like a deer: you had to be careful not to surprise her with too many words, otherwise you could startle her and she'd bound away from what she was going to say. She sipped her tea and then turned to Rainbow.

"How was school this week?"

"All right."

"Are you still being bullied?"

Rainbow thought about home tutoring. "No."

There were a few seconds of silence.

"Does anyone know about your gift?"

"No." Not anymore. "Why?"

"I've been thinking," said Mum.

She finished her tea and gazed over the curly head of the woods.

Rainbow waited, but Mum said nothing more. "Thinking what?" she asked.

"How about trying again this morning, love?"

Rainbow looked down at her wet pyjama trousers. She'd been hoping to do it alone. "I'm not dressed yet."

"Bob won't bother us."

"Okay. I'll be back in a minute."

She ran back to the house, where she threw off her pyjamas and slipped into jeans and a sweatshirt. She hadn't worn these particular jeans for a while, and she noticed with glee that they were too short. She kept them on. It was satisfying to look down at the ankle gap and see proof that she'd grown.

Back in the orchard, she walked around the fruit trees. She'd already tweaked the apple and pear trees last

September. Mum stayed on the bench. Rainbow turned around, wondering whether she'd fallen asleep, and saw that Mum was watching her intently.

She decided on the walnut tree. It was too high to climb into, so she fetched the stepladder from the shed.

"Won't the metal affect your contact with the tree?" asked Mum.

Rainbow shrugged and leant the ladder against a branch. Mum came over and insisted on holding the bottom, despite Rainbow's protests that she was fine. She climbed up to the first horizontal bough and, keeping her feet on the ladder, ran her hands over a slim, vertical branch.

"This one is happy to move."

Mum leant against the ladder and watched her, shading her eyes. Rainbow ignored her and let her concentration funnel: from the calls of chiffchaffs and magpies, from the distant road and faraway voices, to the murmur of leaves and the pulsing of the trunk. She stretched and bent the branch towards the outer canopy of the tree.

She opened her eyes and examined her work. The branch looked odd, curving from vertical to horizontal. She corrected the angle to an easy bend and jumped down from the ladder.

"Hands," said Mum.

Rainbow held them out for inspection. Mum ran her fingers over the palms. There was a responding murmur from her nerve ends.

"I can feel you!"

Mum smiled. "This is better than on Tuesday. They're happy hands today."

Rainbow rubbed them together to relieve the tickling sensation.

"I can't feel my own hands, but I can feel yours. Isn't that strange?"

"It's because I'm your mum."

"Have you got healer's hands too, then?"

"No, but I know a man who has," said Mum.

"Do you? Who is it? Do I know him? Can I meet him?"

"We'll see."

"But–"

Mum's eyes widened in warning and her finger flew to her lips.

Rainbow stopped short. Bob was shouting Mum's name. Mum caught her hand and pulled her behind the boudoir, where they wouldn't be seen. They huddled side by side, their lips pressed closed, eyes locked on each other.

Bob's voice faded away. Rainbow peeped around the edge of the boudoir. The pumpkin patch was empty. There was no sign of Bob at the back door. She let out her breath and turned to ask Mum about the healer. But Mum stood up and spoke first.

"What else can you do with your hands?"

Rainbow frowned. "What do you mean?"

Mum led her back inside the boudoir.

"Can you bring dead wood back to life, or cure a tree weakened by illness, or make new shoots grow?"

"I don't know."

"You need a guru," said Mum.

"Do I? Where can I get one?"

Mum smiled. "I'll find one for you."

"You won't tell anyone about my gift, will you?"

Mum stroked her hair. "Only someone who can help you."

"I don't need any help."

"You've got a very special gift, Rainbow. We have to find the best way to use it, and you need to be protected."

"So that no one exploits me," added Rainbow. "Can't you and Bob protect me?"

Mum hesitated. "If you want to use your gift you'll need a special kind of protection. Otherwise, your only protection is to forget it."

"I can't do that. I need the contact with trees."

"So I must find you a guru. But, whatever you do, don't mention it to Bob."

Rainbow didn't need to ask why. If Bob disapproved of gurus, they must be spiritual, like the crystals and tarot cards Mum hid in the King Edward box in the locked bottom drawer of her desk. She kept the key in the pocket of her silver and orange belt. Rainbow had spent many hours playing with the contents of the box when she was younger. She would lay out the intriguing tarot cards, shuffle them and put them into groups, running her fingers over their dimpled surfaces. As for the crystals, they were as smooth as air. She loved to stroke them. Often she'd find one in her pocket without realising she'd taken it.

They left the boudoir and picked up the ladder. As they carried it back to the shed they bumped into Bob and Fraser, who were walking round the garden. Bob told Mum they needed her voice before they could progress with the recording. Rainbow sidled away.

"I'll deal with you this afternoon," he shouted to Rainbow's back.

Rainbow pretended not to hear him. From the darkness of the shed she listened to Bob fend off Fraser's question about what she'd done. Bob didn't mention anything about trees, and she was relieved to hear him change the subject.

🌿 🍃 🌿

That afternoon, back in the wood with Bob and his tape measure, Rainbow was unable to make anything grow.

"You're a dirty trickster," Bob said, "and you're wasting my time."

"I couldn't care less," spat Rainbow. "If your time's so precious, do something useful with it instead of harassing me."

Mum laid a hand on Bob's arm. "Stop trying to measure. Just watch."

As soon as he did so, the hazel tree responded to Rainbow's touch. Her dismay turned to relief and she mentally filed this discovery to write in her book later on. She moved away from the trees and sat down on a log, hoping Bob would leave her alone now.

"You see?" Mum said to Bob. "You and your science!"

Bob ignored her.

"Stop messing around, Rainbow. Go back and do it where I've measured."

"There's no point. It won't work," said Mum. "Why is it so important to measure it, anyway?"

"There's no proof otherwise."

"Who needs proof?" Mum's voice was suddenly sharp. "Newspapers? Doctors? Who exactly are you planning to prove this to, Bob?"

He glared at Mum and stroked his chin. Their silence was

heavy with sounds: dripping leaves, insects droning and a tractor rumbling in a nearby field. Rainbow buried a hand in the reassuring moss of her log.

"She'd be better off forgetting this mumbo-jumbo," Bob said at last.

"You mean that *you*'d be better off," said Mum.

"Come off it, Jaz. It's like she's a freak or something."

"Only to narrow-minded scientists. I think it's beautiful and natural."

Rainbow sensed unsaid words fly over her head. Why couldn't they let her get on with it instead of turning every incident into an excuse for an argument? She was sick of hearing them argue all the time. Mum had coped fine with the discovery of her gift before Bob got involved. She hadn't even got spiritual. It was Bob who was determined to ruin everything with his stupid tape measure.

Bob turned to her: "You don't want to be a freak, do you?"

Rainbow shrugged. She was pretty much a freak to her schoolmates already.

"Well, I don't want my stepdaughter to be called a freak," he said.

"She's not a freak. She's just different," said Mum.

"I don't want to see her suffer."

"She needn't suffer," said Mum.

"If she forgets this tree mumbo-jumbo, she won't."

"There's another solution," said Mum.

The chill expanded between them. Bob narrowed his eyes. "No way!"

Rainbow sighed. Her gift caused nothing but bother. "It's freezing here," she said. "I'm going out into the sun."

She stood up.

There was no reaction from either of them. They faced each other, their eyes locked like wrestlers' arms. Bob's hands were clenched into grubby fists. The tape measure swelled his right fist, making him seem even more threatening. Mum's long neck and pointed chin jutted out in accusation, like a witch's.

Rainbow had had enough. They were as bad as each other. She marched out of the clearing and went to find Acrobat.

CHAPTER TWELVE

Mum and Bob fought non-stop for the whole of the following week. They broke half the crockery – this time Rainbow's increasing clumsiness wasn't the cause. Their arguments passed from silence, in which saucepans were banged and guitars played at full volume, to slanging matches and muffled crying on Mum's part.

One evening Bob yelled over Rainbow's head that he couldn't stand spending seven hours so close to Jasmine, even if she was asleep. From that moment on, he slept on the mattress in the recording room. Mum locked herself in her creative room as soon as she'd made her morning tea. This didn't stop Bob bawling insults through the door. The only positive point for Rainbow was that they were no longer arguing about her. Everything was brought up except her name, so she knew she and her gift weren't the cause.

When she arrived home from school on Friday evening, everything was calm. She crept into Mum's room and found her sitting on her bed, sorting out her clothes.

"Where's Bob?"

Mum held out her arms. Sadness rolled out of them. Rainbow sat down and hugged her.

"He's gone to stay with Fraser while he calms down," said Mum.

Rainbow wasn't sure if this was better or worse. Mum's eyes were bright and glittery from something stronger than tears.

"We don't need him anyway," said Mum.

"No. Not while he's in a bad mood."

Rainbow knew they did need him. They needed him to look after the garden so they had vegetables to eat. And they needed his music to bring in money for beer and car repairs, and Acrobat's food. But for the moment she had Mum to herself, and the house was peaceful at last.

That evening, Mum curled up on the settee with her and drank hot chocolate instead of sloping off to write or play. She talked about an old friend of hers called Domi, who lived in a commune in France and healed people.

When Rainbow yawned, Mum seemed reluctant to let her go to bed. She got her to help sort through the cassettes and CDs to find their favourites to play while Bob was away.

"This is like *Desert Island Discs*, isn't it?" Mum said.

Rainbow nodded and started to put the chosen music at the front of the CD wardrobe. Her arms felt heavy and she yawned.

"Mum, I need to get some sleep," she said.

"Okay, love." Mum stretched like Acrobat and stood up. "By the way, what would you take with you to a desert island?"

Rainbow sat back on her heels and rubbed her eyes.

"I don't know. My tree book, of course. And sketch pads

and pencils. And Acrobat. What about you?"

"My crystals and tarot cards, I expect. Now, off you go to bed."

⚘ ⚘ ⚘

Rainbow was late waking the next morning. She let her mind float around a little in the unusual peace and then jumped out of bed. Today she would break into Michael's house. Her instinct told her that something was waiting to be discovered. She didn't know exactly what, but she was sure she'd recognise it when the moment came. And breaking in was an adventure. Yesterday at school she'd heard Rebecca say a new family was due to move in. It may take a long time to be invited into the house by the new occupants. And her keepsake would no doubt be thrown out as soon as they arrived.

She peeked around the door of Mum's bedroom. She was still asleep, fully clothed and splayed out on the bed, taking up much more room than when she was upright or lying next to Bob. Rainbow backed out of the bedroom, tiptoed downstairs and breakfasted quickly. She scribbled a note saying she'd gone for a walk. Then she picked up her rucksack and jogged out to her tree.

There was no sound from the cat family. By now, the kittens' eyes had all opened and they squirmed further away from their nest each day. She'd tipped the box onto its side to make it easier for them to come and go, and had propped a plank on the floor against the doorway so they couldn't fall out.

She climbed into her tree house. The box was empty. She glanced about, wildly. Where had they gone? Then she remembered Patti saying how cats will move their kittens if they feel endangered. Acrobat must have realised that a tree house, with its long drop to the ground, was no place to bring up wandering kittens. He was a really good mum.

She had to find where he'd taken them so she could keep Bob away. It shouldn't be too difficult. She would follow Acrobat after he'd finished his dinner that evening.

She slid down the rope ladder and went into the lane. The sun was high and the dewy green foliage surrounding her sparkled in its reflection. Her shoulders lifted and she threw back her head to catch the warmth. She loved the wild, windy days of mysterious autumn, but spring was the season that made everything feel better. It was the mending time of year. Light breezes whispered new beginnings to her and she basked in hope. Everything would be fine.

There was no movement in Michael's house yet. She hummed as she sidled through the brambles to the oak tree. Humming was the closest she allowed herself to singing. Her tuneless voice had been the object of Mum's despair for years.

She sized up the oak, anticipating the movements she'd use to climb to the branch that led into the ash's arms. The first branch was high. She began to doubt her ability to climb up alone. If only she were as tall as Mum it would be easy. She didn't know whether the ash branches would be strong enough to bear her weight either – but by that point she'd be over Michael's garden. If she fell she'd be on the right side of the wall, and she would use his water butt for the return climb.

The problem was going to be the first oak branch. She might have to sneak a ladder down here once it got dark. This would be her last resort: the empty Drunken House at night wasn't a pleasant prospect.

She searched for a log to stand on. There was nothing. Nobody ever came so close to the Drunken House, and the coppice was overgrown. She stood against the trunk and reached as high as she could. Even on tiptoes she couldn't get a grip on the branch.

The oak tree gave her the answer. One second she was flattened against the trunk, searching for a hold. The next, her hands had found a growing spot and she was communicating with the oak. It made her aware that she could shrink the trunk rather than stretch it. She smiled. Who'd ever have thought it would be useful to shrink a tree?

She shook out her arms and released the tension while she concentrated on the oak. Then she placed her hands on the growing spot and let her body press into the safe solidity of its trunk. The internal fibres let her tune into them.

It was a wise old tree. Although it had given her the answer to her problem, it wasn't easily pliable to her will. She had to explain why she wanted to shrink its trunk. She had to persuade it that it was vital to enter the garden. Silently, she pleaded her case through her hands: her love for Michael; her need for a keepsake; her guilt over her greed for power; her willingness to dedicate her life to repairing the terrible mistake she'd made.

The reasons poured from her mind to her hands and into the oak's cells. In return, its sympathy rose through its network of pensive roots. It radiated melancholy for the beech she'd damaged, allowing Rainbow's guilt to subside into sadness. It exuded concern for the hosts of trees that protected the planet and showed Rainbow how they had maintained this responsibility for millions of years, long before man or dinosaur had appeared. Images of tropical forests, hazel thickets and solitary sequoias flashed through her mind. She felt her importance in the world dwindle, shrinking at the same time as the oak's trunk shrank in her hands. Yet the oak insisted she was important, like every one of the planet's trees, from the smallest sapling to the oldest pine. She had a role to play, a belief to defend. She could help, as could every human that grew from earth and returned to its soil.

The oak's voice receded and she brought her aching arms slowly to her sides. Although she didn't understand everything the oak had told her, she felt like a new person. No, not a new person: an older version of the same person; filled with ancient knowledge; more solid, more sure of herself. Wrinkles of age seemed to spread over her skin, but when she touched her face it was as smooth as usual. Nothing had changed on her surface. Inside, however, she felt a knot of new respect for the wisdom of trees. How could she still be only thirteen years old? Well, nearly fourteen. The number that represented her age didn't justify the centuries she'd lived through during the last minute, nor the understanding she had gained.

She sat down on the oak tree's roots and let the ripples inside her spread out until her awe calmed into gratitude. This was a much more effective way of learning than school. On the new scale of things, her mission in Michael's house now seemed insignificant. Yet the oak had approved what must be a tiny, meaningless detail to it. Her resolution grew stronger. She took a deep breath and started climbing. It was easy now she could grip the lowest branch. She clambered up, groped along the branch to the ash and then slithered down its trunk into Michael's garden.

The first thing she noticed was how overgrown it had become. The garden had always been weedy because Michael's sculptures had made it impossible to mow. Nature, now unhampered by metallic carcasses, had crept over the small yard between the house and the workshop. It looked even worse than Mum's bit of garden, because the neat, red-brick walls here demanded order. At home there were no walls, only broken wire fences, so it seemed natural when, each summer, the sagging strand of barbed wire on each side of the front gate disappeared into swathes of swishy grass.

She knelt and parted last year's trailing dead grass, revealing a lively new growth underneath, and then ran her fingers through the eager blades to see if anything had been forgotten. The garden was small, yet it took ages to brush the whole area. She found nothing. Michael's relatives had been thorough. Rainbow wondered what they'd done with his sculptures. Had they been thrown onto a scrap heap like squashed old cars or taken lovingly into houses and looked after with pride? Michael had never talked about his family, other than his grandfather and great-grandfather. Rainbow had been stuck at home on crutches when they'd come to clear the house. Perhaps a cross landlord had thrown everything into a skip.

She pushed open the wooden door into the workshop. It was dark and damp inside. And empty. He hadn't had time to renovate it completely in the months he'd lived there. Instead of the smart installation he'd wanted, he'd used a plug-in light over a scrap-wood bench. Had he sacrificed his workshop-refurbishment time in favour of helping her? Rainbow shook the thought from her head. Her eyes adjusted to the gloom and she searched the room.

There were some loose tiles on the sill by the frosted-glass window. He'd talked about a hiding place under a roof of tiles, and she'd presumed he meant the loft. But maybe this was it. She picked up a tile and looked underneath. There was a cavity between the outside and inside walls of the shed, and the tiles covered a deep hole as wide as her hand.

She squinted into it. She couldn't see anything. She pulled up her sleeve and slid her bare left arm into the cavity.

Her fingers touched something smooth: a cylinder. She lifted it out. It was a cardboard tube. She'd seen it before. She brushed off the cobwebby dust and held it tight against her chest. Tears pricked in her eyes and she staggered, abandoned, in the desert Michael had left inside her.

Outside the shed, she eased the rolled-up sheet of paper from the tube. It was their joint drawing project. She and Michael were supposed to have opened this together, side by side, once they'd each finished their half of the picture. She blinked back her tears. She wanted to hear his booming laugh. She wanted to share this with him. She wanted him back.

She jerked up her head. There was a noise in the lane. A car slowed down in front of the Drunken House and stopped. She rolled the paper back into the tube and shoved it into her rucksack. Voices approached.

The water butt was lying on its side near the house. She dragged it over to the ash tree and climbed out of the garden the way she'd come. Then she cut through the coppice and joined the road around the bend, where the people wouldn't see her.

❧ ❧ ❧

In the middle of Saturday night she was woken from a deep sleep by a hand shaking her.

"It's time," came Mum's voice.

Rainbow couldn't focus her sleepy mind on the question she needed to ask. She rolled over and covered her head with her quilt, only to be shaken again.

"Come on. Put your jumper on and I'll give you a piggyback."

Clothing was eased over her head. She draped herself onto Mum's back and dropped her cheek onto her shoulder.

"Where're we going?" she managed to mumble.

"Away."

They shuffled down the stairs, out of the house and over to the Mini. Through a half-open eye Rainbow saw it was packed full of bags and boxes. Mum released her into a small nest lined with her sleeping bag in the rear seat.

"But Mum—"

"Snuggle down and go back to sleep, love." Mum pulled a blanket over her. "I'm going to lock up."

Now she could go back to sleep, she was irreversibly awake. They were going somewhere. Bob wasn't with them. Maybe they'd collect him from Fraser's on the way. More importantly, she hadn't got her keepsake.

She pushed back the blanket, climbed out of the seat and picked her way back to the house, her feet bare.

Mum was standing by the kitchen door, searching through her pockets for the key.

"I must get something," said Rainbow. She yanked open the door and squeezed through the gap.

"Hurry up then. Nothing too big."

She retrieved the cardboard tube and stuffed a Yorkie bar into her pyjama pocket. Her bedroom was full of things she wanted to take with her. Her eyes alighted on a photo of Mum and Bob and herself, dating from her childhood, when they'd been happy. She picked it up. Knowing Mum, they may be gone a while. She was half-excited, half-scared by the thought of an adventure. She pushed her feet into her trainers and reached for her tree book.

It had disappeared from her bedside table.

She ran downstairs. Mum was gazing around the kitchen, the key in her hand.

"I can't find my tree book," said Rainbow.

"I've packed it. Come on, it's time to go."

"Where are we going?"

Mum looked surprised. "To find you a guru, of course. We discussed it the other day."

Rainbow didn't remember discussing anything. She didn't even know exactly what a guru was. It was typical of Mum to think that by mentioning something she'd discussed it.

"Hurry up, love. We've got a ferry to catch."

CHAPTER THIRTEEN

The yellow Mini bumped out of the ferry's backside into Cherbourg at dawn. Rainbow's first thought was for Bob. Here they were, she and Mum, fleeing the weeks and months of fights in a little Mini. They were alone on the European continent. Bob would be worried about them. First, he'd be angry and then he'd be grumpy. Anxiety would seep through his bad mood and leave him stroking his chin as he tried to work out where they'd gone. She could see him doing it. A shadow of regret dulled the view of the busy port around her. He'd have loved this adventure.

She stretched her leg up over the back of the passenger seat. From the little Mum had said about the trip, Rainbow suspected it had stemmed from an impulse. It was probably a good thing. Mum and Bob would be nicer to each other after a few weeks' break. And she was definitely on the best side. It was her first time abroad, and she was even missing school. Things couldn't be better, though she'd have preferred to bring Acrobat and his kittens. As soon as she could, she'd phone Bob and remind him to feed them.

Mum hunched over the wheel and concentrated on driving on the right-hand side of the road. She ignored Rainbow's pleas to sit in the front seat, and made no response to her excited exclamations about the foreign things she spotted. There were advertising boards everywhere. The writing on the road signs was skinny compared to the reassuring fat letters on English signposts. And although she knew it was perfectly logical, it still seemed strange to see the French words from schoolbooks on the shop fronts.

They drove around Cherbourg three times and then stopped at a service station. Mum asked her to go and buy a road atlas.

"Me? I can't speak French," said Rainbow.

"Don't you learn it at school?"

"Yes, but it's not the same as real-life French."

Mum unfolded her long limbs from the driver's seat and walked into the garage shop. Rainbow wanted to follow, but was afraid Mum would force her to speak. Mum gesticulated at the little brown-haired, moustached man and then pulled out the plastic bag full of the francs they'd bought on the ferry. She emerged a few minutes later with a wide smile and a Michelin map the same colour as the car.

"Now we can find Domi," she said.

She checked her face in the rear-view mirror, started up the engine and passed a crumpled card over to Rainbow.

Rainbow smoothed out the postcard. In the photograph there was a brown liquid in a pear-shaped glass, an old-fashioned checked slipper, and the word 'Cognac' in swirly letters. The image didn't say much for the man they were going to visit. She'd never heard of him before Mum had mentioned him on Friday night. She wished she'd listened more carefully. All she remembered was that he was a French friend from her university days.

On the back of the card were a hand-drawn map and a message:

Come back and see us soon – you know we love you. You're always welcome here. Yours forever, Domi.

Rainbow scrutinised the writing. It sounded suspicious. Only Bob was supposed to love Mum. She conjured up a face for Domi: it was Fraser-shaped, with the garage man's hair and creepy moustache.

The sketch of lines on the postcard led to the centre of Domi's world, called 'Le Logis de Châtres'. And there was a date. 1977. The year she was born.

"Have you heard from him since?" she asked Mum.

Mum was struggling to wind down the window that was still stuck.

"Since when?"

"It says 1977 here."

"As long ago as that!" Mum gave up with the window. "So can you find it for us, love?"

Rainbow sighed. She liked adventures, but didn't have much experience with maps. She negotiated a place in the front seat and opened the Michelin book. The index gave her the names on the postcard sketch and she began to piece the journey together.

It took Mum twenty minutes to find her way out of Cherbourg. By the time she was on the road leading south,

Rainbow had listed the towns they'd need to pass in order to arrive at Le Logis.

🍃🍃🍃

Maps were like numbers. They looked simple but bore little relation to reality. Mum said the journey would take seven hours. But each time they arrived in a town, they went round and round until the signposts eventually relented and revealed an escape route.

They stopped for lunch at an *aire de repos*. When Rainbow rooted around the car for the food basket, she discovered a tent and the little gas camping cooker. Mum had been surprisingly efficient. It had been the same for the passports on the ferry: Rainbow had stiffened in horror when she'd heard the ferry check-in man ask for them. She was sure Mum hadn't organised passports. But then Mum had whipped out two from her sequinned bag. She buried them just as quickly afterwards. When Rainbow asked to look at them, she refused on the grounds that she didn't want Rainbow to disorganise the important papers.

She'd also packed Rainbow's favourite objects. Rainbow would have added a lot more things if she'd known the real reason for Mum's question about *Desert Island Discs*. But she and Mum were rich now. They had a wad of francs with lots of promising zeros, and could afford to buy anything.

They arrived in the small town of Cognac in the early evening and followed Domi's sketch towards Le Logis in the nearby countryside. It was impossible to find. Half an hour later they'd almost given up hope when, as they bumped along a potholed white track that wound through a wood, they passed some parked motorbikes and noticed a group of buildings a dozen metres from the track.

This could be it. The house was completely hidden from the road, as in Domi's notations. Mum parked the Mini in a passing place next to the motorbikes. A battered vehicle – a cross between a car and a van – took up most of the space. Rainbow read 'Renault 4 TL' on its boot door.

"Suppose he's moved? It was a long time ago," said Rainbow.

"Moved? Why would he do that?"

Mum smoothed down her hair. Rainbow got out of the car, stretched and looked around. It was a paradise of trees. She was overwhelmed by green: the smell of green tree sap, the grass, the budding vines and the cow parsley that peppered the banks of the track. It was like wearing green-tinted sunglasses.

An odd-looking tree caught her attention. It grew on the edge of the wood beside the house. There was something familiar about it, as if she'd seen it in a dream. She breathed in the sweet air of warm, French April and walked over to the odd tree. At the height of her forehead the trunk had split into two, and a long, deep scar gouged its cleavage. Above the split, the trunk became two branches. One was strong and straight, and led up to the sky. The other curved angrily from left to right as if avoiding the sun.

Intrigued by the tree's singularity, she reached out and touched the bark with both hands. An image of Amrita flashed into her mind. It was like coming home! Then an icy current raced through her nerves and chilled her whole body. She wrenched her hands away.

Mum came up behind her.

"Nice tree to hug," she said. "It's a silver maple." She patted its trunk.

Rainbow looked at her in horror.

Mum didn't flinch. "It looks strong and weak at the same time, doesn't it? I want to protect it."

"Not me," said Rainbow. "It gives me the creeps."

Mum was no longer listening.

"Let's see if Domi's in," she said.

The house and its outbuildings lay in a clearing of several acres. They walked across the flattened grass towards the buildings and Rainbow spotted part of a vegetable patch, an orchard and an animal pen. There was a slight smell of farmyard waste. Chickens, ducks and geese clucked and squawked, mingling with a family of goats that was climbing in and out of a lopsided grey van parked under some alders. The front of the house had a ruined feel to it, but when she looked more closely, she saw it was in a good state. The repairs simply didn't match the original stone architecture of the smallholding. The place looked heavenly for a holiday. It was as friendly as home in its overspill of clutter, with the added bonus of pets.

Mum pulled the chain of a huge cowbell that hung from the arch over the grand, cobwebby front door. There was no answer. She pulled again.

Rainbow went round the side of the house to look into the garden. Some adults were sitting around a table made from an upturned electricity-cable wheel. Behind them, standing in a ragged circle in the vegetable patch, she counted seven children. It looked like a scene from one of their parties at home, apart from the children. There were never children at their own parties, to Rainbow's simultaneous relief and regret.

The French children were moving towards each other to catch something in the centre of their ring. They advanced a few steps at a time and made 'shushing' noises. In the centre she could just make out a small, furry animal.

Rainbow beckoned to Mum, who joined her. They both peered at the glass-chinking group.

"Can you see Domi?" Rainbow whispered.

Mum squinted. "That could be him; the long-haired one on the left in a red-checked shirt. Yes, I'm sure that's him."

There was a chorus of whoops. A teenage boy, a little older than her, swung a rabbit triumphantly into the air.

Mum started to walk towards the group of adults. She reached for Rainbow's hand. Rainbow deftly avoided the movement by sticking her hand into the pocket of her jeans and trailed after her. Mum would normally switch into her social mode and ignore Rainbow at this point. Today, she waited for her and placed her hand behind Rainbow's back so that they approached side by side.

A lady with wavy grey hair looked up. "Bonjour," she said. "On peut vous aider?"

Rainbow saw that Mum hadn't understood the second part of the sentence either. This didn't seem to worry Mum. She replied in English. Her voice was slow and clear like the nurses at the hospital on Rainbow's first day there.

"Hello. Is Dominique here?"

Rainbow heard the word '*anglaise*' muttered several times. The man in the checked shirt stood up and walked towards

157

them. He was short, with a wiry, tanned body. His long, thick hair made him look younger than the wrinkles on his face showed him to be. He seemed comfortable and wise, like a shrunken oak. He smiled, his eyes fixed on Mum.

"Jasmine?"

His voice was deep and calm. His tongue rolled slowly around every letter of Mum's name as if he were tasting a treat.

"Domi?"

Their smiles became a stereo laugh. Domi opened his arms wide and Mum launched herself into them. They hugged and then pulled back to examine each other more closely. Rainbow took a step back to avoid being knocked over by Mum. She folded her arms. Domi looked ridiculous so close to her tall mum.

"And this must be–?"

"Rainbow," interrupted Mum.

Domi looked surprised. He hesitated. Rainbow waited, unsure if she was supposed to do the French thing and kiss this stranger. Then he stretched out his arm and shook hands with her.

The contact made them both jump. Rainbow tried to pull her hand away, but Domi held on tight.

"Rainbow," he said. He lingered over her name as much as he had done with Mum's. "Don't fight it. Let yourself go. I won't hurt you."

Rainbow opened her mouth to say she wasn't fighting anything. But Domi was looking at Mum, his eyebrows raised in question. They appeared to be having a telepathic conversation. Mum nodded slightly. Rainbow closed her mouth without saying a word.

"Welcome to Le Logis," he said, letting Rainbow's hand go at last.

"Thanks." Rainbow massaged her hot right hand with her left one.

Domi turned back to his friends, who were watching, and introduced Mum and Rainbow to them in French. They all stood up and flowed forward in a wave to cheek-kiss and practise their limited English. Only Domi spoke English without an accent. Rainbow was intrigued. She wanted to know more about him.

🌿 🌿 🌿

Later, as Rainbow unrolled their sleeping bags onto the bouncy double bed in the big room upstairs, Mum told her that Domi was half-English and half-French. That explained why he didn't have the *'Allo 'Allo* accent she'd expected.

Mum leant out of the window and stared at the moonlit vines on the other side of the track. Rainbow crawled into her sleeping bag and yawned.

"How long are we staying here for?"

Mum closed the windows and turned around. "Don't you like it here?"

"It's all right, but the kids aren't very friendly," said Rainbow. "And I'm worried Bob might forget to feed Acrobat."

"I'm going to ring him now. I'll remind him."

"Can I speak to him?"

"Another time. I don't want to talk for too long because it'll cost a bomb."

"Okay."

Rainbow closed her eyes. Mum came and sat on the bed, and her weight tipped Rainbow towards her. It was nice to have Mum to herself like this. She mustn't let Domi steal Mum away.

"Do you love Domi?" she asked. She opened her eyes to see everything Mum might not say.

Mum smiled. "A long time ago I did. We're friends now; old friends who haven't seen each other for ages."

She paused. Rainbow held her breath. Mum was going to make some kind of revelation.

A knock on the door killed the moment. Mum told the woman, Chantal, that she'd be down in a minute. She pulled a blanket over Rainbow's sleeping bag, leant forward and kissed her on her forehead.

"Sleep tight, my little healer," she whispered. She stood up and left Rainbow in the silver shadowed room.

Rainbow closed her eyes again and wriggled inside the sleeping bag. So Mum and Domi had been lovers, like Lady Chatterley and her gamekeeper. Lovers. The word sent pleasant shivers along her arms and down her back. It must have been back in 1977. That would explain the postcard. Domi had sent it when Mum left the commune to go back to England. To England, where Rainbow had been born.

Rainbow opened her eyes. She stared at the cross of the window frame. 1977. She could have been conceived here, in the commune. Her dad had been here. Domi must have known him. But if Domi and her mum had been lovers, then Domi must be her dad.

Rainbow's heart thumped. She sat up. Suppose Mum had

lied to her, and her dad wasn't really dead? Suppose Mum had invented his death so Bob wouldn't hassle her with his jealous fits? Now that she was fed up with Bob, she'd come back to Domi. He was short like Rainbow. He had brown hair like Rainbow. He had magic hands. She was sure he was her dad. She knew it in the same way she'd known there would be a keepsake in Michael's house.

She lay back down and tried to calm the excitement surging through her. What could have happened? In 1977 Mum might have had a mega-argument with Domi and left the commune. She'd gone to England, where Rainbow was born. Then she'd met and married Bob and told him that her baby's father was dead.

Mum must have been on the point of confessing the truth just now when Chantal knocked on the door. When Mum said she'd loved Domi a long time ago, it was her typically vague way of telling Rainbow that Domi was her father.

Rainbow repeated the words out loud. "Father. Dad." She smiled to herself. There was kindness in his wrinkles and heat in his hands. She didn't care about Mum's lie. France was so far away that he might as well have been dead. The lie didn't matter anymore. The important thing was that she'd found Dad.

She decided to act in the same way as Mum: she would keep this important discovery unspoken. It would be like Domi and Mum's silent conversation earlier on. They must have been acknowledging that she was their daughter. Being grown-up was all about keeping quiet about important things.

Rainbow hugged herself in delight. She was still smiling when she woke the next morning.

CHAPTER FOURTEEN

The following afternoon, Domi invited Rainbow for a walk in the woods. He'd spent the morning showing Mum the property while Rainbow helped feed the animals. She jumped at the chance of having some time alone with him.

They walked along the track under the canopy of leaves and he told her about Le Logis. Twenty people lived in the old Charentaise stone farmhouse Domi's mother had left him when she'd died. Domi had lived in England for most of his life and used to come here for the holidays. Rainbow asked him how he'd met Mum.

He smiled at Rainbow and the wrinkles around his eyes multiplied.

"At university in England. She was interested in spiritualism and we became friends."

"Like, *special* friends?" she said.

"Yes, very special friends." He tweaked Rainbow's ponytail.

"So why didn't you stay together?"

"My mother died. I left university to set up a healing business here. Little by little, other spiritualists joined me.

We built up a good reputation in the Charente. The French are more open to spiritualism than the English. They're closer to the earth; more rural, more able to accept truths beyond those explained by science." Domi's eyes sparkled with enthusiasm.

"So why didn't Mum come with you?"

"She had her music. Anyway, she did come – later."

"In 1977."

"That's right." Domi raised an eyebrow at her.

"And you were ... um, together again?"

He frowned.

"Listen, it feels wrong for me to tell you what happened with Jasmine. You should ask her."

She considered explaining that Mum never answered her questions, but it felt disloyal. She didn't know him well enough yet.

He cleared his throat. "Why don't we talk about trees instead?"

Rainbow looked at him in surprise.

"Yes, I know about your gift," he said.

"Oh."

He must be the guru, otherwise Mum wouldn't have broken her promise.

He led her onto a small path and stopped in front of a tree. She recognised the smooth, lipped-up bark. It was a beech.

"She told me about the accident, too. Perhaps it'll help to share what you know with someone you can trust," he continued.

Fraser. Michael. Now Domi.

"How do I know I can trust you?" she asked. Perhaps he

would tell her he was her father.

He raised his shoulders and arms and turned his palms outwards, in a French gesture that seemed to mean 'who knows?'

"Fair enough," he said. "Let's get to know each other better before we talk about trees."

They turned away from the French beech tree. Rainbow, in an anticlimax of regret, answered his questions about her life at home. He didn't mention trees again.

❧ ❧ ❧

On the third day of their stay, Rainbow decided it was time to lead Domi back to the subject of trees. They were outside the house and Domi had just finished his espresso.

"How did you know you wanted to heal people?" she asked.

He put down his cup.

"I've always known. My mother was a clairvoyant and she encouraged me to heal. When I set up Le Logis for spiritualists, I realised that it was my destiny to save the world."

She giggled. "Your arms," she reminded him.

He had a habit of raising them in an all-encompassing gesture when he talked about the people who needed to be healed. She called it his Wild Fanatic look.

"Oh yes." He lowered them. "Still, I do believe people need to be saved. Spiritualists can guide them towards an alternative to today's greedy, materialistic society."

She thought about the oak she'd communicated with outside Michael's garden wall. Her first impression had been right: Domi really was like a human version of the oak.

"What about saving the environment? You know, trees and stuff."

"That's where you have a role to play."

They looked at each other. Rainbow was the first to break the silence.

"Shall I show you?"

"If you're ready."

She nodded. "Can we go back to that beech tree? I want to touch it, but I may need your help."

She'd felt the power in Domi's hands. If the beech wanted revenge for its English kin, she'd feel less vulnerable with him beside her.

"Haven't you touched a beech tree since your accident?" She shook her head.

He laid an arm round her shoulders and squeezed her gently. "I'll be right beside you."

They left the commune and followed the path to the beech tree. It was dressed in lime-green spring leaves. He helped her climb into it and then waited at the bottom while she selected a slim branch. She wondered whether all French trees had the creepiness she'd felt in the silver maple tree by the house on the day of her arrival. Then sensation overran her thoughts. Her hands opened the beech's spirit.

The beech knew what she'd done to its English brother, despite the geographical distance. Trees didn't have a language barrier, unlike Mum and herself. They had a system much older than language. It was something in their roots: a current that travelled through the earth, rock and water of the planet. And it was something in the air: a current that travelled from leaf to leaf in the breeze. She felt warm generosity flowing from the beech. It responded to her silent plea for forgiveness. There was a slipping of fibre over fibre, a reaction to her embrace. She opened her eyes and felt tears on her cheeks.

"Rainbow?"

"It's fine. I feel so ... well, great. And so humble. They've forgiven me. I want to smile at everyone. This is all I need in the world."

"Arms," laughed Domi.

Rainbow smiled sheepishly and dropped her arms. "Seriously, Domi. It's amazing. This beech knows all about the one I hurt."

🌱🍃🌱

The beech's forgiveness broke a dam in Rainbow's mind. Over the next week, waves of words poured out of her. She told Domi everything she'd learnt about trees – though nothing about Michael. He listened patiently and accompanied her around the woods while she learnt everything the French trees passed on to her.

To begin with, Domi simply watched. Then he started asking her questions while she was in a tree: Did the tree explain what it wanted? Was it looking for help? Did she feel a sense of the role the trees expected her to play?

"It's not about wanting," she tried to explain. "It's about being and not being."

When she wasn't in the boughs of a tree, they studied the spiritual books in his library. They also researched tree diseases.

She learnt about how insects bored holes in the bark, about fungi and about Dutch elm disease.

Domi encouraged her to heal diseased trees. She spent hours on branches, poking worms out of holes and then massaging bark over the wounds to seal them. Dutch elm disease was the most difficult because it weakened the tree's spirit. She felt helpless when faced with this depressive illness. The trees were trying to cure themselves, but she sensed that their efforts to kill the fungus were killing their own tissues too. The energy she guided through their bark was too feeble compared to the mass of the sick tree. A day spent on an elm left her distressed and flat. Domi said Dutch elm disease was like cancer.

One day, the stifling heat gave way to a huge storm. Domi seized Rainbow, settled her on the back of his motorbike and whizzed her off to the Dordogne. The storms there were more violent than in the Charente. On the storm-ravaged hills they found trees struck by lightning, and she soothed and smoothed ripped fibres back into place. Thanks to Domi's guidance, she was at last doing something useful with her gift.

CHAPTER FIFTEEN

A fortnight after their arrival, Rainbow was perched precariously in the dancing branches of a spruce tree when she had a disturbing thought. Suppose she wasn't special at all. Imagine everyone had the same gift as her and hadn't yet discovered it. Perhaps that is what the English oak had meant when it insisted that every human could help. She shared her thought with Domi, who was meditating with his back to the spruce's trunk.

"It would be fantastic if everyone could heal trees in return for all that trees do for humans. But I think if that were the case, it would be documented," he replied.

She thought of Michael's warning about exploitation. The first person to mention it would have a hard time. But if he or she had the bravery to make their gift public knowledge, it would encourage others to come out into the open. Then it would become acceptable, even normal. And they'd be able to heal whole forests instead of one tree at a time.

"Why don't you try, Domi?"

He placed his hands on the spruce trunk and followed

Rainbow's instructions to concentrate on feeling the interior of the tree. Nothing happened, even when he moved his hands elsewhere.

"I can't sense anything at all," he said. "It's just as well: I've got plenty of work with my children."

Parents came from all over France to bring their spiritually gifted children to Domi. When she'd learnt this, she'd asked if he'd met other people with the same gift as hers. But he hadn't. No child had anything remotely similar.

She looked down at him leaning against the spruce. "Why are you more interested in children than adults?" she asked.

"Because they're our future."

She'd heard this at school, and it was usually coupled with a monologue about the importance of exams and career choices.

"There are so many old spirits coming back," he continued.

This was far more interesting than exams. She slithered down the trunk and sat beside him.

"What have old spirits got to do with children?"

"They're born into children," he said. "I help my children explore their spirituality and come to terms with it so they can apply their old-spirit wisdom to their lives. Many spiritualists agree there's a collective spirit heaven made up of all the souls that aren't currently on earth. From time to time these old spirits have missions to accomplish, missions to guide mankind. So they are born into chosen children. You know how sometimes you feel you've already been to a place, even though it's the first time you've visited? This is one explanation for that feeling."

"Really? Do you think I've got an old spirit?"

"Yes. That's why I need to understand the scope of your gift. Then I'll be able to interpret the meaning of it in the scheme of things."

Now she understood why he spent so much time with her. It wasn't simply because he was her dad. She wondered if he treated her specially, compared to the other gifted kids.

"What do you do with the children?"

"It depends. Mostly, they need to be reassured that they can trust their intuition. For children to grow up in spiritually healthy environments, their parents need to encourage intuition. Adults have spent years being trained to be logical, so it can be difficult to return to an intuitive state. To convince them, I heal their illnesses and show them science is only part of the truth. Then there's more chance they'll follow their intuition, accept situations they don't understand and make the right decisions."

"What happens if they make the wrong decisions?"

"Look around you. Anything that leads to destruction is the wrong decision," he said. As if to prove his point, a Mirage fighter plane passed overhead. "It's a universal truth, which means it's true in all our parallel worlds."

"What parallel worlds?"

Rainbow was intrigued. The Amrita conversation she'd had with Mum when she was younger came into her mind. Mum had mentioned parallel worlds and suggested that Amrita's soul had split into two, creating an Amrita who lived and an Amrita who died.

Domi continued. "My mother believed that spiritually sensitive people had a capacity for dividing. In fact, I think she said everyone could. When she looked into people's futures she would see several versions of the person, each doing different things. She called these versions 'parallels'. According to the decisions her clients made, they became one of the parallels. The other versions still existed, but in parallel worlds."

Rainbow looked around and shivered. She half-expected to see a host of parallel Rainbows floating behind her shoulder.

"Where are the parallel worlds?"

"I don't know. It's not a concept I've ever studied. Maybe science will stumble on the answer one day. I do remember that parallels should never meet, though."

"Why not?"

"I'm not sure. They were my mother's theories, not mine. I don't remember what else she said, though she probably wrote more down in her memoirs. I've got her notes somewhere in my office. She did tell me a story once about someone being destroyed because they'd touched their parallel. That was when she was old and suffering from senility. She told lots of dramatic stories then, and people stopped listening to her."

Domi looked sad. Rainbow took his hand.

"Let's do something fun together," she said. She pulled him to his feet. "Let's go to the beach."

Rainbow loved the seaside. They were an hour away from the Atlantic coast, with its long, empty beaches and powerful waves. It was hard to imagine them crowded with holidaymakers, as they apparently were in summer. She'd be home in Dorset long before the summer.

Domi had already taken her to the coast several times on his motorbike, to the envy of the other commune children. They would speed along the smooth roads dotted with late-spring beachgoers, Rainbow gripping Domi's solid back. When they arrived at the Côte Sauvage, they'd park in the shade of the pine forest and walk on the cool, sandy path to the dunes. They raced barefoot up the steep dune and down the other side to the splendour of the sea.

They always swam. The sea was cold: freezing cold. The shock of icy water on sweating skin made Rainbow hyperventilate and gulp the warm air like a fish. She and Domi shared a sense of exhilaration in the sea. The energy of the great mass of living water was phenomenal. She loved the battering of the waves as they thundered into her and bowled her over in a sandy wash. If she had a gift to communicate with waves, she'd make them huge and powerful every time she came.

Domi became a boy at the beach; a boy without worries for mankind or the planet. He flung her into the waves, rolled her in the sand, chased her through the sea foam and raced her along the dunes. At the beach he was no longer her guru; he was her dad.

Beach days were always rounded off with a *crêpe*, spread with Nutella for Rainbow and sprinkled with icing sugar for Domi. The more time Rainbow spent with her dad, the more she saw they had lots in common. It was all evidence. She stocked up the proof inside her head and let it float out at night-time when she stretched out in her sleeping bag and waited for sleep, or for Mum – whichever came first.

When Mum arrived before sleep, they would whisper together until she fell asleep. Mum was discovering vegetarian cooking. She spent hours experimenting with the herbs and vegetables planted in the garden or stocked in glass jars in the cellar. She helped Céline, a middle-aged

French woman who'd travelled all over the world as a cook. Céline, who had an eccentric grasp of English, had taken Mum in hand. When she wasn't contributing to work on the commune, Mum would wander off along the tracks, often with Virginie, the commune clairvoyant. Sometimes she disappeared alone. She'd started to come back with songs in her head that she would tease out of the old piano in the evenings.

There were few musicians in the commune. Only Gérard and Lilas played an instrument – the guitar. Aziz played an African drum, which didn't count as a musical instrument. The commune people liked to assemble in the living room when Mum was giving birth to a song. Rainbow kept out of the way. It turned her stomach upside down with worry when she heard Mum work here. They were supposed to be on holiday, not settling into this way of life without Bob.

While she waited in bed for Mum, a froth of thoughts about Bob and Acrobat would bubble in her mind. She missed Acrobat's fluffy dimness, and the kittens were growing up without her. In her memories, Bob's grumpy side disappeared. He called her 'Rainy'. She helped him in the garden. She would hold the other end of planks of wood and fetch the tools he asked for. He would hammer and whistle, and talk about jazz festivals while they rebuilt the leaking woodshed. Acrobat and the four kittens played around their feet, and the woodshed became an ornate house for the cat family. There would be embroidered cushions. The cats would eat dinner in five silver bowls and curl up on her lap. She would stroke them and they would purr her to sleep.

Three weeks after their arrival, Céline's son Christophe let slip that he knew how to speak English. Up to this point he'd either ignored Rainbow or glowered at her from a distance. He kept the other children firmly by his side, as far away from her as possible. At fifteen, he was the oldest and the only teenager. The others ranged from ten down to two years old. His role in the commune was to keep the little ones out of mischief, supervise their games and make sure they fed the animals. He'd do this from a chair, where he would lounge and give them orders. Rainbow was sure he hated his duties. She would have offered to take his place if he'd been friendlier towards her.

One day, early on in their stay, his mum had pushed him towards her. He'd taken a few steps, his hands thrust into the back pockets of his baggy jeans, and mumbled something indistinguishably French at her. Then he'd shuffled away to where Alain was dismantling a broken machine. Rainbow had shrugged and turned back to her tree book.

Most of the time the children were at school. When Domi was busy, Rainbow would help milk the goats, take the dogs for walks, mend fences with François – the animal whisperer – or play with two-year-old Marine. Marine was almost as good company as Acrobat. The only problem was that when Rainbow stopped playing and sketched, Marine would follow her and spread her sticky, chubby hands over the pages of Rainbow's pad. As soon as the children came home from school, Christophe whisked her away to play proper games under his bored supervision.

The evening Rainbow discovered Christophe's linguistic skills, he'd come home with two black eyes and blood all over his face. He scowled at everyone. It reminded her of the embarrassing fuss Mum and Bob's friends had made when Lucy Carter had beaten her up. While the children crowded around Christophe and tried to touch his swollen eyes, she crossed the garden and opened the rabbit hutch door.

"The rabbit's escaped! Come and help," she called.

The children ran over, shouting at her, and she saw Christophe slope into the house. When they cleared the dinner table, a couple of hours later, Christophe stood in her path with his arms full of books.

"Here's some BDs for you," he muttered in English.

"BDs?"

"Bandes dessinées. Comic books," he said. He shoved the pile of *Boule et Bill* comic books into her arms.

Rainbow was so amazed to hear English words twist out of his sullen mouth that she couldn't think how to reply. He turned back and was deep in conversation with Alain before she could recover and thank him.

❧ ❦ ❧

She struggled to read one of the *Boule et Bill* comic books that night while she waited for Mum to finish the bottle of wine she was drinking downstairs with Chantal and Céline. The other adults had left for various appointments with clients. In the daytime, their palm-reading, tarot-card interpretations, healing and other spiritual services took place in three special rooms in the house. But in the evenings the children made the atmosphere too hectic for clients to be able to relax in intimacy. Evening appointments were held in clients' homes.

Two of the reception rooms, which doubled up as bedrooms, were small and overstuffed with furnishings. They smelt musky and a nebula of incense hung in the air, like Mum's workroom at home. The third room was Domi's. It looked like the physiotherapy unit where Rainbow had exercised to awaken her leg muscles in the long months after her accident. The clean brightness made her feel healthy as soon as she stepped inside.

She'd asked Domi if she could watch a healing session with him, but he'd refused. He'd told her that people weren't the same once they were alone in the room with him. They relaxed their stubborn defiance and let themselves be carried away to belief. He said this wouldn't be possible if a third person was present. And he added that allowing yourself to believe was a very private action, especially in today's scientific world. He'd finished by saying that one day, if she turned to healing people, she'd understand. Rainbow had nodded, but she knew it was trees she wanted to help, not people.

At last she heard footsteps on the stairs and Mum entered their bedroom. Rainbow put down *Boule et Bill*.

"Are you drunk?"

"No, just deeper," Mum replied.

She undid her chignon and let her black hair tumble free.

"It's been three weeks now," said Rainbow. "When are we going home?"

Mum picked up her hairbrush. She turned towards the

177

window and began the long strokes that were now familiar to Rainbow. Rainbow didn't like her silence.

"We *are* going home, aren't we?"

"I thought you were happy here," said Mum.

"I am. But I miss Acrobat," replied Rainbow. "And Bob, a bit."

Mum sighed. "Bob's not ready for us to go home yet, love."

"What do you mean?"

"He's still in a bad mood with us. If we go back now, we'll be returning to more fights. It's nice and peaceful here, isn't it?"

"Why doesn't Bob come here, then? With Acrobat and the kittens. He'd feel better and not want to shout all the time."

"You know what he thinks about anything spiritual. He wouldn't agree with this kind of life. And there's no proper music."

Rainbow pushed the comic book off the bed. "When will he be ready, then?"

"We'll have to wait and see."

"But I want to go home."

"Aren't you better here? You were being picked on at school and you said yourself that you were fed up with our fights."

"But—"

"And you've got Domi here to help you with your gift."

That was true. Her real father. But as much as she liked Domi, he wasn't Bob. She couldn't understand herself. She'd have given anything to swap Bob for a proper father, yet now it had happened she found she missed him.

Mum was in full flow. She sat down on the bed beside Rainbow, squashing her leg. "We should make the most of our stay here. You can learn to speak good French and heal trees. We could even enrol you at school with Christophe."

"School? But it's all in French."

"That could be fun."

"No way."

Rainbow caught a strand of hair and twisted it. School? Fun? French school would be even worse than English school. She'd be more of an outsider here.

"Let's enrol you for September, just in case. We can work on your French this summer, here at the Logis."

Rainbow yanked her sleeping bag out from under Mum's weight.

"Bob will be ready by summer."

She wriggled down inside, turned her back on Mum and squeezed her eyes shut. She would have to take things into her own hands.

CHAPTER SIXTEEN

It wasn't easy to use the Logis telephone. It hung on the wall under the main staircase in the entrance hall, which had doors to the front, back and sides of the house. The twenty residents passed continually through. Private conversations were only possible at night.

Rainbow waited until Mum was snoring. She crept out of bed and sneaked down the stairs. The house was quiet apart from the scurrying patter of rodent feet and the creaking of a loose shutter in the wind.

She dialled her home number. There was no ringing tone, just emptiness down the line that separated her from Bob. On the noticeboard beside the phone there were dozens of slips of paper. She looked through them while she waited and saw that Mum, in a fit of efficiency, had written their home number on a scrap of envelope. Rainbow hadn't recognised it at first because it had a code in front. She added 00 44, dropped the zero, and redialled their number.

The ringing tone began. Bob had been at Fraser's when they'd left England, but he would be back home now that

Mum had left. She held her breath and pictured the chaotic kitchen.

It was a long time before she heard a click. Then Bob's sleepy voice asked who the hell was ringing at this time of night. Rainbow had no idea what time it was – there were no clocks in the house – but she knew it would be an hour earlier in England.

"Bob, it's me."

"Speak up. Who?"

"Rainbow," she hissed.

She turned around and peered into the darkness around her. There was no sign of movement.

"Rainbow! What's up? Are you all right?"

"Yes. I mean, not really. I want to know when we can come home."

There was a short silence before Bob spoke.

"Right now, honey, if you want to. Where are you?"

"In France."

"France? What the hell are you doing there? Where's Jasmine?"

"In bed. She said you weren't ready for us to come home yet."

There was a growling noise on the end of the line.

"Bob? Are you still there?"

"Yes. Look, what's your address?"

"I can't tell you. Mum said it's a secret. I just want to know when we can come home."

"Poor Rainy. I bet it's some kind of weirdo place. She's so selfish–"

"No, it's fine. Totally normal. So can we come home tomorrow?"

"Give me your address and I'll come and pick you up."

If Bob came, they'd have to leave. She wouldn't be obliged to enrol at a French school.

"Okay. It's Le Logis de Châtres, near Cognac." She whispered more directions and asked when he would arrive.

"As soon as I can. Don't tell Jasmine or she'll bolt."

"Okay. How are Acrobat and his kittens?"

Bob seemed not to have heard. She repeated her question.

"Everything's just fine. See you soon, honey."

Rainbow replaced the receiver and listened for suspicious noises from eavesdroppers. Everything was quiet. She tiptoed back upstairs. It was a shame Bob had told her not to say anything. Mum would be pleased to know he wasn't angry anymore.

❧❦

Domi was playing a game of *chat perché* with the children, which appeared to be a French version of 'tag'. Rainbow sat on the swing and sketched the garden while she waited for him to finish. Mum swanned over to the table and perched on the edge. Beside her, Virginie was sorting through a bag of embroidery threads. Rainbow could hear them talking. Virginie was encouraging Mum to find a music band that needed a singer.

There was no television at Le Logis. The adults listened to classical recordings or pop music in the evenings. This had branched out into jazz and blues with Mum's addition of tapes and CDs. They also sang along with the guitars at the weekend parties – the old chart-toppers would have made

Bob cringe. Mum didn't seem to mind though. The others would break off to listen as her voice resonated across the clearing. Once she had everyone's attention she'd sing her new songs. Rainbow could tell they were new because major tones had replaced the sad minors of England. It didn't sound like blues anymore.

Mum threw her head back and laughed with Virginie. She hadn't cried since they'd arrived. Rainbow stopped sketching and nibbled the top of her pencil. Maybe she shouldn't have given their address to Bob. Suppose Mum didn't want to go home?

Domi called Rainbow's name. He was crouched in the vegetable patch between the tomato plants with the three youngest children: Sandrine, Rachelle and Marine. Rainbow fumbled with her sketch pad and shoved it back into her rucksack, and then raced towards him. He was pointing something out to six-year-old Sandrine. Rainbow heard him say 'serpent' and 'pas' and 'mal'. Beside them lay a curled-up snake. Sandrine slipped her hand into Domi's.

Sandrine was the daughter of Alain, the mechanic, and Virginie, the clairvoyant. She was often silent because her mum was a depressive. This is what Céline had told Rainbow. She'd added that Virginie had cheered up since Jasmine's arrival. Virginie was teaching Mum more about crystals, and had pocketfuls of the mysterious coloured stones. She was far less interested in her daughter. Sandrine hung onto Domi as much as she could, or onto her dad when he wasn't engrossed in car and motorbike repairs. Rainbow felt sorry for her. When she came across her sitting her own, she took her hand and chatted to her in English. It didn't matter that

Sandrine couldn't understand. She seemed to like the sound of the words and perked up at the attention. After a while, she started to head straight for Rainbow when the children piled out of the van after school. The other kids were a hostile band but Sandrine was a loner.

Domi stood up and backed away from the snake. "Time for work," he said, in English.

"Domi, reste avec nous," whined Rachelle. She grabbed his other hand. Rainbow understood from her body language that she wanted Domi to stay.

"C'est l'heure du travail," replied Domi, and gently unwound her hand.

"T'es toujours avec elle. C'est pas juste!"

Rainbow quizzed Domi, who translated for her: "They're complaining that I spend too much time with you."

"Tell them I'll be gone soon."

Domi translated and they fell silent. Then Sandrine spoke up. Rainbow didn't understand what she said, but it seemed to have a bad effect on the other two. They started to whine again and Marine curled herself around one of Domi's legs.

Domi disentangled Marine, but his eyes remained fixed on Sandrine. He was silent as he and Rainbow walked towards his motorbike. Rainbow shoved her hands in her pockets.

"What did she say?"

"That you're here to stay," he replied.

"No wonder the others were upset. It's not true, anyway. We're going home soon."

Domi collected the helmets and came back. "You know you can stay as long as you like."

"Thanks. It's nice here with you, but we ought to go home.

We can come back to visit in the summer holidays."

"Missing your school friends?"

"No way. I told you, I'm the school weirdo."

"So why the hurry to get home?"

"Mum isn't very practical about school stuff. She even suggested I go to school here!" Rainbow grinned at him.

"Well, why not?"

She frowned. He was on Mum's side. "I can't speak French for starters."

"You're a bright kid. You'll learn."

"Do you want me to stay?"

Domi laid his helmet on the seat of the bike.

"Listen, Rainbow. You've got a gift that you want to develop. Life isn't easy for people who choose to do things differently from the majority. If you stay here, you'll have the support of everyone in the commune, and the reputation of the commune to help you. I don't know exactly what work you could do with your gift, but that doesn't matter for the moment. The answer will come. If you're serious about wanting to work with trees, I think you'd be better off staying here. Has anyone in the commune treated you as a weirdo because of your gift?"

"No. But I'm still an outsider."

"Only because of the language. That's a tiny hurdle to overcome compared to the barriers against anyone with a spiritual gift. It's tough, even as a group. If you're on your own it's worse. You're lucky your mum's prepared to help you. She's brought you here to us, which is a start. But ultimately it's up to you to decide what you're willing to sacrifice to follow your vocation."

"You make it sound scary. I thought I'd just learn a bit about working with French trees and then go home again."

"And what will you do at home?"

"I don't know."

She felt stupid. Bob wanted her to forget her gift, to become a normal person with a normal life. Part of her wanted to be normal, more than anything. But she knew she'd never be normal like Patti or Lucy Carter or Rebecca. She wanted to work with trees for Michael's sake. The trees needed her and she needed them.

Domi raised her chin with his hand. She was forced to look into his eyes.

"The most important thing is that you feel right within yourself," he said.

Rainbow nodded.

"You don't have to decide today. Take your time. Listen to your heart. Don't try to weigh up the logical advantages and disadvantages. Trust that you'll know what to do when the time comes." He let her go. "Now, let's get to work on some decorative trees. Hop on."

They straddled the motorbike. Domi eased it along the rutted track and accelerated into the lane. It was all very well for him to tell her to take her time – he didn't know Bob was on his way to come and pick her up.

The ride didn't last long. They stopped a few villages away at a chateau that dominated the valley where the River Charente idled from Jarnac to Cognac. Domi introduced Rainbow to a perfumed lady, who welcomed them with three dry kisses on their sweaty cheeks. Her garden reminded Rainbow of a dusted and hoovered parlour in a Jane Austen book. The lady hobbled around the flower beds and shrubberies, leaning on Domi's arm, and pointed with a trembling hand to a plantation of ornamental trees.

Rainbow had never worked on cultivated trees before. There were olives, their backbones gnarled and crooked; black mulberries, their leaves big enough to cover Eve's nakedness; and several Judas trees and mimosas. She laid her hands on a crusty palm tree and sensed fragility. It shivered from the memory of winter frosts. Cultivated trees felt different from free ones. They were less grounded than the trees in the woods. She could sense more concern for their individual welfare than for the collective interest of trees. And they were bitter about being uprooted from their origins and plonked into a hostile environment.

The wild Charente trees were similar to their English counterparts, although the woods around the commune were small and had limited undergrowth. Domi told her this was so that mushroom-pickers could scavenge. It was rare to see an old tree standing alone in a field, like the solitary oaks at home, or a park of wise hundred-year olds. There were lots of new varieties to learn about, and Domi brought books home from the library to help identify the different species. It reminded her of her time with Michael, except that Michael had been interested in her as a person whereas Domi was obsessed by her gift and its meaning.

She loved holm oaks. They carried the name 'oak', but didn't lose their leaves in winter. There were several along the lanes, standing proud between the edge of the vineyards and the tarmac. Their twin trunks reminded her of the alder on which she'd demonstrated her gift to Bob. Often, one side of the canopy was smoothly rounded in silhouette, while the side growing over the road had been squared off by passing lorries.

During her first fortnight she'd stopped to get to know a holm oak that grew within cycling distance of the commune. When she'd run her fingers over the crevices in the bark, she'd found a slot. Inside the slot was a piece of paper. Words had been written in beautiful looping letters on notepaper: it was a letter. She couldn't understand the message, but she loved the idea of a tree holding people's secrets.

That evening, while she was piling cutlery and plates onto the outside table, Christophe strolled over with his hands in his pockets. He was chewing gum. The kids were intent on their game of *un, deux, trois, soleil*, stopping and starting in their race to touch the wall of the outhouse without the leader seeing them move.

Rainbow paused, a knife in her hand, and waited for him to speak. He said nothing. She carried on with her work. A glass slipped in her grasp and broke, and she cursed her clumsy hands.

"You like *Boule et Bill*?"

Christophe's voice was barely a squeak in English. When he spoke French, he made a slow, loud drawl that sounded like a single word.

"S'all right."

She had time to gather the broken glass and finish laying the table before he spoke again.

"In England you have BDs?"

"Uh-huh. Comics. *The Beano. The Dandy*. They're for kids."

She picked up the tray and hesitated. Should she help him

out with his English? Nothing came naturally, so she went back to the kitchen to fetch the baguettes and jugs of water and wine.

Christophe was scuffing a hole in the hard earth surrounding the table when she returned.

"Don't bother helping," she said.

He looked surprised. "I'm not."

"I know. I was being ironic."

"Ah. The English humour."

He nodded and watched as she unloaded the tray.

"So where did you learn English?" she asked at last.

He raised his shoulders and spread out his hands.

"Every place. In kitchens. America, Canada, Hong Kong."

"So you should be able to speak well."

The sarcasm snaked cruelly through her words. She lowered her eyes.

"Better than your French," he said. He grinned in triumph, then turned and shouted at the children.

She blushed and hurried back inside the house. It didn't matter. She didn't care. In a few days she'd be gone.

CHAPTER SEVENTEEN

The days passed and Rainbow's vigil over the entrance to Le Logis proved fruitless. There was no white van. Bob must have been held up by some important gigs.

April had unfurled into May. Rainbow lost count of the numerous bank holidays the kids cheered about. There were fewer wet days, and the dry ones were hot. Soon it would be June. The bag of francs was almost empty. Rainbow was sure they'd have to leave when they could no longer contribute to the Logis expenses kitty.

One evening, Mum pulled out their money bag and counted out the notes onto the bed. Rainbow leaned over the bedpost and watched her.

"We've only got enough to stay for a week longer," she said.

"Don't worry, love. Jeff's agreed to buy my happy songs. We'll be fine for the summer."

"Don't you think it's time to go home?"

Mum looked up at her. "Do you?"

She shrugged. "Bob will be missing us."

Mum counted out the coins and slipped them back into

the plastic sachet. "I thought we'd celebrate your birthday here."

Rainbow would be fourteen on the eighth of June. Birthdays had been a disappointment since her sixth year, when Mum had made her an ace dragon cake. The problem hadn't been the cake. It was Mum's timing. She'd brought it into school on the wrong day. Mrs Brown had pointed out – in front of the whole class – that Mum was too early. Rainbow had melted into a puddle of embarrassment. After this, she became used to having her birthday on different dates around the month of June each year, according to when Mum remembered. Mum tried unsuccessfully to persuade her that this added to the excitement. For the last few years Rainbow had stuck a note on the kitchen notice board so Mum and Bob wouldn't forget completely.

Mum caught hold of Rainbow's hand and snapped her back into the present.

"We could all go to the beach, have a party and sleep overnight in hammocks under the pines."

"Really? That would be cool!"

"Good. Let's think about what we need to take, then," said this new, organised Mum.

Rainbow tore a sheet off her drawing pad and they began to jot down their ideas.

🌱 🍃 🌱

The next morning Rainbow woke alone in the bed. She threw on her clothes and jogged downstairs to the kitchen, her birthday party list in her hand. Mum and Domi were sitting at the table. They were leaning towards each other and Domi was drawing a shape on the table top with his finger. Jasmine was nodding in agreement. Rainbow paused in the doorway. Had she interrupted something?

"Hi, Mum, Domi. Sorry," she added as they lurched apart.

"Hello, love. We're planning your party," said Mum. She pulled her dressing gown more tightly around her.

Rainbow collected a bowl and sat down beside them.

"You got up early specially for me?"

"Well –" Mum stood up and went to turn on the kettle.

"Or were you up all night working on a new song?"

Mum would often do this at home when she was going through an inspired phase.

"That's right," Mum said.

Céline arrived in the kitchen and kissed Rainbow good morning.

"Has your mum told you about the French lessons?" she asked Rainbow.

Rainbow shook her head and frowned at Mum's back. Céline sat down.

"Christophe's going to teach you."

"I don't want lessons. Anyway, he'll never agree."

"Oh yes he will," said Céline. She patted Rainbow's shoulder.

Rainbow shrugged her off. "Here he is now."

"Bonjour." Christophe stopped as they turned towards him. "What?"

"You're too busy to teach me French, aren't you?" Rainbow said.

Christophe glanced at his mum, then at his wrist. He was

wearing a new digital watch. He must have struck a deal with his mum.

"I find time," he said, his cheeks reddening slightly.

Rainbow looked at the watch. It was a beautiful metallic blue. There were mini-dials around the face, promising predictions of beginnings and ends. She could imagine it lying heavy on her wrist and proving that she was in control of her life.

"Well, *I* don't have the time," she said.

"Rainbow, love–"

"There's no point, Mum. We're going home after my birthday."

"That gives you a fortnight," said Domi. "We'll relieve you of domestic duties if you like."

Rainbow took another look at the watch. "Okay. We'll start now," she said to Christophe. "Come on."

Christophe's mum nagged him to have his breakfast first. Rainbow stalked out of the kitchen.

He followed.

When she reached the outdoor table, she judged that they were out of earshot and turned around to face him. He shoved his hands into his pockets and looked defensive.

"Right, here's the deal," she said. "You give me the watch and I'll pretend to learn French."

"No."

She glared at him. "I'll look after the children and animals as well. That means you'll have time to play mechanics with Alain. I get the watch."

He folded his arms and grinned. "You want my watch very much."

"No, I don't. I just don't see why you should get a watch and I get nothing."

He laughed. "You get the French. You understand what people say about you."

"Huh! I don't care what they say." She bit her lip.

"Here's the deal," he said, and paused to search for his words. "You stop to be sarcastic with me, and I borrow you my watch one time."

"Half the time. And it's *lend*, not borrow."

"Ah yes: lend, *prêter*; borrow, *emprunter*. You repeat."

She raised her eyes towards the sky.

"And don't treat me like a kid or I'll break your watch."

He looked smug. She kicked the table support and refused to look at him while he undid the watch.

When he passed it to her she slipped it onto her wrist. It had looked great on him, but on her skinny arm it seemed unnatural. He was studying her, so she pretended to be pleased. She pressed the buttons and examined the dials. It was a lot less interesting than it had appeared. She smiled through her disappointment. There was no way she'd give him the satisfaction of thinking he'd got the better of her.

Over the next two weeks Rainbow turned from a reluctant student into a reluctantly eager one. The lessons were more like games than schoolwork and she started to look forward to the evenings, when she and Christophe would sit out of the earshot of the others.

At first he laughed at her accent. He made her pronounce '*un*' a hundred times before the resulting grunt sounded French enough for him. She was surprised by the seriousness with which he attacked his duty. He'd hardly speak a word of English, so she was forced to concentrate and guess the meaning of the French words he used. Gradually, the lessons lengthened until one or the other was called away to help with the evening meal, the animals or the kids.

❧ ❧ ❧

On her birthday morning, Rainbow woke up alone in her bed again. This was another piece of evidence to add to her theory that something was going on between Mum and Domi. She was pleased, because he was her dad, yet she was angry with Mum for betraying Bob. And it was another reason for Mum to delay going home. She should be cross about this. But she was starting to feel more comfortable at the Logis. If it weren't for Acrobat and the kittens, she wouldn't have minded staying a while longer.

The previous evening her fantasy of Bob coming with Acrobat and the kittens, finding he liked it and deciding to stay had shattered. She'd heard Mum tell Virginie about the bad experience he'd had with a spiritualist. Ever since, the sight of her tarot cards, Ouija board or crystals would throw him into a fit. In bed last night, Rainbow's fantasy metamorphosed into a version where Bob arrived ill and was healed by Domi. This would change the way he felt and make him want to stay for the summer. But this morning, in the clear light of day, she knew she would have to call him again and tell him not to come. She would sneak down on their return from the beach expedition.

Mum and Domi were in the kitchen. They stood close to each other as they made coffee. Close, but not touching.

Mum wished her a happy birthday and passed her a tiny package. Rainbow told herself not to get excited. She undid it quickly. It was a battered ring box. She snapped it open and saw a ruby crystal.

It was the one Virginie had tried to give her a few days ago. Rainbow had refused because the silkiness, which she could only feel through the skin on the back of her hands, made her more aware of the roughness of her palms. She'd loved to handle crystals before she discovered trees. Now, they represented the sacrifices her gift demanded.

She kissed Mum and slipped the ruby crystal into the pocket of her patched jeans. She knew it was the only present she would get this year. Domi had already explained that the commune inhabitants didn't exchange presents at birthdays. Instead, they made the birthday person feel special and tried to create a memorable day.

She was finishing her breakfast when Christophe appeared in the doorway.

"Come with me. I've got something to show you," he said in French.

On the third repetition Rainbow understood. She followed him outside.

"It's my birthday, you know. You could say happy birthday."

"It is?" He grinned at her in his irksome fashion. "Hurry up."

So much for making her feel special. She dragged her feet as he led her into the wood, along a twisting path and into an area she didn't know. He stopped where a huddle of dead oak branches reinforced the sides of a hazel thicket. It was a den.

"Is this what you wanted to show me?"

He nodded.

"Well, it's—" she searched for the translation of 'unimpressive'. Nothing came to mind, so she spoke the English word with a French accent.

He laughed. "That doesn't work. Try: 'c'est pas impressionnant'."

She spoke the hissy phrase while he rooted around under a table of wooden planks. He pulled out a big, plastic barrel.

"This is where we have our private affairs. The adults don't know it," he said in English.

Rainbow was shocked. Then she understood.

"Where we *keep our things*, not have our affairs," she said.

She liked the idea of a communal den. A warm glow spread inside her. This is what it felt like to be accepted. She ran her hands over a worn log that served as a seat.

He took a flat, rectangular package out of the barrel. "This is for you. It's too big for take at the beach. Happy birthday."

She blushed, embarrassed at the way she'd nagged him about her birthday when he'd already planned this. The present had been carefully wrapped. She opened it equally carefully. Would it be one of the comic books he liked so much? Yesterday he'd shown her his collection of fifty hardbacked comic albums stacked on a shelf above his bed. She couldn't be bothered to read the titles. It wasn't that she didn't like books: she just preferred sketching and thinking her own thoughts to letting a book dictate what she should think. And comic albums were childish, no matter what Christophe said.

She saw the back of the present first. It was a photo frame. She turned it over and looked at the front. A collection of tree leaves faced her. They had been dried, pressed and arranged artfully on a piece of dark pink paper. Rainbow waited for her emotion to pass so she could speak in a normal voice. Christophe ran a hand through his brown hair.

"Do you like it? Sorry it's made home. I didn't find something you like in the shops."

"It's beautiful, Chris. Thanks loads." She looked up and saw doubt in his face. "Really, I love it. It's much better than a comic book."

He looked puzzled. "But you don't like comic books. Did you want one?"

She assured him he was right, and kissed his cheek. He smelt faintly of leather and engine grease.

His doubtful expression vanished and they hurried back towards the house, the picture under Rainbow's arm. She was thinking about where she would hang it in her room, and only noticed Christophe's preoccupied air after a few silent minutes.

"Are you all right?" she asked.

He glanced at her, then looked away again.

"Actually, there is a thing I must tell to you. There is the man here, in the woods."

She glanced behind her. "Where? What man?"

"He is English, I think."

She stopped walking. "When did you see him?"

"Yesterday. And this morning."

"What did he look like?"

He screwed up his face. "Old ... long hair."

She sighed. He was useless at recognising people. His stares, while he tried to determine if he knew a face or not, sometimes ended in him being punched.

"He looks at the house and the people here. I think he is your Bob which you told me about. He drives a white car. English car."

"Yes, that sounds like Bob."

Why did he have to come today, of all days? Perhaps if they left for the beach quickly, they would avoid him.

"He's come to take you home, you think?"

She nodded. He frowned at the ground and fell silent again.

When they arrived in the clearing of Le Logis, she glanced towards the cars. For a second she saw the van parked, askew. But there was no van. No Bob. Only the commune people packing up bags and baskets and blankets.

She threw herself into the activity and helped prepare children and belongings for the outing. Alain and François were staying at the house to look after the animals and repair Domi's motorbike, which had broken down again.

When everyone jumped into the cars, Christophe lingered behind with Alain. Rainbow could see he was tempted to stay so he could spend all day and night making merry with oil and metal. But he turned his back on them and joined her, Domi, Céline and Mum in the yellow Mini. Domi, in the passenger seat, had the job of telling Mum when she could overtake. Slim Céline sat in the back seat by the window and contrived to wedge Rainbow next to Christophe. Rainbow was mortified to feel her leg pressing against his. As soon as they stopped for a sick child or toilet break she would move to the other side of Céline.

Mum drove at the head of the four-car procession. They bumped along the track and Rainbow stared outside the window to avoid looking at Christophe. The track gave way to the tarmac lane. There, parked in a field entrance, was a white van. Christophe nudged her and nodded towards it.

Rainbow willed Mum to drive on. But the English registration plate caught Mum's attention. She slammed on the brakes.

"What the–!" she gasped. "How did he–?"

She yanked up the handbrake and threw the car door open. Then she climbed out and stood defiantly in the road. Rainbow pushed up the front seat and scrambled out after her.

Bob was sitting inside the van, drinking out of a thermos cup. He opened his van door, stretched and then sauntered towards them. He was smiling. Rainbow smiled back. It was going to be all right. He was in a good mood.

"Hey, Jaz. Hi, Rainy. Nice place for a holiday. You could have invited me too, though."

Mum folded her arms. "So what are you doing here, since you're not invited?"

Bob's eyebrows shot up into his messy hair. He looked as dishevelled as the tramps who begged outside the Post Office in Cognac. Rainbow felt sorry for him.

"It's my fault, Mum," she said. "I asked him to pick us up."

Mum ignored her. Her narrowed eyes were fixed on Bob.

"Come on, Jaz. Let's sort things out. For Rainbow's sake."

"There's nothing to sort out. It's over."

Rainbow glanced from Mum to Bob and back again. Over? She suspected Mum and Domi were having a love affair, but she didn't think it meant that Mum and Bob were finished. No more Mum and Bob?

She reached out and leant against the Mini. If there were no more Mum and Bob, where did she belong? Here with Mum and Dad, which wasn't her home, or at home with Bob, who wasn't her father?

Bob didn't look at all shocked by Mum's revelation. He nodded towards the line of cars.

"Hippie outing? Or are you all off to raise some spirits?"

He laughed at his own joke, though his voice sounded strangled.

"Go home, Bob," Mum sighed.

"What? And leave you both here with this bunch of creeps?"

Mum slapped his cheek.

He caught her hand and wrenched it down to her side. She cried out in pain.

Rainbow threw herself between them and tried to push them apart. They turned away and she fell into the dust. Domi's bare feet appeared on the tarmac by the Mini. He put a restraining hand on Mum's arm and helped Rainbow to stand up.

"Can't we sort this out like adults?" said Domi.

"Get away from us," shouted Mum at Bob. "We're never coming home."

"Don't be so goddamn selfish. Think about Rainbow for once," replied Bob.

"She's happy here," said Mum.

"I think she's old enough to know where she wants to be." Bob turned towards Rainbow. "A girl needs her home, her school and her friends, doesn't she, honey? Not some hippie dropouts. I bet they haven't even taken you to school since you got here."

Mum and Bob looked down at her. There was silence.

"It's my birthday," she said, lamely.

"I know, honey," said Bob. "I've got a big present for you. It's at home."

Rainbow didn't know what to say.

"You don't want us to go back, love, do you?" asked Mum.

Domi put an arm around Rainbow. He turned to Bob and Mum and cleared his throat.

"This isn't the kind of thing you decide in the middle of a road. We're on our way out. Come back tomorrow evening, Bob, and we'll discuss things properly."

Bob seemed to see Domi for the first time.

"I don't know who you are, mate, but you're not discussing anything. This is between me and Jasmine."

"And Rainbow," said Domi, unperturbed. "I'm Dominique, the owner of Le Logis."

He held out his hand. Bob spat onto the road.

"So you're the con-man from her past. I can see why she left."

Domi's jaw clenched, but he said nothing. Rainbow felt braver with Domi's arm around her.

"I'm sorry, Bob," she said. "This is all my fault. I meant to phone you and tell you not to come."

Bob looked uncertain. "But I thought you hated it here. You wanted me to pick you up."

"I was homesick when I phoned you. And you took so long to come. I'm kind of used to it here now."

"I couldn't come any quicker, honey. I had gigs and the garden to see to. And the ticket to book."

She had been stupid to think he would come immediately. He never did anything on an impulse. Not like Mum.

"Who's looking after Acrobat and his kittens?" she asked.

"Ah," said Bob. He scratched his chin.

"What do you mean, *Ah*?"

"Well, I couldn't look after all those animals on my own."

Dread clutched Rainbow's chest. Her vision slipped sideways.

Mum gasped. "What have you done with them?"

"The cat's back with the Bellamys."

"And the kittens?"

Bob ignored Mum.

"Look, Rainbow, are you coming home with me or not? I can't hang around here for ever."

Blood thumped in Rainbow's head. She wrenched herself free from Domi, launched herself at Bob and grabbed his T-shirt.

"What have you done with the kittens?"

"Hey! Calm down." He pulled himself away.

"The kittens," she shrieked.

"Well, they had to go for a little swim."

"You drowned them," she screamed. "How could you?" She threw herself at him and pounded his chest.

"I hate you! How could you? I hate you! I hate you. I never want to see you again."

Tears spilt over her fists. Mum and Domi eased her away, one on each side of her.

Bob stomped back to his van. He revved up the engine and roared away. Rainbow didn't bother to watch him leave.

PART FOUR

PART FOUR

TWIGS

Mary, 1992-1993

CHAPTER EIGHTEEN

Mary's first sensation as she wakes this spring morning is anguish. It drains her vitality and leaves her vulnerable, like a little girl whose mum has left her at school for the very first time.

She struggles from sleep into empty consciousness. Eighteen months have passed since the accident. She tries not to think about *before*. It still hurts too much. What more is she obliged to do for freedom from her memories?

Last night she lay in bed for hours, listening to cars swishing along the wet road under tired streetlights. Memories of Michael slid unwanted into her head. She tipped them straight out again. But when she crossed the quagmire between awake and asleep, he was lurking there. He trapped her in his arms and pulled her into sleep, and so she was forced to succumb to his presence in her dreams.

She's missing him badly this morning. She knows she'll lash out and create a tornado today; anything to spin herself away from her internal wound. She has to regain control, even if it means inflicting pain.

She rolls from her bed and stares out of the window into the busy street below. The view of concrete and metal reassures her. It hardens her and helps her make the transition from green dreams to grey reality.

She's been living with Mother in this semi-detached house in the local town since the divorce a year ago. They are known here as the Hubbards. When Mother divorced Bob and dropped his surname, Mary helped herself to her mother's maiden name. She was glad to change the Linnet as well as the R–.

Mary approves of towns. There is continual movement and no time for reflection. It's all about getting to your destination. There's no looking back and wondering, no stopping to think about things like she used to in the countryside. Here, roads, cars and houses are laid down on the face of nature. They squash it back to where she wants it to be: underground, out of sight.

Occasionally, creeping fingers of green weeds appear between the concrete paving slabs in the front garden she walks across every day. She has weed killer for this problem. In springtime she kills every seven days; in the summer, every fourteen; in the winter, once a month.

She turns away from the window and dresses in her usual ripped jeans and moth-holed jumper. In the cold dampness of the bathroom she coaxes the bolt on the door into its sleeve. Then she pours hot water into the basin and scrubs her face with her rough flannel. She cleanses the pain that is too close to the surface, forces it to seep out through the pores of her skin. Once her face is bright red, she counts her spots and backcombs the crown of her head so she looks a mess.

She's as ugly and unfashionable as she can be. She feels stronger now, in control again.

She thumps down the stairs, looking out for signs of Mother. Without Bob to anchor her, Mother has become dependent on Mary. It's a desperate need, unimaginable *before*, and it drives Mary out of the house. Her only breathing space is when Mother goes on her inspirational creativity retreats or to her meditation meetings. She has given up singing and song-writing, and works in a supermarket. In the evenings she writes fantasy stories in the company of a bottle of wine. Mary wonders what'll happen when she leaves home. Mother will probably crumple up and die in a nest of empty bottles and failure. Mary could feel guilty about this, but she refuses to let herself feel anything. Guilt was for R–.

She opens the door into the kitchen. Mother is hunched over a mug of tea at the table. Mary changes her mind about having breakfast. She picks up her scruffy denim jacket and walks straight out of the front door.

She begins the familiar walk to school. Mother bought a house in this area of the town so that Mary didn't have to change schools. Mary would have preferred the anonymity of a new school. She always was the odd one out in her class, but when she returned to her Year 9 class after the accident she quickly earned a new respect as the school rebel. The kids loathe and admire her. She's almost fifteen now, nearing the end of Year 10. The teenagers – even Lucy Carter and Rebecca – hang around with her in hope and fear of her ruthless moments. They cling and follow, copy and hang back, support and desert her. She never refers to them as her friends.

Trish Bellamy is her only friend. Although they no longer live in the same village, Mary spends most evenings at Trish's house. She cycles there after school on her rusty, old-lady's bicycle. Trish's family, particularly Trish's mum, is her only weakness nowadays. Trish is the most unpopular girl in school. She's intelligent, shy and gullible. The others tease her because she wears glasses and has more spots than skin. They ask each other what Mary sees in Four-Eyes and why she hangs around with her.

Trish is unfazed by Mary's spectacular mood swings. She sticks by Mary, whether she's beating up a Year 7 pupil or sharing stolen sweets with her hangers-on. Trish knows exactly where she's going in life and precisely how she'll get there. Mary envies this hidden strength. She has no idea where she's going.

It's a half-mile walk to school. This morning it looks as if she's going to be early, so she decides to stop for breakfast and kill time until she's late. McDonald's is just ahead. She hates it for its popularity, but today she's too hungry to care. Besides, she's alone and eating from necessity, which isn't the same as choosing to eat there with friends.

She sits in a corner where nobody can look at her without her noticing. She watches the losers chewing on stodgy egg and bacon muffins. There are dozens of them, mostly rushed men in suits. Several boys her age are sitting at the bar. She hears them discuss where they're going to hang out while they skive school.

She has never skived. She can't be bothered to find an alternative to the daily punishment of school. She's never had a boyfriend either. No one she knows is worth associating with. The boys at school are lemmings. Nothing separates one from another; they are as predictable and blank as cardboard cut-outs in their dull uniforms.

She sucks up her watery orange juice and thinks about the other boyfriend possibilities. Trish's boring older brothers bring home snooty fashion-sheep undergrads. Jimmy, Trish's younger brother, is still a kid. The youth-club boys are the same as those at school. That leaves Mark Flint, her boarding-school-scholarship neighbour, who is stuffed with nervous tics. He has a phobia about things falling on his head, which could be quite interesting. But he's never around.

No, it seems that a boyfriend is out of the question. She will stay single forever and end her days as a spinster, eating rats in a freezing attic. Or she could become a nun and dedicate her life to blaspheming. Yes, that would be ideal. She could wrinkle up in a convent for the rest of her life. She would kneel for eighteen hours a day, her hands folded, and silently tell God what an arsehole he is. She would become a saint. No one would know what she was saying in her prayers. She could sail around in her robes, being nastily holy to brats and goody-goodies. She could develop a love for singing loudly and test the godliness of the other nuns by massacring hymns in her out-of-tune voice.

There is a loud shout at the next table. Her daydream shatters. An angry, six-foot heavyweight punches a young man. The young man falls towards her. He cracks his head on her table, rolls over and drops into her lap like a gift from heaven.

She leaps up and pushes him into the puddle of Coke on the floor.

Mr Heavyweight makes a single-minded beeline for the young man's prostrate body. She's in his way. He slams into her.

She swears at him and kicks him hard in the shin. He swears back at her, hopping on one leg.

She snatches her bag and elbows through the rubberneckers to the exit. Outside, she dashes across the road without looking. No one is chasing her. She stops. She's shaking. She leans against a shop front and counts thirteen passing cars.

In the distance a siren blares. It approaches and a flashing police car hurtles up to McDonald's door. Three policemen jump out. Within minutes the two trussed-up fighting cocks emerge from McDonald's and are shoved into the police car, ready to be grilled. She walks away.

The police car brakes at the pedestrian crossing in front of her. A pair of narrowed eyes glares at her from a Cokewashed face of stubble. Then the police car jerks the boy away. She rubs her goose-pimpled arms and continues onwards to school. The real world is harsh and unforgiving. It's a step beyond the safe environment of teachers and kids where she has played the rebel for the last eighteen months. Is it time to take that step?

❦❦❦

The vulnerability from last night's dreams niggles Mary all day. Two detentions and Joanne Clark's broken nose only allow the pain to subside momentarily.

At break she sits alone in the physics lab. Mr Higgins is supervising her detention. She tries to answer the science questions he's given her in an effort to divert her mind from her simmering anguish. Words glare, numbers accuse, units of measure mock.

Mr Higgins alternates between sharpness and sneers. He reeks of dislike for her. She can smell the invisible, silent aura of disgust flowing like sour milk from his mind. It seeps through the skin of his face and down his arms, and then spills across the bench and envelops her. He probably thinks she pretends not to understand physics because she wants to rebel. In fact, the science labs and maths classrooms are the only places she doesn't need to act in order to appear stupid.

He grows tired of lecturing her on her behaviour and shuffles papers at his desk. There are two test tubes of transparent liquids at the far end of her bench. She tries to calculate velocities. Her tongue clicks against the roof of her mouth as she mantras the mesmerising words 'ticker tape'. The test tubes intrigue her. The mantra changes: one tube, two tubes; one tube, two tubes.

Her heartbeat accelerates. Like a reaction to extreme thirst in the night, she sees herself stand up, take hold of the test tubes and … and then what? Will they explode if she mixes them? Is one of them acid? Would it burn through his papers if she threw it over his desk? Over him? She wonders what he would do if she drank them. The two phials of glass represent entry to a whole new category of reactions.

Mr Higgins glares at her. "Five minutes, Hubbard."

Mary picks up her pen. The knowledge that she could create havoc with the test tubes helps relieve her frustration. She concentrates on the worksheet. There are fourteen questions. In a burst of imagination, she scribbles down the six formulae her brain has scraped up over the last year. She fills in numbers randomly and slams her pen onto the bench.

Mr Higgins' lips curl in disdain as he walks over. He takes one look. Mary stands and folds her arms. The test tubes are between her and the door.

"Pathetic," he says. "I'm looking forward to telling your parents how lazy you are when I see them this evening."

Mary sneers internally. Even if the sneer were visible, Mr Higgins wouldn't see it because of the long fringe of hair she hides behind. She doesn't care what the teachers say at parents' evening.

He leans close to her.

"But we'll tell the headmaster your behaviour is satisfactory, all right? So I don't have to put up with you again. You're dismissed."

She walks towards the door. When she reaches the test tubes, she swings her bag out and knocks them to the ground.

The simultaneous explosions of shattering glass and Mr Higgins' temper are icy spring water to Mary's thirst. She smirks. Under the bubbling puddle, three of the floor tiles are revealing their original colours. She wishes she'd had the nerve to drink the contents.

CHAPTER NINETEEN

"Your teachers tell me you're good at languages," says Mary's mother.

She'd almost forgotten to attend the parents' evening, which would have suited Mary fine, but had remembered at the last minute and turned up late. Without Mary.

"They say you could be a translator," she adds.

Mary doesn't want to think about careers. She's annoyed at being assessed and categorised. Hunched in the plastic kitchen chair, her body all angles, she pretends not to listen to her mother.

At school she's wallowing in academic failure. She refuses to drop sciences and spectacularly fails everything set. She measures and mixes in chemistry lessons, chanting the proportions: three to one; five to two; seven to ten. No matter how carefully she measures, the results hiss and spit in rebuke. Sometimes they turn strange colours that provoke detentions.

In French lessons it's different. She has to work to hide her delight as she learns the foreign code. In her head the sentences form themselves, while on paper she mixes them up. She'd like a penfriend, but can't weaken her position as a dud by risking discovery. She'd been tempted to sign up for the French exchange trip in Year 9, when Mother and Bob were going through the divorce, but Mother had approved of the idea, so Mary had refused to go. When, in French lessons, she lets slip a correct answer, she sees Mrs Beacon's eyes light up. This is a warning to shut up and she counts the number of each type of accent on the page in front of her instead. So far, she has managed to avoid living up to the hope in Mrs Beacon's face. She does like languages though, despite her studied indifference. Sometimes, when she locks herself into her bedroom at night, she pulls out her French textbooks. She speaks the words aloud and invents conversations with Pierre and Marie-France. Tomorrow she'll discuss careers with Trish. Perhaps she'll be a nun in France.

Mother continues her monologue of the teachers' opinions. Damp creeps up from the cracks in the tiled floor. It passes the imitation wood cupboards and condenses on the translucent windowpanes. The asthmatic fridge, cramped between the cracked enamel sink and the work surface, wheezes an accompaniment to the monotony of Mother's voice. Mary stares at the wallpaper, where neglected kittens are forever frozen in their play. She drums her fingers to the rhythm of 'Deeply dippy' that she can still hear inside her head and closes her eyes.

Her mother's voice stops on the word 'gifted'. She's talking about languages. But, for Mary, the word will always be associated with *before*. White noise blocks out all thought and feeling. She counts to seven. There is no way she will risk being gifted again. She opens her eyes.

"I hate languages," she says.

🌿🌿🌿

Next morning, Mary has the impression that a man is tailing her to school. She slows. He slows. She crosses the road. He's behind her. She spins around. He continues towards her and then stops a few metres away.

"Get lost!" she spits.

His face is familiar. It's framed by the red and yellow 'M' of McDonald's behind him, and she realises he's the young man who was taken away by the police the day before. He looks closer to her age now his face is Coke-free and shaved.

"Nice to meet you too," he replies. "My name's Gus. And I'll only get lost if you come with me."

"Why would I go anywhere with a loser like you?"

"Because you're bored with going to school every day?"

She restrains a smile. "Not as bored as I'd be if I was with you."

He laughs; a short, sharp bark. "Nice. I like your sharp corners. What's your name?"

Mary turns her back on him and continues walking towards school. He follows. She speeds up. He starts to whistle. When she arrives at the school gates she turns to face him once again. He's skinny, shaggy-haired and undeniably cool in his faded leather jacket and dirty jeans.

"Leave me alone, loser. Find someone else to stalk," she says.

"I'm quite happy stalking you. See you soon, kiddo."

She enters the school grounds and then glances over her

shoulder. He's strolling back the way they'd come, his hands in his pockets. Gus. She smiles to herself. He comes from the real world, far from the petty restrictions of her life.

She waits for Trish in the bike sheds. A Year 11 boy offers her a toke on his fag. She accepts and blows smoke moodily towards the tin roof, thinking about the waste of a school day that lies before her. What is Gus doing now?

Trish arrives with Helen. Mary greets Trish and ignores Helen. She holds Trish's bike while Trish searches through the tangled intestines of her bag for the lock. Helen stares at her, chewing gum. Mary stares back and blows out smoke.

Helen is new at school. She moved into Manor House in Trish's village a few months ago. She's blond, pink and girly, and she dresses like the models in Topshop. She has latched onto Trish, who's flattered by her attention. Mary knows they meet up regularly in the village playground to drink Coke, eat crisps and read *Cosmopolitan*. Helen wants to take Trish in hand and has advised her to get contact lenses and to cut her ginger hair. Jimmy, Trish's eight-year-old brother, told her this. He doesn't like Helen because she pinches him.

"Hey, Trish, I've got a new game," says Mary.

She takes Trish's arm and steers her away from Helen, pretending not to see the look Trish exchanges with her. Helen follows them.

"Go on then," says Trish. "It's not another false-fashion thing, is it?"

False-fashion is a game Mary invented last month. She would start a new trend, rant about how cool it was and then count the number of girls who followed it. The more that followed, the higher her score. She soon lost interest, however, because she dislikes being copied. She dropped the game when Helen pointed out that Mary's trend of growing long armpit hair was stupid because magazine models all have shaved underarms. Mary had primed Trish with an answer to this. But Trish had stuttered and gone red when she recited the counterargument about the hairy underarms her older brothers' girlfriends sported. It was obvious to everyone that she was lying.

"No, my new game's much more interesting than false-fashion," says Mary.

Trish giggles nervously in anticipation. Mary smiles at her and squeezes her arm. Trish revels in being the safe ally in these games. She has forgotten Helen in her excitement and dread of the day's titillation.

"It's called crush-crushing," says Mary. "Watch what I do today."

There has been a change in her classmates over recent months. Lucy Carter's gang, who used to fill their time Trishbaiting, have turned to flirt-and-chasing. For the past three years they have jeered at the boys in their year. Now the same boys are subjected to eyelash fluttering, blushing and provocative body postures. Their names are lovingly inscribed in folders and adorned with hearts, arrows and smiley faces. The boys puff out their chests and raise their voices in response. They spend as much time as the girls working on their hair and image. Mary's ashamed of being a girl when she sees how the others preen themselves in front of the spotty boys they fancy.

During the morning's English lesson, Mary has to choose three people to make up her group of four. She selects Lorraine,

David and Trish. Stupid Lorraine fancies dull David, who reciprocates the feeling. Everyone knows this because they throw regular, surreptitious glances at each other and avoid direct contact. While the four of them read the *Lord of the Flies* worksheet together, Mary talks about French kissing. David and Lorraine squirm in embarrassment. Mary winks at Trish. Later that afternoon she corners blushing Grant and flatters him until his ears burn. She tells him that Judy has a crush on him and wants him to be her sex toy. After a minute, Trish pulls her away, whispers to her fiercely to stop the torture and then huffs away to Helen's side. Mary laughs out loud.

She feels like a saucepan of milk that's about to boil over, frustrated by the mediocrity of her life. She wants something to happen. If she keeps up this crush-crushing long enough, she should get beaten up or lynched. This tingling of danger, more meaningful and worldly than detention, excites her. She continues crush-crushing. By the end of the day she can feel a hostile buzz when she approaches people. No one does anything to stop her, not even Helen. She decides to find out who Helen fancies and seduce him. Helen is bound to react.

The bell rings at the end of the day and they flock to the gates. Mary falls into step beside Trish.

"You've gone too far this time," says Trish. "You can't play with people. It's evil."

Mary studies her friend. She is really upset. "You're not worried I'll do it to you, are you?"

"Of course not. Anyway, I don't fancy anyone," she adds. She flicks back her brushed hair. "I just don't want you to get expelled."

"All right, I'll stop. It's a stupid game in any case. Can I come back to yours?"

"If you like."

Trish pushes her bike and they head towards Mary's home to pick up hers. After a few steps, Trish stops and stares across the road.

"There's a bloke over there trying to catch your attention. Look! In that old van."

It's Gus. Mary makes a 'V' sign at him and continues walking.

"Who is he?"

"Some crazy idiot," says Mary.

"What does he want?"

"To go out with me, I think."

"But he's a man," says Trish.

Trish's reaction accentuates Mary's impression of the huge gap between the safe life of school and the dangers of the adult world. Gus must be at least seventeen because he's driving. Although Mary is fed up with school, she's not sure she's ready to step into adulthood. Trish is happy in the padded cell of her life. She's lucky: she has a family that cares about her. She hasn't been lied to all her life. She doesn't need to search for meaning in the way Mary does.

Gus drives up and kerb-crawls to keep pace with them. "Want a lift?"

Trish clings to Mary's arm.

"No. Get lost, creep," says Mary. She shakes Trish off.

"Too bad. It's your loss." He drives away.

Mary feels strangely deflated.

❧❧❧

Her arrivals at the Bellamys' are the closest Mary feels to coming home. Trish launches her bike into the dark chaos of the shed's interior while Mary stands her bicycle against it and then pushes open the kitchen door.

The kitchen is a large, overflowing nest, scented with fresh bread. Both the Aga and Mrs Bellamy are the source of its warmth. The table is never cleared; a meal is constantly in preparation and there are ceaseless voices from changing sources. Brothers, uncles, aunts, cousins, friends, neighbours and streams of pets flow across the room like air currents. Like the ghosts in Mary's house. Here, she feels part of a whole, even if it's not her own whole. Her corners and hard, flat surfaces become as rounded and soft as the flesh on Mrs Bellamy's comforting arms when she's here. In years to come, a fleeting aroma of strawberry jam will bring the Bellamys' kitchen to mind and reassure her.

Mary gives Mrs Bellamy the daffodils she stopped to pick out of Rebecca's front garden. She winks at Jimmy, who knows where the daffodils come from. He's lounging in her favourite armchair. It has ladders in its nylon stretchcover and creaks like old bones when she shifts her weight in it.

"Did your mother talk to you about yesterday's parents' evening?" asks Mrs Bellamy.

"A bit." She picks up a handful of cutlery and starts to lay the table. "How many of us tonight?"

"Just us five for the moment. Did the teachers give you any advice for your future, then?"

Trish comes into the kitchen. She kisses her mum, pushes Jimmy off the chair and takes his place.

"No," says Mary, "though I'm tempted by science."

She smiles at the thought of how Mr Higgins would react to her words. She knows she'll never get the GCSE grades needed to go on to A levels.

"Science? You?" Trish is stark-eyed with shock. "I thought you were going to leave school as soon as you could."

Mary shrugs. She wants to hear Mrs Bellamy's opinion.

Trish's eyebrows gradually settle back to rest, making her glasses slip down her nose. "It would be cool to be in A-level classes together."

"Smart girls choose science," says Mrs Bellamy, at last. "But are you sure you'll make the grades?" Worry creases her sweat-beaded forehead.

"Probably not. Maybe I'll become a nun instead. You don't need qualifications for that."

"You must think carefully about your studies. I can give you a hand when the time comes. I've been through all this with my boys, remember," says Mrs Bellamy.

Mary nods. It's easy for most people. They simply choose what they're best at, or what they enjoy, but she doesn't deserve to do something she likes. She doesn't even know what she likes. She doesn't want to know.

"Shall I help with dinner?"

"No, it's fine, thanks, Mary. Go and get on with your homework until dinnertime."

Mary and Trish help themselves to a glass of orange juice

and then traipse upstairs like sisters.

Later, they sit at the table while Mrs Bellamy bustles across the hall to the office to collect her husband James. He's a whisper of a man who lives for his academic work, which takes him into London for long periods of time. Mary has never established exactly what he does. She isn't sure that anyone in the family really knows. She's intrigued by how he manages not to be swallowed up by the rest of the noisy Bellamy family. Despite his fragile exterior, he exerts a quiet authority over the tumultuous household. He rarely addresses Mary directly and she wonders whether he notices that she's not his daughter. She prefers his absence to his presence: seeing him reminds her that she's fatherless.

After dinner Mary prepares to leave. Mrs Bellamy accompanies her to the gate and offers her help again in choosing suitable studies. Mary thanks her and declines. She's got some thinking to do before she's ready to discuss the future.

CHAPTER TWENTY

Over the next few months Mary starts to consider the world of jobs. She has to find something punishing, something completely different from anyone else. Above all, it must annoy Mother and be the opposite of what R– would have chosen. For the moment, nothing beats being a nun.

Despite Mary's refusal, Mrs Bellamy becomes her career advisor. She swings her rotund form into the office chair and browses through brochures of job possibilities with the same gusto with which she processes fresh food into meals. Mary, perched on a stool beside her, admires Mrs Bellamy's sleek analysis of what is suitable for a girl who can't stand science on its feet, and who is too lazy to bother with languages. Watching Mrs Bellamy lick a beetroot-stained finger as she whips through page after page of a well-used career guide, Mary feels a sudden urge to confide. She's compelled to explain why she has this need to turn against everything expected of her. But it's been too long. She wouldn't know how to start.

"Don't end up a powerless housewife like me," Mrs Bellamy

cautions. "Get out there in the world and make a difference." Her elder sons are both at Oxford.

Mary takes to wandering around town on her own. She studies people in suits and examines brass plaques on austere doors. She slips into newsagents and pores over jobs pages, mentally noting new words to discuss with Mrs Bellamy. She career-hunts by elimination. First, she crosses off every career she hears her schoolmates discussing enthusiastically, and then every job that seems fulfilling. If the discovery of a job creates a wave of affinity, she immediately rejects it. Her choice must be calculated, not spontaneous. A job with numbers would be ideal.

During one of these outings she sees Gus again. He doesn't notice her. He is walking a step behind a brash businessman in a dark suit. The Suit is speaking loudly into a mobile phone as he walks, obviously proud of his coveted status symbol. They look as if they're together. Mary joins the crowd on the pavement and follows. She's intrigued by Gus's unlikely relationship with his companion.

They arrive at a zebra crossing and stop. Gus's attention is caught by something to his right and he bumps into his stationary partner. The Suit snatches his phone away from his head and barks a rebuke at Gus. Gus regains his balance and apologises. Then he crosses the road and continues along the street on his own, his hands shoved deep in the pockets of his baggy jeans.

Mary whistles in admiration at the slickness of his theft. She hurries to catch him up.

"Are you going to buy me a coffee with your stolen gains?"

Gus stops and grins at her.

"Hey, kiddo. Nice to see you again. What stolen gains?"

"It was pretty obvious to the whole crowd that you were nicking his wallet."

Gus frowns, then laughs. "Right. So you do it better, do you?"

Mary shrugs. "Are you buying me coffee or not?"

Gus takes her arm and steers her into a side street. "Let's have a look at the winnings before I decide."

They cross the town and enter a dingy café, where Mary relents and tells him her name. In exchange, Gus shows her how to pick pockets and then takes her to the warehouse where his rock group is rehearsing.

🌿🍃🌿

Mary's mother accidentally meets Gus when she comes home early from her shift at the supermarket. Mary and Gus are raiding the fridge, thirsty after an afternoon of hanging around town.

Mother enters the kitchen and stops short. Gus is silhouetted like an alien in the light of the open fridge. Her sloping shoulders straighten and her expression brightens. Mary feels the old jealousy from *before* rear up.

"Hello, love," she says to Mary. "Who's this young man?"

"Gus." She turns her back on Mother and speaks to Gus: "This is her."

Gus turns around and they sum each other up. Mary hasn't been kind in her description of her mother to Gus.

Mother oozes social charm. Mary is afraid Gus will be taken in by Mother's fraudulent demeanour. He is going to find her mum more interesting than herself.

"Help yourself to a beer," Mother says.

"No, thanks. I don't drink the rats' piss you've got in stock."

Mary is delighted by his rude reply.

Mother looks surprised, but isn't put off. She asks him what he does.

Gus flops into the settee. "I'm a musician."

Mother eases off her coat and perches on the settee arm. "That's my background too. What kind of music?"

He yawns and stretches, taking up all the room. "Classical violin." He winks at Mary, who smirks.

Mother frowns and stands up. "Well …" She looks lost for words. She glances at Mary, then folds her arms. "And how old are you?"

"Forty-five," he lies. "And you, Mrs Hubbard?"

Mother's chin rises and her eyes flash in anger. Mary's smirk becomes a wide grin.

Mother draws herself up like a cobra. "Mary is only fifteen. She must concentrate on her schoolwork. I don't want anyone to lead her astray."

Mary snorts. "Schoolwork! Since when have you been interested in my schoolwork?"

Gus is unfazed. "I have four A levels, Mrs Hubbard. I know how important school is."

Mary knows he's only just eighteen and that he left school before his A levels.

"Come on, Gus," she says. "Let's get out of this dump."

She pulls him to his feet and out of the house before Mother can embarrass herself any more.

❧ ❧ ❧

Mary admires everything about Gus. He's daring, smart, rude and, most of all, he pleases himself. He is everything she wants to become; a kind of mirror of how she could be in the future. She feels naive beside him and drinks in his worldliness. School, Trish, her mother; all fade into black and white beside the colour of this new scene. It's not love, flowers and hearts; it's adventure, freedom and real life. Gus treats her like an adult. He talks about the fulfilment that creating music can bring, and explains how futile it is to search for comfort in hard drugs.

She goes to see him in concert with his group Augustus. Cramped in the tiny club with sixty sweaty fans, she's intoxicated. She's liberated from everything she's ever been. Free, invisible in the crowd, she is the music. She is the thrashing drums. She is the shrieking electric guitar that reverberates through her body and bursts her into a thousand radiant fragments. On stage, Gus strips to his waist, throws his drenched T-shirt into the horde and blows her a kiss. She screams out his name. Her voice is exquisitely lost in the screech of whistles, the stamping and bellowing of heavy-rock junkies. She's neither Mary nor not-Rainbow anymore; she just is.

They spend the summer shoplifting, heckling strangers and hanging out together. Inside the warehouse his group has rented to live and work in, she lolls on his mattress and watches them rehearsing. Sometimes, in the protective haze of the musicians' smoke, a long-ago memory seeps in. She has to drag her thoughts away from comparisons.

This is an adult environment, different from the baby world of school. She feels good here. The musicians accept her without asking questions or telling her what she should be doing. Her contact with this underworld excites her. R– would never have done this. It's exactly the kind of life that squeaky-clean people are afraid of.

At the same time, she's aware that Gus protects her from the darker, easy-sex-and-heroin world she has heard about and seen on television and in films. If she could sing, she'd choose musician as a career. Since she can't, she'll be a groupie. The simplicity of this idea ripples with clarity. The obvious answer to which career is the non-career.

Social conversation isn't necessary with Gus. She learns nothing about his family or his childhood. After several weeks, however, she knows he hates the seedy slime inside tomatoes. She knows he loves the sound of heavy rain on the metal warehouse roof, and that he'll hit a man bullying a weaker person.

He laughs when she acts the rebel. He smiles when she tells grannies to get lost. He applauds her when she crouches down to relieve herself in a flower bed in the town centre. He joins her when she lights up in no-smoking zones. And he approves when she runs her keys down the sides of posh cars. It's impossible to shock him.

Once, she started to skirt around the black pools of *before*. He stopped her. "Your past doesn't matter," he said. "Who gives a toss about it? It's what you do that makes you who you are."

She thinks about this. It suits her to forget her past. Ever since the accident she has been rebelling against everything that was instinctive to her *before*. She is no longer the same person. Thanks to her rebellious acts, she has become a rebel. And now, by following Gus, she can become a groupie.

CHAPTER TWENTY-ONE

After the best summer since *before*, Mary lurches into Year 11. Trish is motivated and works hard for her exams, but Mary finds school is more of a waste of time than ever.

She's in a maths lesson, and is so lost it seems pointless to even try to follow. Before Gus, there was no alternative. She amused herself as best she could in the only life she knew. Now, the time she spends in overheated classrooms with giggling girlies and mummies' boys is time she could be living real life with Gus.

She yawns, slouches in her chair and counts the numbers and squiggles that dirty the white of the board. Trish and Helen are sitting in front of her. Trish's eyes water constantly because of her new contact lenses and she has to sit closer to the board. Mary refuses to sit any closer to the teachers.

Trish balls up another soaked tissue. Mary is speared by annoyance with Helen for her vanity. How dare she make Trish suffer? Trish is perfect as she is. But Trish and Helen swap pens and smiles. A few months ago Mary would have split up their deepening friendship. Now it doesn't seem important.

Outside, the October sun beckons her. She thinks about Gus hanging around in the town, ready to follow up anything that interests him. There's no reason to stay here. She'll pretend she's ill and skip the afternoon's lessons. Her decision made, she leans forward in her chair and flicks tiny balls of paper into Helen's perfect hair.

When the bell rings, she grabs Trish's arm and tells her she needs to speak to her alone. Helen looks sour. She gives Trish a commiserating look and stalks off to the canteen alone. Trish's eyes linger on her retreating back.

"What is it?" Trish asks Mary.

"I'm going to skive this afternoon. Can you say I'm ill?"

"Mary! You'll get done. Mam said this would happen."

"What do you mean?"

Mary pushes her fringe to one side and studies Trish's face. She hasn't seen Mrs Bellamy for months, not since she started hanging round with Gus. As much as she loves the friction between Mother and Gus, she doesn't want Mrs Bellamy to meet him.

"She said you'd start skiving," says Trish. "Your mother phoned her and they had a long conversation about you."

"Interfering busybody. She's my mother, not my owner," mutters Mary.

"Mary! Anyway, now Mam keeps nagging me to look out for you. She's always asking where you are and what you're up to. What am I supposed to say? You don't tell me anything anymore. It's like it's my fault. She'll be really fed up if she finds out you're skiving. I'm the one who'll have to listen to her worrying."

"If you don't say anything, she won't find out."

Mary can't bear the idea of Trish and Mrs Bellamy discussing her. She knows Trish adores her mum, but – really! She should keep at least a few secrets from her.

"And tell her to mind her own business," she adds.

Trish backs away. Her eyes are wide and teary. "You've changed, Mary. Again. All you're interested in is Gus, Gus, Gus. Mam's worried about you, that's all."

"I can look after myself. I don't need anyone telling me what I should and shouldn't do. Not even your mum." Mary lets her fringe drop back down. "I'm not hanging around here any longer. Don't bother covering for me."

She heads for the school gates and leaves the complications behind her.

🌿🌿🌿

A week later, when Mary comes down for breakfast, Mother is waiting for her.

She has skived most days after the morning register. Trish has told her no one is bothered about her absence apart from Mrs Beacon, the French teacher. But Mary knows that at some point she'll be challenged.

She sees the letter in Mother's hand and smiles to herself. Mother used to skive school too.

"This is Gus's fault," says Mother.

Mary snatches the letter, skim-reads it and then drops it on the table.

"It's nothing to do with Gus."

"You didn't skive before you met him."

"What do you care about whether I skive or not? You just

can't accept that someone likes me more than they like you."

"Don't be ridiculous! If you don't go to school, you'll end up like … on the streets."

"Like Gus?" Mary snorts. "Well, it's better than ending up like you."

Mother fills the kettle. Her hand is shaking. "How do I reply to the headmaster? Do I tell him you're hanging out with a lout and ask him to put the police on you both?"

"Tell him whatever you like. In any case, we're thinking of leaving altogether. The police won't find us in London."

She pushes back her chair, picks up her bag and strides the three steps out of the kitchen. Mother pleads for her to come back. Mary ignores her and slams the front door shut.

She's fed up with people interfering in her life. With London in her thoughts, she marches to Gus's warehouse. She needs some action to calm her down.

Gus is always ready to search out adventure. Today, they head towards the new lingerie shop, discussing the best strategy for stealing the bra, knickers and suspender belt set that Mary fancies.

The shop is designed so that people can hide their embarrassment from other shoppers. The high racks form a maze that is ideal for shoplifting. Mary strolls along the aisles and then stops. A voice she recognises is coming from the discreet fitting rooms. But she can't place the low, masculine growl that accompanies it.

She sidles along the nightwear aisle and peers between lilac and pink negligees. On the other side she sees a plump hand emerge from a cubicle and pull back the heavy curtain. It's Trish's mum. Mary ducks down and watches Mrs Bellamy's face fold into a shy smile.

Mary has never seen her with such a dreamy, girlish expression. She looks blithe. A short man is sitting next to her cubicle. He's wearing a nylon jacket and his hair is combed into a Playmobil cut. He springs up and reaches for the crimson bodysuit in Mrs Bellamy's hands. She shields it with her handbag, but Mary has already seen its G-string cut.

They kiss. It's an appreciative, tasting kiss – the kind young people like her and Gus share – not the quick, routine dry pop she uses with her husband James. Mary counts to five before their lips separate.

The flimsy hangers in her hands ping under the strain. She gropes back along the aisle to Gus. He is fingering the magnetic anti-thief discs on the black lingerie they have chosen. There's a volcano in her stomach. It threatens eruption. The person she trusts most is betraying her family with a slimy stranger. She's going to be sick. She has to get outside.

"Run," she hisses to Gus.

She snatches the lingerie from him and bolts to the door. Gus is a couple of seconds behind her. The burglar alarm pillars shrill into action. Behind the cash desk, the shop assistant drops Mrs Bellamy's purchase and rushes to the door.

A few streets away Mary slows down. She wrenches the underwear from the hangers and stuffs it into her jacket. Gus catches up.

"Why the hell did you do that?"

"I know her," says Mary.

"Who?"

"The woman in the shop. The customer."

"So what? You could have given me more warning. That old cow of an assistant almost caught me."

"Get yourself some new legs then." She starts to stalk off.

Gus grabs the back of her jacket. "What's this all about? We were going to do it properly."

"Let go of me."

Gus keeps hold of her. She glares at him. He examines her face.

"You wanted to shock her," he says. "Who is she?"

"Mind your own business."

She could explain, but he will think she's being petty. He won't care that her ideals of what a family should be have just crashed down into the gutter.

"It *is* my business. Why did you run?"

Mary, her hair lowered over her face, refuses to answer. Gus shakes her.

"You've no idea why, have you? D'you know what your problem is? There's no substance to you. You're empty inside. When I think about what you're like, all I can see is what you're not like."

That's exactly how she feels: a non-person. She glares at him. "Let go. You're hurting me."

He takes his hands away.

"You're like a black hole," he continues, "an inverted black hole; a black hole that rejects everything instead of attracting things. You rebel against everything, but there's no real *you* underneath. You can't live your life like that."

"I'll live my life the way I choose. If you don't like it,

get lost."

"I may just do that. Hanging out with you is getting boring."

He turns around and marches off.

"I thought you liked rebels," she says. She raises her voice. "You liked my sharp corners."

"There's usually something interesting behind corners," shouts Gus over his shoulder.

"You're not exactly the world's most interesting person either," she shouts back.

Silence.

"And your music's crap!" she screams.

He has gone. She's not going to run after him. She yanks the stolen lingerie from under her jacket and slams it into a nearby bin. Then she walks off in the opposite direction, her hands stuffed into her jeans pockets. So much for Mary the Rebel. It would have been better to risk him thinking she was petty, to have confessed how knotted up she's felt since the accident.

She hides in the playground close to the school for the rest of the afternoon and counts the passing birds. She doesn't want to bump into Gus. She certainly doesn't want to go to her lessons. Sitting on the swing, she tries to figure out what she can do about being an inverted black hole. Her concentration is plagued by images of Mrs Bellamy sporting her new underwear in a hotel room with that creepy businessman. What will the family do if Mrs Bellamy leaves them? Flash visions of James Bellamy heating up his single-portion lunch alone in the big kitchen haunt her. How can she look Trish in the face when she talks about her wonderful mum? Trish is going to need her support. She should go back to school.

CHAPTER TWENTY-TWO

The morning after her argument with Gus, Mary doesn't skive. The headmaster calls her into his office. He spends twenty-three minutes telling her he'll expel her if she doesn't attend her classes. Mary exceeds all her previous records by uttering just four words during the whole interview. After his lecture the headmaster leaves her in the corner of his office to meditate on her attitude until break-time.

At break she searches for Trish. She finds her sitting, huddled in her coat, on a bench with Helen. The wind whips the dead leaves into eddies around them. Mary sits down next to Trish and hands her the caricature she made of the headmaster.

Trish giggles. She shows the picture to Helen, who looks down her nose at it and then walks away. Trish turns towards Mary.

"Not with Gus today?"

"No. Had a domestic."

"Never mind. Plenty more fish in the sea."

Mary grimaces. "What would you know about that?"

"That's what Mam says." Trish slides her arm through Mary's.

Mary conjures up an image of Trish and her mum cosily discussing her over their bedtime hot chocolate. She unlinks her arm and stretches. Trish rolls up a corner of the caricature.

"So why did you split up?"

"We haven't split up. I told you. We just had a row."

"Oh. Anyway, you could find someone much more suitable than him."

"What? Two-time Gus, you mean? Is that what your mum suggests?"

"Of course not. Mam would never suggest such a thing. I mean you could chuck Gus and go out with someone who isn't such a bad influence on you."

Trish's faith in her mum is unshakeable. Mary can't tell this naive kid that her mum is an adulteress. She realises she has missed their chats over the last few months of being an inverted-black-hole groupie. There's an innocence she's never appreciated in Trish's comments before, a kind of playing at being grown-up.

"Gus is all right. He's not as bad as he looks. Why don't you get yourself a boyfriend and leave mine alone?"

She nudges Trish to show her she's not upset. Trish doesn't react. She's studying her new patent leather boots, the ones Mary saw Helen choose for her at Curtess's. Her cheeks are pink.

"I don't believe it! You've got a boyfriend," Mary says. She squints at the boys playing football or loitering near the bicycle sheds. "Who is it?"

"Shh. Stop ogling."

"Which one is it? Not Rob. Don't tell me it's Rob."

"Stop it." Trish pulls her back down onto the bench. "Why don't you come round tonight and I'll tell you?"

"I don't know. I planned to sort things out with Gus, but maybe I'll let him stew for a bit longer. Will your mum be there?"

"Stupid question. Of course she will. Why?"

"Just wondered. So you'll tell me who your mystery man is tonight?"

"If you're good."

Something isn't quite right. Trish looks guilty. Mary folds her arms and waits.

"Actually," Trish says after a few seconds, "I haven't got a boyfriend. It was just an excuse to get you to come home with me. Mam wants to talk to you. About skiving, I expect. She's promised me a new stereo if I persuade you."

Mary considers backing out. But Trish looks happy – though this may just be the prospect of a new stereo. And Mrs Bellamy might have a logical explanation for the incident in the lingerie shop. Maybe she won't lie, unlike some mothers.

"Okay. I'll come if you promise to lend me the stereo."

🌲 🌹 🌲

Mrs Bellamy turns from the Aga to greet her. Mary holds her breath. She's not sure she can control her disgust. They exchange cautious hellos. Mrs Bellamy says she's glad to see her after so long. She looks her in the eye and darts a warning glance towards Trish.

"So," Mrs Bellamy continues, "how are things with your

boyfriend? Gus, isn't it?"

Mary teeters on the edge of a crevasse. Vertigo presses her to drag Mrs Bellamy into the emptiness with her.

"My boyfriend's fine. How's–?"

"James is fine too."

"I was going to say 'your family'," says Mary.

Trish looks puzzled.

Mary takes her arm. "Let's go upstairs, Trish."

The telephone rings. Mrs Bellamy goes into the hall to answer and then comes back into the kitchen.

"It's Helen. Take the phone upstairs, Trish."

Trish leaves. Mary and Mrs Bellamy are alone. Mrs Bellamy closes the door. She pulls a chair out from the table for Mary and perches on the edge of another.

"Can we talk?"

"All right." Mary leans against the worktop and prepares to glower her way through a lecture about stealing.

"Okay. I'm in love with the man you saw. My husband knows, but the younger children don't. We've been seeing each other for years and I'm not planning to leave my family. I'm sorry you had to see us. We're usually more discreet."

She wags a finger at Mary, whose mouth has dropped open. "Of course, if you hadn't been skiving, you wouldn't have seen us. Now, I'm going to ask you not to tell Trish. I will tell her, when she's older. I don't think she'd understand yet. I'm not sure you understand either."

"Of course I understand. I'm not a kid."

"No, so I see. That's why I'm talking to you as an adult."

There's a pause while Mary considers Mrs Bellamy's duplicity and her honesty. A thought hovers in her memory:

the accident; Mother; the lie.

"Don't you hate yourself?" she asks.

Mrs Bellamy leans back in her chair and tucks stray hairs behind her ears.

"Why should I hate myself?"

"For lying to everyone."

"Mary, nobody's perfect. Most people have a secret they're ashamed of, or something they wish they hadn't done. It's not a reason for us to hate ourselves. We have to learn to accept our shortcomings and make the best of what we are."

"That's the easy way out."

"It's the *only* way out."

"Well, that's your business, of course." This is what Gus would have said.

"Exactly. But I really want to talk about your business. Can we do that?"

Mary shrugs and sinks into her chair. A slice of fringe has slipped out from behind Mrs Bellamy's ear again. Mary concentrates on counting the separate hairs as they fan over her cheek.

Mrs Bellamy monologues about the threat of being expelled, about being caught stealing and put in a remedial school, about mistakes made by young people because of the company they keep and the help they don't have. She makes it sound as if Mary isn't responsible for her multiple failings. She implies that with some help Mary could turn her life around and become a happy, successful woman. She suggests there's an alternative colour for the canvas that Mary has been painting black since the accident.

It's as if everything that's happened can be wiped away.

Perhaps Gus's lifestyle isn't the only option for Mary after all.

"Mary, be honest," says Mrs Bellamy. "You hang around with Gus because your mother disapproves of him. Don't throw your life away to spite her. You've got so much more going for you."

The mention of Mother brings Mary back to reality. "It's nothing to do with her."

"She's worried about you. She even phoned me to ask for my help. You should try to talk to her. I know you don't get on with her at the moment. But you know she loves you."

Mrs Bellamy is on Mother's side. There's no sincerity in her pep talk, she was just trying to get Mary to stop seeing Gus. Mary scrapes back her chair and stands up.

"It's none of your business who I hang out with. Maybe you should sort out your own life before moralising over mine."

"Mary–"

"Tell Trish I've gone to see Gus."

She rushes out of the kitchen and slams the door behind her. Gus may be bad news for her mother and Mrs Bellamy, but he's the best thing that's happened to her. She's got to tell him that there's more to her than a barren core. She can be better than an inverted black hole. She's got to find out how he wants her to be. She'll do everything it takes to become that person.

At the warehouse she bangs the code on the door: two slow and three long beats. There's no answer. She waits and then repeats the signal.

Twenty-five thuds later, she's still waiting. She climbs onto

a bin, pulls herself up to a window and looks inside.
The warehouse is empty.

CHAPTER TWENTY-THREE

Mary builds a cocoon around herself. Inside, Gus and Mrs Bellamy spin endlessly around her head. They throw criticism and advice at her like tennis balls. She tries to catch the words and tally them: thirty for Mrs Bellamy; forty for Gus.

Outside, Trish, Mother and the teachers create air currents. They blow the words from side to side, rendering her mathematics erratic. She has to keep starting again: love all. She stays in the cocoon for 2 weeks; 14 days; 336 hours; 20,160 minutes.

A butterfly breaks out of the cocoon. This Mary has decided to please herself. She's going to find out what's in the layer between the secret of *before* and the superficial shell she has developed since the accident. She's not going to look back – that's too hazardous. She's going to spread her wings and discover what she really likes.

On her first morning, the new Mary listens to her teachers. There are eight months before the June GCSE exams. Trish is stupefied. She abandons Helen at break and comes to sit with Mary.

"Aren't you well?"

"I'm fine. I've decided to work for my GCSEs. Can you lend me your notes?"

Trish hesitates. "Okay, but only one subject at a time. I need to keep up my revision programme. Why don't we work together?"

Mary shakes her head. She needs to be alone.

Trish crosses her ankles. "Too bad. D'you want to talk?"

"No, thanks. I told you, I'm fine."

"Well, I do. Mam's been acting weirdly since you came over. She's all pensive and jumpy. Do you know why?"

"No idea."

"You're weird, too. What's going on?"

"Nothing. Gus has gone," says Mary.

"Oh. Sorry. Was it something to do with what Mam said to you?"

"No."

There's a silence. Trish is the first to break it. "Why aren't you talking to me anymore?"

"I am talking to you."

"No, you're not."

Mary closes her eyes. The cocoon beckons her back, but it has served its purpose. It's dried-out, bereft of nourishment. She has to go on.

"Well, cut me out if you like, Mary. I don't care."

Trish stands up and stamps off. When Mary sees her next,

she's with Helen. After a few weeks, Mary learns that Helen spends her evenings in the Bellamys' kitchen.

She asks if she can change her options. The headmaster, a smug smile breaking through his beard, tells her it's too late. Mary suspects that the teachers are gossiping about her new attitude. Mr Higgins keeps staring at her, despite the fact there's no difference in the quality of her science work. And Mrs Beacon is delighted with her sudden interest in France.

She still can't talk to Mother, though she has stopped avoiding her and no longer does the opposite of everything she suggests. Mother isn't worth bothering about. She didn't seem to notice Mary's two-week silence. But she did notice the headmaster's telephone call. He thinks his tough lecture paid off because the teachers have remarked a positive change in Mary's behaviour. Mary shakes her head in disgust and watches Mother tiptoe around the house. Mother never asks her why her behaviour has changed so drastically.

☙ ❧

Spring arrives and Mary lifts her eyes from her books. Out of her rain-dusted window she counts thirteen people hurrying along the street. Some raise their heads to the sun in appreciation of the gentle warmth. An elegant woman in her twenties is staring at something in one of the gardens. She bumps into a lamppost.

Mary follows the line of her gaze. It's a tree: a cherry tree in blossom, voluptuous with perfumed petals. The lady is mesmerised. She rubs her head, drops her plastic bag and opens the garden gate. Under the tree, she tips her head back and bathes in its scent. She's in love with it. This morning, when she set out to the shops, she was probably indifferent to the power of cherry blossom. Now, there she is, enraptured, because she's let herself be transported by a glimpse of promise.

It's time to change gear; time to grind out of neutral and move forward. Mary jumps up from her desk and clatters down the stairs to the telephone. She remembers Trish's number even though she hasn't rung it for months.

"Let's go on a get-lost bike ride," she says to Trish.

There's a silence. Then, "Like before?"

"No, like today."

Another pause.

"I can't. I'm going out with Helen."

Mary hangs up and looks outside. The wind is stripping the cherry tree of its blossom. Petals spin down to rot on the wet grass. It begins to rain. She throws on her coat and spends the afternoon alone, counting the laps she accumulates in the ice rink.

Later that spring, Mrs Beacon asks Mary to stay behind after one of her French lessons. Once they're alone, she mentions that her French friend, Madame Murville, wants an English girl to stay with her in Paris for three weeks this summer. Her daughter Katia needs to improve her English.

When Mary asks Mother whether they can afford it, Mother smiles. She says that if everything works out as she hopes, money will no longer be a problem. Mary wonders briefly what Mother is up to, but lacks the curiosity to pursue the subject.

For the first time since losing Gus, she feels a hiccup of excitement. She and Mrs Beacon ring Madame Murville and they organise the trip together. Katia Murville, who is the same age as Mary, will stay with Mary and Mrs Beacon at Mrs Beacon's Devon holiday home for the three weeks after the trip to France. Mary is more motivated than ever to work on her French. For the rest of the term she stays behind after school for extra tutoring.

Mrs Beacon encourages her to write to Katia. Mary finds little to say, and fills her letter with questions about life in Paris to hide her boring life and lack of hobbies. Katia takes weeks to reply. She ignores all Mary's questions and simply tells her she likes visiting museums and art galleries, and that she listens to opera and classical music. Perhaps Katia's English is too basic for friendliness. Mary doesn't write again.

🌿🌿🌿

In July, Mary flies towards a totally new experience. She knows she likes the French language, but what if she hates France?

On the plane, the French she hears is completely different from the language Pierre and Marie-France speak on the lesson cassettes. It flows much faster than Mrs Beacon's articulated words: each sentence of real French seems to be made of one long word. She realises she is truly alone.

The Murvilles are waiting at the arrivals hall. At least, Monsieur and Madame Murville are there, standing behind the first row of enthusiastic greeters, holding a board with her name on. Madame Murville smiles at everyone. She is small, slim and chic in a skirt and blouse with a Hermès scarf around her neck. Her hair is a perfect bob. Beside her, Monsieur looks at his watch and keeps glancing behind him. Katia is nowhere to be seen.

They don't know who she is and she considers walking right past them. But Madame Murville catches her eye and her smile widens into sincerity. Mary holds out her hand to shake. Madame Murville stretches out her arms, grasps Mary's shoulders and kisses her cheeks four times. Monsieur Murville also kisses her, mutters a sentence with the word 'Katia' in it and rushes away.

Madame Murville takes her case and they head through the crowds towards the exit. She speaks slowly, asking about the flight and Mrs Beacon, and Mary tries out her first words of French with a real French person. Madame Murville smiles even more, and speaks a little faster.

There's a flurry of movement in the crowd and Monsieur Murville comes towards them. He's clutching the arm of the girl who must be Katia. She is almost as tall as him, and appears to be gliding. When Mary looks down at Katia's feet she sees she's wearing ice skates. No, not ice skates. They're a strange kind of roller skate, with little wheels in a line. They must be the inline rollerblades the Americans are apparently crazy about. Mary looks up and meets Katia's eyes. She looks defiant and is an unsmiling version of her mother, dressed in jeans and with long, brown hair.

She glides forward, bends and kisses the air beside Mary's cheeks. Then she spins around and precedes them to the terminal doors. Madame Murville fills the awkward gap with talk about the traffic jams. Monsieur frowns at his daughter's back as she weaves expertly between the people and trolleys. She manages to appear disdainful and sophisticated even though rollerblading should qualify as a kid's activity.

From the moment Mary steps outside the airport and smells the sweet aroma of brioche in the air, she suspects she's found her home. The Paris streets have the same effect on her as the Bellamys' kitchen, with added tingles of excitement. There is so much to discover here. She doesn't care if Katia resents her presence. She has a whole country to befriend.

🌺🌿🌺

"Do you prefer sport or culture?" Madame Murville asks Mary. "In France, people tend to lean more towards one than the other."

They are in the car, driving from the airport to their home. Katia has slung her rollerblades into the boot on top of Mary's case and is sitting, barefoot, in the far corner of the back seat. She's staring at a page of a paperback book.

"Well, I like both," says Mary.

Katia looks up. Mary raises an eyebrow at her and then turns and looks out of the window. She can feel Katia's scrutinising eyes on her back. She ignores her and asks Madame Murville to tell her about the monuments they pass.

At the apartment, Monsieur Murville takes Katia by the shoulder, leads her into a grand dining room and closes the door. Mary unpacks in the huge guest room. She has just finished putting her clothes away when Katia knocks and asks coldly, in French, if Mary wants to come rollerblading. Mary shrugs and then nods. She might as well see if rollerblading is as easy as it looks.

They take the lift in silence and walk out to a paved square near the apartment. Mary pulls on Madame Murville's K2 rollerblades and asks if rollerblading is popular in France. Katia shakes her head. Then she says, reluctantly, that her dad brought these ones back from America.

"Cool," says Mary.

"He's over there a lot for his business," Katia adds.

"Really?"

"He always brings back lots of presents."

Now Katia has started speaking, she seems to have forgotten her sulk. Mary doesn't understand everything, but she nods and Katia gradually unfreezes into a torrent of chatter. By the time Mary has struggled to her feet, Katia is offering her shoulder as support for Mary's first steps.

Mary shuffles around the square, falls several times, and can soon let go of Katia.

"You're really good," says Katia. Her voice is a mix of admiration and resentment.

"It's quite like ice-skating," says Mary.

Katia does a half-turn and skates backwards in a circle. Mary claps. Katia bows. After her third tour of the square without falling over, Mary begins to relax. Rollerblading is even better than ice-skating. Unlike the ice rink, there are no restrictions as to where she can skate. She glides towards the low wall, her hands outstretched, and stops.

"Shall we go, then?" she says.

"Go? Go where?"

Mary laughs. "Anywhere! Take me around Paris."

"Seriously?" Katia actually smiles. "Okay. Why not? You're on!"

Mary discovers that her dislike for butter and milk, which make her difficult in England, are standard here, where bread is served without butter, and tea and coffee without milk. There are endless cheeses to taste, and a little red wine with dinner. She even looks French. Many of the French girls have dark hair and are petite, like her. It doesn't matter that Mary's black hair is dyed. For once, she doesn't feel short. France is definitely her natural home.

On her second day she visits the Eiffel Tower. They leave the rollerblades behind and Katia guides her through the Métro. They approach the heart of the nation on foot. She knows the shape of the tower from photos, but the size of it astonishes her. It dominates the whole city. She feels a burst of apprehension as she sums up the number of triangles there are to count. This is a place to come to when things are difficult. But Katia is by her side, chattering about the history of the tower. They climb up one of its legs and Mary overcomes her compulsion to count the hundreds of steps.

When she looks down from the first floor, the belly of the monster, she is struck by vertigo. There's a sensation of lightness in her head. She closes her eyes. Workmen, close by, are listening to a radio. She latches onto the lyrics of a song while she waits for her mind to stop spiralling. It's a French song. She understands the words 'Petite Marie' within the spaghetti of syllable strings.

"It's Francis Cabrel," says Katia, and sings along.

Although her eyes are closed, Mary can see French countryside unfurling beneath her: greens and browns; curly-headed trees; stripes of vineyards; and a wide, slow-moving river. It's as if she were in an aeroplane. Everything whirls, yet her overall feeling is one of peace. Then her view parachutes towards a focal point: an ancient cedar tree in the middle of a hot, sleepy town.

The dizziness passes. She opens her eyes and shakes the strange images out of her head. The tranquillity remains and she feels happier than ever. She is still smiling when she joins Katia in the queue to climb as high as possible towards the Parisian sky.

Katia turns out to be the twin sister Mary always wanted. She chatters through Mary's silences, yet this difference doesn't stop them having similar impulses at the same time. She accompanies Mary to every corner of Paris – on their rollerblades when the streets are suitable – and answers all her questions. With Katia's help, Mary reads through the visitors' guidebook Madame Murville brings home from the tourist office where she works.

The evenings at the Murville apartment are lively. Once Monsieur Murville has flown back to America, Madame Murville forgets she wanted Katia to speak English and they use French most of the time. Mary turns her admiration for the Parisian architecture and the friendliness of the people into French words, with Katia's help, and they laugh over her

French errors and the Murvilles' accents when they speak English.

Three weeks later, Mary and Katia wave goodbye to Madame Murville at the airport. Mary links her arm through her new friend's and promises herself she'll be back one day. For the first time since becoming Mary, she's found something she wants. This isn't simply rebellion against her mother or the R– she used to be. She's Mary, and she's determined to become a Parisian.

PART FIVE

BUDDING

Rainbow and Mary, 1993-1995

CHAPTER TWENTY-FOUR

Rainbow

Rainbow failed her first year at *lycée* – in England it would have been Year 11. She was already sixteen and would have to retake the whole year after the holidays. The thought of adding more time to her prison sentence of sweat-infested classrooms made her body cry out for greenery.

From being an outsider at school in Dorset, she'd progressed to the status of foreigner and 'commune freak' at school in Cognac. It was an improvement. English was in fashion in France and she was in constant demand to translate song lyrics and to help with homework. She set up an informal business doing English exercises in exchange for maths and science, which didn't help her pass the regular tests. It did, however, reduce her number headaches. She never managed to give the answer the teacher expected, no matter what the subject, and blamed Mum for her missing 'right-answer' gene.

But school was over for the summer. She wouldn't have

to think about it for months. She was determined to enjoy the freedom of the precious holidays by spending as much time as possible outside, preferably in the arms of one tree or another. The July sun was hot and today she was harnessed to a cedar tree in a Cognac garden. She crawled along the horizontal branch, five metres above the ground, towards a stranded cat.

Halfway along the branch she became aware of a strange sensation under her skin. It started in the nape of her neck and shivered its way down to her coccyx. She froze, her eyes fixed on the cat. It made a long, howling miaow. Another wave washed down her back. Below her, on the car maintenance garage radio, Francis Cabrel continued his metallic rendition of 'Petite Marie'. The lyrics wove through her body and buoyed her up towards the sky. She felt her spirit rise through the canopy of the cedar top. Gripping the branch, she let her inner self go and floated up. She could see the whole town, the whole of the Charente, the whole of France below her. She could see Paris, the Eiffel Tower.

She gasped. There was a sense of endless, countless triangles of metal. Then, before the cat could finish the last syllable of its miaow, a heavy weight of foreboding thrust her back into her clenched body. The vision was over.

She clung to the branch. Her eyes refused to focus and she was overwhelmed by the sense of depression that had accompanied the vision. The cat, tuning into her sudden fragility, took a nervous step towards her and nuzzled her neck, its howls of fright turning into mews of reassurance. She sat up, let it climb into her arms and stroked it while she recovered. Then she eased it into the rucksack and lowered herself slowly down the smooth line of the climbing rope.

Sylvia, her English school friend, had belayed her while she climbed up to the branch. Sylvia was a rock climber who, under Rainbow's influence, had taken to climbing trees. She had taught Rainbow the art of climbing.

When her feet touched the ground, Rainbow crouched to release the rope tension and then unclipped her descender. The handful of onlookers had already left, leaving Sylvia standing alone at the foot the cedar. Before Rainbow had even peeled off her harness, Sylvia had put away her equipment and hoisted her cat and rucksack onto her back. She jumped onto her mountain bike and sped away, shouting over her shoulder that she'd see Rainbow later at the train station.

Rainbow, still in a daze from her vision, looped the rope into chains and piled it into her bag. She laid the slings and carabiners on top and added her harness. Then she sat and gazed up into the tree, her drawing pad on her knees. It was far easier to draw its branches now she had communicated with it. She'd been trying to persuade Sylvia to let her cat get stuck in this tree for months. She needed a valid, non-spiritual reason so that the owners would allow her to climb it. Finally, a short negotiation involving an English film showing in Angoulême was all it had taken.

The men from the garage had watched her climb the tree to rescue the cat. She hated having to pretend she was doing something normal, but at least she didn't get hassled this way. They were only interested in looking at her bum as she climbed and at Sylvia's boobs as she belayed. They didn't heckle. They didn't accuse her of being a witch. And now she could add the cedar's intimacy to her collection. The cedar was special. It was the first time she'd had an out-of-body trip. What was it trying to show her?

On her return to Le Logis, Rainbow parked her moped and joined Domi in his meditation corner of the garden. He was sitting on the improvised decking under the shade of the walnut tree, his eyes closed. She couldn't understand why he meditated here. Walnut trees had a reputation for being unhealthy.

He spent increasing amounts of time meditating and she suspected he was searching for a solution to her tree problem. She tiptoed towards him and stopped under the leafy canopy. He'd aged. His face was beginning to sag and the despondent expression that had begun to settle there was noticeable, even with his eyes closed.

She sat cross-legged with her back against the trunk and tried not to bubble over with excitement. An out-of-body experience! He'd be delighted.

"Rainbow," he whispered. His eyes remained closed.

She knew she shouldn't jolt him to full consciousness. "Yes, it's me."

"You're perplexed about something. No … excited."

Rainbow smiled. It had been over two years now. Two wonderful years shared with her father – not that she'd ever told him she knew who he was. They had an intuitive understanding that went beyond the need for words and explanations. She appreciated him all the more because he'd been missing from her life for so long.

He opened his eyes, took a second to focus on her and then spoke.

"Tell me. I'm ready."

"I think the answer is finally coming," she said.

Domi sat upright. "What happened?"

"I had an out-of-body. In the cedar."

"At last! Give me your hands."

Rainbow held them out. He took them in his own and fixed his eyes on her face.

"It's definitely a sign. What did you feel?"

"It was like being in the heart of France, but it wasn't very nice. There was an awful feeling of depression. It was like an unbearable weight."

"That's strange. People usually feel light. You must look for signs next time."

"Okay. I saw Paris and the Eiffel Tower. Were they signs?"

"Perhaps. Write them down." He pulled her up and hugged her. "You see? There *is* a spiritual future for you, after all. This is great, Rainbow! Let's celebrate."

A glint of hope had displaced the dejection in his eyes. She hugged him hard. She so wanted to make him proud of her, to dam the flow of disappointment he tried to hide.

CHAPTER TWENTY-FIVE

Rainbow

Rainbow was frying courgettes for dinner when she heard the growl of Christophe's motorbike. It had been his first day working at the motorbike shop. She turned down the gas and asked Sandrine to watch the pan. He'd looked nonchalant that morning, but she'd noticed his fingers worrying the loop of elastic on his jeans pocket while he drank his bowl of coffee. She hurried outside and met him under the red leaves of the silver maple.

"How was it?" she asked.

Christophe's brown eyes glowed. "Génial!"

He always spoke English when they were alone. His slip into French jolted her. She had a sudden vision of him moving away and out of reach.

"What's up, Rainette? You look sad," he said, reverting to English.

"No, it's just strange, you being at work now. I feel left behind."

He ruffled her hair. "If you don't put more effort in at school you'll certainly be left behind; condemned to live eternally in the commune."

He'd told her that the baccalaureate was the best escape route from the commune. But she didn't want to escape and hadn't bothered with schoolwork, especially as she was retaking her first year at *lycée*. She didn't need to understand physics or read literature to work with trees.

"Anyway," Christophe continued, "you're working too."

During the summer she'd offered her services to the regular Logis spiritualism clients. They could hire her to heal sick trees and to stretch branches into more convenient directions as an alternative to chopping them off. She'd also offered fruit-tree reshaping to facilitate harvesting, as long as the tree's balance wasn't endangered.

"Not anymore," she said.

"What? You didn't tell me you'd stopped."

"You've been busy with your smelly engines. The clients don't like what I do. They were fine with the healing, but my tree-shaping work made them ill at ease. The ones whose trees I shaped stopped coming here at all. I pulled out before the commune lost all its clients."

"Merde!"

"Yes. Anyway, I didn't like changing the shape of the trees just to suit people."

"Yeah, I see what you mean. What did Domi say?"

"I didn't tell him." She put a hand on Christophe's arm. "Don't say anything to him. He'll be upset if he knows people won't accept my gift."

He nodded. It wasn't the first secret she'd shared with him. She would trust him with her life.

🌿🌱🌿

During dinner, Christophe announced he'd been offered the flat over the motorbike shop and that he'd be moving there at the weekend. Rainbow felt his eyes on her as he spoke. She concentrated on watching Mum wink at Céline. In some ways it would be a relief not to have him around. She often sensed him watching her and it made her uncomfortable.

She joined in the toast to his independence, already wondering what would happen to his old bedroom. She was the second-oldest child, so maybe she could take it over. It was a huge room. They had converted it the previous year from the former hay attic. Although Mum now slept with Domi, she used Rainbow's bedroom for everything else, and her makeup and clothes were scattered everywhere. Rainbow wanted her own space.

After the meal, Christophe volunteered to wash up with Rainbow. But Domi told Sandrine to take Rainbow's place because he wanted her to participate in his healing session. He'd never invited another person before. She agreed quickly and followed him to his healing room.

"What's this all about, Domi?"

"I want to see if you're tuned into human energy," he replied.

"I'm not interested in healing people."

"I know. Let's just see. There's no harm in checking out

the possibilities."

"It won't work."

Domi sighed, which accentuated his worry lines.

"Okay, we'll give it a go," she said. "What do I have to do?"

His client arrived. Rainbow watched and listened while Domi relaxed the woman with his voice and hands. The client had a problem with her stomach. Once she was lying down, her eyes closed, Domi beckoned Rainbow over and showed her how to lay her hands on the woman's belly.

Rainbow's palms were so gnarled she could hardly feel the client's skin. The woman flinched. Her eyes sprang open and she protested.

Domi calmed her. He laid his own hands on her stomach and motioned Rainbow to do the same. This time the woman was ready. Rainbow felt her relax. She sensed Domi's energy pour into the woman but she could feel no flow from herself. She concentrated. There was no contact at all. She kept her hands in place so Domi wouldn't complain that she hadn't tried. When he took his hands away, she did the same.

After the session, Domi washed his hands and sat down. He looked dispirited. Rainbow considered lying, rekindling the hope she'd seen in his eyes after her out-of-body experience a few months before.

Domi sighed. "Well, that didn't work. We'll have to try something else," he said.

"What's wrong with the tree healing I already do?"

"At some point in the future you'll need to earn a living and I'm not convinced you'll get paid to work with trees. You said there was no interest in tree-shaping or healing. So I thought we'd try out some classic commune work."

"I'm useless with everything except trees."

Domi didn't answer immediately.

"It's my fault for having big ideas. I think I've been too ambitious for you," he said eventually.

Rainbow bit her lip. She was a continual disappointment to him. He carried on.

"I told you my destiny is to save the world, but my contribution is miniscule because I can only treat one family at a time. When you arrived with your unique gift, I was sure it was a sign. I realised that my destiny was to lead you to yours. I believed you had a role of coordination. I saw you as a focal point for trees' voices and I thought they would communicate with humans through you. And I imagined you tapping into a network that would tell us how to save our planet."

Rainbow eyes lit up. It hadn't occurred to her that she could lead a tree revolution. She thought about her contact with trees. The oak beside Michael's garden had been wise and given her its history. The beech in France had reassured her of the trees' forgiveness for what she'd done to the English beech. But she'd never received any messages about the future. For the first time, she wondered how much of Domi's faith was simply ideas in his own head.

He was still talking. "The problem is that you haven't seen any sign of collective communication. You haven't sensed anything other than passivity, have you?" he said.

"No."

"I'm starting to think your gift is the same style as my mine. I'm afraid your destiny may just be to heal one tree at a time."

She frowned. Destiny was supposed to be something great,

something to die for. She didn't just want to carry on as she had done for years. Of course she wanted to help trees. But she'd thought Domi was going to find her something on a heroic scale. She'd thought she was going to save the planet. What was the point of her gift if she couldn't do anything worthwhile with it?

CHAPTER TWENTY-SIX

Mary

Mary looks around the refectory at the other students wading through the bland food. It's close to the end of her first term in sixth-form college. Usually she feels bright and engaged in the adult atmosphere that's so different from secondary school. Not today though. She drums her fingers on the table. She's just told her squash partner Caroline that she's giving up squash. With the prospect of a free afternoon ahead, the old rebellious itch crawls to the surface.

She's sitting with friends from the eleven clubs she's already enrolled in and then left. From climbing to sewing, from book clubs to motor mechanics – nothing outlasts the pointlessness that attacks her after a few meetings; nothing corresponds to what she really wants, to who she really is. When she came out of her cocoon and decided she was going to please herself, she expected to find lots of things to interest her. But the only thing that means anything to her is Paris.

She's conscious of the familiar itch, but hasn't felt it for so long that she's forgotten the force of its acceleration. Her friends have all finished eating. She places her plate on her glass and begins to build a crockery tower. As she positions her neighbour's glass on the top plate, the tower wobbles. The lively chattering around her peters out. The tower is now as high as their faces, and is attracting attention from the other tables in the vicinity.

"It's going to fall," says Caroline.

Mary picks up the salt and pepper pots.

"Here comes trouble. You're in for it," says Deb.

One of the refectory staff in her blue-checked overalls is hurrying towards their table. Mary dangles the salt pot over the tower, lowers it delicately and counts the approaching steps. The rise of adrenalin is the fresh air of spring kissing her into life.

"What's going on?"

The voice of authority sounds so familiar that instead of ignoring it, as she had intended, Mary looks up. Mrs Bellamy is standing opposite her. Mary hasn't seen her since their confrontation over Gus a year ago. The tower looms between them.

"What are you doing here?" Mary asks, her voice quiet. She nonchalantly replaces the pepper pot on the table.

Caroline lets out her breath, which intensifies Mary's itch. She picks up the pepper again. The expectant hush is a soothing balm.

The refectory woman in her blue checks puffs up to the table beside Mrs Bellamy and starts to speak. Mrs Bellamy silences her with a hand on her arm.

"I'll handle this, Jean."

The woman looks uncertain, then relieved. She shuffles away, ordering the onlookers to get back to their meals. Mrs Bellamy waits as Mary's friends leave. Mary positions the pepper pot on the tower.

"Don't forget that children's games always end in tears," says Mrs Bellamy.

"I'm not a child."

"Really? Then why the childish attitude?"

"My attitude is my concern, not yours," Mary replies. "As I told you once before."

"Actually, as a member of staff, your attitude *is* my concern. Take down the crockery and then come to my office."

Mrs Bellamy's order inflames Mary's irritation to a level of fury she hasn't felt since Gus left.

"I'll come when I'm ready."

Mrs Bellamy turns around and walks towards the door. Mary watches her leave and then adds a serviette to the crown of her creation. She leans back in her chair and admires the structure for nine seconds. Then she picks up her bag and leaves the refectory. Nobody stops her. By the time she has pushed through the swing-door she feels flat. What is it about Mrs Bellamy that makes her feel so cantankerous? Their argument was ages ago. She should be able to put it behind her, like she has done for the rest of that rebellious period.

Her friends are waiting for her outside the refectory. They stop talking as she approaches. She refuses their offer of a trip into town and walks on her own to the squat cube of the library.

The librarian looks up from her computer and beams at her. She worked in Paris for a year, and Mary has spent hours reliving her stay with the Murvilles and learning about France from her. The librarian holds back French course books for her so she doesn't have to race the other students to grab the few copies.

"How's Baudelaire?" she asks Mary.

"A bit stuffy. I'm so glad you gave me the translations. They really help. Listen, I've just seen someone I know who must be a lecturer now. Is there any way I can find out what she teaches?"

"Easy. What's her name?"

"Bellamy."

Mary pulls out the French *carambar* sweets she received in the post from Katia that morning. She shares them with the librarian, who scrolls through computer screens, and looks around the familiar huddles of tables. The glass ceiling panels and large windows give the cosy top-floor library a heady giddiness. It's like a nest. Her French and English A levels don't amount to many hours of lectures, and she spends more time here than in the classroom block.

"Here we are," says the librarian. "Mrs Ada Bellamy, careers advisor."

All the help Trish's mum gave Mary eighteen months ago must have motivated her to get her own career.

"Yes, that figures," she says.

She thanks the librarian, sits down and takes out her copy of Baudelaire's poem '*Les Hiboux*'. She whispers the words out loud, letting her ears linger on the swishy sounds of the language and take in its rhythm. Then she reads the translation. What a bore Baudelaire was: it sounds as if he's warning people they'll be punished for wanting to change places. She puts the paper back into her folder and flicks through the different sections. All her homework is done. She stares out of the window at the concrete blocks of classrooms. Everything is a monotonous December grey. The sky is mustering its energy to hurl snow and hail towards the icy ground.

She needs to move. She slings her bag over her shoulder and leaves the library. Maybe she'll go and hang out in the common room with Jed. He might let her ride his motorbike around the car park again.

The offices adjoining the common room belong to the careers department. Mary pauses at the door, and then pushes it open a little. She's never been inside. There's a cramped waiting room with three scruffy doors leading off it. It's empty. A photocopier stands below a noticeboard overflowing with tacked-up leaflets. She opens the door a little further. On the office doors she can make out small, white rectangles bearing people's names, but she's not close enough to read them. The whole area is silent. She steps inside. She only needs five seconds, just enough time to read the names and then slip out again.

She tiptoes across the chipped squares of lino. *No, no, yes.* The third door is Mrs Bellamy's. It's ajar. She approaches and listens at the crack. There's no noise. She nudges the door a few centimetres open. Still no sound. She'll just see what it's like, and then she'll go. She pushes it right open.

Mrs Bellamy is sitting opposite her, at her desk, reading a book.

"Ah, Mary. There you are. Come in. Would you like a coffee?"

"No."

Mrs Bellamy stands up and walks around her desk towards Mary. Mary backs away. Mrs Bellamy stops.

"I'm not going to eat you."

Mary decides she might as well get it over with. She steps inside and shuts the door behind her.

"How long have you been working here?" she asks.

"Since September. What do you think of my office?"

Mrs Bellamy sits down on one of the two easy chairs and motions Mary to join her. Mary ignores her and perches on the edge of the desk instead. She inspects the room. Papers are organised neatly into four piles, the walls are decorated with seven colourful careers posters and there's one plant on the windowsill. It's convivial and snug.

"It's a bit of a dump," she replies.

"Good. I don't want anything too formal. How are your studies going?"

Mrs Bellamy looks crisp. She's dressed in a neat suit and her hair is cut short. She's still plump but she comes across as energetic and motivated. Mary has a twinge of jealousy. She wishes she felt as good as Mrs Bellamy looks.

"So-so," she replies. "How's Trish?"

"Very well. She's enjoying her sciences, especially physics. I think she's leaning towards engineering. How come you two don't see each other anymore?"

Mary shrugs. "She's at school, I'm at college."

"It's a shame you've drifted apart. Old friends are important – they're a bit like family. And how's your mother?"

"Same as ever."

"I thought I spotted her with a gentleman in town."

"Probably Graham, her new man."

"Ah. What's he like?"

"All right. Keeps Mother occupied."

Actually, when Graham arrived in her mother's life in the summer, Mary had felt a great weight lift from her. She's careful not to frighten him away. This isn't difficult because he's quiet and totally uninteresting. He reminds her of a lizard: he's dull-brown and dry-skinned, and he merges in with the furniture.

Mary and Mrs Bellamy look at each other. There's a short silence.

"You're growing up, Mary."

"That's not what you said earlier in the refectory."

"No. What was that all about?"

Mary sidetracks. "How's your lover these days?"

The word 'lover' slips off her tongue without raising the slightest sickness.

"Wonderful. And are you still shoplifting?"

Mary looks directly into Mrs Bellamy's crinkly eyes. She opens her mouth to reply, but no words come out. Instead, she and Mrs Bellamy burst into laughter simultaneously.

"Goodness gracious," says Mrs Bellamy. "Wasn't that an awful situation?"

"Terrible. I'm sorry about being so rude to you."

"That's all right. It's behind us. We're different people now. Look at me: a smart, working woman. And goodness, look at you: a beautiful young lady who's going to dazzle the world with her success."

Mrs Bellamy stands up and clasps Mary's hands in her own.

Her delight is infectious. Mary throws her arms around her neck and hugs her. They spin around the small space between the desk and the door, laughing.

"Well, what an exciting day this is turning out to be," says Mrs Bellamy. "Let's have a coffee and you can tell me what college life is really like, from a student viewpoint."

"Okay, as long as you give me the lowdown on the staff side."

"It's a deal. Oh, and you must call me Ada."

Mrs Bellamy bustles out of the office to the coffee machine and Mary sits down in an armchair. She drags a hand through her hair, which she's let grow out of its shaved back and long fringe style. Beautiful? Success? She's never heard these two words applied to her. She's charged by a bolt of confidence and is still smiling when Ada returns with two hot plastic cups of coffee.

For the next half hour they discuss college, Trish and Ada's new career. Not once do they touch on the past. When Mary leaves the office to make room for the nervous boy who has a careers appointment, they arrange to have a coffee together the following morning.

"Say hello to Trish from me," finishes Mary. "It'd be good to see her again after all these months."

"Will do. And you must come for dinner."

CHAPTER TWENTY-SEVEN

Mary

Things have changed at the Bellamys' house. Last time Mary was here she had been fifteen and Mrs Bellamy stayed at home all day to look after Trish, little Jimmy and her husband James. Now that Ada works full-time the kitchen feels different. It's hollow, even though six people are eating dinner this evening. The Christmas decorations, which Jimmy, Trish and herself used to drape over every bookcase and framed picture, are still in a box.

James, the academic, now cooks many of the meals. He's still learning how to interpret recipe books. Tonight's *saag gosht* isn't altogether revolting, though Mary doesn't like spinach and can see tails of it curling around the lumps of meat. There's a soapy aftertaste. Two ingredients must have reacted together – surely James hasn't put soap in the dinner? And the rice is stodgy. Ada is the only one to comment on it: she points out he's used pudding rice instead of long grain and says how well it complements the runny curry.

Mary concentrates on the food because Trish, sitting opposite her, keeps sending killing looks across the table. Beside Trish, Helen smiles in a condescending manner each time she catches Mary's eye.

Ada didn't tell Mary that Helen would be here tonight. If Mary had known, she'd have found an excuse not to come. In fact, Ada looked as surprised as Mary to see Helen sitting in Mary's favourite armchair. Trish had ignored Mary and told her mum that Helen was staying to dinner.

"No problem, as long as Pop has made enough," Ada had replied.

"*Dad*, not Pop," said Trish. She'd turned her back on Mary and started whispering to Helen.

At the dinner table, Ada and Jimmy are the only ones talking. Mary watches Ada. Is she is unaware of the hostile atmosphere, or doesn't it bother her? During the past few weeks they've seen each other regularly. Mary pops into Ada's office on her way to the common room, and sometimes eats with her at the refectory. She's impressed by Ada's transformation from a housewife into a careers advisor, and wonders how many other people reshape themself like this. Ada has told her that the most difficult part is to pinpoint what you want. Once you know, you can overcome all the hurdles to get there.

They clear the table together. Jimmy mooches away and James wanders back into his office. Ada looks at her watch.

"Helen, it's time for you to go home," she says.

Trish glares at her mum. "Mary too."

"I'll run Mary home as soon as I've done the ironing."

Helen says goodbye to Ada and smirks at Mary. She pulls

Trish out of the kitchen, leaving Mary and Ada alone.

"I think I'd better go too," says Mary. "Trish obviously doesn't want me here."

Ada plugs in the iron. "She'll be fine once Helen's gone. Give it a go. Please?"

"Why do you want us to be friends so much?"

"Neither of you has any sisters. You can count on old friends in a way you can't count on new ones."

"She's got Helen now."

"Exactly."

They laugh. Trish appears and they stop.

"I see you're having fun," says Trish, and turns on her heel. "I'll leave you to it."

Ada grabs her arm. "Wait a minute. I'd like you to show Mary the university guide you borrowed from school before she goes."

"If you want. I'll go and get it."

"Take Mary upstairs. I want to listen to my Spanish tapes while I'm ironing."

Trish looks Mary up and down. She doesn't smile. Puberty hasn't treated her kindly. Her skin is pockmarked and greasy. Her make-up, however, is expertly applied, and her contact lenses allow her green eyes to illuminate her face. Mary decides she must try make-up. Trish dresses better too. Her fitted blouse and tight, zipped jeans are an organic extension of her body. She's passed through the experimental stage and found a style that suits her. It's a chic, elegant look. Mary would feel clumsy if she wore the same tight, classic lines. Trish has definitely found herself since Mary saw her last.

Trish jerks her head towards the staircase. "The quicker

you come, the quicker you can go," she says, and flounces out of the room.

Mary follows.

Trish has spread her personality over every centimetre of her redecorated bedroom. She is fashion-conscious, colour-coordinated and as untidy as ever.

"Trendy," says Mary.

Trish searches through her school bag. "Helen helped me. She's going to be an interior designer."

"I thought she wanted to be a doctor."

Trish gives her a Helen-like condescending look. "That was ages ago. Anyway, she failed biology."

"Oh. Ada–" starts Mary, "that is, your mum – says you want to be an engineer."

"What's wrong with that?"

"Nothing. I didn't say there was anything wrong with being an engineer."

"I suppose at college you all have arty careers lined up. I can't imagine my mum is much help, never having had a career herself."

"She's a brilliant careers advisor, actually. She really cares about helping the students find the right job."

"Yeah, I see you hang off her every word nowadays. I suppose it's because you haven't got any friends."

Mary holds herself back from slapping her. "What's your problem? You haven't stopped being spiteful since I arrived."

"It's your fault for being so superior. Us school kids are obviously below you. You know what, Mary Hubbard? We don't need you."

"By *we*, you mean Helen and you?"

Trish glares at her. "At least Helen's around. We share stuff. She doesn't pick me up and drop me as it suits her."

Mary looks out of the window. There are thirteen cows in the field below.

"I'm sorry. It was a difficult time," she says.

"Story of your life, Mary. Get some therapy or you're going to use up a lot of friends. And while we're on the subject of friends, keep away from Mum. She's my mum, not yours. I don't like you sneaking round her and sucking up all the time."

"What?"

"I'm sick and tired of hearing her raving about you. It's non-stop 'Mary this, Mary that'. I've had it up to here with you."

"But—"

"I know something's going on. That business with whatshisname – Gus. You told her some secret or other. I know. I can read Mum like a book. She's too honest to be able to hide anything."

"That was over ages ago. I didn't tell her any secrets. I was just fed up with her because she and Mother ganged up and tried to warn me off Gus."

Mary remembers Ada's shy smile in the lingerie shop. She blocks the memory.

"But that's over. We're friends like before, when she helped me choose my studies. Before Gus came along."

"*I* was your friend, not Mum."

"You're still my friend. It's you who doesn't want to be friends anymore. I'd be happy to do stuff with you again."

Trish sniffs. "I'll think about it."

Mary hides a smile and waits. Trish finds the university guide and holds it out.

"Anyway, what stuff?"

"Whatever," says Mary.

"I suppose we could go to the cinema."

"Cool. When?"

Trish smiles grudgingly and they decide on Friday evening.

Mary opens the university guide and they look through it together. Trish gradually relaxes into friendliness. They flick through the guide, but university seems so far away that they soon drift into talking about the differences between school and college. Before long, Ada knocks on the door and tells Mary she'll take her home.

Mary waves goodbye to Trish and they drive away from the house in Ada's Astra.

"I take it that went well," says Ada.

"Yes. Thanks, Ada. It's true that there's nothing like old friends."

There's a short silence.

"Did you mention Philip?" asks Ada.

"Is that his name? No, of course not."

Ada sighs. "She's bound to find out one day. I really should tell her, but she's still so young and innocent. Sometimes I think college would have helped her grow up. The teachers are so good at the comprehensive though. And the classes are half the size."

"Maybe she resents being left behind."

"Do you think so? She agreed it was best to stay at school."

"Of course she did. It was your advice," says Mary.

"She's a sensible girl. Too sensible. Perhaps she shouldn't

listen to her mam quite so much."

"She's lucky to have a mother who supports her."

"Thanks, Mary. What about your mother? Do you get on any better?"

She will never get on with her mother, not like she does with Ada. She has tried. No doubt she loves her in an instinctive way, but there will always be a distance between them because of *before*.

"Things are okay," Mary says.

"Only okay?"

"What do you expect? She's a mythomaniac and she's wrapped up in her own life."

"It's a shame about your father."

Mary's sure her heart misses a beat. She swallows. "You mean Bob?"

"No, your real father."

They are on the outskirts of town. Mary counts the passing lampposts and pretends nonchalance.

"What about him?"

"If you can't see eye to eye with one parent, you often get on with the other, if he's there."

"Well, he's not."

"No." Ada hesitates. "What actually happened to him? Do you mind my asking?"

"He died."

"Is that what your mother told you?"

"Why? Should she have told me something different?"

"It's not my place to talk to you about your father. I think you should ask your mother about him again, now you're older. She may be able to give you more details."

Mary sits upright in her seat. "Did you know him? I mean, when he and Mother were together?"

"No, Mary. I never met him."

Mary slips into silence. She stares out of the window at the houses gliding past, their Christmas lights winking garishly.

When they arrive in front of Mary's home, Ada puts her hand on Mary's knee.

"Do try to talk to your mother."

Mary says goodbye and slithers out of the car without responding. She counts fourteen steps to her front door.

CHAPTER TWENTY-EIGHT

Mary

After the cinema on Friday evening, Mary and Trish drop into the King's Head for a drink. The pub is crowded and they weave in single file around the groups of students. Many of them nod or wave at Mary as she passes, and she exchanges a few words with several of them. She stops when she sees Jed, and introduces Trish to him.

Jed is her closest friend at college. Their relationship is based on lighthearted banter and irony, with which they cover their secrets. Sometimes she's tempted to talk seriously to him, but she never finds a way to start. She can taste fear too. She's afraid he'll become important to her and that he'll find her empty compared to his expectations. It's better this way.

"Is he your boyfriend?" Trish asks as they sit down.

"No." She scrutinises Trish over her glass. "Do you fancy him?"

"No, it's not that. It's you, actually."

Mary chokes and spits shandy over the carpet. "Me?"

Trish laughs. "I don't mean I fancy you!"

"Good. What do you mean, then?"

"I've never seen you so sociable. It's weird. You're like a bird: you hop to one friend, chirp merrily and make them laugh, and then hop to another. You've changed. You always used to be so angry with everything."

"Maybe I seem different because I know what I want now."

"Do you? What?"

"I want to live in France, in Paris."

"Because of that holiday with whatshername?"

"Katia. Yes. For the first time I felt I'd found my destiny."

In fact, it was the second time, but the first was *before*, so it doesn't count. She steers her mind to the Eiffel Tower and its interminable triangles. There's a companionable silence. They sip their drinks.

"Do you ever feel something is missing from your life?" asks Mary.

Trish swills her Coke around her glass. "Missing?"

"Forget it. What about you? Are you happy?"

"You're kidding. How can I be happy when I'm stuck at school? I can't wait to get to university and start real life. Everything is so boring here: home is mundane, Mum and Dad are stuck in their ruts, Jimmy is a pain and nothing ever happens in the village. Helen is tedious. She boasts she's already done everything there is to do. She brags that her mum is pretty and young, though she's a real tart because she cheated on Helen's dad and got married to another bloke."

Mary twists her empty glass in her hand. "Shall we go home?"

Trish looks surprised. Then she checks her watch and agrees.

🍂🍃🍂

Christmas morning arrives and Mary does her best to ignore it. She sprawls under her quilt and thinks about Trish. She can understand her anxiety to move on: Trish always focuses on what she wants and advances in a straight line, impatient to reach her target. Mary moves transversally. She slips from one channel to another as if by accident, always moving outwards and never going back. Her thoughts about Trish spill into thinking about Ada's words in the car.

Mother and Graham are already up. They never lie in, even at Christmas. Before Graham moved in with them, Mother would stay in bed on weekend mornings. She'd leave notes on the breakfast table for Mary: *Out with G. tonight*, or *Where's dishwasher salt?* The dishwasher had been Graham's first gift to Mother, which said a lot about their relationship. Mary would throw away the notes, or find the item and bang it on top of the paper. Sometimes, if she felt particularly annoyed, she would scrawl an unhelpful answer underneath: *Out too*, or *Salt is in cupboard*.

Graham bought the neighbour's house within weeks of meeting Mary. In a whirl of efficiency, he employed workmen to join the two half-houses and transform them into a big new house. He and Mother live mostly in the new part of the house. They drift around their old-fashioned sitting room and kitchen–dining room. Mother stopped swiping boxes and jars across the red eye of the cash-till laser last summer, and now looks after their home. She calls herself a writer. Mary sees no evidence of any writing actually being done in Mother's old bedroom, which they converted into an office.

Mary likes the extra space because it's easy to hide from Mother and Graham. She has her own little sitting room and bathroom, as well as her old bedroom. She thinks of it as her flat. There isn't a kitchen, but she has a personal front door. Better still, Mother now fusses over Graham rather than her.

She can hear the depressing sound of cheerful Christmas music. She turns over in bed and counts the muffled creaks of footsteps on polished floorboards, willing the numbers to lull her back into a doze. But the creaks are too slow. She keeps coming back to Ada's hints about her father.

Perhaps it's time to give Mother another chance. Will she tell the truth now Mary is older, or will she stick to her old lies? Mary sighs. The pain is behind her. It no longer matters. She doesn't want to sink back to where she was three years ago. She's dealt with it. There are rarely any dreams nowadays. She no longer picks fights with Mother in revenge for her lies. It isn't worth the bother. *Your actions make you the person you are, not your past.* Thanks Gus.

There's a knock at her door. Mother tells her lunch will soon be ready. Mary mumbles that she's coming and glances at the clock. She's managed to use up the morning. Now there's the afternoon and evening to get through.

"Happy Christmas, love," says Mother, when Mary walks into their sitting room. She takes advantage of Mary's sleepy movements to hug her.

"Mother," groans Mary. "Morning, Graham."

Graham is sitting in his armchair in front of the open fire, a glass of sherry in his hands and a book on his lap. He closes his book, puts down his glass and stands up.

"Happy Christmas," he says.

Mother stands by Graham's side. Mary stares dully at them. Late mornings always make her heavy-headed. She feels like a spectator of a play where only the actors – Mother and Graham – know what's going to happen.

"I'm off to the kitchen for some tea," she says.

"Just a minute, love. We've got something to tell you."

Mother is dolled up for the day in a sweeping black blouse over burgundy corduroy trousers. Her dark hair has been trimmed into a matronly bob and she looks respectable. Her bohemian side only seeps out through her daring lines of kohl eyeliner.

Next to Mother, slightly smaller, stands the Reptile. He is beige and cream with a stoop that tilts him to the left. Mary has never discussed anything with him. He is proud of his patience, and she can tell he's waiting for her to open up to him. She doesn't want to get close because she suspects she despises him. She can't afford to scare him away from Mother.

"Go on then. Tell me."

They exchange smiles. "We've decided to get married."

Third time lucky, Mary thinks. "Congratulations," she says. "Can I get my tea now?"

"You could show a bit more enthusiasm. Graham's been good to us."

Mary's chin raises in defiance. She didn't ask for his charity. "Am I supposed to sing and dance?"

Graham clears his throat.

"Please don't be sarcastic," says Mother.

"You're getting married. That's cool. But it's not as if I'm a kid. You haven't got to pass him off as my new father."

Why the hell did she say that? Mother's cheeks start to crumple at the edges. Mary is reminded of her reaction after the accident, when Mary had announced her new name. She's unable to drag her eyes away from Mother's face. She counts four wrinkles under the right eye, five under the left. Ada's words are hot in her head.

"Though I suppose that's what he'll be," Mary hears herself add.

Mother's eyes plead for silence.

"A new father," Mary continues, "because my real father died when I was a baby, didn't he?"

"Do we have to bring that up again?"

Mother's voice is weak. Graham clears his throat again. "Mary, you know I'll never try to replace your biological father. This is about your mother and me. Not about you. As you say, you're not a kid. You'll be heading off to university in less than two years. You'll always be welcome here – this is your home – but I don't expect you to treat me like a father."

"I see. It's not about me. The question about what happened to my father is nothing to do with me."

"We're talking about our marriage, not about your father," says Graham. His voice is annoyingly dry and calm.

"Well, I'm talking about my father, which is between my mother and myself. Not you."

Graham folds his arms. Mother leans against him.

"We talked about this when you were little," she says.

"Exactly. I was little. I'm sixteen now. Maybe you'd like to add more."

Graham's tortoise head swivels towards Mother. So she hasn't told him either. Mother's face pales.

"What more can I add? He left us and then died." She grasps Graham's arm.

Inside her head, Mary screams at her mother. *Lies! Liar!* She clamps her mouth shut and presses her hands to her temples. The words are trapped. They crash around and dent her brain, unable to escape into the open air. She strides out of the room and slams the door behind her.

In her sitting room, she sweeps the books off her bookshelves. She wrenches open the window and hurls seven cushions outside. She kicks her CD tower and watches it crash to the floor. The room resonates with the rage of her crying.

At last she collapses into her chair. She bangs her head onto her desk and counts the blurred grains of its yellow wood. At seventy-four, her mind starts to empty. The tiny kernel at the very centre of her being shivers in the cold air. She was wrong to think she was over it. It still hurts. Enormously.

CHAPTER TWENTY-NINE

Mary

January is bitter cold. Every day, Mary swallows mouthfuls of chilled air and lets them freeze inside. They numb her perfectly. She feels nothing but the stillness of her frozen routine: to college; back from college; out with friends; home to bed.

Mother is wrapped up in Graham and the wedding. Mary wonders if her relief at not having to endure Mother on her own anymore has turned into loneliness. She phones Trish and they spend hours moaning about the masses of homework they're expected to magic out of their minds. The differences between school and college now seem few. Mary invites Trish for coffee in her sitting room with her college friends without worrying that she'll feel left out.

Now she sees more of Trish, Mary feels awkward with Ada. The renewal of their relationship seems to have been a stepping stone to finding Trish again. She goes back to thinking of her as Mrs Bellamy.

Mary's tutor has arranged an appointment for her with the careers office. Mary sits on the hard chair opposite Mrs Bellamy's desk and they talk about university choices and career possibilities with a Modern Languages degree. Mary has already confided in Mrs Bellamy and told her she'd like to work in Paris. The question is which career to aim for. Translators or teachers are all very well if she works in England. But to work in France, she must choose a career that will be suitable over there.

"The French are very hot on qualifications," says Mrs Bellamy. "Before you choose a course, you could take a gap year and work there. Then, if you discover you don't like the French way of life after all, you can do a different degree course."

It's an ideal opportunity to escape from the lies in the love nest at home.

"How can I find a job from here in England? Are there listings or something?"

"Don't you want to think about it first and discuss it with your mother?"

"No."

Mrs Bellamy lifts a hand to arrange her stray hairs behind her ears, remembers her hair is short and lets it drop back into her lap. "I'll look into it for you. I think schools take language assistants. Alternatively, you could go to a French university for a year and study French on a foreign students' course."

This second idea sounds even better. She's never worked before – she always resisted the popular trend of Saturday jobs. When Graham arrived and showered Mother with money, he opened a bank account for Mary and pays a meagre allowance into it. She spends as little as possible. She doesn't want to be any deeper in his debt than necessary.

"I'll find out about both," says Mrs Bellamy. "But you must talk to your mother about it. You'll need her help to fund a gap year."

"Mother's only interested in her wedding."

"Oh? She's marrying Graham?"

Mary nods.

"Isn't that good news?"

"I suppose so."

"Hmm. Have you had a fight with them?"

Mary nods again.

"Oh, Mary. Was it about the wedding?"

Mrs Bellamy's manner is cautious. Mary can feel her tiptoeing towards what she really wants to know.

"No. It was about my father."

"Did you ask–?"

"She says there's nothing more to add."

Mrs Bellamy jumps up and bangs her hand on the table. "She promised, dammit!"

Mary leans forward. "What did she promise?"

Mrs Bellamy folds her arms and then unfolds them again. She grips the edge of the desk.

"I'm going to tell you, since your mother hasn't. I've been trying to persuade her to tell you for years, but she's been too scared of your reaction. She knows she should. She even promised me she would."

"Surprise, surprise," mutters Mary.

Mrs Bellamy takes a deep breath. Mary's mind detaches

from her body and drifts a little above it. So the cliché is true: people really do take a deep breath before saying something difficult.

"Your father ... well, he didn't die when you were a baby. He and your mother split up after your birth, but he didn't die."

Mary wills her on.

"I never knew him," Mrs Bellamy continues, "but I met your mother just after he left. She was alone with you, so I'd go up Wymer Hill every day and help her out. She was so angry with him that she swore she'd tell you he was dead. She wouldn't even say his name. I tried to persuade her it was important for you to know the truth, but she wouldn't listen. I'm afraid she only ever thought about herself. She didn't want you to find him when you were older and let him have the pleasure of enjoying a relationship with you. She resented him skipping the hard bit at the beginning. She wished he was dead, and in her mind I think she imagined him dead. She had awful post-natal depression – that wasn't your fault, of course. Anyway, we had a row about it. She refused to speak to me until last year, when you were seeing Gus. That's when she promised me she'd tell you the truth."

Thirty-six, thirty-seven. Mary notices a persistent pain in her leg and realises she's pinching it. She forces her hands into her lap and carefully interlinks her fingers. "Did she tell you why they split up?"

Mrs Bellamy looks puzzled. She sits back down. "No. Listen: what I'm trying to tell you is that your father is still alive. He's out there somewhere."

She looks expectantly at Mary. She's waiting for an

excitement that Mary can't summon.

"I'm not interested."

Mrs Bellamy strokes Mary's arm. "You poor thing. It must be a shock to learn you have a father after so long. You need time to digest the news."

There's a knock on the door. Mrs Bellamy calls to the person to wait for a few minutes.

"Think about what I've told you. If you want me to help you trace him, let me know. I'm here for you, even if it's just to talk."

"I don't want to delve into the past." Mary closes her notebook and slides it into her bag.

"But–"

"Look: thanks for telling me the truth. I appreciate it. Honestly. But I can't look backwards. It's not important anymore." She stands up. "So you'll find out about the France business for me?"

"France?" Mrs Bellamy looks lost. "Oh, yes, of course."

Mary opens the door. Mrs Bellamy hurries around the desk.

"Are you sure you're all right?"

Mary nods. She would like to be honest with Mrs Bellamy, but being honest would mean reliving the past. She can't risk that.

She leaves the building. As the door closes behind her, Jed calls to her to come and play pool. She ignores him and counts the seventy-six steps to the library. How many more lies are left to discover?

CHAPTER THIRTY

Rainbow

When Rainbow scored fifteen out of twenty in the first history test of her second year at *lycée*, Sylvia was amazed. They left the classroom block together and Sylvia demanded to know who in the commune specialised in miracles. Rainbow laughed.

"Nobody yet, unfortunately. I've decided I need my bac."

"What for? Is your mum nagging?"

"No, she couldn't care less. And for Domi, a bac is a boat."

Rainbow felt great. She never imagined she'd get such a buzz from succeeding in anything so unnatural as a written test. It had been much easier than she'd thought. Schoolwork was simply a case of learning textbook words and then regurgitating them. It was nothing to do with finding answers.

"Why, then?" asked Sylvia. "We've still got this year and next before the bac finals."

"I'll show you in the library. Madame Cartier is helping me

research careers."

"Careers? Libraries? What about your trees?"

"Careers working with trees, stupid. With the French Forestry Commission, for example."

"Do you need a bac for that?"

Sylvia had decided to be a sports teacher because she was crazy about sport. Everything was straightforward for Sylvia. The other students found Rainbow bizarre because she lived in the commune, but Sylvia accepted her gift and treated her like anyone else.

"I don't know what qualifications I need. That's what I'm about to find out. Don't mention it to anyone from the commune though." Rainbow grimaced. "Domi wants me to be a palm-reader and live in the commune for ever."

"Oh, can you?"

Rainbow glanced sideways at Sylvia. "Can I what? Read palms?"

"Yeah."

"Of course. There's nothing spiritual in that. It's just a question of learning what the lines mean and tuning in to your client. It's not like healing."

They walked towards the library. Sylvia often ran or cycled to the commune on her training circuit and had become an extension of the family. She'd been the only one to show any signs of disappointment when Christophe had left. The other commune members, after a few months of adapting to only seeing him once a week when he popped in, were pleased he'd found his vocation and was building his own life. Sylvia had admitted that she found him cute and missed him. She was tall, blonde and pretty, and although her sporty aura attracted lots of boys, she never noticed them. You had to say things straight to Sylvia. Rainbow had never met anyone with such a limited field of perception. Sylvia didn't get vibes. Rainbow, who depended on vibes, could tell that Christophe wasn't romantically interested in Sylvia. He was more likely to want a mysterious, secretive girlfriend; someone weak who needed his strength and stability.

"So Domi's given up on trees?" said Sylvia.

"I think he's lost. He's been waiting for a sign for so long that he's finally decided I should heal one tree at a time, for free."

She looked at Sylvia to see if she was really listening, and decided she was.

"I need to do something more than healing the odd tree here and there. I'm sure I've got a bigger destiny than that. But I'm not going to find it by sitting in the commune and waiting."

"Bravo," said Sylvia. She applauded and then ducked into the library to avoid Rainbow's punch.

Back at Le Logis, Rainbow took the librarian's documents out of her bag and slid them into the top drawer of her desk. There was no chance anyone would find them in her bedroom. One of the useful aspects of having Christophe's old room was that people had already established the habit of not entering.

The commune people were so entrenched in their habits. Time passed slowly here and nothing exciting ever happened. She had to get away and begin her real life. Christophe had gone through this phase too. As for Sylvia, she had always been restless. She'd talked about leaving home the whole time Rainbow had known her.

Rainbow didn't want to waste her life, not like Mum, whose life had been completely pointless. She still wrote songs, sold some and sang with bands in the surrounding towns, but she wasn't growing. Domi was the same: he wasn't advancing in his quest to save the world. If anything, he was retreating. The commune, which had seemed to be a stepping stone to her destiny, now felt like a broken bridge. She wanted to do something important, to make something of her life and her gift. She had to do it for Michael. She closed her eyes and saw his face as if the accident had been yesterday and not four years ago.

That evening in bed she took out the Forestry Commission leaflets. Her excitement mounted as she read through the possible career paths. At the end they listed the necessary qualifications. Her heart plummeted. You needed science to work with trees, for some reason. They wanted a scientific or specific agricultural baccalaureate. You also had to be French. The only baccalaureate stream possible for her had been literary, given her dread of science and numbers. A career with the French Forestry Commission was out of reach.

Each attempt to find a job in which she could use her gift finished in failure. Her tree business had scared people away. A month ago, she'd managed to organise an interview with the journalist from the local newspaper. She'd planned to publicise her work in the paper and invite offers to hire her. But the meeting with the journalist had ended in disaster. She was never going to succeed.

That weekend, Christophe took Rainbow into the motorbike shop below his flat. There was an object shrouded by a bedsheet in the middle of the oily workshop. He whisked the sheet into the air and exposed the project that had obsessed him for the whole summer. Rainbow drew in a breath and whistled. The motorbike was red, chrome and black. It was beautiful in its glossy cleanliness: silent and powerful. She mistrusted its perfection.

"It's yours," he said.

Rainbow turned slowly away from the motorbike and looked up at him.

"What? You can't give it to me."

"It's an early present for your eighteenth birthday."

"I can't accept it. It's far too big a present. I haven't even got a licence."

"I'll drive you around on it until you get one."

"But you've spent so much time rebuilding it."

Christophe reddened. "It's a present, okay? You don't refuse presents."

"Sorry. I mean, thanks." Rainbow's cheek colour matched his. "Thanks loads. Shall we go out on it now?"

He grinned, eager to demonstrate its prowess. "Of course. The beach?"

He knew she loved the coast in September, and she knew he loved the stretches of road leading to it. They knew a lot about each other. But since he'd moved away from the commune the year before, she found it difficult to read him. It had been novel to visit her 'brother' in his independent life at first. Then she began to feel awkward with him, and he seemed less brotherly. They were no longer the kids who'd grown up together. They still saw each other regularly, at parties in his flat and at the Cognac festivals, but she hadn't expected this present. The weight of it squashed her intestines flat.

He threw her the leathers he'd borrowed and opened the garage door while she pulled them on. Then he started up the engine. He ran his hands over the bike's body and examined the chrome tubes lovingly before beckoning her to sit behind him. She hesitated, then slipped her arms around his waist.

It was a perfect Sunday. The sun warmed her back as he steered the bike through the streets of Cognac and onto the main roads. He liked speed. So did she, and the exhilaration dispelled her uneasiness. Unlike Domi, Christophe rode with abandon. He was part of the bike, a predator, weaving and racing through forest and plain.

When they pulled into an empty car park under the pine trees an hour later, she was high on recklessness. She slid off the warm leather, aware of his eyes on her, and stretched her legs. Then she unfastened her helmet and shook out her long, brown hair. The nerves throughout her body were still vibrating.

"That was brilliant," she said.

The bike looked less threatening now. Dust and heat had softened its shining expectations.

Christophe remained silent. He was staring in her direction. She glanced over her shoulder to see if something behind her had captured his attention. There was nothing obvious.

"What is it?"

He picked up a spiral bike lock and held out his hand for Rainbow's helmet.

"Nothing."

She made sure their hands didn't touch when she passed it to him. And she kept a step ahead of him when they crossed the road and walked towards the dune that separated them from the sea.

"Let's dune-jump," she said.

"Okay. First one to the top can choose the dune."

She raced up the shifting slope of warm sand, but he overtook her and reached the summit first. Rather than admiring the expanse of the Atlantic, as Rainbow always did, he turned and taunted her as she puffed towards him. She collapsed a few metres away. He laughed.

"You should do more sport, Rainette."

"I climb with Sylvia. That's sport."

She refused the hand he offered to help her up. The view captivated her, and she reached for the sketch pad in her pocket.

"Come on, daydreamer. We're jumping from that one." Christophe pointed to the lip of a dune with a huge drop beneath it.

"No way. It's too dangerous."

"I'll jump first. If I break a leg you needn't follow."

"Why do you always choose the biggest ones? We'd have loads more fun doing lots of smaller ones."

"I like watching your face when you're on the edge."

He turned and led the way. She stuck her tongue out at his back and followed him.

"This time I'll jump straightaway. You'll see."

He reached the edge, waved at her and then flung himself into the air with characteristic disregard for the danger. Her chest constricted and she rushed forwards to watch. He landed, rolled and whooped.

"Enorme! Your turn now."

Despite her intentions, Rainbow hesitated. "You're in the way. I might land on you."

He grinned up at her and slithered to the left.

"Is that a log sticking out of the sand?"

He pulled out a knobble of driftwood and threw it to one side.

"There aren't any glass bottles, are there?" she asked.

"Not that I can see. There are probably lots of broken ones under the surface, though."

"Shut up! Right, I'm coming."

"Really?"

She ignored his laugh. With a frown of concentration, she stepped over the edge.

Thud! Her eyes sprang open on impact and she rolled into him.

"Congratulations. That was record time," he said.

He was sitting on his heels, his back to the sea. She looked up at him. His brown eyes were fixed on hers. She couldn't look away. This wasn't the Christophe she'd grown up with. She had no idea who this man was.

"Rainbow," he whispered.

He took her hands to pull her up and leaned forwards. Their lips met. The crash of ocean waves was the clash of cymbals at the climax of a symphony. Rainbow cringed at her clichéd thought and opened her eyes.

The mysterious stranger had disappeared. All she could see was the vulnerable fifteen year old she'd met years before.

She drew back. He was watching her. The soft brown of his irises turned brittle. She stood up. A heavy pain pulsed beneath her breasts.

"I'm sorry," she said.

He winced. Then he turned his back to her and pulled his knees up to his chest. She placed a hand on his shoulder. He shrugged it off.

"Is there someone else?" he asked.

"No. It just doesn't feel right. I'm sorry."

"Stop apologising. It's not your fault."

She sighed. "You know I really like you–"

"But only as a friend. I'm not your type and all that." He stood up. "Come on, let's walk."

As much as she wanted to console him, she knew the subject was closed. They started to walk along the sand. She felt as if her centre of gravity was in her ankles.

After ten minutes, they turned in silent consensus and returned to the motorbike. It stood, lonely, under a pine tree, its optimistic brightness out of place among the greens and browns of the forest.

CHAPTER THIRTY-ONE

Mary

Spring always has this effect on Mary. Sap rises in her bloodstream and swells her energy levels until she feels the need to blossom. But she doesn't know how to blossom, and so the pressure builds up. For nearly two years she has retained a polite veneer with Graham. She must prevent it from cracking at all costs.

He'd promised not to act as a father. Yet the minute he and Mother were married, his stale presence bloated until it filled the atmosphere at home. He has started having talks with her: talks about her future (pretend to listen); talks about drugs (nod and look suitably impressed); and talks about boys (control that snigger).

The worst talks are those about Mother. He lectures Mary about being respectful and then advises her to humour Mother's literary dreams. It's all right for Mary to ridicule Mother's writing but she bristles with annoyance when Graham says Mother needs her 'little scribbling activities' to keep her healthy. He's never heard her sing properly. He's never seen her surrounded by admiring fans. Does he say this to gain popularity with Mary, to pretend he's on her side? If so, he has miscalculated.

She's now on the lookout for any other slyness concerning Mother, and is more determined than ever to keep her distance from greasy Graham.

⁂

One Saturday night in April, she switches on the television to see if any French films are being shown. She's been revising for her A levels, which are in a month's time, and deserves a treat.

She is lucky. Manon is running across arid scrubland with her goats. Mary turns up the volume and lies back on her floor cushion. She props her head against the settee and closes her eyes. She knows *Manon des Sources* by heart, and wants to avoid cheating by unconsciously reading the subtitles. There should be a village scene now. But Mary can hear someone knocking hard on wood.

She opens her eyes. No one on the television is knocking. It's her front door.

She jumps up, flicks off the television and hurries towards the frantic banging. The panic she can sense through the heavy wooden door is contagious. She wrenches it open without checking the spy hole.

Trish bursts into the room.

"Shit! Oh shit!" She paces around the settee.

Mary closes the door. "What is it?"

Trish doesn't seem to hear her. On her third tour of the settee, Mary grabs her arms and forces her to stop. Trish glares at her. Then she sinks onto the settee and drags her fingers through her unusually dishevelled hair.

"Shit, shit, shit!" she moans.

She slumps forward, her head in her hands. Mary drops to her knees in front of her. "Tell me, Trish. What's happened?"

Trish groans, wails "Shit!" and bursts into tears.

Mary sits beside her and squeezes her clenched shoulders. She feels inadequate. Her "there, there" sounds ridiculous. She waits. Eventually, Trish's wails calm to sobs. Mary pours her a glass of water.

"Tha-anks," hiccups Trish.

She takes a gulp, chokes and then goggles wild-eyed at the ceiling as she gasps for breath. Mary snatches back the glass and thumps her on the back until she recovers. Trish takes another sip.

"It's Mam," she says.

"What? Has she had an accident?"

"No."

Mary lets out the breath she'd held.

"It's worse," says Trish.

"What could be worse? She's not ... dead, is she?"

"No, but I wish she was."

Mary bites her lip. She thinks she knows what's coming.

"She's having an affair," says Trish.

Mary isn't sure how to react. She decides not to feign surprise.

"What makes you say that?"

"I've just seen her. In the pub." Trish shudders. "With a

horrible salesman-like bloke."

"Maybe he's just a friend."

Trish looks scornful. "They were snogging, Mary."

"Oh." There's a silence. "Which pub?"

"Who cares which pub?" Trish sniffs and snatches the tissue Mary offers her. "The Queen's Arms. We don't usually go there because it's full of oldies. But Helen wanted to try it out tonight."

"Where's Helen now?"

"At home. She's got a horse show tomorrow. She spotted them snogging when she went out to the toilets."

Typical Helen. She could have kept her big mouth shut.

"Did your mum see you?"

Trish shook her head. "How could she do it? What about us? Don't we count for her anymore?"

"Of course you do. You know she loves you all."

"Yeah, right. Not Dad though. Do you think she'll leave him, like Helen's mum did? And will she take Jimmy and me with her, or will she leave us too?"

"You should ask your mum. Tell her you saw her in the pub."

"No. I'm never, ever going to talk to her again." Trish picks up a cushion and hugs it.

"You poor thing. I can guess how terrible you must feel," says Mary.

"No, you can't."

Mary remembers how she felt when she saw Mrs Bellamy with Philip. She can't explain that to Trish. But if she can get Trish to talk to her mum then at least Trish will know her mum has no intention of leaving her family.

"I really think you should talk to her."

"What if she says she's going to run off with him?"

"She won't do that."

"How do you know?"

"Because she's not like that; she's not like Helen's mum."

"Maybe she is, after all. How can I ever trust her again? I thought I knew her, but she's not the same person anymore." Tears reappear in Trish's eyes and she blows her nose.

Mary stands up. "Look, you won't know if you don't speak to her."

"Thanks for your sympathy." Trish's voice is sarcastic.

"I *am* sympathetic. But there's no point speculating about what may happen when you could simply ask her outright."

"It's all right for you. It's second nature for you to demand explanations," retorts Trish. She narrows her eyes. "You ask her. Then you can tell me what she says."

"Trish! I can't do that. This is between you and your mum."

Trish sighs and looks around the sitting room. "Let me stay here tonight and I'll talk to her tomorrow."

"Well … All right, then."

She makes up a bed for Trish on the settee and offers to sleep in the room with her. Trish says she wants to be alone. She turns on the television and climbs into the sleeping bag. Mary creeps up to bed.

That night she debates whether to be completely honest with Trish. She doesn't want to make things more difficult for her. As she drops into a fitful sleep, she wonders whether Mother had the same debate with herself *before*.

Sunday is the only day Graham doesn't work. He likes to have his Sunday roast at lunchtime, and calls it the family moment of the week. For Mary, it highlights everything her family lacks. She tries to have an activity planned so she doesn't have to eat with them.

Today, with Trish lying red-eyed on her settee, she cancels her planned trip to the ice rink and encourages Trish to go home and face her mum. Trish looks miserable as she leaves. Mary silently wishes Mrs Bellamy luck as she watches Trish stumble through the rain to her car. When Trish has gone, Mary wanders into the kitchen.

"Isn't Trish staying for lunch?" asks Mother.

Mary shakes her head and avoids further questions by asking Graham if he needs any help with the cooking.

"No, thanks, it's all in hand. Go and sit down."

She pours herself a glass of water and forces herself to take it to the table rather than following her instinct to disobey him and drink it at the kitchen sink. She mustn't antagonise him. She wants to broach the subject of funding her gap year in France.

She's received details from several universities that advertise 'FLE' courses: "Français langue étrangère," she says to herself. The words set off a buzz of anticipation. It'll be another new beginning. She'll be a new Mary. "Marie," she whispers, lingering over the husk of the 'r'. She'll shed her Englishness with her clothes when she arrives in Paris and become a French Marie, with a French haircut, French friends and French clothes. Katia Murville won't recognise her.

Graham and Mother join her at the table. Mother says how nice it is to be together for a meal, and Mary sighs.

Sometimes she thinks she preferred the dizzy mother to this Graham-friendly version of her. She waits until both Graham and her mother have their mouths full, and then launches into her mission.

"I'm going to take a year out before I start uni."

There are surprised noises in reply. Neither of them would speak with their mouths full, so she's able to explain her plans without interruption. She doesn't stop until she gets to the delicate part about money.

"If you'd like to support me, you could fund my year. Otherwise I'll get a job to pay for it myself," she finishes.

She's not used to asking for help, and doesn't think her words sound particularly persuasive. She hopes they'll finance her. If they don't, she'll need to work for a year to save enough.

"Can we see the details?" asks Graham.

"Of course we'll pay, love," says Mother.

"But we'd like to see the paperwork first," insists Graham.

Mary jumps up from the table. She ignores Graham's suggestion to wait until they've finished eating, and runs upstairs to her bedroom. She pulls the brochures from her bedside table, hurries back to the table with them and sits down again. She hands them to Graham.

"We'll look through them over coffee," he says.

He tosses them onto a chair behind him. One slips to the floor. Mary controls her urge to slam it back onto the chair with the others. Let Graham play his power games; she doesn't care as long as he pays.

The meal drags on forever. Graham chews at least sixteen times on each mouthful. Mother talks about a new character that has arrived in a story she's either writing or reading – Mary can't tell which. Graham nods at Mother and manages to ask Mary questions about her studies without interrupting the flow of Mother's monologue.

"Do stop tapping against the table leg," he says to Mary at one point.

Mary stills her leg. She concentrates on the gobs of rain slithering down the windowpanes to distract her from her forced state of obedience.

At last the meal is over. Mother makes coffee while Graham and Mary go into the sitting room. The brochures remain unopened on Graham's lap. He launches into one of his talks, this time about the increase in teenage clinical depression and the possible link with drugs (nod from time to time). He's so interested in teenage downfalls that she wonders whether he only married Mother so he could study Mary's behaviour and compare it to his statistics.

She pulls back her sleeve as if glancing at a watch. Graham reacts to the hint. He looks at the covers of the three brochures and then stretches out his wrinkled neck to look at her.

"Paris, eh? Did I ever tell you about my time there?"

"No. Do you know the universities?"

Graham shakes his head and opens the top brochure with his scaly hands. He studies the first page. He intends to read every single word of each brochure. She closes her eyes and takes a deep breath.

"Shall I come back when you've finished?"

"No, stay there. I may have some questions as I read." He looks up and smiles humourlessly at her. "Patience is a virtue, young lady."

She waits. Rain drums against the new, double-glazed windows. Mother washes up and listens to classical music in the kitchen, probably swigging from the sherry bottle in secret. Graham sits and plays with Mary's future, his legs crossed effeminately and his glasses barnacled to his nose by his perpetual frown. She criss-crosses her nails on the leather armrest in series of eights and waits for his verdict.

She won't be surprised if he refuses to pay. He's bound to believe that young people should work to pay their way. He thinks she's flighty, impatient, rude and spoilt, all of which can be cured by his life lessons and good, hard work. And probably a war. She hates this feeling of dependence, especially when it ties her to someone she doesn't like.

It takes an hour for Graham to satisfy himself that she's serious about studying in France. He suggests she should find a university in a small town, where day-to-day life is cheaper than in Paris, and agrees to pay.

"I'll increase your monthly allowance to pay for lodgings, food and books. It'll only just be enough to live on. You'll have to be careful. Money doesn't grow on trees," he says.

Mary agrees to look into other destinations, thanks him and pulls her stiff body from the armchair. She can't remember ever having sat still for so long.

Her heart is set on Paris. She'll wait for a few weeks and then tell him that only Parisian universities teach French to foreign students. She stretches, picks up the brochures and leaves him to his Sunday afternoon snooze. It's time to call Trish to see how she fared with her mum.

CHAPTER THIRTY-TWO

Mary

Mary rings Trish straight after leaving Graham to his Sunday afternoon nap. James Bellamy answers and tells her that Trish is at Helen's that afternoon and is staying the night. Mary doesn't trust herself to keep her temper with Helen. She decides she'll skive her English class the following afternoon so she can catch Trish at her school gates.

Monday passes slowly, with Mary's thoughts circling around Trish and Mrs Bellamy. Her lecturers spoon out advice in preparation for A levels, using the same words she heard for her GCSEs two years earlier. At school the teachers had said that GCSEs were the most important exams for their futures. Now, the lecturers are telling them it's their A levels that really count. More lies. More twisting of facts to suit themselves. No doubt at university they'll be told their degree exams are the only ones that mean anything. She's sick of being continually tested to prove she exists.

She's eating lunch with Jed when Mrs Bellamy walks into

the refectory and looks around. Mary slips out of her chair and hides behind the tray trolley. Jed raises his eyebrows, but he doesn't ask any questions. As soon as Mrs Bellamy has gone, she sits back down. Jed knows Mrs Bellamy is Trish's mum, and he tells Mary he saw Trish in town last night. She was crying her eyes out and looked drunk. A blonde chick was holding her up. Mary curses Helen. Who needs a friend like that?

At four o'clock she arrives at the gates of her hated school. The bell rings, and children push and shove their way out of the doors. She retreats across the road to sit on a wall and flattens herself into the brickwork. She dreads seeing Mr Higgins.

The younger classes, in strict school uniform, leave first. The Year 11s, boasting customised touches to their navy and white, saunter out after them. The Year 12s and 13s, who have no uniform, leave a suitable interval before revealing their fashionably dressed selves.

Mary spots Trish. She jumps off the wall and dashes across the road between the buses. Trish's top is crumpled, there are stains on her jeans, and her denim jacket has a rip at the elbow. As for her hair, it's loose and hangs in dank, ginger rats' tails. The way she's walking shocks Mary the most: her shoulders are slumped, and her face, which is usually fixed on the horizon, is turned miserably to the ground. Mary calls out her name. Trish looks up and manages a pathetic smile. There are dark circles under her eyes.

"What are you doing here? Haven't you got lectures?"

"Not this afternoon," lies Mary. "I've come to see how you are."

They walk towards Trish's car. Mary links arms with her, and she stoops a little less.

"Where's Helen?" asks Mary.

"That bitch? Who cares?"

Mary rubs her arm, overwhelmed by a rush of protectiveness.

Trish drives them to Mary's flat in her Fiesta. As soon as they're inside, Trish drops her bag, puts *Brothers in Arms* in the CD player and collapses onto the settee. She squashes a cushion in her arms.

Mary doesn't listen to music anymore. Not since Gus. She prefers silence. In silence you can feel things happening around you. There's potential in silence. People are more attentive and quicker to react. She doesn't need this aural drug that hides possibilities like make-up. She only puts on CDs when visiting friends insist. Most of them are ill at ease in silence.

She makes two cups of tea and then sits on a floor cushion opposite Trish.

"So? What did your mum say?"

Trish closes her eyes.

Mary sighs. "You didn't even go home, did you?"

"Not exactly," says Trish.

No wonder Mrs Bellamy was looking for Mary at college today.

"So you haven't said anything to her yet? You didn't ring her?"

Trish shakes her head. "I told you: I'm never going to speak to her again."

"You won't get anything sorted by burying your head in the sand."

"There's nothing to get sorted. She's cheating on us. She doesn't deserve to have a chance to explain herself."

"You can't live with someone and not speak to them–" She stops. It's what she did with her own mother for years.

The thought of Trish treating Mrs Bellamy as she has treated her own mother shocks her. Then her shock shocks her again. Why should she feel differently towards Mrs Bellamy? There's really no difference. Mrs Bellamy has done the same thing as her own mother. She has lied; lied by not telling the truth. Mary pinches her thigh in anticipation of the usual bitter wave of hate.

There's nothing. She thinks about Mother's words when she was unconscious. Still nothing. No bitterness. No reaction at all.

Trish is staring at her. Mary releases her thigh and rubs her forehead.

"Sorry? What did you say?"

Absolutely nothing. No emotion, not even a trickle of acid. This authentic nothingness is new and strange.

"I said I'm not going to live with her," repeats Trish. "I'm going to move in with you."

"But–"

Trish stands up. She is taller, heavier and more determined than Mary has ever seen her.

"I don't give a toss about what Mum and Dad will or won't let me do. I'm eighteen. I can do what I want. I'm not going back there to listen to her lies. So can I stay here or do I have to find a doorway to sleep in?"

There are tears in Trish's eyes, despite her tough words. She plumps back down onto the settee. Mary comes and sits beside her.

"Why don't you listen to what your mum has to say? Then, if you can't bear to live with her, you can come back here."

"I need some time to think about things before I can look at her." She sniffs and takes a tissue.

"All right. You can stay here a couple of days. You'd better go home for your toothbrush and school things, though."

Trish hugs her. "Thanks, Mary. You're a true friend. I'll go now. She won't be back from work yet." She squeezes into her jacket and grabs her bag. "See you later."

Mary follows her to the door. So much for not getting involved.

"Don't forget to leave a note saying where you are," she adds.

Trish is already running towards her car, her energy restored. Mary sighs and leans her head against the door. Its solid wood is strangely comforting.

🌿🍃🌿

Mary's flat changes appearance overnight, and by Tuesday afternoon the atmosphere is no longer one of empty secrecy. Trish's clothes drape over cushions, a sleeping bag curls up on the settee and books and pens are wedged between candles on the shelf. Make-up spills over the surfaces in the bathroom. Even Mary's bedroom has altered: she has fixed up the old wallpapering board on two trestles in a corner to give herself a place to study away from Trish's noise. Her flat has come to life.

On Tuesday evening they rush to eat in the shared kitchen

with Mother before Graham gets home from work. Mary warns Trish that she won't be able to avoid Mrs Bellamy at college for much longer, and Trish promises to talk to her the following evening after school.

Graham arrives from work. They stop whispering and stand up to leave. He kisses Mother on the cheek and then lays his scaly hand on Mary's arm.

"I want to speak to you. Alone."

Trish goes into Mary's sitting room and Mary sits back down at the kitchen table.

"If it's about the universities, I haven't had a chance to find other towns yet."

"No, it's about your friend."

"Trish? What about her?"

"May I ask how long she intends to stay?"

Mother looks up. "Has she been sleeping here?"

Mary raises her eyes to the ceiling. Some things never change.

"She's going home tomorrow."

Graham loads his fork with a little carrot slice, a tiny dollop of mashed potato and a cube of lamb chop. "I presume her parents know what's going on?"

"Of course."

"I hope so, Mary. I don't want to harbour any runaways under my roof."

How can Mother stand such a pompous git?

"She's not a runaway."

"Indeed? If she's still here after tomorrow, I'll consider her a runaway. And I'll have to think again about France."

Mary clamps her lips shut, squashing the insult before it leaps from her mouth. She pushes back her chair and walks out of the room. It doesn't hurt him to have Trish in the house. He's mean, manipulative and power-crazy.

There are no lessons on Wednesday afternoons at college. Mary hurries to the library to write an English essay in her favourite corner. She doesn't like English much. There's no connection between the poems they study and real life. And the novels were written so long ago that they're irrelevant to today's problems. Her lecturer gives her Bs. He says she lacks the zest of passion to bring her up to an A. She doesn't care. Who can feel passionate about girls in long skirts who didn't dare speak their minds? She's only taken English because she passed the GCSE and she needs two A levels to study French at university. It's a means to an end. University is a means to an end too. The end is a life in France, far away from *before*. If she finds work in Paris, she may not even bother with university.

It's difficult to concentrate once she starts thinking about Paris. She stares out of the window. Twenty-four students are lounging on the college lawn. Mary squints to see if she can recognise anyone, but she's too high up. She wishes she were back in the Eiffel Tower, looking down over the Champ de Mars and its precise green shapes. The French know about keeping nature in order: their public gardens are nicely under control. She turns back to her English folder and gasps. Mrs

Bellamy is standing there, her hands on her hips.

"I thought I'd find you here. Do you mind?"

She lowers herself into a chair without waiting for an answer. Mary fixes her eyes on her folder.

"I must talk to you about Trish," says Mrs Bellamy. "She hasn't been home since Sunday. Is she really staying with you?"

Mary nods.

"Is she in some sort of trouble?"

"No."

A student nearby makes an annoyed 'tut'. Mrs Bellamy leans forward.

"She's guessed about Philip, hasn't she?"

"I can't say anything," whispers Mary.

"Has someone told her?"

"Can't you see the difficult position you're putting me in? She's coming to talk to you this evening. You can ask her then."

A ripple of 'shushes' riles Mary. She stands up and strides into an empty aisle of books. Mrs Bellamy follows.

"If the problem's Philip, and she refuses to understand when I tell her about him, will you look out for her?"

"Of course. That's what I'm already doing."

Mrs Bellamy looks relieved. She pats Mary's shoulder. "Thank you, Mary."

Mary watches her bustle away. Despite Mrs Bellamy's anxiety, she's as robust as ever. There are no signs of a breakdown. No tears. Just an admirable 'let's get this sorted' attitude.

When Mary gets home that evening, Trish has already left. Mary tidies her flat and wonders how Trish and Mrs

Bellamy are getting on.

At 9 p.m. her front door swings open. Trish is back.

CHAPTER THIRTY-THREE

Mary

Out in the garden behind Mary's house, the grass needs cutting. It's Saturday, a week after Trish saw her mum and Philip in the pub, and Mary has to do her house jobs. She pushes open the kitchen door and shuts it on Graham's voice telling her to mind the pear-tree roots. He's home for lunch.

Of the tasks he has allocated her, gardening is the one she dislikes the most. She's responsible for mowing the lawn and weed-killing. Both are destructive, which pleases her, although she'd rather not go into the garden at all. The rest of the gardening is left to Mother, who spends hours on one tiny job and then does nothing for weeks. Graham regularly inspects the level of perfection of the flower beds but doesn't appear to take any pleasure from them. Mary has never seen him smile spontaneously. He probably only does that at his golf club.

She unlocks the shed and wheels out the electric lawnmower. The lawn is on the original house's side. It's a long, thin strip, divided into two by a wobbly stone path that grates on the lawnmower blade as she pushes it along. At the far end of the lawn are some withered pear trees. Their roots make knobbles in the lawn, exposing themselves to the sharp lawnmower blade.

She navigates the first length of the lawn. It's hot under the late April sun and she stops to take off her jumper. There's movement next door. The Flints must be out in their garden. She peers over the fence to see if Mark the phobia weirdo is there. Only his parents are in sight. Mark must still be at boarding school. She imagines him sitting indoors, wearing a tin World War II helmet and preparing for his A levels.

She nods at Mrs Flint and continues mowing. It's a shame Mark isn't there because she's sure Trish would like him. Trish could do with a boyfriend to take her mind off her relationship with her mum. He's supposedly intelligent, which is one of Trish's boyfriend criteria. She'll introduce them when Mark comes home for the holidays.

Trish confronted her mum last Wednesday and was told the truth. Mrs Bellamy had been right: Trish refused to accept that her mum had a long-term lover. She's staying with Mary while she digests the lie she feels her whole life has been. Mary empathises. She tried to share the truth of *before* with her, but it proved impossible to distil her emotions into words.

Graham appears on the patio, on cue, the moment she turns to cut the last strip – the difficult one next to the flower bed, where she has to be careful not to let the mower slide off the lawn and cut up the plants. His presence unnerves her. She has to yank the mower back into line several times before she finishes. The damage isn't too bad: only a few leaves hashed and a couple of flower heads flattened.

Putting off the moment she'll have to walk past him and hear his complaint, she bends down and examines a mangled French marigold leaf. Why is it French? In a translation she did a few weeks ago she learnt that the French call it 'Indian': *l'oeillet d'Inde*. She takes a dark green leaf and rubs it between her thumb and forefinger.

The contact with the bleeding leaf is repulsive. She drops it, wipes her fingers on her jeans and shivers. It reminds her of the accident and the shock of waking up afterwards. Until last week, she had always been overcome by hate for her mother when her memory arrived there, and she would flounder in its force. But now the hate has receded. In its place, she sees an image of Michael. *Please, not Michael.* She counts thirteen marigold flowers before the image fades.

"You could have cut the grass shorter," says Graham. He kicks lumps of damp cuttings to spread them out. "And used the bag attachment to pick up the bits."

"If I'd cut it shorter, I'd have damaged the pear-tree roots," she retorts.

Graham takes the mower from her. He wheels it backwards and then passes three times over a corner Mary hadn't bothered with. She turns to walk towards the back door.

"Wait a minute, young lady. I've got words to have with you."

Why can't he speak normally? Mary stops and pulls a neutral expression over her sullenness. Graham will enjoy his power more if she lets her resentment show.

"Where's your friend?" he asks.

"Out."

"I don't understand why she's still living with us. Didn't I make myself clear last Tuesday?"

"She's going through a difficult patch with her parents. They know she's here."

"I think I'll ring them and check."

The strain from cheering up Trish and resisting the memories of *before* overcomes her.

"Are you calling me a liar?"

She can no longer keep everything inside. It all needs to come out, even though she knows he won't cower before her and that her provocation will only result in her losing. She wills him to retaliate. He almost smiles as he takes up her challenge.

"Are you lying?"

"Ring the Bellamys and you'll find out."

"I'll do that. Meanwhile, you can tell her to pack her bags. The best thing for a teenager going through a difficult patch is to be grounded."

"She needs some space at the moment. In fact," Mary takes a step closer, "her mum asked me to look after her. She understands, unlike you."

"In that case, Mrs Bellamy should have come to me. Not to you."

"What for? To hear you lecture her on how to deal with Trish?"

"I only lecture disobedient children."

"Well, lecture away. I'm not listening."

She puts her hands over her ears and hums loudly and tunelessly. Graham shakes his head and turns to push the mower back to the shed. She can't believe he has given up already. What sort of fighter is he? She takes her hands away from her ears. Some reptilian instinct makes him glance back right at that moment.

"It's a shame you insist on being disobedient, Mary."

"It's a shame you're such a control freak."

His back stiffens. He swivels slowly around to face her. "If that girl is still here tonight, you can forget your trip to France."

Mary doesn't reply. She strides into the house and kicks off her trainers. His smug smile burns into her back. In her sitting room, she marches to her bookshelf, picks up a book and throws it across the room. *Damn him!* Another book. *Damn his money!* A third. *Damn his power over her! Damn the day her mother met him! Damn them both!* Within seconds, the shelf is empty.

🌺 🌿 🌺

Trish refuses to go out that evening. She mopes in front of the television while Mary fingers through the promises of the local *Gazette's* jobs pages. She can't let Trish down now by sending her home, even if it means Graham won't pay for university. And she'd promised Mrs Bellamy she'd look after her.

Trish has stopped looking after herself. She no longer uses make-up and has been wearing the same clothes for days. And in the middle of some absorbing activity, like a comedy show on television, she'll spurt out an unrelated question: "What'll Jimmy do if he finds out?" or "Poor Pop. How can he look at her?"

Every morning, she drives to school and is back at the flat by the time Mary arrives home. She told Mary that Helen has betrayed her. They no longer speak to each other and she has no other friends at school. She seems to have stopped working for her A levels too.

Mary has no choice. She's the only person Trish believes in at the moment. Trish must stay, which means she has to find a summer job in order to get to France. She needs to earn enough to buy a ticket to Paris, pay the university fees and finance a couple of months' rent. Once she's there, she'll find work so she can support herself for the rest of the year. She continues to flick through the *Gazette* pages. Perhaps talking about the future will jog Trish out of her stupor.

"Any ideas for summer jobs, Trish?"

Trish stares at the television and doesn't reply. She could have been immersed in a programme, except that it's just a boring car advert.

"Trish!"

"Uh, what?"

Trish turns around, her eyes dull, and Mary repeats her question. Trish shakes her head and picks up an old *Cosmopolitan* she brought from home. After a few minutes, Mary suggests a trip to the cinema.

"What's the point?"

Trish needs time to assimilate the truth, but she also needs to understand that it's her mum's problem, not hers. At least Trish's mum has acknowledged the truth, unlike her own.

"It'll do you good to think about something else."

"I can't believe Pop says nothing. How can he carry on like

that, knowing she's screwing that other bloke?"

"It's their decision, Trish. Your mum loves you all, but she loves Philip too."

Trish lowers the magazine and stares at Mary. "What did you say? Who?"

"Your mum said his name the other day."

This sounds even worse, as if she and Trish's mum have been chatting casually about her adultery. She rushes on to explain.

"It was at college, when she was asking if I knew where you were."

Her cheeks redden under Trish's scrutiny. Trish's eyes narrow.

"So you've been talking to her behind my back?"

"No!"

"Yes, you have. And she's even told you his name. I don't believe it!"

"We just–"

"You're on her side, aren't you? I thought you were looking out for me, but all the time you've been her little spy. When did she tell you his name? While you were having a cosy drink with them both at the pub?"

"Trish! It's not like that at all."

"Then what is it like? And don't you dare lie."

Mary hesitates. "All right. If you really want to know the truth, I saw her with him a couple of years ago, when I was with Gus."

"What?" Trish lurches to her feet and draws herself to her full height. "You've known about it for two years?"

Mary jumps up and tries to lay a hand on her arm. "Look–"

Trish shrugs it off.

"And you didn't say anything?"

"What could I have said?"

"If you'd been any kind of friend, you'd have told me."

Trish turns her back on Mary and snatches up her coat.

Mary grabs the sleeve. "Trish, please–"

"I can't believe you've known her secret all this time. You've been plotting together. Now I understand all those private whisperings between you two when you were with Gus."

She yanks her coat away and strides to the front door. "That's it, isn't it? Mum was worried you'd tell. That's why she was always sucking up to you. And why you're always defending her. You don't give a toss about me."

"No–" Mary tries to prevent her opening the door. "Let me explain."

"Let go! You're no friend of mine."

"Trish–"

Trish seizes her handbag and wrenches open the door. She slams it behind her, in Mary's face.

Mary opens it and rushes after her.

Trish throws herself into her Fiesta and starts up the engine. Mary tugs the car door handle, but Trish has locked it. The engine revs. Mary's nails drag down the wing of the car as Trish screeches out into the road without looking behind her.

Mary screams out her name. But there's no reply. Trish has gone.

PART SIX

BLOOMS

Rainbow and Mary, Summer 1995

CHAPTER THIRTY-FOUR

Mary

Mary studies herself in her bathroom mirror, looking for signs of her entry into adulthood. It's the eighth of June, her eighteenth birthday, and her A-level exams are over.

There's nothing new. Her short black hair glosses around the same pixie-thin face. She has no wrinkles, no baggy skin and no wisdom in her eyes. There isn't even an interesting scar to show for her childhood. She looks completely ordinary: a skinny, flat-chested adult-girl. The temporary piercings and the half-shaved head from her rebellious period have left no history on her features.

Her college friends say she's 'pretty', whatever that may mean and hide. She looks it up in the dictionary and reads, 'having superficial attractiveness but not striking beauty'. Superficial and not striking – that figures. Gus would probably have described her like this. She looks up 'superficial'. 'No deeper than the surface,' says her dictionary. She snaps it shut. She can't allow herself to be anything but superficial. Going any deeper under her surface would mean unearthing what she was *before*. Despite the soul-searching and discoveries of the last two years, she still doesn't really know who she is. If she continues to feel blocked like this, she may have to come to terms with what she was *before*. But not yet. Not until she's forced to.

It's been six weeks since Trish disappeared. Mary thinks constantly about her. Mrs Bellamy called in the police that awful night. They found her car by the train station, but there were no more traces. Mrs Bellamy says they haven't been particularly helpful in their investigations because she's eighteen. The hospitals haven't seen her and she's sent no word to anyone to say where she is.

The Bellamys have hired a private detective, a bland man who isn't the slightest bit like Hercule Poirot. Mary has stopped dropping in to see Mrs Bellamy and relies on the telephone to ask for news. She can't bear to see her. After blossoming for two years, Mrs Bellamy has now faded into an old lady. Her sole aim is to find Trish. Her relationship with Philip is over because, as she told Mary, she felt paralysing guilt each time she saw him.

Once Mother and Graham have left the house, Mary comes downstairs and eats her breakfast in the kitchen. She picks up the *Gazette* and turns to the jobs page. Graham has said she must get a summer job now the exams are over, as it's good for young people to work. Her place at university in Paris has been confirmed and he has agreed to fund her year there, perhaps because he feels guilty about Trish. But he insists she contribute to her living costs.

What she'd really like to do is to spend the summer in

France. But Graham will never let her have a three-month holiday until term starts. Too much free time is bad for young people and encourages them to be lazy and live off society. She closes the paper and wonders if she has enough money in her bank account to buy a ticket to Paris and find a summer job there. The prospect of arriving in Paris with no plan is daunting. Perhaps Katia Murville could put her up until she finds work.

She telephones the familiar Parisian number. Katia answers and wishes her a *joyeux anniversaire*.

"I was going to call you today, Marie."

Mary smiles at the pronunciation of her name. She kicks her French into gear and catches up with Katia's news, and then tells her about her place at university. Katia is delighted. She invites Mary to spend the summer with her in France, saying her mum can get Mary a job in her tourist office doing guided tours in English. There's no reason for Graham to refuse her this opportunity. They work out the details of times and flights for the following week. Mary is happier than she's ever felt on any birthday.

A week later, she arrives home from her shopping trip to find a slip of paper on her front door mat. She bends down, picks it up and reads it. Her hand shakes. She forgets all about her new possessions for Paris. She drops her bags and dashes into the other half of the house.

"Mother!"

"Your mother's out," says Graham. "Do you have to shout like that?"

He doesn't even look up from the encyclopaedia balanced on his crossed legs. She waves the note under his nose.

"It's Trish! She's back. I must go and see her at once."

He slowly closes the book, adjusts his glasses and frowns at the scruffy writing.

"I see she's come to her senses at last," he says. "I hope her parents punish her properly for everything she's put them through."

Mary snatches back the note. "I have to see her before I go."

"Make sure you're back early, then. You must get a good night's sleep before tomorrow's trip."

She hates the way he forces her to ask for a favour. He knows her bike is broken.

"Could you drop me off, please?"

He glances at his watch. She bites her lip.

"Please! I'm sure Mrs Bellamy will bring me back."

"I must get dinner ready first. She's been away for nearly two months. I'm sure she can wait another two hours."

🍃🍃🍃

The girl who opens the front door of the Bellamys' house doesn't look like Trish until she smiles. She's wearing glasses again and, instead of the stylish blouse and skirt sets, she's dressed in a long, draping wrap-over skirt of muddy brown and a pastel-green cheesecloth top with winged sleeves. Her ginger hair is loose around her shoulders. She looks serene.

"Trish?"

Trish whoops and pulls Mary into a hug, swinging her around and off her feet. Mrs Bellamy appears in the doorway.

"Hello, Mary. Isn't this great?"

She winds an arm – now much bonier than it used to be – around Trish's waist and hugs her to herself. "Doesn't she look wonderful?"

Trish squeezes her in return. There's a silence as mother and daughter look at each other. Mary feels tears in her eyes. Mrs Bellamy releases Trish reluctantly.

"I expect you two would like to talk."

Mary links her arm through Trish's. "You bet."

In an unspoken consensus they head off to the circuit they used to walk around when they were kids. Mary can't stop looking at her friend.

"You look so zen. What have you been doing all this time?"

Trish smiles. "I guess I've come to terms with life's ups and downs. Now I'm back with a vengeance."

She tells Mary about being homeless in London and how meeting up with some people from an ecology group saved her life.

"They're wonderful guys. Really sorted."

"It's rubbed off on you. What did you do with the greenies, then?"

"We lived in trees. The council wanted to uproot a forest and we managed to stop them by refusing to come down. Can you imagine me living in a tree? I've got to introduce you to them. Mary? Are you all right?"

A hot flush creeps up Mary's back and steals her senses away. The thought of being in such close contact with a tree makes her feel sick. She sees a vision of Amrita trying to save a tree, sitting on a branch, her arms wound around its trunk. She pictures the Maharajah's men, axes brandished, threatening her, attacking. She imagines the slicing of sharpened blades, a rush of sap and spurting blood, Amrita collapsing into a sticky, sappy, bloody pool, the tree folding on top of her. She remembers the beech tree. The accident. *Before*.

Trish puts an arm around her. "You've gone all white."

It feels as if her soul is being sucked out through her skin. She takes seven deep breaths in an effort to curb the sensation.

"Let's sit down for a minute," says Trish.

They sit down on the grass.

"Sorry." Mary's voice is weak. She has to divert her thoughts from trees. "So, what are you planning to do now?"

"I'm going to start by taking my A levels, then I'll get a university degree, and after that I'll head into the world of marketing. I'm going to do lots of voluntary work with the gang at the same time. They're trying to raise awareness about the importance of trees to the environment. The idea is for me to work for them once I get my marketing degree. It's really worthwhile. I can get you involved if you—"

"No!"

"Oh." Trish looks taken aback. "What are your plans now your A levels are over, then?"

Mary visualises the Eiffel Tower and begins to feel better.

"I'm spending the summer with Katia. Then I'm going to university in Paris for a year. I'm off tomorrow."

"That's great. You've wanted to live in Paris for ages."

"We'll only be in Paris until the middle of July. After that we're going to stay with Katia's cousins for the rest of the summer. They've got a farm in the countryside, near a little town called Cognac. You know, like the drink."

"Cognac. Whereabouts is that?"

Mary stands up and links her arm through Trish's.

"I've no idea, but it sounds cool from Katia's description of the summer festivals there. I feel as if I know it already."

CHAPTER THIRTY-FIVE

Rainbow

Rainbow's second *lycée* year finished in June and she immediately started a summer holiday job in the local garden nursery. It was an escape from the dullness of the commune and a breathing space before she entered her third and final year. If only she hadn't failed her first year, she'd be free now.

Domi had suggested she work as a palm-reader during the summer holidays. She felt a fraud when she read palms. People thought it was magical, whereas she simply analysed lines and sensed the client's personality. At least the work in the nursery meant she was in touch with nature. Plants were honest. Her gift only worked on trees, but garden plants responded well to her handling. Her boss said she had *la main verte* – which was the French term for green fingers.

This morning she was at the cash till. It was the part she least liked. While she waited for customers, she usually read through the gardening books or sketched. When they arrived, spilling the earth from her baby plants over the hardwood counter, she would silently bid the plants farewell. She scarcely noticed the people buying them.

Today, she was finishing a drawing while she waited. She closed her eyes and visualised the small-leaved elm she'd found at the weekend. The bark of its tender branches was characterised by corky ridges, which made the young boughs look old and wrinkled. They reminded her of her hands. She opened her eyes and sketched, consulting the outline sketches in her scruffy notebook.

When she'd finished the tree she added a caricature of Amrita. She smiled to herself. The picture of Amrita comparing her hands to the tree's bark had a hint of humour in it. She'd sketched Amrita for years now and felt she understood her personality. She added a touch of red and pink to Amrita's sari. This made Amrita leap to the forefront of the picture and become its heroine, its focal point.

"Can I have a look?"

Rainbow jumped. She snatched the sketch pad towards her chest and looked up. The French voice belonged to a boy of her age. His eyes were the blue of jays' feathers and he had a stubby brown pencil tucked above his right ear.

Her back began to tingle. She gasped. It was stronger than the other time she'd experienced it, in the cedar tree two years ago. The shivers ran down her spine, tripping on each vertebra. She clutched her book in anticipation of her soul lifting far into the air. It was slower this time, as if her soul was heavier. She stared at the boy, poised for spiritual flight. But there was nothing more than a continual ripple that raised the hairs all over her body. It was unpleasant, actually. Not like last time at all. She shook herself.

"Are you all right?" the boy asked.

Last time the tingling had gone on for less than a second. This time it wouldn't stop. It was like waiting at a level crossing for the carriages of a goods train to trundle past.

"Mademoiselle?"

The boy glanced backwards and then passed his hand in front of her face. She blinked and managed to ignore the sensation.

"Oh. Sorry about that. Can I help you?" she asked in French. He was holding a yucca plant.

"Would you like me to call someone?"

He reached out and touched her arm. The tingling stopped. She looked down at the hand that had worked magic on her. He had bitten nails, long, stained fingers that looked as if an ink cartridge had exploded on them, and he smelt of lemons. He took his hand away and the tingling returned, though in a lower key. It was a manageable hum now. She smiled at him, lighting up a dazzling reflection of a smile on his lips.

"Are you one too?" she asked.

His smile quivered. "Sorry?"

"A healer. Are you a healer?"

A frown extinguished his smile. "Certainly not. I'm an artist, not a con artist." He smiled again. "My name's Nicolas Lalande."

Rainbow opened her mouth to argue that not all healers were dishonest. But she didn't want him to turn off his smile again. And the tingling was increasing.

Nicolas slid the yucca plant onto the counter and held out his hand. Rainbow eased her hand into his and shook it. The tingling stopped.

"I'm Rainbow Linnet."

"Rainbow," he repeated. He didn't ask the usual follow-up questions about her strange name. "Can I look at your drawing?"

Hours seemed to have passed since he first asked the question. She laid the sketch pad flat on the counter and turned it to face him.

"Wow!"

He picked up the pad, held it close and then at arm's length. Rainbow could sense him fizzing with excitement. He shifted his weight from one foot to the other and ran his hand through his hair.

"Wow! I can really feel those colours. It's her."

"Do you know her?" asked Rainbow.

"She's just what I've been looking for. She's my character; the girl in my graphic novel."

He waved the pad at her as if this explained everything.

"You've got to work with me," he said.

His enthusiasm was infectious. "Yes!" she said. She wasn't sure what he was talking about, but she knew the answer was yes.

"Good. What time do you leave work?"

She dragged her eyes from his face and looked around her. She was still in the nursery.

"Oh. Six o'clock."

Nicolas nodded furiously, pulling out the pencil from behind his ear and a tiny sketch pad from his back pocket. He scribbled down his address in the town of Saintes and tore out the page.

"Bring all the stuff you've done with this character," he said, and passed her the page. He reached out to shake hands, changed his mind and kissed her on each cheek. "I'm so glad I've found you."

He picked up the yucca and swept out of the door.

"See you later," murmured Rainbow.

She sank into her chair. It was only when the next customer arrived at the desk that she realised Nicolas hadn't paid.

꽃 ꒰ 꽃

Sitting in the train to Saintes that evening, she resolved to ask Nicolas for the yucca plant payment. The moment he opened the door and kissed her, however, she forgot about it. He whisked her into his world of pencils and paper in the studio shed at the bottom of his parents' garden. The room smelt lemony from his deodorant and was deeply silent apart from an intermittent scratching from a branch against the window. She hardly noticed the shelves of comic books, the pots of ink pens and water, trays of crayons and piles of drawing paper on the floor. Her mind and spirit were overpowered by his effervescence.

He sat her at the drawing board in the centre of the room and circled her, pulling out volumes of comic books, showing her his first graphic novel, pointing out the framed, signed pictures on the walls. He told her to call him Nico, shortened her name to Renne, went through page after page of sketches from his current graphic novel and electrified her with excitement for his project. She soon grasped the storyline: a gipsy boy called Enzo loses his memory in an accident and meets a traveller girl. This girl takes Enzo through pages of different scenery and helps him pick up the pieces of his memory. Nico used scenery to show emotion. His problem was how to depict the messianic quality of his traveller girl and integrate her into his backgrounds.

"Draw her for me," he said. He whipped a piece of paper from one of the piles and slapped it onto the drawing board.

The paper was big, white and empty. "Doing what?"

"Let's have her meeting Enzo. Standing. Looking enlightened."

Rainbow sketched. With Nico standing beside her, she worked faster. Her lines were defter than usual and Amrita looked more confident.

"Good. Now let's have her walking."

Rainbow sketched.

"Great! Now running, her hand in Enzo's, pulling him forwards."

The evening continued. *Sitting.* She sketched. *Lying down.* She started a new piece of paper. *Looking sad. Crying because Enzo has just recounted something terrible he's remembered.*

It was dark outside by the time Nico was satisfied that they had worked enough. Her fingers were numb and her stomach was growling. He grinned at her.

"I'll come to your house tomorrow evening. Then we can really get started."

It wasn't until she had kissed him goodbye and he'd closed the front door that she realised she was exhausted.

She rigged up trestles and boards in her loft bedroom the next evening so they could work in peace. She waited outside the commune and, as soon as he'd parked his grey Peugeot 205, she led him indoors before Mum could see him. The kids, sitting at the outdoor table, looked up. Nico didn't appear to notice them and they returned to the board game they were playing. Only Sandrine stared. Rainbow paused on the threshold. Sandrine's expression was horrified. Rainbow never invited friends home, apart from Sylvia. This would be the first time a boy had come into her bedroom. Was Sandrine worried about what they might do together? Or was she having a bad clairvoyant moment?

Nico turned around to see what Rainbow was looking at, and she quickly led him upstairs. She didn't want him to suspect that Le Logis was a spiritual commune.

"This is perfect," he said. "Plenty of light. Lots of room. And a long way from your family."

She opened her mouth to correct him. But in some ways he was right. The commune was her family. He needn't know about their line of work. She helped him lay out his pencils and inks, and listened to him enthuse about the ideas he'd had for the graphic novel after she'd left last night.

Once his tools were ready, he started to sketch Amrita in the doorway of a caravan. Rainbow watched him. He stopped moving when he was drawing. His energy became focused on his pencil and he seemed to disappear, devoured by his work. She sat close beside him, wanting him to look up and notice her. But it was only when she started to draw a panel with Amrita swimming in a river pool that her connection to his intensity returned.

"Merde! She won't come," he said.

Rainbow looked at his panel. The girl he'd drawn wasn't Amrita. There was something wrong with the shape of her face. Or was it her eyes? Each feature individually was correct. The problem was her overall demeanour: she looked ordinary.

He slid the sheet of paper towards her. "You draw her."

She rubbed out his work and replaced it with the familiar lines. It worked. She sat back and smiled at Nico.

He was almost buzzing with excitement again. "You've got something dead special there."

"Really?" She glanced down at Amrita and then back into Nico's shining eyes.

"Really. You'll have to draw her in the panels and I'll do the rest."

She could feel herself glowing in pride, glowing from the current he was discharging. This was going to be the best summer of her life.

CHAPTER THIRTY-SIX

Rainbow

Rainbow and Nico worked together most evenings and every weekend. Rainbow concentrated on encouraging Amrita to express the ideas Nico demanded of her. Each time she succeeded, he rewarded her with a burst of excitement and an exclamation of pleasure. She basked in his admiration. If only it would last more than a few seconds.

He drew page layouts, wrote scenes and explained the concepts of *la bande dessinée* until Rainbow dreamt in panels and speech bubbles. He wanted to enter the student section of a local comics competition being held in August. Their entry had to be ready by the end of July.

She no longer sketched Amrita as an afterthought to her tree drawings. Instead, she spent hours putting her into different situations. Away from trees, Amrita paled. Rainbow struggled to fit her into the traveller-girl role without losing the essence that shone through when she was in contact with trees. Then, one evening, she had an idea that would make things easier with Amrita and also allow her to tell Nico about her gift.

"You know you want to show the traveller girl as a kind of messiah?"

Nico nodded without looking up from his paper.

"Well, why don't we make her into a tree spirit? Enzo can discover the truth at the end of the story."

Nico frowned. "No. We don't want any freaky stuff to spoil our story."

"It needn't be freaky. Just a little spiritual."

"It's out of the question. I don't want my name associated with rubbish like that."

She bit her lip. How would he react if he found out he spent most of his time in a house full of freaks?

Eventually she managed to bend Amrita to her will. When she added her to Nico's settings, their strength brought Amrita to life. And Amrita transformed his pictures from beautiful landscapes into a story. Rainbow was envious. She had given Amrita a destiny.

Sometimes they met at his house but most of the time they stayed in the commune, where she'd asked everyone to respect Nico's attitude to spiritualism and not mention their work. Occasionally, she managed to persuade him to leave her bedroom and work in the woods or beside the River Charente. He took more notice of her when she was outside. She loved it when his sparkling eyes looked into hers. It compensated for all the things he didn't ask about her and for the brief answers he gave when she encouraged him to talk about himself.

The weeks passed and Rainbow began to plot as much as Nico, although her plot didn't concern Amrita. She was plotting a way to make him see how much she wanted him to kiss her. However sensitive he was to the appearance of the people he drew, he seemed to be completely ignorant of what went on inside real people.

Sylvia couldn't understand Rainbow's dilemma.

"Tell him you fancy him," she said. "Or just kiss him. Then he'll realise how you feel."

Rainbow remembered the disastrous kiss with Christophe. "What if he pushes me away or says he doesn't fancy me?"

"You could do a striptease. That'll catch his attention – though, knowing him, he'll probably just try to draw you."

Sylvia was the only person Rainbow had confided in about her feelings for Nico.

"Being with him is like drinking a fizzy drink," she'd said.

Sylvia hadn't looked impressed. "Maybe. But once the fizz goes, they're flat and tasteless. And Renne is a stupid nickname."

When Sylvia had met him, just after this, she'd immediately asked him whether he had a girlfriend. Rainbow, red with embarrassment, had whisked him away. Sylvia had taken an instant dislike to him, although Nico barely noticed her. After a while, she accused Rainbow of being weak, girly and boring in his presence. And she'd told her she was wrong to drop her best friend for a selfish git.

Rainbow also felt a chill from the other commune members when Nico was at Le Logis, although nobody had said they disliked him. It was probably just because he didn't share their beliefs. Mum had asked if she was in love with him. Rainbow had hotly denied it but Mum had insisted on embarrassing her with talk of unwanted pregnancies and protection against diseases.

Domi was silent when Nico stayed for dinner. The few times he did speak, he usually let drop a reference to trees and she would have to shut him up before Nico suspected something. She didn't have the time for trees anymore, especially as Nico knew nothing about her relationship with them. Luckily, Nico didn't pick up on hints. He was quite like Sylvia in that respect.

Sandrine was also quiet. She refused to utter a word when he was there, but this was easy to explain to Nico: Rainbow told him she was going through a pre-teenage crisis. He'd replied that it was one of the drawbacks of living with your uncles, aunts and cousins.

🍃🍃🍃

Sylvia's striptease suggestion was intended as a joke, but the idea caught Rainbow's imagination. One day, when Nico was in her bedroom mulling over the end of his story, she saw an opportunity to put her plan into action. He was wondering what the traveller girl could do once she'd helped Enzo remember who he was.

"How about them getting together?" she suggested.

Judging by his surprise, Nico obviously hadn't considered this an option.

"Enzo and Marielle?" he said.

"Yes, Enzo and Amrita."

"Marielle, not Amrita," he said.

"I'm sure it's their destiny. Look how well they get on."

"It might get in the way of the story."

"It *is* the story, Nico. Look: Enzo could burst into her caravan one day. He sees her lying naked on the bed and realises he's in love with her."

Nico looked doubtful.

"It's not much of a setting, though I suppose it would be good to get in a nude panel. I can't see how it would move the plot along, either."

"It's obvious. He kisses her and understands she's the last missing part of his story."

"Wouldn't he just say sorry and leave her caravan?"

"No! Imagine it. Amrita is lying on the bed like this."

Rainbow jumped onto the bed and lay in what she hoped was a provocative position.

"Now you're Enzo. Go out of the room, wait a few seconds and then burst in on Amrita."

"Marielle, not Amrita," said Nico.

He stood up and left Rainbow's bedroom.

Rainbow whipped off her T-shirt and bra, and then pulled the sheet over her jeans so she appeared naked. Then she leaned slightly forward on her arm so her small breasts looked fuller.

The door opened and Nico came in. He stopped in surprise and stared.

It looked as if everything was going to go wrong. She swallowed.

"Now Enzo comes forward and kisses Marielle," she said.

Nico took a step towards her.

"Gosh, Renne. Look how your skin swallows the light," he breathed.

Rainbow resisted looking down at her shoulder, where his gaze was fixed. He took another step towards her, his head tilted to one side. She raised herself onto an elbow and slid the other arm around his neck. He didn't resist. She drew his face to hers and kissed him.

"You're beautiful," he said, afterwards. "How could I have missed seeing that?"

CHAPTER THIRTY-SEVEN

Mary

Life can get no better than it is in Paris. As soon as Mary sees Katia, it's as if they've been parted for two hours rather than two years. She immediately slots back into the Murvilles' family life, and she and Katia delight in repeating their rollerblade visits. This time, Katia introduces her to some friends and they spend whole nights at parties. She feels surer of herself here in France, and completely free of any obligation to conform. Any mismatches with people's expectations are easily explained away by her British nationality.

She works at the tourist office alongside Madame Murville and learns all about the landmarks on the themed, guided circuits the tourist office provides. The more she learns, the more fascinated she becomes with the history of Paris. While she's learning, she helps out in the back office. She takes photocopies, arranges leaflets on the stands before the tourists arrive and helps organise the participants in the costumed visits. After two weeks her French has improved enormously and she starts to accompany Katherine, the American guide, on her guided visits. She can't believe she is being paid to have so much fun. Katherine lets her give the historical speeches about the Trocodéro, then the Eiffel Tower and the Champ de Mars, until she is doing a whole visit alone. This has to be the perfect job, the perfect city, the perfect life.

The only part she dislikes is the interaction with the visitors. Many of the English-speaking tourists want to show off how much they know, and it's rare to find a group who are truly interested in historical details. She loathes the way some Brits speak so loudly and elbow their way to the front. The French are more considerate about letting smaller people or children take their places.

🌱🌿🌱

She has discovered that Cognac is in the south-west of France, nearly three hours from Paris by the fast TGV train. Katia begs her to accompany her there, and assures her they won't be doing any farm work. But she's reluctant to leave the city of her dreams, especially for a place that is a 'symphony of greenery', as Katia describes it lovingly. How will she cope, being so close to nature for a month? The thought brings back daggers of memory from *before*.

Yet something about Cognac attracts her, and Paris without Katia wouldn't be the same. So, after a few weeks of work, she agrees to visit the farm. She can always catch a train back if it's too much to bear.

When she and Katia squeeze onto the TGV at Montparnasse station on the eve of national Independence Day, she's already mourning the safety of stone and tarmac. They whizz through the plains south of Paris. Katia rhapsodises about their destination. She always spends her holidays with her cousins Frédéric and Corinne in a drowsy village near Cognac. Mary listens to stories of sunny days spent swimming in the river, going to outdoor music concerts, sleeping on the beach, picnicking in the woods, playing *pétanque* – the French game of boules – and cycling around the vineyards.

"You may be a bit daunted by my aunt," says Katia. "She comes across as surly and uncultured, but she's an angel underneath."

"Don't worry. It takes a lot to intimidate me," says Mary.

The flat fields turn into hills and valleys, trees and hedges. Her stomach tightens, though it's not Katia's aunt who worries her. She starts to count the stations they rush through. There aren't enough of them to occupy her brain, and she's reduced to concentrating on the polka dots on Katia's T-shirt.

When they reach the hilltop town of Angoulême, they bang their suitcases down the steep step onto the platform. It's hotter and quieter than it was in Paris. Mary sweats.

Katia's uncle meets them at the station entrance in his car. He's a smiling, jovial man, as hearty as a folk-story farmer – which figures, because he spends his life tasting the cognac he makes. He kisses them and asks after Katia's family. Katia's chattering eases the drive through small villages of stone houses and vineyards.

The countryside is nothing like west Dorset. Here, it's tame and ordered. The vines stand to attention in lines, perfectly controlled by humans. Everything, other than the green vines, is dry and dusty. Mary relaxes. There's no risk of being attacked by damp tendrils of grabbing greenery. Yet her unease persists. In fact, it increases as they approach their journey's end. She must be more worried about the aunt than she thought.

The farm lies on the outskirts of a village a mile from Cognac. The huge, double wooden doors at the stone entrance arch are closed and look far too heavy to open. Mary unsticks herself from the car seat and gets out. A high wall surrounds the buildings, and Katia's uncle tells her proudly that it was a protection against the English during the Hundred Years' War.

He leans his shoulder against one of the heavy doors. She imagines him whispering a secret French word. The door shudders a little way open, revealing a courtyard filled with tractors, trailers and a well. A rambling buddleia bush, aflutter with butterflies, fills the air with honey scent. Two hunting dogs bark and bound forwards. Someone shouts at them. There's a clatter of garden tools falling to the floor and then some swearing at the confusion. Katia's aunt appears.

"Oh, it's you," she says. "Well, get yourselves indoors out of this heat."

Katia hands her aunt the odourless roses they bought at the station and kisses her four times. Then it's Mary's turn.

"Ça – va – Ma – rie?" Katia's aunt asks between the kisses.

"Oui, merci. Et vous?"

"Ouf, ça pourrait aller mieux." *Things could be better*, Mary translates to herself.

Katia has already explained that few country people of her aunt's generation speak English. Some don't even speak French among themselves. They use the colloquial patois language, or insert patois words into each sentence. Katia is sure they do this on purpose to confuse Parisians like her.

In the 1970s kitchen, Katia's aunt plonks the roses into a vase and orders Mary to call her 'Tata' – which means 'aunt' – and her husband 'Tonton'. In this blunt way, Mary is accepted disinterestedly into the heart of a new family. She winks at Katia to reassure her that Tata doesn't frighten her at all.

Tata pushes them out of the back door and instructs them to greet the cousins. They walk into a kitchen garden and through to an orchard. A stepladder stands under an apple tree and four legs are just visible. Two of them are female, and must belong to fifteen-year-old Corinne.

Mary's attention lingers on the other pair of legs. They are tanned, muscular and masculine in their sleek hairiness. Mary has an urge to run her hands up the legs. She wants to brush the silky black hairs in the wrong direction. On the feet of these legs, unlaced, is a pair of cream canvas deck shoes. They are dust-free, despite the grime of drought. This has to be eighteen-year-old Frédéric.

Tata shouts to Corinne and Frédéric to come down and say hello. Mary thinks she hears Tata say the words 'roast beef', but she can't see how that corresponds to the situation. She must have mistranslated something.

The branches swish and a deep voice curls around the sexiest English 'Hello' she has ever heard. She curbs her desire to say 'Pardon?' just to hear it again, and watches as the taut calves gradually give way to chunky thighs in cotton shorts and a dream of a naked torso. She holds her breath and wills the face to match the body and voice.

The face that turns towards her is olive-skinned, blackhaired and brown-eyed. He is an exotic Greek god. Mary holds his gaze. The holiday in Cognac may be more interesting than she'd anticipated.

CHAPTER THIRTY-EIGHT

Rainbow

Rainbow had always felt a little disappointed that her gift had never elicited the least excitement. Michael had worried she'd be exploited. Mum had accepted it as natural. Bob had been spooked, and Domi had only been concerned about its meaning in the grand scheme of saving the world. Nico didn't even know about it.

Her success as an artist, on the other hand, elicited excitement from dozens of strangers. It was intoxicating to see her glory reflected in other peoples' eyes. She'd never felt this with her other gift, as she now called it.

She stood beside Nico and the judges while their photographs were taken. Opposite was the young journalist who'd refused to take her tree-growing gift seriously. He didn't remember her from their disastrous meeting last summer, when she'd persuaded him to meet her in a wood and had demonstrated her gift to him.

He'd been less polite then. He'd demanded measurements

and statistics. Photographs weren't enough, he'd said. The public will think there's trickery. Rainbow had wanted to use the newspapers to get her message across to the world. *Take care of trees*, she'd wanted to say. *Respect them. Stop deforestation.* This journalist from a local newspaper was the only one who'd agreed to meet her. In the woods, she'd discovered that he was more interested in her body than her story.

Now, like the other journalists at the press conference, he was looking for an original angle to report their win in the student category of the comics competition. Rainbow smiled while Nico enthused about their graphic novel. They were a good team. Nico possessed the technical knowledge, and her mysterious Amrita had seduced the judges. The colours were 'astonishing'. The protagonist was 'convincing'. The judges claimed that the Lalande–Linnet team would 'go far' if they continued to study art.

That evening, exhausted after the excitement of the day, they lay on Rainbow's bed and discussed art school while they waited for dinner. Nico knew the details of all the art courses off by heart. She enjoyed sharing his vision of their future together. She hadn't needed to research art schools: she would follow him. He stared up at the ceiling as if he could see their success webbed between the wooden beams.

"Now we've got the prize, I bet we'll get a place at the Emile Cohl School in Lyon next year," he said.

"Lyon? But that's on the other side of France."

Nico rolled over and kissed her. "It's the best school, Renne. And don't argue. You're coming with me."

He talked about his ambitions for them to work in

America. He'd planned everything. They would get several comic albums published in France. She would translate them into English and catch the attention of the American market. They'd live in Los Angeles, move from comics into animation and have three children.

After two months of living in Nico's sparkling world, she was still inspired by him. She laid her head on his smooth chest, closed her eyes, breathed in his lemony essence and listened to the magic of his voice. She no longer needed trees. She had Nico. They were surfing the wave of France's ninth art together. He was in front. She just had to hold on behind and enjoy the ride. Life was easy.

❧ ❧ ❧

The next morning Rainbow came down to breakfast to find Christophe drinking coffee at the table with the Sunday late-risers. Nico had already arrived and was sitting with them.

Rainbow bent and kissed Christophe's cheeks. He mumbled his congratulations. She continued around the table, kissing her greetings, and then sat on Nico's lap. There was an uncomfortable silence. Then Domi asked Rainbow to tell them all about the prize-giving ceremony.

"It was cool," replied Nico. "It gives you a taste for fame."

Rainbow nodded in agreement and turned to Christophe. "That journalist was there. You remember, the one from last summer?"

Nico looked surprised. "You should have told me you knew him, Renne. We could have played on it."

Christophe eyed him sourly. "I doubt that reminding

him of his attempted rape would have done much for your publicity."

Rainbow concentrated on spreading jam on her croissant so she wouldn't have to look at either of them. Christophe finished his coffee and put down his bowl.

"By the way, Rainbow, I saw your double the other day," he said.

She looked up. "My double?"

"A girl who looks like you. In Cognac."

Rainbow felt suddenly sick. She pushed her jam croissant away. "How weird. Did she really look like me?"

"I didn't see her close up. You know what I'm like with faces. But I really thought it was you for a second. Luckily, I didn't shout your name. When I tried to catch up, I couldn't find her anywhere."

"Poor girl, looking like Renne." Nico squeezed her thigh to show he was joking.

Christophe pushed back his chair, announced he was leaving and marched out of the room. Nico looked round the faces at the table.

"What's up with him?"

Mum and Céline exchange glances. Rainbow sighed. The sooner she could move away from this place, the better. How was she going to wait a whole year until art school?

Nico cleared his throat. "Coming back to Renne and me, we've decided to apply for the comics art school in Lyon after our bac exams. Now we've got our prize, we're pretty sure of getting a place."

Domi's bowl slipped out of his hand. "Lyon?"

"I don't know if we can afford to send you to Lyon, love,"

said Mum.

"The judges think Renne needs to work on her technique," said Nico. "Emile Cohl is the best school. My uncle lives in Lyon. We can stay with him."

A pool of coffee dripped unheeded into Domi's lap. He turned to Rainbow.

"What about your trees?"

"What about them? The experts say I should study art," said Rainbow.

Nico frowned. "Trees?"

"It's nothing. He just thinks it will be difficult for me to live in a town and not see many trees."

"We're talking about a career here, Dominique," said Nico. "Renne must develop her skills. Don't worry, I'll look after her."

He slid an arm around Rainbow's waist. Rainbow averted her eyes from Domi's ageing face. He wouldn't say anything in front of Nico, but she knew he was shocked and disappointed. He saw her drawing as a hobby. Céline was the only one to show any enthusiasm.

"I think it'll do you good to get away."

Rainbow smiled at her, grateful for her support. Then she realised why. Céline was Christophe's mother. Of course she wanted Rainbow out of the way.

CHAPTER THIRTY-NINE

Rainbow

Rainbow and Sylvia walked up the steep slope towards the disused quarry with their climbing equipment on their backs.

"You're going to have an easy final year," said Sylvia. "You won't need to bother working for your bac exams now you've got a place in Lyon."

Sylvia had dragged her away from Nico and was determined to take her climbing, despite the searing temperature. Rainbow hadn't talked to her properly for weeks. She had plenty of free time now because the garden nursery was closed until September. She stopped to catch her breath.

"It's not like some *beaux-arts* schools. Our places are conditional on us getting our bacs."

"Are you sure it's what you want?"

"Of course. Nico's taking me to see it next week."

They reached the rock face and dropped their rucksacks. Sylvia tugged the route guide out. It fell open at their current location, La Font qui Pisse. She stroked the rock and tipped

379

her head back to study the routes to the top of the ten-metre rock face. Then she turned back to Rainbow.

"You don't sound very excited about it."

"Of course I am. But it's not the same when Nico's not with me."

"Exactly. I'm surprised he let you out today, actually. And that he hasn't ordered you to live with him so he can control you even better."

"He's not like that. We did discuss moving in together, but it's too far from the *lycée*."

Sylvia shook her head despairingly.

"Let's forget Nico. Are we going to climb Suicide Intellectuel or not?"

"If you lead. I haven't climbed for ages."

"Too much work, not enough sport. Haven't you even climbed any trees?"

Rainbow shook her head and concentrated on pulling on her harness. No trees. Not since June, when she'd met Nico and stepped onto his two-seater rocket to her destiny. That's why she was here at the quarry, rather than in a wood. She daren't touch a tree for fear of falling from the rocket back into the complications of spiritual obscurity.

"Why don't we go further round and try some new routes," she asked. "I'm sick of always doing the same ones."

They studied the guide. Rainbow lifted her head every so often to catch up on the dry smells of late summer around them. Everything was beginning to wither and turn yellow. She relaxed. There was no tempting call of rising sap.

She loved sitting at a drawing table with Nico. Never before had she been so inspired or felt so important to a person. She was going somewhere, at last. But here, outdoors among the half-asleep bushes and grass and wild flowers, she was serene and safe.

"How does Domi feel about your choice?" asked Sylvia.

"He doesn't want me to go. I don't know if it's because I'm leaving the commune, or because I've given up trees."

"Both probably."

Rainbow kicked at a loose stone. Bloody Domi. He'd relegated her to a shelf. He wanted her to sit and heal one tree at a time in between reading peoples' futures in their grubby hands. Who wouldn't have preferred a glittering career in art? She could hardly look at him without feeling resentment interweaved with guilt, these days. And she couldn't get anything right for him anymore.

Sylvia decided on a series of French-graded '5a's to warm up. They picked up their rucksacks, scrambled around the rock face and began to climb. Once they'd conquered these, they moved further along to a harder route.

"It's your turn to lead," Sylvia said. "Go for it!"

The route looked difficult. Rainbow's palms perspired as she studied it from the ground. They were still rough and ridged, despite the lack of contact with trees for two months.

The crux was three-quarters of the way up. She raced up the first half, clipping into the bolts as she climbed. She knew she had to do the easy bit fast, before her arms tired. Pausing on a small ledge, she dropped her arms to her sides to bring the blood back into them and studied the crux. It was a flake, an upside-down triangle of rock that stood proud of the rest of the face. A fig tree grew out of a crevice in the rock above it. She would need all her arm strength for the layback technique she'd have to use to climb up the side of it. Apart from the physical difficulty it seemed straightforward. She remained wary, nevertheless. Cruxes often looked simple from below.

Sylvia shouted up and encouraged her to make a move. Her suggestions for holds were often impractical because their size difference meant they rarely used the same holds to climb a route.

Rainbow took a deep breath. She side-stepped, pulled herself up to the next hold and started to lay back off the flake. After three moves, she was stuck. She groped for a hold with her left hand. All her weight was on her right arm. Her feet, cramped into the little rubber-soled slippers that usually worked miracles on rock faces, had no holds. They simply balanced her against the face.

"I can't do it!"

"Yes, you can! There's a jug up to your left."

"It's too far away."

Sweat trickled between her breasts. The fig bowed down above her, enticing her. She swore. It was unethical to use a tree. Sylvia would never let her forget it if she cheated.

"Bring your feet up," called Sylvia.

Rainbow felt the rope tighten as Sylvia prepared for a fall. She scrabbled with her toes. There was nothing for her feet.

"I'll be off in a second. Have you got me?"

"Yes. If you really can't go on, grab the tree. I'll forgive you, just this once."

Rainbow hesitated, then grabbed.

Her fingers curled desperately around a thick root. She pulled her body upwards, her feet smearing against the rock.

The fig tree took her weight. Sylvia's voice seemed to float up from a thousand metres away. Rainbow hugged the trunk: it was like coming home.

Suddenly, an excruciating pain flashed through her insides. The fig was outraged. The trees were outraged. She had betrayed them with her decision to study art.

She cried out, wrenched her arms away and fell.

The rope snapped her up a few metres below and she smashed into the quarry face. The pain from the rock was nothing compared to agony of the trees' anger.

CHAPTER FORTY

Rainbow

Domi loitered at the door to Rainbow's bedroom while she packed her bag for the journey to Lyon. She was going to stay at Nico's overnight and leave early the next morning.

"You're set on going to that school, then," he said.

She nodded.

"You know, it feels all wrong."

"I have to do something positive. I'm not like you, Domi. I can't sit around and wait for a destiny to appear. My gift with trees is useless, whereas important people are excited about my drawing."

"Important people? Those are Nicolas's words, not yours."

She stuffed a jumper deeper into her bag and searched for a way to justify herself. Domi continued speaking before she could think of anything.

"Still, it's your decision to make, Rainbow. If you feel you need to do this, then you must go."

She straightened up and looked directly into his eyes for

the first time in months.

"Thank you, Domi."

🌿🌿🌿

"So you're off," said Christophe.

Rainbow heaved her bag down the stairs. He must have taken time off work to drop in and say goodbye.

"I'm only going for a week."

"It's the first step of your escape from the commune. This time next year you'll be off for good. To live someone else's dream."

Rainbow paused mid-step. "It's not someone else's dream."

"Are you sure? You're not just following Nicolas because it's the easiest way to leave?"

She scowled at him. "My art is as good as his. We were both accepted."

"I'm not questioning that. I just wonder if you're really interested in it. What happened to the girl who was determined to save trees, no matter what?"

Rainbow pushed past him and tugged her bag out to the parking space.

🌿🌿🌿

"I'll miss you, love," said Mum. She helped Rainbow load the bag into the Mini.

"Of course you won't. We don't spend time together anymore, Mum. In any case, it's only for a week. I don't know why everyone is making such a fuss. I'll be back before you have time to miss me."

Mum settled in front of the steering wheel to drive her to Nico's house. Rainbow dropped a kiss on her greying hair and then walked around the Mini and opened the passenger door.

"I suppose it's not really a surprise," said Mum.

Rainbow slid into the passenger seat and yanked on the stiff seat belt. "What isn't a surprise?"

"That you've chosen art. Your father was an artist."

Rainbow stopped pulling the seat belt. "My father was an artist?"

"Kind of. Anyway, it shows these things are in the genes."

Rainbow slotted the buckle slowly into place. "You mean that Domi's not my dad?"

"Domi? Of course not. What makes you think that?"

It was a good question. Rainbow searched for what had made her think Domi was her dad. The date, that was it. The date on the postcard: 1977. Now she thought about it, her deduction seemed ridiculous.

"I don't know." She swallowed. "So who was my father?"

Mum opened her mouth. Then she closed it again. She slammed her car door shut. "We'd better get going or you'll be late."

"Mum! I've got a right to know, surely?"

"Trust me, you don't want to know," said Mum.

She put her hand on Rainbow's thigh and shook her head. Her eyes swam with sadness. Or was it pity?

Rainbow pushed Mum's hand away and glared out of her window. She felt disorientated. The perspective of her past had shifted with Mum's words. She drifted back to the question she thought she'd resolved years ago: if Domi wasn't her father, then who was?

Mum turned the key and the engine burst into life.

"Are you all right?" asked Nico. He took her bag and carried it up to his bedroom. "You look pale. I suppose it's the first time you've left your mum."

Rainbow followed him up the stairs. "It's nothing. I'm fine."

He dropped the bag and caught both her hands in his. "This is it, Renne. Our second step towards our dazzling future. You'll see. Lalande and Linnet! We'll be greater than Goscinny and Uderzo."

His eyes sparkled. Rainbow felt her spirit lighten. This was the most important thing now: being with Nico, feeling inspired and alive, feeding on his confidence in her, making him proud. She missed this when he wasn't with her; she felt lost and unsure. His presence beside her was vital for her to know who she really was. When she looked into his blue eyes they seemed to reflect back her true self.

But was this her true self? All she could see was a wavering image of herself. Did she really need Nico's eyes to see who she was? Nothing seemed so certain anymore. Perhaps all she could see was a possibility.

She let go of his hands and took a step backwards.

It was difficult to carry her bag back downstairs alone.

"Good for you," said Sylvia, once she'd overcome her surprise at seeing Rainbow standing alone at her front door. She took one handle of the bag and shared the heavy load.

Rainbow shivered.

"I'm not at all sure I've done the right thing. Can I stay the night with you? I can't face going back to Le Logis and hearing them get spiritual on me."

"Of course. How did Nico take it?"

"Badly. He accused me of ruining his career."

Sylvia put an arm around her.

"I think you're better off without him. Maybe the real Rainbow will come back now."

Rainbow grimaced. "What have I done? I must be crazy."

"Ah, that's the Rainbow I know. Welcome back!"

CHAPTER FORTY-ONE

Mary

Mary discovers that Frédéric – or Fred, as he likes to be called now he drives his own car – doesn't have a personality to match his Greek-god appearance. Why is it that the best-looking guys turn out to be the least interesting?

It took her ten minutes to realise this. Those ten minutes proved fatal. He sensed her infatuation, latched onto the way they stared at each other and took it for love at first sight. He can't accept she was simply dazzled, like a rabbit in car headlights. Yes, he's good-looking, but he's also arrogant. He can't pass a window without admiring himself in it. And he only ever talks about himself and his political ambitions.

The worst thing is that he has taken her subsequent disinterest in him as an encouragement. The more she ignores him, the keener he becomes. She doesn't want to upset him and risk ruining Katia's holiday. For weeks she has been thinking up ruses to keep him at a distance. She's worn-out. The activities with Katia and Corinne have been fun:

the riverside lounging, the parties and the music festivals. She should feel fulfilled now she's living in France. But she's becoming more and more aware that something important is missing – and it's certainly not Fred.

She thought she would like being a foreigner and having the opportunity to reinvent herself once more. But the French Marie she has become isn't really her. She's just a token English girl; a girl whose English label hides her personality. The French only relate to the stereotype she represents. They can't relate to a person who lacks the language to express herself in any depth. She still doesn't fit in.

In a few days she and Katia will head back to Paris and their new lives as university students will begin. One final ordeal remains: tonight's party with Fred's friends. Then she can return to Paris and hope she'll find the missing key to fulfilment there.

Fred's Cognac gang have a house to themselves for the evening, because the parents are away. They're going to celebrate the end of the summer holidays before they scatter over France to continue their studies. Mary knows it will be difficult to integrate. This wouldn't have bothered her in England, where she often chose to be aloof. But this French Marie feels a desperate need to be accepted in her adoptive country. If France doesn't work out, what's left?

She's alone in Fred and Corinne's house at the moment, waiting for Katia and her cousins to return from their bike ride in the woods before they head off to the party. She turns on the television and chooses a quiz rather than one of the badly dubbed American soaps. With a slice of Nutella-smeared baguette in one hand, she reads the French subtitled clues to each question before they disappear. It's hopeless. By the time she's read and loosely understood the question, the answer has already been given. There's so much she doesn't know, even when she manages to understand the words. Learning the language is the easiest part of changing countries. The hardest bit is digesting the culture: the names of actors and TV presenters, the cult films, the French songs, the politicians, the history, the geography and the proverbs.

She takes a shower, mulling over the incredible fact that the death penalty existed in France until the early 1980s. Then she dresses herself carefully in jeans, high heels, a shirt and open waistcoat to attain a casual look. In an hour a cluster of chic French girls will be looking her up and down. She refuses to conform to the image of the badly dressed English girls in fleeces and jogging trousers that Fred's gang of Cognac girls gleefully cling to.

🍃🍃🍃

Fred drives them to the party house. Within seconds of him ringing the doorbell, his friend Nathalie opens the door. She throws herself into his arms with a squeal of delight. Fred looks pointedly at Mary while he hugs Nathalie. He's trying to make her feel jealous. All she feels is a spark of hope that tonight he may attach himself to another girl.

Given Nathalie's excitement, Mary presumes the party is well under way. Nathalie is more reserved with Mary and Katia – one kiss only – and then she urges them all indoors. She jigs to the salsa music and flings her arms into the empty space around her. The room is completely bare. Mary realises they're the first arrivals.

"Wonderful, isn't it?" cries Nathalie.

"Very. Where's your furniture?" Mary asks.

"Pardon?"

"Your furniture, where is it?"

The problem isn't the loud music. It's the three-sentence interval the French need in order to accustom themselves to her accent and the sequence of her words.

"Oh, our *furniture*," Nathalie corrects.

Her words sound exactly the same to Mary.

"We've moved it into the garage for tonight," says Nathalie.

They follow her into the kitchen and help her serve packets of crisps, peanuts, dried sausage, olives and a savoury cake. This will be the only food they'll see until after midnight – or even for the whole night.

Before long, the front door swings into action. The guests are the same age as Mary, but many of them are already in long-term relationships. Everyone here has known each other since primary school. She can't imagine an equivalent English party being so full of couples. The parties at home are mostly about getting off with someone you fancy.

The norm at parties like this seems to be one kiss instead of the standard two. She embraces the people she's already met this summer and tries to recall the seed of a detail that will allow a conversation to germinate. She exhausted any references to their visits to Britain long ago. They've all been to England, meaning London, and have terrible memories of the food, especially the shock of being served a wobbling jelly in its glory of artificial colour.

"Ah, our favourite Rosbif," says a girl called Carine, and

kisses Mary.

Mary has learnt that this is a slang reference to the English. *Ah, my favourite Frog*, she wants to say. Instead, she recalls the mysterious-sounding illness Carine was complaining about the week before, when their paths had crossed in town.

"How are you feeling?" Mary asks her.

"Much better, thanks."

Carine turns towards Nathalie and they launch into a long discussion about B.B. King. He visited Cognac during the Blues festival earlier in August. Mary listens and stumbles on a key word.

"Sorry, what did B.B. King reply?" she says. Carine stops in mid-flow.

"Basketball," she says, after a moment. "Where was I?"

"Telling me how to apply to work as a volunteer," Nathalie fills in. "Go on."

Mary has missed the link between the two parts of the story. She gives up trying to follow. In the kitchen, she helps herself to some crisps and then goes into the lounge in search of someone who's alone. She can manage to hold a conversation with a single person; it's when there are two or more that it gets difficult.

Fred is in the lounge with the boys. They stand in a tight circle, their backs facing out. She eavesdrops and pretends to examine the face sculpted in the stone chimneypiece. The boys assume the girls will want to gossip together, and that by separating themselves they're doing the girls a favour. This is fine when the girls know each other well, but Mary prefers masculine company. The boys are easier to understand. They generally have more patience and listen right to the end of her slow sentences.

There's no way she can enter their circle. She goes back to the girls in the kitchen and joins Katia, who's talking to someone she appears to know well. Katia dashes away to dance and the girl smiles at Mary.

"You must be Katia's penfriend," the girl says. "It's Marie, isn't it?"

Mary nods. "And you're–?"

"Agnès. I'm a Parisian like Katia, nowadays. I used to be Frédéric's neighbour."

"So are you down from Paris for the end of–?"

"For the weekend?" she finishes. "Yes, I'm going back tomorrow. How are you finding farm life?"

She indicates the dusty paw marks Mary hadn't noticed on her sequinned jacket. Mary brushes them away self-consciously.

"Those dogs. Always jumping up," she says.

"Yeah. They're cute though. I remember them well."

"I'm more of a cat–" Mary starts.

"Lover? Frédéric's family aren't, though, are they? He's more into dogs. What about his mum? She's a real one."

Mary giggles. Katia's aunt hasn't improved over the weeks, and Mary has seen no sign of the angel beneath her grumpy exterior.

"Yes, she is a bit."

"A bit what?" Agnès looks puzzled.

"Well, a bit of a dog."

"Is she? I always got on brilliantly with her. She's a real character."

That makes seventeen misunderstandings on Mary's

mental list. Before she can explain her mistake, Agnès turns away and walks into the lounge. Mary is alone once again.

Agnès pulls Fred onto the dance floor. Mary watches her weave like a sleek panther and wonders how the carefree, popular, rebellious Mary in England could have turned into this uncertain, spurned Marie. She needs to move, to get away from her thoughts.

"I'm going to the loo," she says to no one in particular. She goes into the entrance hall to search for the toilet.

Away from the noise and the covert glances, she climbs three steps up the staircase and sits down. She drops her chin onto her arms and counts the paw scratches on the inside of the front door.

The doorbell rings. It startles her out of her counting. She waits for Nathalie to prance out of the kitchen and reply. No one appears, so she answers it herself.

An attractive boy she has never seen is standing on the step.

"Come in," she says in French. "Nathalie is inside."

The boy's mouth drops open. He stares at her.

Mary clears her throat, mentally cursing her accent, and repeats her invitation. He remains motionless. Perhaps he is deaf. She indicates the hall with a sweep of her hand. He takes a step back. The hands that clutch his motorbike helmet are white-knuckled. He looks as if he's seen a ghost.

"You're British too," he says, in lightly accented English.

A surge of eagerness mixes with her confusion.

"Too? Are you British?"

"No, I'm French."

Mary shivers in the swirl of cool September air. The boy

apologises and enters, closing the door behind him. She rubs her shoulders with her hands, warming herself. She's excited. It must be the prospect of a proper conversation in English.

"How come you speak such good English?" she asks.

"I live with an English girl."

"Oh."

"I mean, I don't live with her, but we grew up together," he adds. He smiles and frowns alternately. "This is incredible."

The slight dip in her excitement at his mention of another girl is replaced by a thrill. She has a premonition that this meeting is going to change her evening. Maybe even her life! He's obviously keen to speak English too.

"Well, I'm Mary," she says.

He projects sensitivity coupled with Gus's self-confidence.

"Mary? I'm Christophe," he replies.

He takes her hand to shake and holds it tight. She feels herself begin to blur around the edges, as if she's evaporating in the heat of his touch. Everything around her seems to be faintly doubled, as if she's in two places at once. Yet it's a comforting sensation. She searches for something to say that won't splinter the electric atmosphere between them.

The lounge door opens and Fred appears. Christophe drops her hand. Fred stares at her and then glares at Christophe.

"Ah, here you are, Marie," Fred says. He turns his back to Christophe. "Will you dance with me?"

Mary peers around him to check Christophe isn't about to leave the house. He's pushing the lounge door open with his back. He looks sad. She's hit by a sudden panic that she's going to lose him.

"Sorry, Fred. I've just promised Christophe a dance."

Christophe stops. Fred pushes past him and returns into the lounge. Mary blushes.

"I hope you don't mind–"

"On the contrary."

Christophe smiles at her. She knows she has an idiotic grin on her face, but is powerless to play it cool. For several seconds, they simply look at each other. Then Christophe holds out his hand.

"Let's dance."

CHAPTER FORTY-TWO

Rainbow

It was a dull and windy evening in September. Rainbow's final *lycée* year had just started, and it had been three weeks since she dropped art and Nico. Every day she regretted declining her place at the art school in Lyon. She knew she'd made the right decision, but it wasn't easy to go back to her depressing search for a tree destiny.

She lay alone on her double bed under the creaking roof. The beginning of autumn was thickening her blood. Soon it would be winter, her hibernation period, and she would curl up and let routine drag her through the short days and long nights. Then the rising sap of spring would bring her new ideas and energise her into action. But spring was a lifetime away.

This year the chill had arrived early and she found it impossible to protect herself from the seeping cold. She lay flatly exposed, waiting for its numbing onslaught. She was eighteen and still had no idea what to do with her life. She would spend hours hunched in one tree or another, her ear pressed against the hush of its pulsing bark, and let it lull her into frozen listlessness. Her former energy had been replaced by the heaviness of despondency.

Christophe had suggested working for a tree doctor. A biker acquaintance of his had a tree-surgery business, and he'd been interested when Christophe had mentioned Rainbow. She'd made a list of local tree surgeons and then written to them, mentioning a talent for working with trees without saying more. The idea was that the tree doctors would be curious enough to want to meet her. Last week, she had ridden on her moped to meet the only one who'd responded to her letters. He immediately told her she was too small. She'd demonstrated her gift, nevertheless, only to be told to go back to 'Mutant Land'.

She sat up on her bed and stretched. She was waiting for Christophe. He'd said he would call into Le Logis this evening to tell her whether his tree-doctor friend would see her. If the tree doctor wasn't interested, she would go to agricultural college after her *bac* and get a forestry qualification.

She had started to supplement her occasional palmreading work by reading tarot cards, which demanded an equally low level of talent. Luckily, there was some leeway for perspicacity in both techniques. The clients could feel their own personal questions had been answered and were motivated in one direction or another by the time they left. She'd even developed a couple of regulars. They fed off her confidence in their futures and sucked her dry.

Domi advised her to note everything she told her clients, along with their reactions, so she could revise prior to a subsequent sitting. He thought this would make up for her lack of ability to see the future and tune into humans in the same way she tuned into trees.

She never noted a word. The work disheartened her. And, since she'd discovered Domi wasn't her father, she'd noticed a new obstreperous streak in her personality that made her want to do the opposite of whatever he said. She wanted to punish him for posing as her father for the last four years. But she couldn't say anything to him because he'd never claimed the role.

She stood up and glanced out of the window. There was still no sign of Christophe's motorbike outside. She lay back down with her copy of *The Alchemist* in the hope that Santiago would show her some sign of her own destiny.

Darkness was falling when she eventually heard Christophe say hello to the people in the commune kitchen. The sound of his running feet on the stairs made her sit up. There was excitement in his approach. It had to be good news.

He opened the door. He looked pleased with himself as he kissed her. Then he stood back and studied her.

"You've got your winter blues early this year. Never mind, I've got something to cheer you up."

"Really? He wants to take me on at his tree surgery?"

"Thierry? No, he wasn't in when I phoned. He hasn't called back yet."

Rainbow slumped back down onto the bed. "What's the good news, then?"

"I've got a client for you. Palm-reading."

"And that's supposed to cheer me up?"

"It may be fun. She's your double."

She felt a pulse of curiosity. "My double?"

"I told you last month I'd seen a girl who looked just like you."

"Oh yes. Have you met her, then?"

Christophe grinned and ran his hands through his hair. He looked shy and happy. Rainbow gasped. He was in love. The realisation was like the blow of an axe through her bark. She struggled to understand. She had rejected his love last year. She should be happy for him. So why did she feel this agonising disorientation?

He seemed oblivious to her distress. "I met her at a party yesterday. We talked all night. She needs some answers, so I suggested she came to you for a reading. I didn't tell her she's your double in case it frightened her away."

Christophe was like a brother. She couldn't be jealous of his girlfriend. She shook herself. It would be intriguing to meet her double.

"Do we look exactly the same?"

"Her hair's short and black rather than long and brown like yours. But she's small and skinny like you, and her features are identical. She could be your twin. Her name's Mary."

Given his terrible reputation for faces, Rainbow wasn't sure his idea of identical was reliable. He smiled again. In fact, he hadn't stopped smiling since he arrived.

"So, will you read her palm?"

"I guess I could. When can she come?"

"Actually, she's outside."

Rainbow leapt to her feet and looked out of the window. In the dim light she could make out the figure of a girl perched on the back of the red motorbike. Rainbow's bike, her birthday present that she'd still not learnt to ride. The girl had a helmet on and was huddled into the leather jacket Christophe lent Rainbow when he took her out on her bike.

The old tingling sensation started to caress her spine. It hadn't felt so strong since the day she'd met Nico. There was an ominous sense of anticipation in the air around her. She shivered.

Christophe looked expectantly at her. "Please?"

She ignored the negative vibes, took a deep breath and smiled at him. "Let's go and bring her in."

PART SEVEN

LEAVES

Rainbow and Mary, Autumn 1995

CHAPTER FORTY-THREE

Rainbow and Mary

Mary

Mary sits on Christophe's motorbike and pulls the borrowed leather jacket closer around her shoulders. She eyes the dilapidated house with suspicion. The spiritualists have chosen a predictably spooky place for their business. She can feel the hairs on the back of her neck rising. The buildings are close to whispering trees and she shudders to think how the greenery would encroach in springtime. Doesn't Christophe's friend feel threatened by the creeping vines, the skeleton branches and the roots burrowing beneath her feet? Does she ever think the fate of Sleeping Beauty may befall her?

Yesterday, despite its inauspicious beginnings, had been one of the best evenings of her life. Fred had finally got the message that she wasn't interested in him, and spent the evening snogging Agnès. Mary spent the rest of the party in Christophe's arms.

She smiles as she visualises his honest features. He may not be classically good-looking like Fred, but she's far more attracted to him. He has a deep strength. She loves the leathery, engine-oil smell of him and the way he moves with such assurance. They talked non-stop last night. Katia had to drag her away from him at five in the morning. Then, this afternoon, he picked her up on his gleaming motorbike. They picnicked beside the river, on a rug, and lounged side by side in the cool September air. And they talked even more. Mary has never said so many words to one person. Not even *before*.

There's something enigmatic about him. He seems to know her better than she knows herself, as if he can sense her essential core. She wonders whether he's the key to help her face who she really is: not the Mary she became after the accident; nor the Marie she has become in France. No, something older: the missing part of her life; the buried side of *before*.

A dizzy lightness engulfs her. It's like the whirling sensation she had in the Eiffel Tower. She shivers. It must be the thought of *before*. She's not ready yet. She counts the grip-marks on the handles of Christophe's motorbike.

It's a stunning bike, a perfect example of Christophe's talent for anything concrete. Jed had taught her to ride his motorbike in the college car park in England, and so Christophe had let her drive this beauty along the track before they arrived. She wants to disappear into the evening sun on the bike, her arms around Christophe. How can she go back to Paris now? If only she'd met him when she first arrived in Cognac.

She rubs her arms in an effort to warm herself. She mustn't get carried away. Christophe may be less smitten than her. After all, he had suggested the palm-reading. Will his friend see a future with Christophe in Cognac, or at university in Paris? Or is she a fake who will see nothing at all? He hasn't told her his friend's name. He's not said much about her at all, except that she's English. And he's taking a long time to persuade her. Night has almost fallen.

At last she hears a door open and he appears around the side of the house. The girl is with him. She has long brown hair and is dressed in loose jeans and a baggy green jumper. Mary had expected dramatic, spangled purples and oranges. She removes her helmet, slides off the motorbike seat and takes a step towards them. Then she stops. She's looking into a mirror.

Her head begins to spin. She reaches behind her for the solidity of the bike. It's worse than a simple mirror; she's looking into a mirror of the past. She's looking into *before*.

There's a scream. By the time she realises the voice is her own, she's astride the bike. She revs up the engine, kicks off and streaks away along the track.

Rainbow

Rainbow had stopped walking towards the girl as soon as she saw her shocked expression. She thought the girl's reaction was rather dramatic, even though her face could have been Rainbow's own. Her features were identical. Rainbow had grabbed Christophe's arm and forced him to stop too. The familiar tingling sensation ran riot up and down her spine.

She suddenly knew it was connected to this girl Mary. Then the girl had screamed – a long drawn-out howl of animal pain. Before Christophe could react, the girl had roared away on the motorbike. There was a gaping hole in the atmosphere where she'd been.

"Merde!" Christophe pulled himself free and raced along the track after her.

The roar dimmed to a hum. He stopped, bent to catch his breath, and then walked back to Rainbow.

"You should have warned her. She freaked," said Rainbow.

"I didn't want to put her off. She's incredibly sensitive."

"You idiot! That's even more of a reason to warn her."

She kicked a shower of stones along the track. Christophe had given her a glimpse of something intriguing, only to handle it so badly that it was immediately snatched away. She could strangle him. The girl really was identical. And now Rainbow had a furious need to get close to her. She had to hear her voice. She was desperate to touch her. Unfortunately, the girl – Mary, she must call her – seemed to feel the opposite.

Christophe swore and punched his hand into the trunk of the silver maple tree.

"She'll never trust me now," he said. "We'll probably never see her again."

She pushed his hand off the maple and glanced up into its creepy, asymmetrical branches. The image of Mary's face and the texture of the maple's bark blurred together in her mind. A distant memory lay on the edge of her thoughts, just out of reach. All she could grasp was a vision of Amrita in her red and pink sari. She shook the thought away. She had to concentrate on what was happening here and now.

"Do you know where she lives?" she asked.

Christophe nodded.

"Come on then. We're going to find her."

She dashed back into the house, picked up a coat and shouted to Mum that Christophe was driving her to his flat. It would take too long on her little moped. Without listening to the reply, she rushed back out and joined him beside the Renault. He was leaning against it, his forehead resting against the roof. She squeezed his arm.

"She's more than a palm-reading client, isn't she?" she said.

He nodded.

"Come on then. Spill."

They climbed into the car and she listened to his tale about the party the previous night as he drove off. She smiled when he said Mary was lost. Christophe liked lost causes. She waited for a pause so she could ask the important things about Mary – like where she came from and what she was doing in France. But he was in full flow about his feelings for her and she didn't want to interrupt. He hadn't spoken so much since the unhappy day when he'd given her the motorbike last year. Even if they never saw Mary again, she'd at least re-established her closeness to him. She was determined, however, that they would see Mary again.

Mary had disappeared. The bike wasn't parked at the farm where she was staying, nor was it at Christophe's flat. They drove around the streets of Cognac, hoping to catch a glimpse of her. Christophe, for all his raving about how deeply he knew her, had no idea where she might be. After an hour of kerb-crawling, he dropped Rainbow off at the commune and went to wait for Mary at his flat. He promised to ring as soon as he had some news.

Rainbow couldn't scratch Mary from her mind. She found Domi in his consulting room and told him what had happened. He was washing his hands and had his back to her.

"She seems to be afraid of me," Rainbow told him. "Why would she be scared?"

He turned around and dried his hands. "Did you feel a sense of foreboding or light-headedness when you saw her?"

"No. Just shivers down my spine. But I've had that before."

"Ah."

"I had the tingling with Nico too. There was nothing spiritual there."

"Was it exactly the same? Or did it lessen when you were with Nicolas?"

She thought back to her first encounter with Nico. "You're right. I felt the tingling when I saw him, but when he touched me it stopped."

"Hmm. A warning."

She perched on the edge of the couch, encouraged by his pensive expression. "So, what does it mean?"

He sat down behind his desk and shuffled through one drawer after another. Eventually, he pulled out a dusty sheaf of papers bound with a faded red velvet ribbon and handed it to her. "You might find an answer in here."

"What is it?"

"My mother's notes on spiritualism. If you do find an answer, remember it's just a possibility. It's not necessarily the sole explanation."

She examined the yellowed papers, which were covered in tiny French handwriting. "Do I have to read all this? Can't you just tell me?"

"No. I don't have any experience of this kind of situation. All I can tell you is that these are the writings of an honest clairvoyant. You may find a clue to help you. But it may also put you off wanting to meet the girl properly. In the end, only you can decide what to do."

She blew the dust off the pages and carried them up to her bedroom.

Mary

Mary can't bring herself to face Katia, Fred and Corinne. She needs to be alone. At the farm entrance, she scribbles a note to Katia telling her not to worry if she doesn't see her for a while. She drops it in the letterbox and then rides away from the roads she knows.

She wants to stay on Christophe's bike forever. If she keeps riding she'll never have to face anything ever again. She cruises along lanes and through villages with names she's seen on signposts but has never visited. From time to time she stops to sit on a bench or stretch her legs.

She sees nothing and hears nothing other than the comforting purr of the engine. Hours of counting pass. Is the faint doubling sensation she's had since meeting Christophe linked to the girl she's just seen? Her mind processes possibilities but she refuses to examine them. She is cocooned in the warmth of the helmet, balanced in the void between the surface of her senses and the depths of her brain.

Midnight chimes and she finds herself in Cognac, outside the motorbike shop. She still can't imagine going back to the farm, but Christophe's face hovers, gentle, in her mind. She won't be able to rest until she's asked him more about his palm-reader. She has to see his lips pronounce that name. She has to hear him say it.

He's waiting for her. He doesn't ask about his bike. He simply makes her a mug of black tea and holds her while she cries.

At last she finds the strength to speak. "Who is she?"

"Her name's Rainbow."

"Of course it is. I mean, who is she? Is she real? How can she possibly exist?"

Christophe looks puzzled. "She's as real as you are."

"Tell me about her. Everything you know. Begin at the beginning."

Christophe doesn't ask why. He talks. After fifteen sentences, Mary knows it is impossible. It's as impossible as her gift. She wants to understand. She has to understand. But to understand, she must face *before*. She can't do it.

Christophe continues speaking. She forces herself to listen. It's like hearing a tale, one she knows by heart. He knows her story. Somehow, this changes things. She isn't as alone as she thought. She listens more easily. The story isn't quite the same. There's a moment of difference, and then a world of difference. She listens and lets his reassuring voice slip into her mind and open the closed box of her memory. There it is, the critical moment when she was unconscious: a moment of shock, like falling into the ice-cold water of the Blue Lake. She slams the lid closed again.

When Christophe asks her if she still wants his friend Rainbow to read her palm, she shrugs. She's in control again. Numb, but in control. He tells her she's not obliged, but he thinks it would help her. He strokes her cheek. She looks into his brown eyes. She agrees. There's no need to tell anyone that she shared the trunk of her life with this girl. She'll get her reading and then leave.

Rainbow

Rainbow found her answer in the wad of notes. She didn't read the whole pack. She was too excited by what she discovered to finish reading. How could it be possible? And if this were possible, how many other things in life that were deemed impossible actually existed?

She read another passage and then stopped to speculate. She compared the revelation in the notes with her own life, and then tried to imagine Mary's. She couldn't understand Mary's name. Surely they should bear the same name. How did it happen? And when? She had no memory of the tearing-apart sensation Domi's mother had recorded. And what could she mean about coexistence only lasting as long as it was necessary?

She was still reading through the important snippets at four in the morning, when Christophe called. Mary had returned to his flat. He told Rainbow she'd better come over.

It only took her a few minutes to find the object she hadn't set her eyes on for years. It would prove the link between herself and Mary. She jumped on her moped and rode to Christophe's flat.

Rainbow and Mary

Christophe introduced them: "Mary, Rainbow; Rainbow, Mary."

Rainbow stared into Mary's distrustful green eyes. Mary showed no shock this time. It was like looking into a mirror, except there was no sign of the excitement she could feel gleaming in her own eyes. Despite a day astride a motorbike, Mary looked smart in black jeans and a body-hugging green polo-neck jumper with a short, sequinned jacket. Rainbow glanced down at her old jumper and baggy trousers. She wanted to touch Mary's hands but they were hidden behind her back. She smoothed away the strands of hair straggling from her ponytail.

"Come and sit down," said Christophe.

He led them to his sofa and armchair. Rainbow and Mary sat face to face, the coffee table between them. Christophe settled beside Mary on the sofa.

Rainbow leant back and sat on her hands. She couldn't risk endangering them both by reaching out to touch Mary.

"Can you tell me who you are?" she asked.

"You're the palm-reader. Ask yourself," replies Mary.

"Are you right or left-handed?"

Mary glares at her, and then decides the question is pertinent. "Left."

"Me too. Let me see your right palm."

"Why not the left?"

"If you're left-handed, the left shows your conscious self. It represents your public face and what you make of your life. The right is your subconscious, inner self."

"Then I'm only interested in the left hand," says Mary. She holds it out.

Rainbow clenched her hands behind her back to control them. Mary's hand was only slightly rough, like a gardener's. It was nothing like her own, scarred palm. She swallowed. She couldn't get any vibes from Mary. Looking at Mary's hand wasn't enough to tell her anything.

"Well?" says Mary. She refuses to feel any curiosity about this impossible embodiment of her former self. She just wants to get her palm read so she can decide whether to go to Paris or stay with Christophe. Then she'll shove this unnerving impossibility to the depths of her mind and forget it.

Rainbow could sense nothing from Mary's hand, but her resistance to Rainbow's presence was like a solid wall. Rainbow knew she'd have to touch her, even though she had no idea what would happen with the touch. Would Domi's mother's dire predictions of absorption prove true? Did she risk disappearing? She released her hands and let them cradle each other in her lap. Maybe there was another way.

"Do you really want me to read your palm?" she asked. "Aren't you more interested in finding out why we look so much alike?"

"Everyone's got a double. There's nothing special about that," says Mary.

"I think it *is* special," said Rainbow.

Mary was hiding something. She should have looked surprised at their identical appearances and asked questions.

Perhaps she'd always known she had a parallel. Perhaps she knew when and why it had happened. Perhaps–

"I don't care what you think," says Mary. "Are you going to read my palm or shall I find a more cooperative palm-reader?"

"You'll have to let me see your right hand too."

"No. Only my left."

Mary thrusts her left palm into Rainbow's hands.

Rainbow looked down at her three hands. Her soul lifted out of her body. Then, like a predator's jaws snapping closed on a victim's neck, her hands clamped Mary's palm. She crashed back into her body. A blinding sadness overwhelmed her. There was an unbearable weight of guilt and a cold, hard fossil of defiance. The honesty of Mary's pain gripped her. She couldn't let go.

For a second, time stopped.

CHAPTER FORTY-FOUR

Rainbow and Mary

And then started again.

Mary's eyes spring wide open. Green innocence invades her. The flow of soothing calm is stronger than any drug she has tried. It's peace: a deep pool of soothing rightness. She wants to drown herself in the pool, even though it is deadly stagnant.

Gradually, the feeling of peace ebbs away. Oh, the cruelty of it! To have tasted this and be denied it. She tugs on her hand to free herself. She is sobbing. Christophe helps wrench their hands apart. He holds her close to his chest and strokes her. Under his caresses, the hurt bottled up inside her surges to the surface. It's time. This Rainbow must know the truth. She'll have to open the door to *before* and speak the words she has never been able to say.

Rainbow fell back into her chair. She hadn't disappeared; neither had Mary. She held her burning hands to her forehead in an attempt to calm the dizziness that was spinning her into unknown fields. They were dark fields: burnt, treeless, raped of nature, barren. Something was wrong. Badly wrong.

"We're connected," said Rainbow. "And it's wrong. I need you to help me understand what happened."

She pulled a scroll of paper from a cardboard tube in her bag and unrolled it onto the coffee table. First, she revealed her own corner, the corner she'd started drawing in when she was thirteen years old. She'd sketched up to the centre of the paper during her art lessons at the Drunken House.

Mary watches her drawing reveal itself, little by little, as Rainbow stretches it out. All those years ago it represented her vision of the future. The joint project had been Michael's idea: they'd each started in a diagonally opposed corner and drawn how they saw the future, without looking at each other's work. She never saw Michael's side. On their last evening together they did her maths homework instead of finishing the drawing. Mary leans closer, her heart thumping, to see what he had drawn.

Rainbow spread the drawing out and held down the corners so Mary could study it. Rainbow had examined it years ago. She was more interested in Mary's reaction. She watched Mary's fingers trace Michael's sketch lines, from seeds to tiny saplings to the power of the dominating baobab in the centre: a future of healing trees, going from strength to strength.

"He was so wrong," sighs Mary.

"We were almost right," said Rainbow.

She looked down at the lines her own hand had pencilled. There were trees, of course. And a badly drawn version of Amrita arm in arm with Michael under an eternally sunny sky.

Mary feels Christophe looking over her shoulder at the drawing.

"Can someone explain this to me?" he asks.

Rainbow looked at Mary.

Mary looks at Christophe.

Christophe turned to Rainbow.

"It could be like this," said Rainbow. "A girl grows up and discovers she has a gift for healing trees. She meets a man called Michael who helps her develop this talent. Unfortunately, during her experiments, the girl breaks the branch of a tree and causes an accident." She stopped. Keeping it factual helped, but the pain was still present.

Mary grips the sides of her thighs. Her fingernails dig into her skin. She's trembling. She counts the syllables in each of Rainbow's words as Rainbow continues.

"The girl loses consciousness. When she wakes up, she learns she killed Michael in the accident. After a few months of avoiding trees because of her guilt, she decides Michael would have wanted her to carry on healing trees. She breaks into his house, looking for a keepsake, and finds the last drawing they worked on together. This drawing. It shows his view of the future and confirms her belief that trees are her destiny. Her mother finds her a guru in France. She spends the rest of her life wondering what the hell she's supposed to do in answer to her calling." Rainbow smiled ruefully at Christophe. "You knew most of that. So let's hear Mary's version."

Mary looks up at the expectant faces. Can she do it? She doesn't understand how the impossible could have happened, but somehow it did. They must have split into two parallel beings the millisecond before Mother's confession. She feels Christophe's hand on her shoulder and takes a four-second breath. This is it.

"A girl grows up and discovers she has a gift for healing trees. She meets a man called Michael who helps her. Then the girl forces a beech tree branch to grow against its will. It falls and kills Michael."

Rainbow nodded.

Mary continues. "While the girl is unconscious, she hears her mother make a confession."

Rainbow sat up straight. This must be it. The split. She had no recollection of any confession. "What did she say?"

"You killed your father," whispers Mary.

Her voice refuses to continue. Years of suppressed anguish spill out as sobs. There is no longer any anger. Now she's spoken them, her mother's words seem to fade out of earshot. She takes a deep breath, blows her nose and looks at Rainbow.

Rainbow froze at Mary's whispered words. Michael? Her father? Michael. Her father. She tried to link the concept of 'father' and 'Michael' to become one single idea. Something in her resisted. If she placed this last stepping stone into the river she'd have no choice but to step onto the far bank. She'd have to face the desecrated fields she'd sensed on touching Mary's hand.

"You didn't know, did you?" Mary says.

Rainbow shook her head.

"That's why you were able to carry on," says Mary.

Rainbow shook her head again. No way. Not Michael. She couldn't take that last step.

"What happened next?" she whispered.

"When she recovers from her accident, the girl blames her mother for lying to her. But she hates herself for killing her father, too. She rejects her gift. She rejects everything, in fact. She renames herself Mary – the name she finds on her birth certificate; the name Michael must have given her – and she tries to make herself into a new person to replace the guilty person she can't bear to be." A long, shuddering sigh escapes Mary. "That's my story," she says.

She is washed-out. She clutches Christophe's warm hand and leans back into his arms. Poor Rainbow. It's her turn to deal with the truth.

Rainbow felt as stiff as a wooden doll. She struggled to her feet. It was one thing to find out you had a parallel being. She could cope with that. But it was another to discover your life had been based on a lie.

"I've got to talk to Mum," she said.

"Do you want me to come with you?" asked Christophe.

Rainbow shook her head. "Stay with Mary."

"I'm not leaving you on your own to deal with this," says Mary.

"This isn't your story. It's mine. I must face it alone."

Mary wants to support Rainbow, but the idea of seeing a different version of her mother makes her hesitate. "Okay. We're here if you need us," she says.

Rainbow

Rainbow arrived at the commune at six in the morning. Her shock had turned into anger towards Mum for her lies, and then into despair. She couldn't understand why she felt so strongly. Surely she'd recovered from the guilt of killing Michael? It had happened five years ago. So why was she in denial?

She parked in front of Le Logis. Suppose Mary was lying. Or suppose Mary had misunderstood Mum's words when she'd been unconscious. She hadn't thought to ask Mary if Mum had confirmed her confession afterwards. If Mary was like her – and surely she must be – she may have believed what she'd misheard without questioning it, like Rainbow had done when she'd believed Domi was her father. This must be the explanation. If Michael had been her father, he would have told her so. Relief swept over her and her pity for Mary doubled.

She tapped on Domi and Mum's bedroom door. A residue of anxiety sweated through her palms. *Please, please don't let it be true. Please don't let me have killed my own father.*

There were a few groans and then Domi told her to enter. She tiptoed in. The importance of knowing the truth outweighed her guilt at waking them so early.

Domi sat up, pulling the quilt with him. Mum didn't move.

"Mum! Wake up. Sorry, but it's really important."

Domi rubbed his eyes. "Did you meet your double?"

"Yes. Are you awake, Mum?"

Domi shook Mum. She turned over, squinted at Rainbow and yawned. "Can't it wait until the morning, love?"

It would be easy to hate her. For a second, she sympathised with Mary. "Mum, I need some answers about my father. Who was he?"

"Don't start that again, love. There's no point."

Domi laid a hand on Mum's knee. "Tell her, Jasmine.

It's time."

Rainbow looked at Domi in surprise. "You know who he was?"

He nodded. His eyes glittered with tears. "He was my best friend."

"Was it ... Michael?" Rainbow turned back to Mum. "Was Michael my dad?"

Mum sighed. "Yes, love. I'm so sorry. I said it was better that you didn't know."

Rainbow looked from Mum to Domi. Her mouth hung open. How could they sit there and just say the words like that? How could they have both known and said nothing to her? She closed her mouth and swallowed.

"You lied to me! You said my father had died. Why didn't you tell me the truth?"

"I always meant to tell you, love, only I never found the right time. Then, when Michael died, I thought there was no point in making things even harder for you, especially as you'd been in contact with him without knowing he was your dad."

"Why didn't you tell me before he died? Why didn't *he* tell me?"

"I'm sorry, love. I had no idea he was living in the village. I only learnt he was there when I saw him in Fraser's car. At that point I was more concerned about you than him. I didn't know he was your friend."

"So how did you find out I knew him?"

All this time she'd thought he was her secret. Her legs refused to hold her upright any longer. She collapsed onto the end of the bed.

"He didn't die immediately. He spoke to Fraser while I was holding you and waiting for the ambulance. Afterwards, Fraser told me what he'd said."

"And?"

Mum swallowed. She had tears in her eyes, but Rainbow refused to relent. Mum deserved this to be difficult.

"He wanted me to tell you he was your dad, and to ask your forgiveness for not having had the courage to tell you himself. He moved to the village to be near you. He'd planned to come to the house and introduce himself. But then he bumped into you accidentally. After that he couldn't find a natural way of telling you. He felt guilty about deserting us."

Tears trickled down Rainbow's face. "He was my best friend. We spent hours and hours together. He taught me all about trees and he helped me improve my drawing. He must have been on the way to tell you about my art lessons when the accident happened," she whispered.

"He was coming to confront me. Fraser said he was furious about me telling you that he'd died when you were a baby. In the end we both lied to you, love. I'm so sorry."

"Why did he abandon us when I was a baby?"

"He was never one for staying in a place for long. The responsibility of being a father was too much for him. That's why I hated him."

Rainbow couldn't feel any pity for Mum. She blew her nose and turned to Domi.

"So how did you know him?"

"We grew up together. He was here in the commune with me when Jasmine came over. This is where they met. You were conceived here."

"Why didn't *you* tell me?"

"You never asked me about your father, and you didn't tell me about Michael. I had no idea he was so important to you. If you'd mentioned him I would have told you the truth, or got Jasmine to tell you. When you first arrived here and Jasmine explained what had happened, I was worried. I thought you'd reject your gift if you knew you'd killed your dad."

Rainbow sighed. Domi laid a hand on her shoulder. "Does it change anything, fundamentally?"

She shook his hand away.

"Of course it does. I feel as if my whole identity has changed."

She told them about the meeting she'd just had with Mary and recounted Mary's side of their story. Domi nodded from time to time. Mum sat silent and white-faced.

"Mary says you confessed Michael was my father while I was unconscious. Is that true?"

"I don't know. I can't be sure of what I did and didn't say. I certainly thought about it. I was in a terrible state. I didn't know if you were going to live. I'd just seen Michael die; seen my white lie come true. I was delirious."

"And what did Mary mean about the birth certificate?"

Mum sighed and shook her head. She suddenly reminded Rainbow of Mary.

"She's right. Michael wanted you to be called Mary, after his mother, so that's the name we gave you. I was so angry with him when he left us that I called you Rainbow instead. You know … the hope after the rain."

"So I'm really Mary."

"No, you'll always be Rainbow," said Domi. "The question is, does this change the way you feel about trees?"

She slowly shook her head.

The old grin lit up his face. "Good, because Sandrine has found your destiny."

She struggled to transfer her thoughts to the future. "Go on."

"She says there'll be a huge gale here on the eve of the year 2000. It will be the beginning of a new life for you and your English tree friends."

Rainbow snorted. "Right. A gale! You think I'll sit around here for the next five years waiting for a prediction to come true? I don't even have any English tree friends."

"Maybe Mary does," said Domi.

Rainbow rolled her eyes to the ceiling, stood up and left them. She went to the kitchen and boiled a saucepan of water for tea. So Mary had told the truth. Michael was her father.

Now she thought about it, it was obvious. She remembered the way their hands had fitted together on the day she'd sold him the tomatoes. And the sepia photos he'd shown her of his great-grandfather, the man with magic hands. Not just his great-grandfather, but *her* great-great-grandfather. She had a whole new history now; a history she'd inherited, along with her gift, through Michael. An unexpected smile alighted on her lips. She had known her father, after all. And he had been the best. How could Mary have overlooked the precious time they had spent together? Poor Mary. She was like a negative to Rainbow's positive.

Her thoughts turned back to the memoir notes she'd read about parallel worlds. Domi's mother had been wrong. Two parallels could coexist. It was like having a twin sister. It would be fun. She doubted Mary had any contact with tree-huggers, though. She would have to ask her.

Tree-hugging always made her think about the Amrita Devi legend. She remembered there was a disagreement about the end of the legend. Some people said Amrita had defended the tree and died, while others insisted she'd lived. But Mum had mentioned the possibility of the two Amritas coexisting, just like her and Mary. The hint of a hazy memory dangled just out of reach. She couldn't quite catch it. Perhaps Mum would enlighten her later on.

She glanced out of the window into the September dawn. Two figures were sitting on a red motorbike. She pulled on her jacket, stepped out of the door and walked around the house to meet them.

Mary rushed towards her. She looked concerned. Rainbow's habitual loneliness evaporated into the cool air. It was going to be wonderful to have a twin sister.

Rainbow and Mary

Mary hurries towards Rainbow, anxious to know how she is coping with the truth. She remembers the disorienting horror she felt when she learnt she'd killed her father.

She stops a step away from the person she could have been, and looks into the face she knows so well. The expression is one she remembers from a long, long time ago: Rainbow looks calm, relaxed and accepting. She has learnt the truth, and yet she looks happy. How can it be possible? Mary is once again overcome by a desire to change. This time, she desperately wants to be Rainbow.

Rainbow saw a silent plea emanating from Mary's sad eyes. She reached out and grasped her hand.

"Come with me," she said. "We need to hug a tree."

The sun was rising. A short distance away, silhouetted by the sun, stood the silver maple tree. It had always made Rainbow shiver in dread. A strong, thick trunk grew straight out of the ground and then, at the height of a thirteen-year old girl, it split into two. Each bough continued upwards. The strong one was vertical, the weaker one bent right and then left in its search for sunlight.

For the first time, Rainbow felt drawn to the silver maple. She led Mary to it. Holding hands, they spread their arms around the trunk and embraced it. Rainbow closed her eyes. Her residual anger over Mum's lie seeped into the bark. It travelled through the phloem network and down into the tree's roots.

An icy shock ran the length of her backbone. It was like the time she'd fallen into the freezing cold water of the Blue Lake when she was twelve years old. Coming out of the water all those years ago, her clothes soaked, she'd felt heavy and cold. This aftershock was slightly different, though. She felt fuller rather than heavier. A hazy knowledge and a patchwork of images flashed into her head. They were pictures of a past that could have been hers. She knew one of the faces. It was Patti. She also knew that Patti was now Trish. Alongside Trish she could see Sandrine and the vision of a huge, desecrated forest awaiting her nourishment. Was this was her future? Did Trish held the key to a lifetime of worthwhile work with trees?

She opened her eyes. She had to tell Mary how much

better the silver maple had made her feel.

But Mary had gone.

Rainbow let go of the maple trunk and looked behind it. There was no one. She scrutinised the fringes of the wood and the vineyard on the other side of the track. Mary was nowhere to be seen. She rested her hand against the maple to balance herself.

The answer was here. She looked up into its canopy and realised she need look no further. The weaker, twisted branch had no sap-beat.

She glanced towards the car park. Christophe was still sitting on the motorbike. How would she tell him that she'd made the girl he loved disappear?

He must have sensed her disarray because he slid from his motorbike and hurried towards her. He was smiling. A tide of heat flushed through her, turning her icy insides into steam. The way he moved made her feel … well, strange.

"I'm so sorry," she said. "You loved her and I've made her disappear."

"No, you haven't," he whispered.

She looked into his enticing brown eyes. He seemed different. Magnetic. She couldn't look away.

"She's inside you," he continued, "back where she belongs."

He was right. And Mary had intoxicated her with an overpowering need for him. She reached out her hands, brought his face close to hers and kissed him. He responded. A cocktail of novelty and familiarity exploded inside her.

When she drew back and opened her eyes, he was smiling at her. Slowly, she smiled back. This time, it was right.

"The beach?" he suggested.

"Yes," she said. "But first there's something I must do."

"You need a tree."

She nodded and turned back to the silver maple. Her hands found the part that fitted her palms best and she laid her cheek against its bark. The maple was silent. She no longer needed to communicate directly with it. Instead, it was an opening, a window she could look through. Outside the window there was a green haven of trees, their branches stretched out in acceptance, their leaves gossiping softly in the breeze. On the edge of the wood stood Amrita, dressed in pinks and reds, her long black hair shining. She was smiling, her arm held loosely around a healthy silver maple tree. Her other arm reached towards Rainbow. *Welcome*, she seemed to be saying. *You're healed. Rest for now and be ready. Our future lies together.* She waved at Rainbow and slipped between the trees and out of sight.

Rainbow opened her eyes and let her hands slide down the trunk.

"All right?" asked Christophe.

She nodded. "Everything is perfect. Let's go dune-jumping."

Rainbow's story continues in...

Tree Slayer (Book 2)

Tree Sacrifice (Book 3)

ABOUT THE AUTHOR

Harriet Springbett lives in the Poitou-Charentes region of France with her French partner and their teenage daughters. Her first literary success was winning an honours award at the Highbridge Festival of the Arts at 10 years old with an essay about spring. Since then, her short stories and poetry have been published in literary journals and placed in several writing competitions.

She grew up in West Dorset and qualified as a manufacturing engineer before realising she preferred people to machines, and words to numbers. She moved to France in 1995, where she studied French and then worked as a project manager, a freelance feature writer, a translator and an English teacher.

She has always written in her free time. Tree Magic is her first novel. She blogs on writing, life in France and French cultural events at:

https://harrietspringbett.wordpress.com

ACKNOWLEDGMENTS

A published novel is the end point in an evolution of ideas and drafts. *Tree Magic* wouldn't have evolved without the help of many people, both directly and indirectly.

In particular I'd like to thank my writing group, Lumineuse: Helen, Fiona, Rhonda, Min, Chris, Barbara and Nola. Thanks also to my early readers: Darylle, Angie, Hester, Rachel, Michelle – and to Fiona, Gwen Davies and Sarah Hutchinson for their interest and suggestions.

For their help with my research, thanks to Anne Hind and Liz Leo, to Emmanuel Perrier of the Emile Cohl School and to the Angoulême Comics Festival team. Martine Fievet, Patrick Chappet, Rity and Dimitri were inspirational, and I must thank Tini and Sprog for living where they live and knowing what they know. Special thanks to Christine Colson-Cecchini for her lesson in positive thinking.

Thank you to the Impress Books team, especially Julian Webb, my editor, for his patience.

Last but not least, my heartfelt thanks to Cycy, who supported me without ever reading a word I wrote. And to my daughters, whose excited demands to hear about Rainbow kept me writing.